MORGAN'S WOMAN

Ram's Tor, high in the hills above Sweyn's Eye, is a small farm with fields sloping down to the cliffs above the sea. There David and Catherine Preece are trying to build a married life and eke out a living in the wake of the Great War. But they have one massive handicap – David is crippled, confined to a wheelchair, and Catherine knowing when she married that she did not love him, faces the intolerable burden of running the farm single-handed.

Into this explosive situation comes an attractive man. Morgan Lloyd, who lost his fianceé through an accident in the munitions factory, is looking for work, and he comes to Ram's Tor to help Catherine with the tasks that are beyond her strength. Gradually, as they work side by side, a passionate attraction begins to flower them – a dangerous attraction that will not only incur the jealous hatred of Catherine's husband, but the hatred and contempt of the whole town.

MORGAN'S WOMAN is the fourth of Iris Gower's sequence of novels set in South Wales at the beginning of the century.

Also by Iris Gower

COPPER KINGDOM
PROUD MARY
SPINNERS' WHARF

and published by Corgi Books

MORGAN'S WOMAN

Iris Gower

CORGI BOOKS

MORGAN'S WOMAN

A CORGI BOOK 0 552 13138 5

Originally published in Great Britain by Century Hutchinson Ltd.

PRINTING HISTORY

Century Hutchinson edition published 1986
Corgi edition published 1987

This book is set in 10/11 Paladium

Corgi Books are published by Transworld Publishers Ltd.,
61–63 Uxbridge Road, Ealing, London W5 5SA,
in Australia by Transworld Publishers (Aust.) Pty. Ltd.,
15–23 Helles Avenue, Moorebank, NSW 2170, and in New
Zealand by Transworld Publishers (N.Z.) Ltd., Cnr. Moselle
and Waipareira Avenues, Henderson, Auckland.

Reproduced, printed and bound in Great Britain by
Hazell Watson & Viney Limited,
Member of the BPCC Group,
Aylesbury, Bucks

To my children
Susan, Angela, Tudor and Paul,
with love.

CHAPTER ONE

The hills swooped softly towards the sea; the tiny fields walled with ancient limestone spread open, lying askew beneath the sun like a loose woman's skirts. In the distance the town of Sweyn's Eye belched and shimmered, but neither the stink nor the abrasive dust from the copper works reached so far as Ram's Tor.

Catherine Preece stood in the sweet pasture of the hilltop; her bright hair hung to the waist of her calico dress and the bloom of her cheeks spoke of a life spent out of doors. She walked slowly past the field of green corn that swayed and moved with a life of its own under the soft, sea-scented breeze. The foliage, which was rich and flourishing, had perhaps grown too early and might prevent the corn coming into ear by May. Catherine shook back her hair — there was little point in anticipating trouble.

As Ram's Tor Farm — named after the jutting peak of the headland — came into her line of vision her steps faltered. She assumed an expression of blandness as she approached the low door of the whitewashed building, mentally preparing herself to face her husband. A crash greeted her entrance and she stood dismayed staring at the floor where a large pool of water spread towards her boots.

'David what's wrong with you, boyo? Can't even get on with washing yourself now is it?' She went forward slowly, telling herself to be calm, but the frustration on her husband's face as he stared up at her from the wheel-chair, distressed her.

'Jesus!' He punched his fist into the roundness of his thigh and the trouser leg beneath shuddered as though in

7

reproach. Then his anger vanished and his thin face seemed to fold in pain; he was so handsome with his hair curling and dark and his eyes fine and blue, it was strange that she had never loved him.

'David, do not blaspheme.' Her voice softened. 'And please, don't torture yourself.' She knew she should put her arms around her husband and hold him close, but she feared the bite of his constant rejection. 'Look, we're going to the Guildhall tonight and you'll be getting your medal — won't you be proud?'

'Don't talk so daft, Catherine!' His voice was low. 'Is a medal going to bring back my manhood? Jesus, you can be so stupid.' He leaned forward, his eyes burning. 'I curse the war and the devil who did this to me!' He gestured towards the lower half of his body. 'I'm a cripple, Catherine — can't you get that into your head? I can't work the farm, I can't make a living for us, I can't do anything!'

As she bent to pick up the tin bowl from the spreading pool of water, she too felt anger burn in her belly. It should not have happened, this dreadful thing which had turned David from a healthy man into a cripple. In the autumn of 1918 the end of the war had been declared, but no one had told the German who fired the shell at the men of the 13th Welch.

'We must go to the ceremony though David,' she said quietly. 'Your mam is so proud of you, and what about young William? You know you're his two eyes.'

David's face softened. 'Aye, you're right about that, girl; at least he was too young to know how the top brass blundered the war, thinks it was a bloody picnic, he does, he can have the medal if it will make him happy.'

'That's my good boy.' Catherine expelled her breath. 'I'll fetch out your uniform and give it a good pressing; you'll be the smartest man in the place.'

David's eyes were hot with pain. 'Don't humour me, Catherine! I'm not senile, I'm paralysed from the waist down, I've lost the use of my legs and I'm not capable of doing what the beasts do so readily — but I'm crippled in body, not in mind or in feelings.'

'I'm not trying to humour you, only to cheer you up.' She knew that her voice trembled and she hated her weakness, but David had been home from hospital for only a few short months and she had not yet found a way through the despair that revealed itself in anger.

He caught her hand and drew her to him, smoothing back her hair as though she was a child. 'You're so beautiful, Catherine; we had such a short time as man and wife and I keep thinking you're too young to live the life of a nun. The decent thing to do would be to go out and shoot myself!'

Catherine put her arms round his neck tentatively and when he did not thrust her away, she pressed her lips against his cheek. The bristles of his three days' growth rasped against her mouth and she felt her heart beat swiftly with the pity that she dare not show.

'Right, then,' she smiled. 'You can stop worrying about the farm, because I've got an idea!' She moved away from him. 'William is coming up to twelve now. isn't he?' She paused. 'Your mam has always said he eats her out of house and home — what about him coming to stay with us for a bit?'

David nodded. 'Aye, he could help with the winnowing and I daresay he could do a bit of seeding, but he's too puny to guide a plough behind the horse. Don't you realise the strength it takes to hold a plough steady? One big boulder could tip the whole thing and throw a man over the handles.'

Catherine squared her shoulders. When David had come home he had turned away the help she had hired, which was a pity, for though Gethin-Sheepshearer was getting old, he was a fine worker. 'I can do the ploughing, I've done it before!' Her eyes challenged him and David stared at her for a long moment in silence before nodding.

'All right, we'll give it another year then.' He sank back into his chair. 'I must admit the corn looks good, even though it was slow germinating, and we should have a decent harvest.' He leaned forward. 'Keep back enough corn for seeding in the autumn and the straw can be mixed with pulped roots as winter fodder for the cattle.' He sighed. 'And let's hope we'll make some small margin of profit.'

Catherine smiled at him encouragingly. 'Since the war, the farm crops have sold well and we've a healthy herd of shorthorns giving good milk, mind.' She rested her hands on his shoulder. 'We'll manage David, don't you worry.' We have to, she thought sombrely, for what was the alternative?

'Come on, boyo, I'll give you more hot water and you can finish washing while I see to the *cawl*.'

Covertly, as she stirred the pot of meat and vegetables, she watched him; his back and shoulders were broad still and the muscles in his arms stood out proud.

But they had been put to much use: levering him from his chair, swinging him into his bed that stood now in the corner of the parlour instead of in the sun-filled bedroom where the roof sloped low on beams blacked with age.

She had been married to him for only a month when David went to war, a strong proud man of thirty determined to fight for a better world. He had ideals and principles aplenty — enough for two of them, since Catherine felt only fear when he walked away from the folding hills of Ram's Tor.

Yet it had been no love match. Catherine had been offered to David Preece just as a bitch is offered to a dog by her father who had too many daughters. At sixteen she had been already used to the backbreaking work on a farm and did not fear hard toil, but she had begged her father not to send her to Ram's Tor for she did not want to be wife to anyone.

David had come courting her with eagerness, for her father's farm was richer than his own, lying on the flatter land that faced the sun. He saw a union that would be practical and perhaps even beneficial, for there was no son to inherit the rich farmlands. And so Catherine had been married with little ceremony and had left her home to go to the bed of a stranger.

Mating — that was all it had been. She had lain beneath the dark beams staring upwards for a long time after her husband had fallen into a contented sleep. She had seen the process of coupling many times — it would be difficult to avoid, living on a farm — and yet she had imagined that between a man and woman it would be different, tender and loving. David had tried not to hurt her — and she had dimly understood that, but she had been frightened and unyielding . . .

'Catherine!' David's impatient voice broke into her reverie and she dropped the spoon she was holding into the pot of stew.'

'I'm sorry, I was far away, there's soft I am!' She smiled at him over her shoulder, seeing that he had put on his shirt and was buttoning it up with stabs of his fingers as though each movement was one of anger. From where she stood, there might have been nothing wrong with him. His eyes were clear, his face newly-shaved, his hair sparkling with droplets of water.

'Is it bored with my conversation you are, then?' He spoke sharply and Catherine had the feeling that if he could have risen he would have lashed out at her physically as well as verbally.

'Of course I'm not bored,' Catherine said a little too quickly, 'I was thinking that I'd better get out straight after I've eaten and fix that break in the wall, or the daft sheep will be falling over Ram's Tor and into the sea.' She hurriedly removed the bowl of water and dabbed at the damp patches on the wooden table absently. 'I don't know why the animals keep heading in that direction, pushing always against the stones; it's as though they *want* to fall over the cliffs!'

'I know just how they feel,' David said sourly. Catherine straightened as anger washed over her, running through her veins like fire. Yet her voice was steady when she spoke.

'Do not talk like that, do you hear me. David Preece? You've come home, haven't you? And you know as well as I do that almost a generation of men from the town were wiped out in the battle of Mametz Wood.' With flushed cheeks she took a snowy linen cloth from the drawer,

11

shaking it out of the creases into which it was neatly folded, so that billowing like a sail it came to rest evenly over the table. Her hands shook as she set out the cutlery; she could not in all honesty claim to love her husband as a wife should, but she respected him and felt affection for him and it pained her to see his soul wither away in bitterness.

They ate in silence and when once Catherine glanced towards her husband she felt him look at her with the eyes of a whipped dog. Pity twisted within her and suddenly the mutton stew had no taste.

'More bread?' she asked softly, rising to saw at the too-fresh loaf so that it crumbled beneath the knife.

'Here, let me do that.' His long arm reached out and then deftly he was slicing the bread with skill and certainty, his forehead creased into a frown of concentration.

Realisation swooped into Catherine's mind. She must find her husband a job that he could do just as well sitting in his chair. She watches his long fingers, strong and spatulate — good hands, farmer's hands, but surely they could be put to another use?

'Remember you made me a pair of boots before you went into the Army?' she began carefully. 'Well, they're wearing thin in the soles; could you ·mend them for me this afternoon? I can work barefoot for the time being.'

His eyes seemed to see right through her. 'Aye, I suppose I could do that if you get me some leather and root out the last for me. Finding work for idle hands, are you, love?'

'I'd rather see you occupy yourself usefully instead of sitting in by here feeling sorry for yourself,' she said sharply. 'Please, David, stop picking on me all the time; none of this was my fault and I'm only trying to help you.'

His voice was subdued. 'I know it's damn wicked of me, but I can't help myself because you've grown into a beautiful woman since I've been away and there is nothing I can do about it.' There was naked pain in his eyes. 'I want to lie in bed with you, to feel your breasts in my hands, I want you to bear my sons and the frustration of it all is driving me insane!'

Catherine went to him and, kneeling before him, put her arms around his waist. She rested her head against the clean linen of his shirt that smelled of sunshine.

'I do understand,' she said softly, 'and I pray that one day you'll get well. Men do walk again and miracles do happen, David.'

His heavy sigh ruffled the curls around her face. 'Don't delude yourself, *cariad*, there's no miracle on earth that can heal a shattered backbone and all the crushed nerve-endings inside. Save your prayers for yourself, for soon you will want a real man — it's only natural, we're like the beasts of the field in that respect.'

'Well, *I'm* not!' Catherine said fiercely, shaking back her hair. 'Women are not like men,' she said more softly. 'This thing that happens in bed, we do not need it. Why, I've heard the wives of other farmers laughing behind their hands, saying they prefer a tune on an old fiddle rather than going to their husbands' beds!'

He touched her face gently. 'You are young and your blood runs hot and if you have not felt the joy of loving, then there is a worse fault in me than I thought, for I should have taught you better.'

'No, the fault is within me,' Catherine said urgently. 'I saw my mother grow old and die trying to give my father a son; worn out she was with childbearing and the shame of bringing forth only girls. That's not the life I wanted, David, can't you see that?'

'You'd better get out and mend that wall,' he said bleakly, turning away from her, the arching of his body spelling out his wish that she remove her arms from round his waist.

Outside, she breathed deeply. The sun was fading and the wind was whipping in from the sea carrying with it the smell of salt. She left her boots in the kitchen and her bare feet curled into the grass as she moved towards the gap in the stone wall. And yet she saw not the swaying green corn or the sea below, a glittering blue sapphire; she was wondering what was to become of her life, for at the moment it spread bleakly before her.

A loud bleating shattered the silence of the hillside and Catherine blinked quickly, lifting up her skirt and clambering over the wall. Lying down and peering over the edge of the Tor, against the white-tipped wash of the waves she saw a young lamb perched precariously on a rocky ledge.

'There's soft you are getting yourself in such a scrape, *bach*,' she said soothingly. 'Just stay still now and I'll be down to fetch you.'

Catherine was not used to the hills, for her father's farm had stretched out along the lower lands of the coast to the west of Port Eynon. But her bare feet found easy purchase on the rocks and she knew no fear as she scrambled down towards the trapped animal. The cries of distress grew louder as Catherine drew close and smiling, she thought that the little creature was just like a babba wailing for its mam.

She paused to look below and just at that moment, the creature made an erratic movement and before Catherine's horrified gaze went toppling off the ledge, legs waving like thin sticks, trying frantically to find a foothold. Then there was silence except for the wash of the sea that moved the small body to and fro in a macabre dance of death.

CHAPTER TWO

Sweyn's Eye slumbered beneath the blue arch of the sky and the soft spring air was filled with the scent of violets. In the gardens bees, woken early, hovered greedily over velvet petals and above, against the blue bowl of the sky, gulls wheeled cleanly in flight.

The day wrapped itself around Morgan Lloyd like a balm as he stepped from the train. A final gust of steam spat cinders as though in defiance before the iron monster subsided into shuddering silence.

Morgan sighed heavily and walked out of the station, smelling the stink of the copper works which vied with the salt breeze from the sea. This, he thought, was home and sanity after the maelstrom of the war. The bloodied fields of France were left behind and Morgan had been determined to let his memories lie there too, for there was little to be gained by resurrecting bitterness.

It was several months now since the German government, with defeat staring them in the face, had sent a note to President Wilson of the United States of America. On the fifth of October, the request was made by the enemy for peace negotiations to be opened and a month later, the war had officially ended on the eleventh day of the eleventh month in the year 1918.

As he walked along the *Stryd Fawr*, Morgan became aware of the bustle of people around him. No one spared him so much as a glance; it was as though he had become suddenly invisible. Home is the hero, he thought with more than a trace of irony, for there was no one left in the world who cared a damn whether he lived or died.

But in that assumption he was wrong.

'Morgan! My fine handsome boy! Let me look at you, then.' Warm hands grasped his arms and eyes full of pride looked up at him from the lined face of Stella O'Connor.

'There's good to see you!' His voice was thick and his eyelids felt as though they were coated with grit, for Stella reminded him so much of her daughter Honey that the knife seemed to turn in his gut.

For a moment he was swept back to his past to the green years of his life when anything had seemed possible. He had fallen in love with Honey O'Connor with her thick golden hair and the slimness of her and most of all the sweetness of the love that shone in her face whenever she looked at him. But Honey had died in an accident at the munitions factory where she had worked.

'I mean't to meet you at the station,' Stella was saying gently. 'There's a fine one I am, arriving too late for the train.' She glanced away from him, her eyes full of shadows, and he realised that for her too the moment was fraught with memories.

The silence was shattered by the strident sounds of a brass band and Stella laughed up at him. 'The men of the town have walked the streets for days raising money for the wounded, but it's like children they are — enjoying every moment of it.'

Morgan smiled as he watched the drummer struggle beneath the weight of his instrument. A tattered leopard-skin that was meant to protect the man's skinny belly flapped uselessly between his legs.

'By God, it's Dai-End-House!' Morgan stood with his arm around Stella's shoulder, aware of the catch in his breath as the sound of the drums pulsated through his veins.

'It's good to be home.' His voice was rough, but Stella seemed to understand for she squeezed his arm encouragingly.

'Come on, don't let's stand here blathering, there's a hot meal waiting for you — that's if that lazy, shiftless husband has looked after the oven for me!'

Together, they moved away from the busy High Street

and Morgan paused for a moment, staring up at the twin slopes of Kilvey and Town Hill. The hills seemed to fold protectively round him and even the blighted, ruined hollows and rises on Kilvey seemed to offer him a welcome.

'My girls are growing up fast,' Stella said steadily, her eyes meeting his. 'Lovely they are too, but not one can take the place of Honey my first-born.'

Morgan forced himself to smile as he took Stella's arm and propelled her across the busy roadway, filled now with motorised vehicles which roared incessantly past. The day of the horse-drawn carts was almost finished, he thought with a tinge of sadness.

'I know it hurts,' Stella was saying. 'It still pains me, God knows, but the time has come to put the past behind you. You are a different man now, handsome and strong into the bargain; you'll have no trouble in finding yourself a wife.'

Morgan felt a great rush of affection for Stella O'Connor. 'Don't you worry about me, I can take care of myself,' he said softly, comforting her for he spoke the truth. He had not denied his natural urges; he was a man and hot-blooded and he had lived each day knowing it might be his last. But his forays into the beds of whores had not brought him anything but temporary gratification. Love was a more exclusive thing.

Green Hill had not changed. The stench from the expanding superphosphate works on the banks of the river had increased the discomfort in which the residents of Emerald Court lived. Abrasive copper dust defeated the brave daffodils that shook blighted trumpets as though in reproof, for they were dying even as they grew.

The bells from St Joseph's Church rang out in the dusty air and Morgan felt a pain in his gut as memories came flooding back. Honey, why did you have to leave me? The words cried out in time to the bells and became a dirge that drowned Morgan's senses.

'Come on inside the house, Morgan — see, there's Brendan peering through the window looking for us.' She

17

laughed. 'The poor auld fool doesn't know how to make the gravy, so he's waiting for me to finish off the dinner; what is it I've been married to all these years?' She spoke in exasperation, but there was a world of fondness in her voice.

Brendan O'Connor had aged almost beyond recognition; gone was the spirited, noisy belligerence of manner he had once shown. The hand which grasped Morgan's was weak and trembling.

'You're to stay here with us for as long as you like,' Brendan said and even his voice was weaker than Morgan remembered. 'By the saints, they were long enough discharging you boys from the Army, but you're here now and most welcome.'

'It's good to see you!' Morgan spoke warmly — he and Brendan had scarcely shared a mutual liking, and yet now they seemed drawn together by ghosts from the past.

It was strange to sit in the achingly familiar kitchen where his first tentative feelings of love for Honey had blossomed. The old clock with its long copper chains still ticked on the wall and the blackleaded grate still shone brightly against the flames of the fire.

'It's good to have you home and well again, Morgan,' said Stella as she laid a work-roughened hand on his arm, her eyes filled with understanding as they met his. 'You have made for us a new place of peace to live in, and you must live in it too and marry and have children, for you're young and young flesh heals quickly. You'll fall in love again.'

Morgan did not answer. How could he tell Stella that the war had left him feeling empty and depleted? But he was a natural born survivor and he would build anew and gradually his life would take on shape and form once more.

'I want you to stay here for a few days — you will, won't you?' Stella said softly. 'But it's all right, I know you've got itchy feet and will be on the move soon enough.'

Morgan nodded. He had no wish to remain in the little neat house in Emerald Court, for it held too many memories. In any case, he needed his independence.

A silence fell over the kitchen and the sound of the clock

seemed magnified as the pendulum swung to and fro, ticking away the minutes. He had been home just one brief hour, yet all the old aches and longings had rushed mercilessly into his consciousness and Morgan felt betrayed by them.

Stella reached behind the clock and drew out a thick envelope. 'This is for you,' she smiled, almost shyly. 'I know what it is though — an invitation to go to the Guildhall.' She handed it to him, watching as he read quickly. 'You will be going down to the Guildhall, won't you?' she asked. 'You must accept, for it's a ceremony to honour all you boys who fought in France. You couldn't have timed your homecoming better,' she laughed. 'Of course, we're all going to come with you to watch.'

Morgan nodded. 'It seems I'm going to get a medal — what do you think of that, then?' If Stella read the irony in his tone, she chose to ignore it.

'Why, that's wonderful, sure it is, and I'll be as proud of you as if you were my own son!'

The door swung open suddenly and the room was filled with a babble of voices. Morgan stared at the young O'Connor girls as they came to a halt shyly grouped together in the doorway, falling silent at the sight of the stranger.

'Well, aren't my girls going to give me a kiss, then? Haven't forgotten me already, have you?'

One by one they pressed soft lips against his cheek, unable to control the giggles of embarrassment. With a sigh of relief, Morgan realised that they were accepting him, perhaps remembering him . . . a little.

'Now let Morgan alone,' Stella said reprovingly, though her eyes were warm. 'I thought I told you lot to stay outdoors for a few hours, but it's a fat lot of good talking to you girls.' She turned to Morgan. ''Tis anxious they are to see a real live hero.'

'I'm no hero!' he protested. 'Just an ordinary soldier.' He pushed back his chair and gestured towards his heavy pin-striped suit. 'Do you think I could get out of these clothes, Stella?'

19

'Sure an' what am I thinking of — go on you upstairs, you know the way.' She met his eyes again and as he saw the warm encouragement that shone in them his tense features relaxed into a smile.

'Oh, yes, I know the way.' Morgan moved slowly into the familiar bedroom, taking a deep breath as memories of his father flooded his mind. It was in this humble room, staring out of the window at a blank wall, that Dad had lived out his last days. He had fought for every breath as the coal-dust in his lungs gradually killed him.

He pushed the unpleasant memories away and looked around, seeing that Stella had made every effort to welcome him. The curtains and bed-covers were new and fresh flowers stood in a vase on the small table beside the bed.

Morgan leaned against the wooden door, closing his eyes. He was weary from travelling, he told himself; he needed sleep and then perhaps he would feel more human.

He undressed slowly and then lay on the sheets which smelled of blue-bag and sunshine, feeling the tension drain from him. Soon he would be asleep, it was a trick he had developed in the trenches. Sleep he did, but in his dreams he saw Honey and she was reaching out white slender arms to him, her golden hair like a sea of sparkling waves about her shoulders. He woke up sweating to a darkened room and a waking nightmare.

CHAPTER THREE

Dusk settled softly over the patchwork quilt of Ram's Tor and the moon silvered the green stalks of the corn so that when they rippled it was as though the sea had claimed the land.

Catherine Preece stood outside the small, whitewashed farmhouse which crouched against the folds of the hills as though for protection from the elements. She sighed softly; she loved this land, this beautiful piece of Wales to which she had not been born but which had adopted her so readily on her marriage to David Preece.

The horse beside her whinnied softly, head high, eyes rolling as though seeing ghosts in the darkness of the night. Catherine patted the warm flanks resssuringly.

'Hush, Sheena, it's all right, everything is all right.' Then why had this sense of loneliness sprung up unawares to confront her? Catherine felt a strange reluctance to attend the ceremony in the Guildhall, for there she would be obliged to smile — to pretend that there was nothing wrong, that her life was nothing but a bed of roses.

'Catherine! What the devil are you doing out by there, girl — haven't you hitched up the horse yet?' David's voice was impatient, the words falling like pebbles hard and merciless, and Catherine took a deep breath to calm herself.

'Aye, we're all ready, just coming. David *bach*.' She drew the cart as near to the doorway as she could and one of the wheels scraped against the whitewashed stone of the wall. She tensed, expecting an outburst of anger, but David merely grunted and edged himself forward. His chair, made especially for him by Elias-Blacksmith, slipped away from

21

him with wheels spinning, leaving David clinging to the sides of the cart. Only the great strength of his shoulders and arms prevented him from falling to the ground.

The horse shifted uncertainly between the shafts as Catherine moved suddenly to catch David round the waist and help him upwards.

'*Daro!*' David muttered an oath as he fell forward into the well of the cart and lay there for a moment, panting, his eyes closed against the world. On an impulse, Catherine leaned over and caressed his face gently.

'There's strong you are, David; it's proud of you I am.' The silver of the moonlight seemed to spin a web around them and there, standing in the soft light, Catherine could almost forget the difficulties which had beset her since her husband had come home from the war. If only they could talk, find some mutual ground where they could come together and plan, then there would be hope for them. David was a fine farmer, he knew the earth so well that she sometimes thought he could see the seed germinating beneath the soil. He was a better farmer than her own father and that was the greatest compliment she could pay her husband.

Between them Catherine and David lifted the wheel-chair into the cart where it leaned drunkenly against the boards. It was a good solid chair, made in friendship, and was the difference between David being imprisoned in one room and being free to roam the lower areas of the farmhouse. With a little help he could even get outside and enjoy the sunshine in the garden.

Catherine caught the reins and clucked softly and Sheena jerked into motion. A soft breeze drifted in from the sea and Catherine drew her coat closer round her shoulders, for even though it was spring the air blew chill along the coast road.

She drove down the sharp incline which led between the rocks into the village of Oystermouth. Dark shapes of oyster ketches lay stark against the sand. The silver ribbon of the Mumbles railway lines gleamed in the moonlight, winding away into the distance.

'Look, David, there's your mam waiting for us and William leaping up and down like a frog that's found it's got legs! *Duw,* there's a pair they make — your brother so long in the legs and so thin and your mam plump as a pudding beside him.'

Catherine smiled as she drew the cart into the roadside. 'Come on, William - give your mam a hand up, there's a good boy,' she said, as she jumped lightly into the road and was enveloped in motherly arms.

'There's a good girl you are; I knew you'd be on time.' Gladys Richards smiled warmly, her twinkling eyes almost lost in folds of flesh as she playfully pinched Catherine's cheek. Then she turned to William and gave him a dig in his thin ribs. 'Come on, do as Catherine says and help your old mam — don't just stand there goggling!'

Gladys was alight with pride in her eldest son as she leaned forward and kissed his thin cheek. Almost in the same movement, she slapped William's hand away from her rotund backside.

'That's enough pushing — I'm in now, aren't I?' She collapsed into the cart and giggled like a girl. 'The boy thinks I'm in my dotage.' In spite of her cheerfulness, Gladys winced as she eased her swollen legs into a more comfortable position, for she had the bone ache and in spite of her liberal use of wintergreen oil, her knees continued to complain at every movement.

Catherine fell into step beside William, the reins slack in her hands, for Sheena was docile and amenable and did not need a great deal of direction.

'Can't give the poor old horse too much weight, can we?' Catherine's eyes flashed wickedly at William and he laughed into his hand. Catherine was always at ease with David's young half-brother, for William had inherited his mother's great humour and was quiet and kindly. They walked side by side in companionable silence, listening to Gladys and David carry on a conversation in the well of the cart.

'I'm coming up to the farm to help you soon, aren't I, Catherine?' William said at last and she smiled at him warmly.

23

'Well, as long as your mam doesn't mind. Are you sure you can spare the time off from your schooling? We don't want you growing up ignorant, do we?'

'There's a thing to say! I'm not ignorant, mind, I can do reading and writing and sums!' William sounded indignant and Catherine squeezed his arm.

'But you're not bred to farming, Will, and you might find the going hard.'

William looked at her levelly; he was tall as she, though thin with the greenness of youth. Yet he had an air of maturity about him that Catherine found endearing.

'Can't help that,' he said, 'and though my dad was a fisherman, not a farmer, I love the land.' He smiled suddenly. 'Can you imagine my mam having two husbands and her looking like a plum-duff at Christmas!'

'For shame on you, Will!' Catherine said, but she couldn't help returning his smile.

'Aye, it's funny that though I love the sea, I'd exchange the ketch my dad left me for the land on Ram's Tor, any day. I should have been a Preece and not a Richards, I suppose.'

'Well, you'll do for me, boyo,' Catherine said quickly, 'and we do want your help on the farm, especially now that the ewes have their lambs. We'll need help when the harvest comes in, too.'

The lights from Sweyn's Eye were coming closer, distinguishable as street-lamps and glowing windows rather than the distant, twinkling stars they had appeared to be from the western curve of the beach. The roadway slid around the rim of the bay, flat and narrow, bounded by hills on the one side and the sea on the other.

'*Duw*, I'm that excited,' William breathed the words, 'you'd think it was me getting a medal, not our David.'

Catherine studied William's thin, earnest face; he looked unfamiliar in his best suit which had grown too small for him. His hands jutted from too-short sleeves and he needed to leave the buttons of his waistcoat open even though his chest and belly were thin and sparrow-like.

'Aye, we're all proud of David,' she said softly, 'but there's

24

many sorts of bravery mind, William — like you offering to help me on the farm. And those lovely old men like Gethin-Sheepshearer breaking their backs in the fields when the younger ones were gone to the war.'

She paused, smiling thoughtfully. 'Never forget Gethin or worn-out old Jonah, I won't — and him without a hair left on his head but using the scythe like a good one.' She paused, remembering the shock she had experienced when David had turned the men away from his door, fearing their pity.

'Denny-the-Stack was loyal to the last,' she continued. 'Always had straw on his clothes he did, and so kind he was to spare time to help me with his own five sons gone off to fight in France.'

The roadway was congested now with a stream of vehicles driving past the Bay View Hotel towards the docklands where the Guildhall stood righteous and sturdy.

'Thank the good Lord we're nearly there!' Gladys said loudly. 'My poor knees feel as if I've crawled all the way from Oystermouth.'

'Stop moaning, Mam,' William said as he stifled a laugh. 'Me and Catherine's walked all the way, mind.'

'Well, and so you should - young, and strong like you are. But I'm a poor old woman with bad legs, don't forget!'

Catherine led Sheena into a small side street, feeling it would be easier for David to alight from the cart and slip into his chair away from the eyes of the crowd.

There were men in uniform on every side although the war had been over and done with for many a month, and the sight unnerved Catherine.

She could not help but notice that there were finely dressed women standing outside the Guildhall and self-consciously, she looked down at her own dress which was plain to the point of severity. Made of unbleached calico, it had been washed so many times that it appeared white and even the rosebuds embroidered on the high neck had lost their colour. But then it was not she who would be in the limelight but David, she told herself firmly.

She was attempting to manoeuvre David's chair from the

cart when strong hands reached over her head, taking the burden from her. Catherine looked over her shoulder and found herself staring into the eyes of the most striking man she had ever seen.

'*Duw*, it's Morgan Lloyd as I live and breathe! How are you, man?' David was leaning from the cart, shaking the stranger's hand, his voice for once free from overtones of bitterness.

'Morgan and me were in the same hospital in France,' David explained. 'Not much wrong with him as you can see, though the man's a damn hero. Going to have the VC then, are you, Morgan?'

'Nothing so grand, just a service medal like everyone else, see.' Morgan was standing so close to Catherine that she could breathe in the clean masculine scent of him. He radiated strength and character, yet she almost resented his instrusion.

'Come on then, David,' she said, breaking the sudden silence. 'Let's get you into your chair, is it?' She placed her arms under David's shoulders and at once Morgan was beside her, expertly lifting and then gently placing David in the chair.

David seemed unselfconscious. 'Glad to see a friendly face,' he remarked. 'I suppose there'll be damned officers everywhere?'

Catherine stood quietly behind David's chair, making it an effective barrier between the stranger and herself. He was handsome, with a strong jaw and deep eyes and a mouth which twisted with humour when he smiled. But he was far too sure of his own charm and somehow Catherine felt irritated by him.

Gladys was walking on ahead, but William came to Catherine's side ready to lend his strength for the effort of wheeling the chair to the Guildhall. The entrance glowed with lights and sound, exuding an air of festivity. As though sensing the tension between Morgan and Catherine, William moved even closer to her, his hands touching hers on the back of the wheel-chair.

'There's daft we are standing by here talking,' he said

26

impatiently. 'We'll be stuck right at the back if we don't get a move on.'

David gave one of his rare smiles. 'The one with the lip is my brother — his cheek will either take him far or earn him a bloody nose!'

Morgan nodded briefly to William, allowing his eyes to move to Catherine. The look was quite deliberate and she had the feeling that he did nothing on impulse.

'I think you've got an admirer, Catherine,' David said cheerfully. 'And more, I think you'd better tell Morgan that you're spoken for.' He gestured with his hand. 'Meet my wife, Catherine.'

She found her hand engulfed in a firm grip and quickly she drew away from him.

'You're very beautiful,' he said. 'David is a lucky man.' As he bent towards her, Catherine glanced up at him almost fearfully, feeling suddenly as though she was suspended above the little scene, an observer rather than a participant. She saw quite clearly that Catherine Preece, respectable married woman, was being made fun of by this cocksure stranger.

How she guided the chair into the Guildhall she could not afterwards remember, for she was trying to come to terms with the sense of pique that Morgan Lloyd aroused in her. Did he not realise that she was no child, but a woman who had been responsible for keeping the farm going during the war years?

The hall was crowded and as William had predicted, the family had to stand at the back. Catherine held her breath as she saw Morgan take charge of David's chair and wheel him to the front to take his place with the rest of the soldiers receiving medals.

'That man fancies you,' William said in a stage whisper. His eyes rested on Catherine and she felt her cheeks grow hot.

'Don't be so daft, he's only this minute set eyes on me. In any case, as far as I can see he thinks I'm quite stupid. He just rubs me up the wrong way; I hope he won't stay around after the ceremony.'

27

'Maybe you're right, maybe not.' William hunched his shoulders, excluding her from his line of vision; obviously he had said his last word on the matter.

Catherine heard names being called out, familiar names in the town of Sewyn's Eye such as the Richardsons who were the copper bosses and Mansel Jack who had run the munitions factory before enlisting. The list of names went on endlessly and after a time she fell into a reverie, thinking of the crop of wheat which seemed to be strong and good and yet about which she had worrying doubts.

As she heard the name of Morgan Lloyd being called she stood on tip-toe to see him move on to the platform. And then she looked away again — the man was nothing to do with her after all.

David Preece was given a standing ovation and men cheered and clapped. When the medal was pinned to his coat, Catherine felt tears burn her eyes. Her husband was right, what good was a medal? It didn't give a man back his health and his strength and all the cheering and clapping was very fine, but he still couldn't rise from his chair and walk.

She realised quite suddenly that David's sickness and disability bound her more tightly than ever her wedding vows could do.

She was his woman, his wife, yet in fact was little more than his nurse and could never be his lover nor bear his children. Suddenly she was washed with pity, though whether for herself or him she couldn't be sure.

*   *   *

The sun was streaming in through the window and outside the birds were calling loudly to each other. To Morgan Lloyd coming awake, it seemed he was in a different world from other people.

He lay in his bed in the O'Connor household and told himself that last night had been much more pleasant than he had anticipated. He had gone to the ceremony at the Guildhall with scant enthusiasm, spurred on by the

28

excitement of the Irish family who had wanted the medal for him more than he had himself.

"Tis proud of you we are!' Stella O'Connor had beamed up at him, the warm expression in her eyes reaching out like gentle fingers to touch him. 'We'll come along later and sit at the back of the hall and you'll be the son I never had.'

And so Morgan had left Emerald Court, striding out down the hill, his uniform chafing and restricting after the freedom of his civilian clothes. He had reflected that he wanted no medal; those who were alive needed nothing except to be allowed to forget the horrors which had taken four years of living, and turned them into a time for killing.

He had been pleased to meet up with David Preece once more and to meet his pleasant if shallow young wife. He had heard David say her name was Catherine and, before he looked away from her, he had not missed the likeness she bore to Honey O'Connor. Yet she was nothing but a pale imitation of Honey, a mousy farmer's wife with no conversation or animation.

He rose from his bed and stood staring out into the dingy court, washed now by sunlight so that the yard below and the flat of the ugly wall opposite him seemed to exude light and warmth, beautified somehow with stark shadows falling like pools in the angles of the buildings. He raised his arms above his head and stretched his lean young body; he was a man and he was whole — not crippled like David Preece — and for that he was thankful.

Downstairs Stella was busy cooking breakfast over the fire; the blackened frying-pan spat and hissed as the bacon turned crisp and the appetising smell made Morgan's mouth water as he walked into the kitchen.

'You're late enough this morning, Morgan, but then I'll forgive you for you supped enough ale to drown a man. Last night meant more to you than you'd thought possible, for you didn't only get a medal but a sight of yourself as you might have been!'

He turned away from the shrewdness of her eyes, seating

29

himself at the white scrubbed table which gleamed clean in the wash of sunlight.

'Aye, it was all right,' he said, leaning back in his chair, his eyes fixed on the fire which glowed behind the gleaming blackleaded bars. The tall clock with long chains swinging sent out a cacophony of sounds and Morgan realised that it was eleven o'clock.

'*Duw*, I am late right enough! You should have called me, Stella, not let me sleep like a pig in muck.'

'Well, let you lie in while you have the chance, that's what I thought. When you've work to go to you'll be up early enough, I daresay.'

She placed the plate of eggs and bacon before him and busied herself making a pot of tea. At last she sat opposite him, her elbows on the table, her fists under her chin. 'Now, what are you going to do with yourself, Morgan my boy? And I don't mean just today, I mean for the rest of your life.'

Morgan felt himself grow tense, though the face he presented to Stella was without expression. He concentrated on cutting the rind from the bacon and put a forkful of the food into his mouth.

'Now don't you go pretending with me,' Stella said softly, 'and please don't look at me with cold eyes like that. I'm your friend and I want what's best for you; I'm not just being a nosy-parker.'

Morgan inclined his head and placed his fork carefully on the table, noticing how the grain of the wood ran away from him and that where the planking met there were grooves which needed to be scrubbed every day to keep them free from grease and spills.

'I'm just about getting the ideas in my head sorted out, and there's you looking into my brain making up my mind for me,' he said gently, his shoulders relaxing. He was too much on his guard, forgetting that he was not at war now but with friends.

'I might just consider working on a farm — there now, what have you got to say about that?'

Stella looked at him carefully. 'That's fine, sure it is,

30

unless you are more interested in the woman than in the land. I know Catherine looks a bit like my Honey, but she's married and not for you.'

Morgan rose from the table and put his hand on Stella's shoulder. 'I know you mean well, but it's nothing to do with the woman. And I'm a grown man now; I've seen other men die screaming for their mothers and wives and sweethearts and I came through it all. I think I'm strong enough to make decisions about my own life.' He moved to the door and relented as he saw her anxious eyes follow him. 'Don't worry, I've no plans to take away another man's wife.' He smiled. 'Be easy, Stella, I can take care of myself.'

Outside, the sunshine was hot upon his face and Morgan closed his eyes, not seeing the shabby court and the windows begrimed with copper dust, nor hearing the voices of the children who played in the street, for in his mind he could see the rolling fields and waving corn of the farmlands on the outskirts of the town. Perhaps a new start was just what he needed.

He moved away from Emerald Court, knowing that he must find a niche for himself for he wanted to live his life his way without interference however kindly meant. And he needed a job — the money he had received from the Army would not last long if he frittered it away. A talk with David Preece would not do any harm, he decided.

He found himself moving down into the town, striding out along the coast road in the direction of Mumbles Head where the outcrop of rocks jutted into the sea and thus created the small inlets of Bracelet and Limeslade. And he looked across the golden sand, he asked himself what better occupation could he have than to work the land on Ram's Tor? The more he thought about it, the more attractive a proposition it seemed.

It was true he knew nothing at all about farming, but he was strong and healthy and he would not be slow to learn. His step quickened as he neared the farm — David Preece would surely take him on, especially if Morgan offered to put money into Ram's Tor. David had taken a

31

liking to him, for they had been bound together by the fortunes of war; but that was before he had received his crippling injuries. Some might say that David was lucky to be alive, but Morgan would have preferred death.

The narrow road was sloping upwards now, a road which had been blasted out of solid rock a few years before the war. Below, he could see the pier pushing out to sea, and, at right angles to it, the arm of struts and planks which held the lifeboat.

The sun was high above him now, the arch of the sky blue without a trace of cloud. He felt refreshed, reborn and although he scorned himself for being sentimental — he, the hard-bitten soldier — he could not help the enthusiasm which gripped him when he thought of learning to be a farmer. For now he would be just a worker, one with a share of the profits if David took him on, but eventually — when he knew all he needed to — he would have his own farm.

Ram's Tor lay over the slope of the cliffs which towered above the sea. A gentle tide was running, darting tongues of foam playfully between grey rocks, as Morgan paused to stare downwards — feeling the tangy salt breeze lift his hair, drinking in the freshness of the air.

The whitewashed building gleamed in the sun and Morgan sighed softly, unaware that his eyes were alight as he made for the open doorway. He rapped loudly and after a few moments, heard the creak of David's chair as the wheels turned against the stone floor.

'*Duw*, There's a surprise, man!' David smiled up at him, yet Morgan saw the lines of pain around his mouth. Poor sod, he was little more than a dead man, Morgan thought, pity welling within him.

'*Bore da*, David, can I come in then?' Morgan stepped into the shadowy coolness of the parlour and saw that there were no mats covering the flagstone floor. No doubt they had been taken up to facilitate the easy moving of David's chair.

'Aye, come in with you, boyo, and tell me what brings you up this way?' David had a pleased smile hovering in his eyes. 'Though I'm glad to see you whatever.'

'I've got a proposition for you.' Morgan felt his throat grow tense as he spoke — what if David turned him down flat? 'I need a job see, something to occupy my mind as well as my muscles. Damn the war, it's got a lot to answer for!'

'Amen to that,' David said in a low voice. He looked at Morgan and shook his head. 'I could do with a man, there's no denying that, but it's money we're short of, see? Take you like a shot, I would.'

'Well, I've got a bit saved — spent little or nothing while I was doing my time in the Army. I'd like you to think of it as an investment, for both of us, for I would dearly love to learn about the land.' Morgan rose to his feet and stared out of the window into the fields.

'I don't want to be shut indoors, working in a factory or grubbing in a pit, I think it's time I did something different and farming seems to me to be the answer.'

David leaned forward eagerly in his chair. 'I'd have to talk it over with the missus, boyo, but you could be just what we've been praying for!'

Morgan smiled easily. 'Shall I go and find her, persuade her I'm just what Ram's Tor Farm needs?' he asked, but David shook his head.

'No, don't do that, Morgan, Boyo. I know you can turn on the charm, but better let me tell her — she's a proud little thing and I don't know which way she's going to turn these days.' He grinned. 'Never did understand her, mind — any man who says he knows a woman's thoughts is a fool or a liar!'

'Aye, I guess you're right,' Morgan conceded, but he was eager for a decision; patience had never been one of his strong points.

'Anyway, boyo,' David continued, 'I could do with a drink of beer. The bottle's in the pantry on the floor there — fetch it and we'll celebrate the prospect of our working together. I must admit it would be good to have another man about the place.' As David spoke he grimaced with the pain which was ever present, jabbing at him with spiteful fingers.

Morgan walked through the passageway and into the spotless kitchen where the fire was burning low in the big grate. He picked up the scuttle and threw coal on to the embers, stirring up the flames and satisfied to see the glow become warm even as he watched. This he guessed was one of David's tasks, and he was saddened that the man who was once so strong had come to the doing of menial jobs in the kitchen of his own home.

He carried the beer and two mugs back to the parlour and as he sat down David gave him a grateful smile.

'Heard you putting coal on — damned well forgot again, didn't I?' He shook his head. 'And Catherine wouldn't have bawled at me if the fire *had* gone out; that's the trouble, she's so patient with me.'

As Morgan looked into the foaming mug, he knew how David must feel — cooped up like a beast, receiving nothing but kindness from those around him, when he probably needed a good blast of manly cussing to clear the air.

'Aye, I suppose it's hard for those who've not been to war to understand that we are different men to the ones who left Sweyn's Eye to fight Kaiser Bill.'

David looked up, his eyes shadowed as he sighed heavily. 'Sometimes I feel strong, as though I could get up and walk away from this damn chair . . . and then when I try, I realise it's all an illusion.'

Morgan was sorry in his gut for the husk of a man seated before him; it would have been easier to work with him if he had been strong and healthy. And yet he would talk to David and learn from him and from Catherine Preece too, for she was part of the new life he was to mould for himself.

He rose. 'I'd better get on then — shall I wait to hear from you?' He stood poised in the doorway, his hand resting on the wooden jamb that was warmed by the sun, the paint peeling and flaking beneath his touch. There was much that had been neglected at Ram's Tor, but he would have all the time in the world to put it to right.

David nodded. 'Aye, I'll no doubt send our William to see you some time tomorrow. Where are you staying?'

Morgan took out a piece of paper and a stub of pencil from his pocket and wrote down the address.

'Emerald Court,' he said softly in triumph, for he knew that David had made up his mind. 'Just tell the boy to ask for the O'Connor household — everyone in Green Hill knows it.'

As he walked through the fields just as the sun was beginning to fall lower in the skies, his eye anxiously scanned the horizon with a feeling of possession and it was as though he already owned the fine land of Ram's Tor.

On the hard slatted seat of the Mumbles train, he swayed to and fro, staring back the way he had come, knowing he had done the right thing in approaching David Preece.

And he would work his guts out to make the farm a success; he was ambitious, needing a better life with a goal on which to set his sights.

'Well, there's the lad home for his dinner at last!' Stella O'Connor's eyes were anxious as they searched his face and he smiled at her reassuringly. 'Foine rabbit stew with carrots and parsnips that'll put the hair on your chest, sure it will!'

He slid his arm around her shoulders. 'I'm so hungry I could eat you between two slices of bread and have the rest of the family for afters.' He smiled down at her, realising he had had no food since breakfast.

'You look very full of yourself.' Stella eyed him carefully as she put out the stew. 'What have you been up to then?' She cut a chunk of the brownish bread and spread it thick with yellow butter so salt that the water broke through the surface like drops of dew.

'I've been getting myself a job, up on Ram's Tor.' He held up his hand as she would have spoken and shook his head. 'There's no point in you saying anything, Stella. I know you mean well and I'll always be grateful to you, but I have to go my own way.'

He began to eat and steadfastly looked down at the table, allowing Stell no room to voice any more of her fears and objections. Tomorrow, word would come from Ram's Tor and then he would be leaving Emerald Court for good.

CHAPTER FOUR

Rain washed down on the town of Sweyn's Eye, turning streets grey and sending flurries of water along gutters, holding low the green cloud of copper smoke that twisted sinuously into dingy courts and humble dwelling places.

Mansel Jack stood in the window of his drawing-room staring out at the lowering skies, his hands thrust into his pockets. The town was all right, but it was not Yorkshire and he wanted to return home.

'There's a look that would turn the milk sour — and you just got a medal!' His wife came to stand beside him and he held out his arms to her, his ill-humour vanishing.

'You move like a whisper, Rhian,' he said softly. 'I didn't hear you come in.' She was just as beautiful as when he had first seen her, working a loom in his mill back home.

'That's because you were far away in a world of your own,' Rhian said firmly. 'You've been in a funny mood for days and I think it's about time you told me what's wrong.'

'And you're far too sharp for comfort!' he said, but he smiled down at her, his eyes warm. Two years of marriage had only served to strengthen the bond between them which not even the war could destroy.

'I'm thinking of returning to Yorkshire, lass.' The silence seemed to stretch endlessly before he hurried on, 'The mill at Spinners' Wharf is doing well and now that I've sold off the site of the munitions factory, there seems no challenge for me in Sweyn's Eye any more.'

Rhian stared up at him levelly. 'If you're asking will I go with you, then of course I will. Don't think I'm going to let you out of my sight for one moment, do you

36

— and let some other woman get her hands on you!'

Mansel Jack kissed her hair. He was past forty, he mused, yet he did not feel middle-aged; perhaps having a young and lovely wife helped perpetuate his strength and virility.

'I know I'll be taking you away from everyone you love, but it's Doreen — she's written to say she's been poorly these last few months. She begs me to return and I can't refuse.'

'Of course not,' Rhian agreed readily. 'She's your sister and she has no one else but us to care for her.'

Mansel Jack kissed his wife's mouth tenderly, meaning only to convey his gratitude at her understanding, but as always when he held her passion stirred within him. His breathing quickened as he touched her breast, so sweet and firm beneath the silk of her blouse, and he loved her with all his being.

'There's wicked, making love in the middle of the day!' She breathed the words softly against his mouth and he knew she wanted him as much as he wanted her.

He lifted her gently and carried her upstairs to their big bedroom, kicking the door shut behind him. 'You're a witch, do you know that?' he said as he set her down on the silk covers. He unfastened her buttons with fingers which trembled, slipping the blouse from her white shoulders.

'You make me feel like a lad with his first lass,' he whispered. 'I love you, Rhian!'

'I know, my lovely.' Her hands cupped his face, drawing his mouth down on hers; their breath mingled and she was as sweet as the spring flowers that grew in profusion in the gardens below.

'Come to me, *cariad*,' she said softly and her eyes closed in the joy of possession, moving with the rhythm of the sea, making them one flesh. Every time Mansel Jack made love to his wife, he felt he was restating his devotion to her, setting his seal upon her and marking her as his own.

As she moaned beneath him pleasure, hot and searing, tore through him and surged through his veins. God, how he loved this woman who was his wife!

They lay hand in hand afterwards, close together, legs

still entwined. He had no need to ask her if she was content, for there was the drowsy after-love look on her face which told him all he needed to know. He sighed softly, nestled down into the softness of her breasts and slept.

It was some hours later when Rhian left the house which stood on the beginnings of the western slope of the town to walk down to Spinners' Wharf. She felt warmed and cherished by Mansel Jack's love, yet there was pain in the knowledge that soon she would be leaving her home and returning to Yorkshire with her husband.

But then she was like Ruth in the bible, she thought pensively — his land would be her land, his people her people. She loved him and that was all there was to it.

Yet how was she going to break the news to Billy? Her brother had grown closer to her than ever in the last few years and he seemed to need to spend time talking to her. Perhaps both of them realised that blood ties could become broken if neglected for too long.

The long low building of Spinners' Wharf came into sight and Rhian paused for a moment, staring down into the rust-red water of the stream that flowed past the woollen mill, reliving memories of the past.

She had met Mansel Jack when she had run away from home, dogged by unhappiness which was eased a little as she worked at the Mansel Mill. There she had designed her own patterns for woollen turnovers and warm winter blankets and first became drawn to the owner of the mill.

But back in Sweyn's Eye, Rhian's aunt had fallen sick and reluctantly, she had returned to her home town. Later, Mansel Jack had come south to run the munitions factory at Sweyn's Eye and eventually asked her to become his wife.

Smiling now, she hurried down the hill and knocked briefly on the door of the mill house before letting herself in. The kitchen had not changed; a big fire roared in the blackleaded grate, the brass fender shone and the same clock ticked in the corner of the room.

'Rhian! There's lovely to see you! Smelled the tea-pot you did — I've just this minute made a brew.'

Gina Sinman's smile enfolded Rhian, speaking of a friendship and trust which could not be broken by time or distance.

'Cerianne and my little Dewi have gone out with your Billy — just for a walk, they said, but they've been away an hour already. Good with the children your brother is, Rhian.'

Rhian sat in one of the high-backed wooden chairs and smiled up at her friend. 'When are you and my brother going to get married that's what I want to know?' She spoke teasingly and her smile widened as she saw the rich colour suffuse Gina's face.

'Now don't start that nonsense again!' Gina smiled to soften her words. 'Billy and me are doing all right, so you just keep your nose out or I'll be angry with you, mind.' She poured the tea and its fragrant aroma filled the kitchen.

Rhian sighed. There were so many memories wrapped up in the essence of the mill that it seemed to be more than bricks and mortar and was almost a way of life. As though reaching into her thoughts, Gina spoke of the past:

'Remember when my Heinz was alive, he used to bumble round the place with wool in his hair and with dye all over him — wonderful husband he was, mind. I'll never know how anyone could have taken him for a spy, just because he was Austrian born but him a Welshman at heart.'

'It was the war,' Rhian said softly. 'Folks were afraid and Heinz was a foreigner, to the townspeople an enemy.'

Gina sighed. 'Aye, it's all over and done with now, best forgotten I suppose.' She was silent for a moment, her expression downcast. 'I meant to come up to see you before now — it's Carrie, she's taken sick. Nothing too bad,' she added hastily, 'just a chill or something. She's gone upstairs to bed now, much against her will, and I'm only surprised that she hasn't heard your voice and come hurrying down — you know what she's like.'

'I'll go and see her in a minute.' Rhian smiled, she did know what Carrie was like, an indomitable woman who had lived her life to the full. It was Carrie who had cared for Rhian when she was a child and Carrie who had comforted her when Mansel Jack had gone off to the war.

Rhian rose to her feet. 'She'll be surprised to see me, I'm thinking.' She spoke with a feeling of guilt; it was some time since she had visited the mill, but there had seemed no need. These days everything ran smoothly with a dozen or more workers to cope with the orders, a far cry from the time when she had worked the looms almost single-handed.

The stairway was dark and curving upward in a spiral and Rhian felt memories press around her. It was here she had delivered Gina of her son more by instinct than skill and it was from the mill house she had left to become Mansel Jack's bride.

Rhian entered the dim room quietly in case Carrie was asleep, but the rustle of bedclothes told her that she was very much awake. 'It's me, Rhian — shall I open the curtains a little?'

'Aye, if you must.' The voice was weak, not a bit like that of the robust woman Carrie usually was.

Rhian looked at her quickly, observing with a feeling of pain that Carrie had changed in the last few weeks and had become frail and looked old.

'There's soft you are to go catching a chill.' She tried to speak normally, but Carrie was too sharp not to see through her.

'Shocked, aren't you, *cariad*? Oh, I know what's happened to me; I'm just like your aunt was.'

Rhian sat beside Carrie and took her hand. 'Now you're not going to be silly about this, are you? My Aunt Agnes was much older and a different kettle of fish too. Good to me she was, mind, but never did pay much attention to the needs of others. You, now, are needed here; little Cerianne loves you and so does Dewi — what would the children do without you?'

Carrie shook her head. 'Look, girl, don't fret about me.' She stared levelly at Rhian. 'I've spoken with the doctor and you know how I trust old Bryn Thomas, don't you?' She paused, her eyes on Rhian's face. 'I'm going to be honest with you, for I feel you can take it in your stride, but I don't want anyone else knowing, mind.'

Rhian felt a chill creep into her bones; the hair prickled on the back of her neck and her mouth was suddenly dry. She wanted to leap up and rush from the room but Carrie's eyes, pleading for understanding, were holding hers and she struggled to be calm.

'I've got six months at the outside, there's a thing for you now. My lungs it is see, *merchi*, nothing anyone can do. But I've had my time and I'm grateful for it, so don't go weeping for Carrie, will you?'

'But doesn't Gina suspect, surely she's noticed how sick you are?' Rhian asked softly.

Carrie shook her head. 'No, you don't notice about folks when you see them every day, like. She realises I'm not getting any younger, of course, but that's all.' She looked searchingly into Rhian's face.

'And I don't want you to go saying anything, promise now? I couldn't stand no pitying looks and whispering in corners.' Carrie pushed herself up against her pillows. 'Now, what's this visit all about then? Got any special news, have you?'

'No, nothing special, do I need something special to come to see you then?' Rhian said quickly. 'I just wanted to visit old friends — nothing wrong in that, is there?' She drew the blankets around Carrie's shoulders, knowing she could not leave for Yorkshire . . . not yet. She owed it to Carrie to spend these last months with her.'

Carrie looked at her waistline meaningfully. 'Hoped there would be a babba on the way. I'd be sort of grandmother to it, wouldn't I?'

'*Duw*, I'll say you would!' Rhian forced herself to smile, though when she looked at Carrie she could not help seeing a dead woman and that was all wrong. Carrie would be alive and spirited and in full possession of her senses until her last breath,

'Like the child I never had, you,' Carrie said wistfully. 'Only too glad to take over from Agnes and bring you up I was.'

41

'I know.' Rhian held Carrie's thin fingers in her own. 'You were wonderful to me, it was to you I turned whenever I was hurting and I've never told you how much I care for you. I've left it pretty late, haven't I?'

Carrie clucked her tongue. '*Duw*, don't you think I knew? No words needed. I'm glad you're here, mind. Gina is a good girl, good as gold, but it's you I want near me when the end comes.'

Rhian tried to conceal the tears that rose to her eyes and blurred her vision, but Carrie was too sharp.

'Don't cry, *cariad*, won't do no good and it pains me to see you sad. Just think — I've had my life, enjoyed it more than most, got nothing to complain of, have I?'

Rhian put her arms round Carrie drawing her close. She was thing as a bird, just skin and bone, her strength and vitality having slipped away unnoticed. Rhian wondered how they could have been so blind, herself most of all.

But now she must be strong and treat Carrie as she had always done, with the casual love of familiarity. And Mansel Jack would have to go to Yorkshire alone — set up house for them, plan for the future.

Rhian felt she would be like an apple cut in half, incomplete without her husband, but she could not leave Carrie, not now.

Later as she sat in the kitchen with Gina, she found it difficult not to blurt out the truth. It would be good to have someone shoulder the burden with her, but that was not what Carrie wanted.

'*Duw*, there's a long face if ever I saw one! What's wrong with you - lost a florin and found a farthing, have you?' Gina smiled, but her eyes held a question and as Rhian drank from the tea Gina had placed before her she searched for something convincing to say.

'It's just that Mansel Jack has to go to Yorkshire,' she said at last. 'I will stay here until he finds a home, but it will be difficult to part with him.'

'Ah, I see.' Gina nodded her head wisely. 'Been as close as burrs on a sheep's back, you two have since your husband came home from the Army — and I don't blame you either.'

Absently Rhian helped herself to more tea. The shock of Carrie's news was wearing off and the pain was a low ache which she found difficult to disguise.

'I'd better not wait any longer for our Billy,' she said at last, rising to her feet. 'Give him my love and kiss the children for me.' She forced a smile as she shrugged herself into her coat. 'I daresay you'll be seeing more than enough of me once Mansel Jack leaves the town; I won't like to be in that big house on my own.' It was an excuse which Gina would readily believe and she smiled at once with sympathy.

'Well, girl, move in here if you like, this place belongs to you and your husband after all. Think it over, right?' Gina smiled as she went with her to the door. 'And don't leave it so long before you next come and visit us?'

As Rhian walked along the road leading from Spinners' Wharf, her thoughts were in chaos. She longed to find relief in tears but as Carrie had said, there was no point in crying.

* * *

Mansel Jack was angry with Rhian. 'Your duty is to me,' he said, his voice level but his eyes narrowed. 'I want you with me in Yorkshire, not here in Sweyn's Eye.'

'I'm not going to row with you over this,' Rhian said carefully, 'but I can't desert Carrie, she has always been so good to me. Please try to understand, my love.'

He shrugged, though his shoulders remained tense. 'Well, it seems that you've made up your mind and there is nothing more to be said.'

Rhian bit her lip, thinking desperately that she was caught in a cleft stick. She wanted to be with her husband more than anything in the world, yet she had a duty to Carrie who had brought her up.

To make up her mind to remain in Wales while Mansel Jack went up to Yorkshire to prepare a home for them was all too easy. To actually say goodbye to him was another matter entirely.

Lying beside him in the great bed, Rhian felt the pain of yet another parting cut deep. She had seen him go to war, lived with the dreadful uncertainty of knowing he was in the trenches and now she could scarcely bear for him to be out of her sight — so how could she endure a separation that might last for months?

Beside her, Mansel Jack stirred and opened his eyes and immediately reached for her. She clung to him, loving him like an ache within her.

'What's wrong, Rhian?' His mouth was close to hers and after he had spoken, he kissed her gently. 'Don't tell me there's nothing, I can see it in your eyes.'

'It's Carrie — when I saw her yesterday she was weaker than ever. Please don't be angry; you must see for yourself that I can't come to Yorkshire with you.' Her voice faded away as she buried her face in the warmth of his shoulder.

'Of course you must stay, if that's what you feel,' Mansel Jack said at once, but his tone was cold. 'I can see how much Carrie means to you. But, I must leave for Yorkshire soon — you know that Doreen is constantly telling me she can't manage the business affairs of the family alone.'

Rhian sighed. 'I suppose it's just as much your duty to be with your sister as it is mine to be with Carrie,' she said as she clung to him, 'but there's awful to see you go without me.'

He kissed her roughly and his breathing deepened. Rhian felt the passion that surged through him communicate itself to her. She crept closer to him and her arms closed tightly round his broad shoulders.

Her love for him was a searing joy which never became diluted however many times she lay with him.

She had known men before. Gerwin Price had raped her, had bred in her such a terror that she recoiled at the touch of a man's hand; it was then she had gone north to Yorkshire to try to make a new life working at the Mansel Mill. But when her aunt's illness brought her back to Sweyn's Eye, her old sweetheart Heath Jenkins had returned to her life . . . she had loved him since she was a young ignorant girl and the depths of his love had taken away her fears, taught

44

her that there was joy in the union between a man and his woman. But Heath was destined to die in the fields of France.

Even Heath's love, wonderful though it had been, dimmed in comparison with the depths of feeling Rhian shared with Mansel Jack. Her husband was her life; every breath she took was for him and she would have followed him wherever he chose to go. But now, Rhian had to hold her head high and endure another separation from Mansel Jack.

When he would have risen from their bed, she held on to his hand. 'Come back to me my love, only for a minute. I want to have you in my arms again just for a little while.'

He kissed her throat and then her eyelids and finally her mouth. She clung to him, drinking in the scent of him, but at last he moved away.

'Now say you won't come with me!' He smiled down at her. 'Because I can't believe you really mean to allow us to part.'

She stared at him. 'Was that the reason you made love to me then?' Her voice was hoarse. 'You thought you would persuade me to change my mind — how could you!'

He took her arm roughly. 'Because I love you, you idiot, and I want you to come with me. I didn't expect to play second fiddle when I married you!'

Rhian slipped into her robe and tied the belt, fighting the anger and fear that his words instilled in her. It was no good arguing with him, he would never understand.

Later, as they sat in the station waiting-room, Rhian could scarcely contain her feelings. She was reminded of the times when Mansel Jack had left her to go to fight the war in France and irrationally, the same fear of losing him washed over her.

He was not going into battle, it was true, but in Yorkshire there was another danger in the form of Charlotte Bradley who had once been engaged to him. Would he perhaps see his life in a different light once he was back in his own home and wish he had not married in such haste?

His background was so different from Rhian's. He was used to a fine house and good living while she had been

45

brought up simply in a small cottage which was not even hers but had been bought up by the Richardson estate and leased to Rhian's Aunt Agnes.

'Why are you so silent?' Mansel Jack's voice sounded cold and hard. 'Regretting your decision to stay, are you?'

Rhian shook her head. 'I was wondering if you ever regretted coming down to Wales to open your munitions factory,' she said, her voice low, 'and more importantly, if you've ever been sorry you used up one of your leaves from the Army to get married to me.'

'Not until now.' He bent his head so that his forehead rested against hers. 'I've caught myself the best-looking woman in the world, Rhian, and I need you by my side.'

The sound of a train clattering along the track froze Rhian into a moment of sheer panic. She wanted to hold Mansel Jack to her or else leap aboard the train with him, but common sense told her she could do neither. So she stood up beside him and smiled, conscious of the pressure of his hand upon hers.

'I'll be back as soon as I can, Rhian.' He spoke firmly, as if sensing the tumult within her. Then he was striding away, his well-loved and familiar figure soon swallowed up inside the waiting carriage.

She could scarcely see as the train hissed and steamed its way out along the line that led away from Sweyn's Eye. She felt alone as she had never been before, because now she was accustomed to having her husband at her side in the softness of the night.

She turned away at last and left the empty platform, gathering her coat around her shoulders, chilled in spite of the warmth of the day. She walked slowly, acknowledging her own reluctance to take on the responsibility of caring for Carrie. But she must appear cheerful and never allow the mask to slip, for Carrie trusted her.

When the long low buildings of Spinners' Wharf came into sight, Rhian consciously squared her shoulders, She hurried past the stream and rapped on the door of the house before letting herself into the spotless kitchen.

Gina was sitting in her usual chair with the children playing round her feet and she glanced up with a ready smile as Rhian entered the room.

'There's lovely to see you again so soon, *cariad*!' She rose at once and pushed the kettle on to the flames of the fire. 'Give me your coat before that little boy of mine gets it all sticky with jam. *Duw*, there's lovely fine wool - I do envy you, Rhian.' Gina fondled the coat, staring at it in fascination, and Rhian suddenly realised how much she had taken for granted during these last few months. Once she would have walked the streets in a good Welsh shawl and thought a fashionable coat an extravagance.

'I've come to ask if your offer to put me up still stands,' she said quickly. 'Mansel Jack's left for Yorkshire and I'm too much of a baby to want to stay in that big house of ours alone.'

'Don't you say another word!' Gina smiled softly. 'I'd be tickled pink to have you stay by here with us in the mill house, you know that!'

She poured the water into the brown china pot, pushing her son aside with a good-natured nudge.

'Billy's coming down here later — going to have tea with us. I've made a big batch of Welsh cakes, special.' Gina's words bubbled over and Rhian smiled.

'You're a daft pair, she said reprovingly. 'Everybody knows you're in love with each other — and as for our Billy's little girl, you've taken the place of her mam these last three years or more.'

Cerianne leaned against Rhian's knee, smiling up at her and looking so much like Billy that on an impulse, Rhian bent and kissed the softly contoured face.

'Why you talking 'bout me, Auntie Rhian?' The little girl clambered up on Rhian's lap and snuggled into her arms.

'You're far too sharp for your own good, do you know that?' Rhian said softly, brushing aside the fair curls.

Gina sat at the other side of the white scrubbed table and stared at Rhian, a frown creasing her brow. She made to speak but paused, staring down into her cup as though fascinated by the swirling beverage and the specks of leaves floating on the surface.

Rhian felt a fluttering of apprehension, for she knew instinctively that Gina was going to talk about Carrie's sickness and tried to prepare herself to dispel the other woman's fears.

'You don't think there's something really wrong with Carrie, do you?' Gina blurted out the words, her eyes firmly downcast, watching the spinning tea as though it held the answer to her question.

'Good heavens, you mustn't worry about Carrie — she's as tough as an old leather shoe!' Rhian hoped that her voice carried conviction. 'I'll go up and see her soon, ask if she wants to come down for tea.' She managed to smile. 'And if your Welsh cakes don't tempt her, then nothing will!'

Gina heaved a huge sigh. 'There's a relief, I was that worried, *duw*, don't know what I'd do without that woman — like a mam to me she's been these past years.'

'And like a mother to me for much longer,' Rhian said softly, almost to herself. She sank back in her chair with her niece clasped warmly in her arms, wondering how she could face the next months without Mansel Jack at her side.

'Drink your tea, it's going cold.' Gina's gentle voice intruded into Rhian's thoughts and she sat up straighter in her chair, holding firmly to Cerianne's small frame.

'There's a bully you are!' As she smiled to soften her words, Rhian knew that in the months ahead she would need all her resources of strength, but the least she could do for Carrie was to ease her dying. She swallowed hard and blinked back her tears.

'*Duw*', she said with forced cheerfulness, 'aren't you ever going to bring out those Welsh cakes then?'

CHAPTER FIVE

There was the sound of birds, loud in a song that was sweet to the ear. Dawn was breaking over the fields where the corn appeared grey in places and touched with a rosy glow where the sun struggled through the morning mists. The sea far below the cliff-face washed inwards, softly pointing fingers of foam between grey rocks. Salt spiced the balmy air and Ram's Tor was coming awake.

Catherine awoke in her lonely bed and covered her eyes with her hand, knowing she must face another hard day. There were the potatoes to be boiled for the pig swill, a job she hated for the smell of potato peel lingered in the kitchen for hours.

And downstairs she could hear her husband stirring, knew he would be impatient to be up and about, wanting first the privy and then endless strong cups of tea to drive away the dullness of mind brought on by his medication.

She rose and stood near the window, staring outwards but seeing inwards, searching her emotions as she had not done for a long time. At last she felt the desolation which had touched her life when David had come home from the war was fading away, and there was an understanding between them that had grown almost into a friendship.

From the top field, the small herd of shorthorns were falling into line, ambling along the lane, udders heavy with milk. Served two purposes, did the cattle, providing both meat and drink. Catherine sighed — there was no more time to stand dreaming, for there was work to be done.

The morning air was clean and fresh as Catherine left the farmhouse and hurried towards the byre where the cattle waited patiently, long lashes curling and coquettishly flicking upwards at her entrance.

'There, there, Sal, let me get hold of you then, that's right, you'll soon feel easy.'

She hitched up her skirts as she sat on the worn wooden stool and laid her face against the warm flank of the animal. 'Keep still, girl, that's the way!' As she spoke softly, she became tinglingly aware that she was being watched. She glanced over her shoulder and saw Morgan Lloyd standing behind her.

'Good, you're up and about early this morning.' She quickly adjusted her skirts and pushed back a strand of hair which had fallen across her eyes, conscious of her dishevelled appearance. 'I hope you're finding your room over the stables comfortable.'

'Aye, the place serves well enough.' He leaned towards her and spoke swiftly, and though his words were ordinary there was an expression in his eyes which for some reason made her angry. It was as though he was in the company of a silly child.

'How about teaching me the milking?' He came close to her and under his watching gaze her fingers usually so deft became clumsy. Quickly, she rose from her seat and gestured that he should take her place.

'No, no, not like that!' she said swiftly as he grasped the teat and pulled. 'You must close your index finger and thumb first — like this, see? Then your other fingers must close slowly. That's right.' Her tone was grudgingly approving as a spray of steaming milk flowed into the pail.

She stood watching him for a little while before turning away. 'Well, if you think you can manage the rest of the herd, there's no need for me to stay. I'll go and make breakfast — come in when you're ready, mind.'

He stared up at her, his eyes clear as though seeing inside her. Startled by the shrewdness of his expression, Catherine took a quick breath, and then turned and hurried back to the farmhouse.

'There's a time you've been, *merchi*!' David said, glancing up at her from his chair. 'Starving to death I am by here, girl.'

As Catherine stared down at him and saw the smile curving his lips her heart was full; he tried so hard to be cheerful.

'Well, you shan't be starving much longer. I'm going to cook you such a big breakfast, the like of which you've never seen before!'

He caught her hand and held it to his cheek and the tan of her skin was highlighted against the paleness of his face.

'Why so carefree, my girl?' he asked, his eyebrows raised in surprise.'

She laughed. '*Duw*, am I usually such a grouse then? I'm happy because I don't have to do the milking today — or perhaps any other day now Morgan Lloyd is here to help.'

'There's glad I am to hear that,' he said softly. 'I know you didn't really want him here.' He sighed. 'But I am envious of Morgan Lloyd because he is whole and strong.'

'That's enough of that!' Catherine said. 'I'll not let you wallow in self-pity. Some men are lying buried in those foreign lands across the sea, mind. Too soft I've been with you, giving in to your moods all the time — well, no more, do you hear me?'

Relenting, she took a deep breath and placed her arms around his bent shaking shoulders, silently aghast until she realised he was laughing.

'You devil! Right, I'm not going to cook you any bacon and eggs until you apologise for making fun!'

Breakfast was eaten in silence. Morgan had glanced around the small kitchen, his shrewd eyes missing nothing, and had settle himself at the table without a word. It was David who finally broke the stillness by dropping his cutlery on the white cloth and pushing away his plate.

'Well, boyo,' he said as he stared directly at Morgan, 'do you think you have made a good investment putting your money into my farm?'

Morgan rested his arms on the table and took a sip of tea from the large china mug before answering.

'I shall have to make changes,' he said and ignored the

surprised lift of David's eyebrows. 'I think we should buy a winnowing machine; it must take a man hours just working with a sieve to separate the grain from the straw.'

'Well, it's the way I've always done it and my father before me,' David said reasonably. 'We get the neighbours in to help at harvest time — this isn't like the town, you know.' He sniffed derisively. 'You're in the country now.'

'And we could do with a motorized plough, too,' Morgan continued, unruffled. 'But there's plenty of time for that, we'll have to continue using the horse for the time being.'

'Now listen here,' David Preece leaned forward, the chair creaking beneath his weight, 'if you think you're going to come in and change everything I've done, you can just bow out again.'

Morgan took another piece of bread from the pile on the plate before him and began to chew hungrily.

'Too late for that,' he said at last. 'We've signed the papers and everything is tied up legally.'

Cathering stared from one man to the other, not knowing what to say. She felt she should be with David — he was her husband and deserved her loyalty — yet she happened to think that Morgan was right. No one could stand still, you had to move with the time or be left behind.

'My father is thinking of getting one of those petrol-driven tractors,' she offered gently. 'They do the work of twenty horses, so it's said.'

David turned on her with sudden anger. 'Your father is in a different position from me, he's got a bigger farm and more money to throw away. We need to keep our expenditure down to a minimum just to break even — you know that as well as I do, Catherine.'

She subsided in her chair with eyes downcast and Morgan's glance flickered across to where she sat avoiding his gaze.

'No need for any of us getting hot under the collar,' he said softly. 'We'll all do what we think is best for the farm.' He shrugged. 'After all, we want to make a living at it, don't we?'

He rose to his feet, conscious of Catherine's large eyes now resting upon him, and smiled disarmingly. 'I'm awaiting my orders, I've milked the cows — now what do I do next?'

'Feed the pigs!' David's voice fell hard and cold into the silence of the room and Catherine made as though to protest, but his glance was enough to make her lapse into silence.

'Aye, all right,' Morgan said easily. 'Where's the food?'

David raised his eyebrows. 'The swill is kept in the bin outside the back door of the farm, it's just boiled potato and meal. Bale some of it out and tip it into the trough. Not beyond you, is it?'

As Morgan stood still, his hands hanging easily to his sides, he reminded Catherine of a man about to pounce on his prey. Then he shook back his thick hair and smiled. 'I shouldn't think so.'

As he left the kitchen, Catherine stared tight-lipped at her husband.

'Do you want him injured, then?' Her voice was mild but there was a world of accusation in her eyes. David shrugged and rubbed his hand across the roughness of his chin.

'I suppose not, it's just that he's so damned cocksure, that's all. Hasn't been here two minutes and he wants to change everything.'

Catherine gave him a quick look and hurried outside just in time to see Morgan step over the wooden fence into the sty.

The sow lay in the straw of the shed, her litter sucking greedily at her engorged teats. She glanced up with baleful, red-rimmed eyes as Morgan tipped swill into the trough.

Catherine saw Morgan half turn at a grunt behind him and the wild boar that was David's pride and joy moved out of the shadow of the roughly-built sty. The long black snout jutted forward and the ugly head was lowered in anger.

'Come out slowly, Morgan boyo,' Catherine said breathlessly. 'Hold the bucket in front of you, that's the way, don't give the *mochyn du* the chance to charge you.'

She waved her scarf, but nothing would divert the animal

from his intention of charging the stranger who had dared to enter his domain.

Suddenly Morgan threw the bucket into the creature's face and leaped quickly over the fence, breathing heavily. Catherine stood staring at him miserably until at last he looked up at her.

'And what was the object of that little exercise?' His voice was tight with anger and she couldn't honestly blame him. She shrugged and turned away.

'I suppose it was David's idea of a joke,' she said lamely. As she pushed back her hair and stared up at Morgan, the bewilderment in his eyes was too painful to see.

'I'm sorry,' she said as she turned away quickly, 'I should have warned you.' She heard him move past her and saw him enter the kitchen and realised there would be a showdown. Morgan was not the type of man to let a matter rest, he would have his say if the devil took him.

She left the farmhouse behind and strode across the small fields towards Ram's Tor.

*   *   *

The peak of rock jutted out over the sea, black and dangerous but offering a breathtaking view of the rugged coastline. She would spend the morning mending the boundary wall and keep out of the way of both men, she decided, tying her scarf around her long hair and fastening it in a knot on her neck. Above her the sun was warming the land and she knew with a dart of triumph that if the weather held, the crops would be good this year.

She lifted warm stones and carefully built up the gap left by the sheep; the foolish creatures were intent upon falling down the sheer cliff-face and into the sea far below. And they couldn't afford to lose any more stock — the sheep would be sheared for their wool and later in the year would be sold for mutton; the money they fetched would be needed to be put back into the land.

She worked solidly for several hours and at last straightened, rubbing her palms into the small of her back to ease the ache. Her arms had caught the sun and freckles were appearing on the golden skin. Catherine sighed and stared up into the cloudless sky, knowing that she must go back to the farmhouse and make a meal for her husband. Her spirits fell and even as she told herself not to be foolish, she dreaded facing David, not knowing if his ill-humour of the morning would still be with him.

As she skirted the edges of the cornfield, she saw a tall figure coming towards her and bit her lip, rebuking herself for the way her heart sank at the sight of Morgan's head bare to the sun and the broad strength of him as he strode towards her. He was a handsome devil right enough, but he just seemed to be giving her more problems.

When he was a few feet away from her he paused, and she too faltered to a halt. His eyes were bright as they rested upon her and when he came slowly towards her, she made no move. Strong fingers drew the scarf from her head and took a strand of her hair, holding it out to watch the effect of the sunlight on it. He would have spoken then, but the silence of the dreaming afternoon was suddenly shattered.

The maroons fired from the lifeboat station shattered the peace of the day and Morgan stared past her in surprise.

'It's the call to the lifeboat crew,' Catherine explained quickly, 'though what could have happened on a day such as this I don't know.'

She turned and hurried to the cliff-top, staring out to sea. 'Look,' she pointed, 'there's a small boat gone aground on the Mixon Shoal. Can't be local people or they'd have known better.'

Morgan seemed to be inordinately interested in the spectacle of the listing boat and watched intently as the lifeboatmen gathered together on the arm of the pier, coming from all directions.

'Volunteers,' Catherine said. 'Perhaps you'd like to join the crew now that you're a Mumbles man.'

Morgan's eyes were alight. 'I'd like nothing better,' he said quickly, 'my life seems to have lacked excitement since I came home from the Somme.'

Catherine stared at him thoughtfully. 'It's no picnic, mind,' she said shortly. 'Oh, it looks fine now with the sun shining and a few silly people stuck on a sandbank. But it's not always like that. Sometimes the waves run thirty feet high over the Mixon and the wind is enough to tear your head from your shoulders. Dangerous, it is!'

Morgan looked down at her. 'And there lies the attraction.' He spoke in a low voice and somehow Catherine had the impression that he was not talking about the lifeboat. She left him staring over Ram's Tor and made her way back to the farmhouse.

David was sitting near the window, trying vainly to see what was happening. She told him of the boat caught on the shoal and he subsided into his seat, interest vanishing.

'You haven't fed the chickens yet,' he said, hunching forward in his chair. 'I've mixed in the stale bread with some bran, but you know I can't get my chair over the step or I'd get out and feed the birds myself.'

Catherine stifled a sigh. He was being his most awkward and yet she could hardly blame him; it must be difficult for him to come up against a hard-headed man like Morgan who wanted to tell him how to run his own farm.

'I'll feed the hens a little bit later,' she said. 'I've got some oyster shells to put in with the bread, but now I want to talk to you. There's to be no more tricks like that one with the wild boar, right? It's lucky no one was hurt — and don't you go laughing at me again for I mean what I say, mind.'

She moved to the deep pantry that lay cool and dark beneath the stairs, the large slab of marble that made up the shelf keeping the food cold and fresh.

'Now what do you want to eat — shall I boil up a bit of salt fish for us?' Turning to look at David she saw he was crouching forward in pain; she went to him and held him close and slowly felt him relax.

'*Duw*, woman do you have to humour me all the time? I've told you before about that.' He caught her hand and

56

made her stand beside him and she sighed in exasperation.

'I'm a good wife to you, David Preece. I am not humouring you, just trying to find out what you want to eat. I'm patience itself and I won't have no one saying any different — but my patience is getting short, mind.' Even as she spoke, she saw a smile come into David's eyes. 'Now let me go, boyo, you were just telling me you are starving.'

He spoke as though he had not heard her. 'I do realise how difficult all this has been for you, Cath, you've been wonderful to me since I got home. I know I put on you a bit, but I do care for you *cariad* — I want you to know that.'

She was sure he did, but only in the way he cared for the hens in the shed or the cattle in the fields. She wasn't, couldn't be a woman to him, desirable and lovely; rather she was part of his hearth, a possession, something he needed. But this was not his fault.

'What's all this daft talk about now when I have to do the cooking, David?' She could not help the fact that her voice was harsher than usual, but she was shaken by his strange mood.

He dropped her hand suddenly as though stung and hunched himself over his chair. 'I'm just trying to get through to you, but you're like one of those Egyptian sphinxes — hard on the surface with God-knows-what inside.'

'That's silly talk.' She moved to the sink. 'I was only thinking how well we've been getting on together,' she said as she began to wash the potatoes, scrubbing away the dirt uncaring of the coldness of the water on her hands.

She boiled the salted fish in a large blackened pan and stood staring at the water that moved and twisted the creature and gave it the appearance of being alive. She shuddered and turned away, setting the table deftly, her movements light and quick.

'I get lonely sometimes.' David's words seemed forced from him and Catherine felt pity drag at her, slowing down her movements. She looked towards him, telling herself to rest her hand on his shoulder, to explain that she knew a little of his pain.

The cutlery dropped from her nerveless hands and clattered on to the table. 'I think there's a danger of the corn running,' she said, deliberately changing the flow of conversation. 'The foliage is becoming just a bit too strong and we did plant a little later than we should have.'

'No, it'll be all right,' David said. 'We put down Square Head's Master and you know that's a moderately quick growing variety of wheat.'

Catherine realised that her mind had removed the veil of pity through which she usually saw her husband. He had become a person to her again, a man who was her friend.

She had given him more of herself than ever a truly loving wife could, for she was apart from him and they never had been in love. She had attended to his bodily needs, bathing him like a child, concealing her revulsion at the withered flesh which once had been a healthy limb. In short she had done her duty by David and now she realised that duty was a cold thing, a despicable substitute for true caring . . . but it had been all she had to offer. Now subtly things had changed and they talked together, even laughed together and still had occasional misunderstandings which were not important.

The door of the farmhouse creaked open and turning quickly, Catherine saw Morgan silhouetted in the shaft of light. He stood tall, his shadow long, and though his face was hidden from her she could envisage the strength of his mouth and the glint of humour in his eyes.

'Go and wash at the pump in the yard if you please.' Her voice was prim and unfamiliar and Catherine hated herself, yet was driven by some feeling she did not understand. 'Supper will be ready in five minutes,' she continued, 'take it or leave it.'

He stood still for a long silent moment and Catherine busied herself scooping the fish out of the pan and setting the food clumsily on the plate, ignoring the splash of boiling water that touched her hands.

As Morgan left the kitchen she swallowed hard, eyes fixed steadily on the bubbling saucepan of potatoes; then she heard the creak of David's chair and glanced at him defiantly.

'Did you have to be so short with him?' David asked evenly, manoeuvring himself into his place at the head of the table. Catherine felt strangely irritated and disturbed as she set out three plates on the snowy cloth. She cut chunks from the fresh loaf and did not speak, for there was no pleasing her husband.

The meal was uncomfortable and as soon as was decently possible, Morgan rose and went outside into the encroaching shadows of the twilight. David pushed his chair away from the table and nearer to the fire and rubbed his hand through his hair.

'Get more coal on by here, is it, girl?' He spoke absentmindedly. 'And you'd best light the lamps, I want to do a bit of reading.'

'Yes sir, no sir, three bags full sir!' Catherine was amazed at the anger in her voice, but she was compelled to go on. 'I only have to wash the dishes, feed the hens and milk the cows and a thousand and one other things around the place — don't mind me!'

She cleared the table with hands that shook, hearing with a feeling of guilt the grating of the coal as David banked up the fire. But he was growing lazy and that was no good for either of them, she told herself in mitigation.

The evening air was soft, the mantle of blue shifting into a sky rich with gold and red teasing out into softest pink. She took a deep breath and stared around her at the land which she had worked for all the years of the war. She had loved Ram's Tor and put herself into the task of farming the good land gladly. And now there was an intruder in her life: Morgan Lloyd had come to disrupt and change and she resented him.

And David, what had he done to earn her ill-humour? Why did she have to remember that she had never loved him, not even when he was whole and strong and had worked by her side? She had never liked the scent of him and his touch had left her unmoved. But no, that was not quite true — his approaches to her in the marriage bed had engendered a feeling of sadness, for David Preece was ashamed of human emotions. And yet now, there was something growing between them . . . a trust, a liking . . . and it was too fragile and lovely to break with her bad moods.

When she finally arrived at the barn, it was to find that Morgan was already installed with the animals. His hands, gentle but strong, were bringing forth the milk to the pail in great gushes.

He turned and looked at her long and hard and Catherine found herself glad of the dark shadows which hid the blush in her cheeks; she had been unpardonably rude.

'Can you manage?' Her tone was conciliatory and Morgan rose to his feet in one easy movement.

'Catherine . . .' His shadowy figure moved towards her and in a moment of blind panic she turned away, her shoulders hunched, her attitude one of rejection. She wanted nothing from Morgan but his loyalty, his help on the farm, for emotionally she was drained and even an overture of friendship would be a strain on her patience.

'I was only going to tell you that I'm going up to Merioneth tomorrow to buy a good Welsh Black bull; I can rear him to serve the herd, it makes good sense. Will you help me to choose an animal, Catherine?' He waited for her reply and when there was none forthcoming, he turned away. 'I'll be finished here soon,' he said flatly.

Catherine looked up at him. 'What will you use for money?' she asked, her voice sounding hard and cold. 'Good stock is an expensive item.' She crossed her arms over her waist. 'I manage the farm accounts, remember, and though I make a good profit on the milk and do quite well on the calves, there's nothing like the money put by for a well-bred beast.'

'I've a little money left from my Army days — enough, I reckon,' Morgan said easily. 'And if you're not prepared to help, then I shall just have to learn what a good animal is for myself.'

She stared at him, bristling with hostility at his arrogance. Let him waste his money if that was what he wanted! She left him and returned reluctantly to the house, staring up at a sky grown indifferent now and grey. Her spirits were heavy as she braced herself to face her husband, knowing that there were unwelcome tasks to perform before she could go to the emptiness of her bed.

Morgan stayed out all night, Catherine knew because she lay awake for a long time staring into the darkness, listening for the ringing sound of his footsteps against the cobbles. She wondered where he could be, anxious that his absence was her fault.

Or was there perhaps a woman, someone with a claim on him? She sighed softly — what Morgan Lloyd did was no business of hers; she must not think of him or worry over him, for he was nothing to her except another pair of hands on the farm. But it was a long time before she slept.

When Morgan did return it was in triumph, leading a fine Welsh Black bull into the yard. He had chosen well; Catherine admitted it grudgingly and then only to herself.

'You're back then,' she said, her tone haughty and Morgan smiled infuriatingly.

'Aye, girl, I'm back and with the best buy in the market, too.' He turned the animal for her to see and in spite of herself, she moved forward and looked more closely at the young bull.

'He's prime,' she said. 'I bet you paid the earth for him?' Her hand went out instinctively to touch the animal's coat and Morgan smiled.

'Not really. I listened to the other farmers talking, learned which animal was the most suitable for stud and then spread the tale that the beast was from a contaminated herd!'

'But that's dishonest!' Catherine said, though her voice trembled with laughter. 'You've done well, boyo, but get him into the field now and let the rest of the herd get used to him, right?'

As she watched Morgan lead the animal away, she felt his triumph as though it was her own. She'd make a farmer of him yet!

61

CHAPTER SIX

Mary Sutton sat alone in the warmth of the conservatory. A spirit of languor had enveloped her all afternoon and she had not added a stich to the pullover she was knitting for her ten-year-old son. She stared out into the garden and beyond to where the sea laved the shore far below. Restless and lonely, possessed by a mood of blackness for days, not even her child's presence had raised her spirits. Indeed she had been relieved when his nurse had come to take Stephan away for his afternoon nap.

She had thought she had come to terms with her loneliness over the years and even though she sometimes cried into her pillow in the darkness of the night, had been convinced she had got over the distress of her past. But that was before her husband had returned to Sweyn's Eye. Since the night of the awards, when she had crept into the Guildhall to watch him receive his medal, she had grieved for him — all the old regrets and longings had risen to the surface and would not be put aside.

She rose to her feet and pushed open the door, moving slowly out into the spring sunshine. The sweet air was like a cloak falling about her and she tilted her head, closing her eyes, seeing not the orange particles of light but the pain in Brandon's face when she had told him the truth about herself.

Fresh home from the battle of the Somme, Brandon Sutton had been eager to take his beloved wife into his arms. And she had gone to him with love overflowing, his safe return filling her with incredulous joy for she had been informed he was missing. The sounds of the railway station had died away as the couple had embraced and Mary clung to her husband, not wanting to let him go.

But the spectre of Mary Anne Bloomfield, who had once been Brandon's fiancée, had forced Mary into a swift honesty with her husband. She could see them now, both of them standing in the warmth of the drawing-room, she knowing that the unutterable must somehow be uttered and that it was better from her lips than from those of Mary Anne.

She had drawn on all her reserves of strength and stared into his eyes, feeling as though she were about to plunge a knife into his heart.

'I'm having a baby,' she began and held up her hand as he made to speak. 'No, hear me out, Brandon, and don't look at me for pity's sake.'

He had moved back a pace, his face suddenly pinched, his eyes dark as though he knew she would deal him a death blow.

'I don't know who the father is.' Her voice was low but clear, her shame bringing the colour to her cheeks. 'When I heard that you were missing, I went out . . . I didn't know what I was doing. He was kind, he took me in his arms — and then . . . then I found out I was going to bear a child.'

It seemed at first, as though he might strike her; he raised his hand and then let it fall. But it was the look he gave her before he turned and left that remained in her heart and mind.

She heard later that he had returned to the front with his battalion and in vain she had waited for some word of forgiveness from him, but it did not surprise her when no word came. And now he was back in town — come only for the presentation of his medal — but he was staying in the Mackworth Hotel in the Stryd Fawr, so near and yet a million miles away.

She wandered back indoors and mounted the stairs to the nursery. Stephan was her love, her boy, the child she had always wanted, yet she had paid dearly for the privilege of motherhood. She entered his room, ignoring the surprised look his nurse gave her for Nerys was an old friend first and nursemaid second.

Mary looked down at the child in the blue-painted cot and shook her head. It was ironic that her son was so like Brandon there could be no doubt of the boy's paternity, for he had the same high forehead and the thick dark brow and hair that were the Sutton trademark. So her honesty had been for nothing; she could have kept her secret and her husband's love if only she had remained silent.

The sound of the doorbell chiming echoed through the house and Mary felt her heart leap in a mingling of fear and elation. What if he had come to her, wanting to talk, bury old quarrels — how would she contain her joy?

'Mary, I hope I've not come at a bad time; there's pale you look.' Mali Richardson was staring up at Mary with concern in her face and slowly Mary's heart settled into its normal rhythm,

'Of course it's not a bad time, it's lovely to see you. Come and sit in the sun.' Mary smiled in genuine warmth, for she had known Mali since the days of her childhood and they had grown closer over the years.

'You're not yourself,' Mali said softly and Mary shook back a strand of hair that drifted over her forehead.

'Once you wouldn't have even noticed that. You've become very mature, Mali, a far cry from the days when you were out tom cattin' with Sterling!'

'I never was tom cattin'!' Mali protested, but a smile curved the corners of her mouth. 'There's strange life is, Mary — have you never thought how odd it is that we two who had nothing as children have become very comfortable?'

'Aye, but with all respect I've had to fight for what I've got, my love,' Mary said quietly. 'How is that husband of yours? I hope he's keeping well.' She changed the subject, hoping she had not offended Mali with her outspokenness.

'Yes, he's well enough, but I've not come to talk about myself. No, I came to ask you why you haven't made an opportunity to see Brandon before he leaves town.'

'Leaves town?' Mary echoed the words faintly, her heart seeming to dip in trepidation. 'Is he going so soon, then.'

'Very soon. Sterling has met with him several times and

he's set on returning to America almost at once, so it seems.'

'But what can I do?' Mary couldn't think straight; her mind raced, her hands trembled and she knew that she could not let her husband simply walk out of her life again, not without a fight.

'Look, I love my husband and there's nothing I wouldn't do to keep him and I know you feel the same way about Brandon, so why are you sitting here doing nothing? Once there's an ocean between you it will be too late.'

'Oh, my God!' Mary stared at Mali in panic. 'What shall I do, go alone or take Stephan with me?'

'Get the boy ready now, right now. Come on Mary, don't stop to think, you must at least try to put things right.'

'But wouldn't he have come up here if he'd wanted to see me?' Mary asked as she rose to her feet, her eyes darting to and fro as if she could find an answer to her question in the overhanging vines that hung heavy with fruit.

'Never mind your silly old pride,' Mali said quickly. 'Come on, you fetch a coat and I'll go up to the nursery and get Stephan ready.'

Mary obediently drew a short knitted coat over her light summer dress and stood for a moment looking at her reflection in the oval mirror in the hallway. Her hair was just beginning to show traces of grey and there were lines now around her eyes. But she would not see thirty again, she told herself sharply, and there was no doubt that the ravages of the war years had left a mark on her features. There was every possibility that Brandon would not want her back under any circumstances. He was a fine handsome man and he might well have met someone else by now. It was a little more than two years since she had told him of her infidelity and during that time a great deal had happened.

Mali was hurrying down the stairs with Stephan held firmly in her arms, though the small boy was sleepily trying to squirm away from her. Mary smiled and took the sweet weight of him and his soft hair brushed her cheek as he nestled into her shoulder.

'Nerys wasn't very pleased,' Mali said, pulling a face, and

Mary laughed even though within her there was a tumult of emotion raging.

'I don't suppose she was — she doesn't like her routine upset, but this is a special occasion after all.'

Mary led the way out into the sunshine that splashed through the trees lining the drive, throwing mottled patterns of light that moved and shimmered as though with a life of their own.

'Get into the car,' Mary said quickly, her voice ragged with nervous emotion. 'I want you to come with me and take Stephan and be firm with him; I can hardly drive with him in my lap.'

Mary started the engine of the Austin and with ease born of long practice set the car in motion. Beside her, Mali sighed.

'Same bossy Mary as used to oversee the Canal Street Laundry — you haven't changed. But I do envy you, Mary, your ability to drive — there's clever you are.'

Mary grimaced, 'Needs must . . .' Yes, she had needed to be independent over the years, but never more so than when Brandon had walked out on her. At first she had grieved, remaining shut indoors, sure that she would never be able to hold up her head in town again.

It was painful to be alone, yet pride played a part in her grief too for she was sure that everyone must know she had betrayed her husband. Mary Anne Bloomfield had learned her secret and she was not a woman to keep her tongue still.

And yet when Stephan was born, no one who looked on the infant's face could fail to know that Brandon Sutton was his father, for the likeness was too vivid to be denied. But Brandon had never seen his son.

She drove carefully along the *Stryd Fawr* towards the Machworth Hotel, a grand and gracious building with *jardinières* gracing the entrance where a liveried commissionaire stood to attention. Mary needed to drive carefully, for the roads were crowded with traffic and peopled with delivery boys on cycles and women shopping with great zeal but no apparent direction.

'Stop just by here,' Mali said unnecessarily, for Mary was already drawing the car to a halt. They could see that the hotel foyer was thronging with people and Mary pulled on the brake with a nervous jerk of the wrist.

'I can't go in.' She felt fear tear at her; could she bear the finality of it if Brandon rejected her yet again?

'Of course you can — go on, don't just sit there making a show of yourself, *merchi*. Here, take your son for I can't do anything with the boy — he's too lively for me!'

Mary reluctantly climbed from the driving seat and took Stephan's warm hand in hers, drawing comfort from his childish grip. He was wide awake now and his eyes held a curious expression as he gazed around him.

'Go on!' Mali urged and it took her gentle push to propel Mary towards the doorway covered by a stone awning.

It was cool inside and dim and Mary stared along the passageway, her heart beating suffocatingly fast. She breathed in the scent of polish and the distinctive smell of old leather and tried to calm herself.

'Yes, madam, is there something I can do for you?' The middle-aged man standing at the reception desk was smartly dressed and eyed her sharply as she approached with Stephan.

'I'm looking for Mr Brandon Sutton — could you tell me what room he's in, please?' Mary was unaware of the wistful quality of her voice, yet she knew that she was being regarded steadily and the man was taking stock of her appearance. She was pleased that her clothes were good and her shoes polished and sound, for she believed she would have met with short shrift had she not presented a ladylike appearance.

'Well, I suppose it's all right since you have the child with you.' He smiled a little thinly. 'Though normally we do not allow ladies into the gentlemen's rooms, of course.'

'I understand,' Mary said a little shakily. 'I do assure you that it's all quite proper and above board.'

After a moment, he nodded. 'Yes, I can see that.' He

picked up a book from the desk and consulted the pages. 'Ah, yes, room number twenty — that's up the first flight of stairs and along the corridor to your left.'

As Mary thanked him, she wondered if she would have the strength of will to knock on the door of Brandon's room and if she did, what could she say to him that had not already been said?

The corridor was dim and chill without the benefit of sunshine and Mary stumbled a little over the uneven floor, straining to see the numbers on the doors. And then she stood outside Brandon's room, her heart beating swiftly, her lips trembling. She tried to picture him, tall and strong, with his leonine head and calm eyes which had always looked at her with love — until that last time they had been together when she had admitted her unfaithfulness. Yet how could you be unfaithful to a man you believed dead?

She took a deep ragged breath and lifted her hand, pausing for a moment and almost inclined to turn away even now. But Stephan stirred, his small arms clinging to her. Before she could lose heart, she rapped loudly on the door then stepped back not knowing what to expect.

Her husband stood in a patch of light, staring out at her, his heavy brow drawn together in a frown, his eyes unreadable.

'Can I come in for a bit of a talk then?' Mary asked softly and before he could reply she was in the bare impersonal room. She seated herself on a hard-backed chair and drew Stephan towards her.

'I heard you're leaving for America soon and I had to come. Look on our son, Brandon — there's a likeness not even you can fail to see.'

He thrust his hands into his pockets, not speaking but he moved closer to stare at the boy and Stephan returned his gaze steadily.

'Yes, he's my son, I'll grant you that,' Brandon said. 'But nothing is altered - you were unfaithful to me.' He moved away abruptly. 'Do you expect me to melt with gratitude because you've borne a child to me and not your lover? Look, Mary, this is getting us nowhere; why did you come here?'

Mary's mouth was dry, there was a pain within her and a sense of hopelessness.

'I really don't know,' she said and her voice shook. 'There's soft of me to think we could somehow make it up. I'd better go.' She took Stephan's hand firmly and would have moved to the door, but Brandon took a step towards her.

'Wait, Mary. I want you to know there's no need for you to worry about money — I'll make arrangements for you to receive an allowance every month. You are still my wife after all.'

'I don't want your money,' Mary said harshly. 'You know I've more than enough to keep myself and to set my son up for life. Mercenary I've never been, Brandon, and you should know that more than anyone on this earth.'

'Don't get uppity, honey.' Brandon's voice was sharp, his eyes narrowed as he stared at her. 'It's you who have done wrong, not me and I'll thank you to remember that!'

'There's no danger of me ever forgetting it, is there?' Mary demanded, trying to keep her voice low, conscious of the open door and the possibility of being overheard.

Things were not going at all as she had planned; she had wanted the sweetness of reconciliation, not renewed condemnation.

'I'm only human, can't you understand that?' she said, shaking her head. 'I was out of my mind with grief and I wanted the comfort of arms around me. Was that so unforgivable?'

'Other women lost men too,' Brandon said harshly. 'Did they all go rushing to find a lover? Ask yourself that, Mary!'

'I did not have a lover!' Mary said shakily. 'I lay with another man for one night, that was all. I didn't even have to tell you about it — I just thought we could be honest with each other, But I was mistaken.'

'*Honest!*' There was a world of scorn in Brandon's voice. 'You don't know the meaning of the word.'

Aware of the hostility in the small room, Stephan began to move restlessly from one foot to the other. He twisted his face in Mary's skirt and with a quick movement she drew him towards the door, brushing back the thick ruffled hair.

'Come on, be a big boy now, there's nothing to be upset about, silly.' She smiled at him. 'You know your mam shouts sometimes, but I don't mean any harm, now do I? We're going home in the car — you'll like that, won't you?'

Brandon had moved closer as though intrigued in spite of himself. Now he held out his hand and rested it gently on Stephan's shoulder and as the boy turned to look at him, he could not help but see his own mirror image.

'He's a fine boy,' he said grudingly, 'and he looks tall and strong for his age. He's a credit to you, but take care not to make a cissy of him.'

Mary glared at Brandon angrily. 'No son of mine will ever be a cissy! You forget that I was brought up hard and reared my brother single-handed into the bargain — didn't do a bad job on him, did I? Died for his country, Heath did.'

'I know that, I shouldn't have spoken.' Brandon thrust his hands into his pockets, his expression less hard, less certain. His eyes rested for a long moment on Mary's face and then turned to look at his son. It seemed he was about to speak and Mary felt a tingling of hope; she even moved a pace towards him, then the silence was shattered by a loud feminine voice with an unmistakable American accent.'

'Of course I can go in, my good man, let me pass at once! Hello there, Brandon, it's me.' The woman swept into the room as though it was her right and then stood still, her eyes suddenly wary. 'I came to discuss the journey home with you, honey,' Mary Anne Bloomfield said more quietly. 'I didn't know you had company — perhaps I should go.' But she had no intention of leaving, for she settled herself into a chair and shrugged off her coat.

As Mary moved to the door, she summoned all her powers of control. Turning, she stared meaningfully at Mary Anne and then her eyes met Brandon's.

'Let him that is without sin cast the first stone — *honey*!'

She left the room and closed the door with precise quietness, though her mouth was set into a firm line of anger. So for all his high-minded moral attitudes, Brandon was going back to America with his former fiancée! Well, she had made her last overture — Brandon Sutton could go to hell and back before she would speak to him again.

So blinded was she by anger that she almost walked past the Austin and it was only because Mali — still sitting in the car waiting for her — called her name that she remembered where she was.

'Don't tell me, it went badly,' Mali said. 'I can see it in your face. I also saw that baggage Mary Anne go into the Mackworth and I knew then that any hope of you and Brandon getting back together again would fly out of the window once that American flossie came on the scene.

'Here, take Stephan.' Mary cranked the car and jumped aboard the shuddering Austin, eager to be away from the town and return to her home where she could be alone with the bitterness of her thoughts.

'He won't forgive *me!*' Mary said hotly. 'He who has consistently carried on with that American woman ever since she came over here. What he did before he met me is one thing, but to keep up his association with Mary Anne now proves to me that the affair isn't finished by a long chalk.'

Staring straight ahead, she was instinctively driving the motor car through the crowded street. She handled the controls with casual expertise, her eyes reading the roadway, her quick mind making decisions even as she spoke of her encounter with her husband.

'They are going back to America together, Mali — now, what do you make of that?' Suddenly her anger evaporated, she felt chilled and vaguely ill. It had taken a great deal of courage to face Brandon again, to lower her pride and ask for his understanding, yet all the time he was moralising to her he was planning to take a trip with Mary Anne Bloomfield!

'I'll take you home,' Mary said dully, 'but thank you for coming with me.' She smiled shakily. 'I suppose it was worth a try, wasn't it? And at least Brandon

71

knows now that Stephan is his son.'

Mali hugged Stephan closer. 'There's sorry I am, Mary, it's my fault you went to see Brandon and whatever you say, I know it was a complete disaster. I suppose that just serves me right for interfering.'

'No, you meant well.' Mary forced herself to smile, though tears were near the surface and she wanted nothing more than to shed them until the pain inside her was dulled.

'Aye, I meant well right enough,' Mali said, 'but then they say the road to hell is paved with good intentions. Drop me at your gate and I can walk the rest of the way home; it's not far.'

Mary guided the motor car away from town and through the narrow streets and courts that lay scattered on the outskirts. The pale sun was slipping into a haze behind the hills as she drew to a halt.

'Take care,' she said softly, 'and come and see me soon.' She smiled ruefully. 'It seems that I see very little of my friends these days — a woman alone is a bit of an embarrassment.'

'You'll never be that to me and Sterling,' Mali assured her at once. 'You're always welcome in my home.'

Mary lifted her hand in a gesture of farewell as she turned the car into the driveway and smiled as she saw that her son had curled up on the seat beside her and fallen asleep. His thick dark hair clung to his forehead damply and his chubby hands clasped the folds of her skirt.'

'I'm all you've got, boyo, but I'll take care of you, don't you worry,' she whispered softly into the gathering gloom. Yet in spite of her brave words, tears trembled on her lashes so that for a moment her vision was blurred.

It was then that the Austin hit a tree-stump and the motor car bucked like a frightened horse, throwing Mary forward over the windscreen. Her head caught on the side of the bonnet as she fell and there was a blinding flash like an explosion that clouded her vision. As she lay gasping, feeling the dew-damp grass beneath her hands, she heard Stephan crying.

'Mammy, Mammy — I'm hurting, Mammy!' His tearful voice drummed loudly in her ears like the sound of the ocean booming in an empty cave and Mary pressed her hands against the ground desperately trying to rise. At first she was on her knees, when moving through the darkness that was inside her head. She felt rather than saw the bonnet of the car and then she was dragging herself upright, reaching over into the seat to grasp Stephan's small hand. He pressed himself against her, his arms clinging around her neck; she held him close, cradling him in her arms, and heard herself making small sounds of distress for something was wrong, very wrong.

Mary felt her knees become weak and the earth seemed to waver and tremble beneath her feet. She could not get her bearings, her vision was blurred and everything was distorted as though she was looking into the convex side of a silver spoon. Even Stephan's face seemed sinister — the nose jutting forward, forehead bulging, eyes sunken and hollow.

She thought she cried out as she sank to the ground, but she could not be sure for the roaring ocean was inside her brain . . . drowning her, forcing her into an oblivion where she was unaware of her son clinging to her hand, staring fearfully into her face and crying into the darkness of the night.

CHAPTER SEVEN

The kitchen was steam-filled and smelled of barley meal and potatoes cooked in their skins. Catherine paused for a moment in her task of pulping the vegetables, to brush the damp hair away from her brow. Preparing the swill for the pigs was a job she hated and she meant to make up enough to last for several days. She used up the damaged potatoes, those which were soured or cut by a spade, and others too small for selling at the market in Sweyn's Eye.

Some farmers gave the animals uncooked potatoes, which was the easier way, but Catherine believed what her father had taught her that pigs flourished on the more easily digested cooked meal. The best mixture, in her experience, was to put three and a half pounds of potatoes to two and a half pounds of barley meal per head. The actual profit per animal was only two shillings, but her pigs earned her a good reputation for fine pork which was important to Catherine.

David had gone out on the cart with Morgan, taking the sacks of new potatoes into town. Catherine had spent several days sorting and grading the crop and now her nails were split and torn and her back ached constantly. But in fairness to David, he had helped as much as he could, leaning down from his chair and laughing as he carved a face on a potato shaped like a man.

Grudgingly, Catherine admitted that Morgan's help on the farm had eased much of the burden and she had been surprised at the swiftness with which he had absorbed the ways of the land.

'There, that should be enough to keep the pigs going for a week at least,' she said aloud and smiled at her own voice ringing in the empty kitchen. She lifted the heavy pan and carried it outside, tipping the swill into a tank behind the sty. It took several more trips before the kitchen was free of the overpowering smell and then Catherine flung open the windows and sighed in relief.

From outside she heard the sound of the bullock bellowing in the fallow field. The animal was magnificent, strong and sturdy and as Morgan had said, would be an investment. But she would have preferred that he kept his money as a cushion in the event of a poor harvest, the sometimes disastrous results of which Morgan knew very little.

There was so much to fear with a crop of corn: the sparrows could be deadly enemies, the rain could kill the harvest or it could 'run', producing little else but foliage. She sighed, it was pointless looking for trouble and at least the small amount of root crops she had insisted on putting down had flourished.

During the war years Catherine had done well with early potatoes, but then she had help on the farm and the picking needed many hands. She had seen the sense in David's wish to cut back on root crops and concentrate more on the corn, yet she knew in her heart that it was a risky business depending so much on one harvest.

She washed quickly at the sink, fearing the return of the men, but she needed to get the smell of barley meal and potatoe peel from her hair and skin. Afterwards, she sat in the window with the sun slanting through and drying her hair to a gleaming cloak. She would make herself some sandwiches, she decided, and then get back to her chores; the very thought made her weary, but she would get over it and find her second wind as she always did.

Later, she made her way up towards Ram's Tor Point to look for stray sheep. The lambing time was over and had gone very well, with only one dead ewe who had fallen over on her back and been unable to rise. But there might just be one or two stragglers and every lamb was precious. Catherine smiled to herself, knowing that 'townies' who came to gaze at the farm saw the lambs as pretty creatures

— and so they were, but they also represented profit in the shape of meat or wool; it didn't do to be overly sentimental about the animals.

It was good to be alone and as she stood on the headland, looking down at the sea far below, she felt more contented and at peace than she had done since David came home from the war.

The birds were singing in the bushes to the west of the slope and the soft washing of the water against the rocks had a soporific effect on her. Catherine sank down into the grass and closed her eyes and in a moment, she was asleep.

*   *   *

The town was much as it had always been, but now Morgan was seeing it through the eyes of a man who had left Sweyn's Eye behind. He was used now to the rolling farmlands and the fresh air untainted by copper fumes and dust.

The narrow road leading to the red brick walls of the market were crowded with vehicles. A large brewer's cart with four magnificent dray-horses blocked one side of the roadway and a woman sitting stiffly in a dog-cart was trying to pass.

'We'll have to take it easy here, man,' David said, leaning over the edge of the cart. 'Hate these busy streets, I do, can't think why anyone would want to live here.'

'It's all right — I'll get us through, don't you worry.' Morgan walked at the side of the cart which was groaning under the weight of the potatoes and flicked the reins encouragingly. The horse moved forward, obedient but slow. 'Come on, Sheena, girl,' he said coaxingly. 'You can do better than that.'

At the side entrance to the market sat the cockle women perched on boxes with their wares set out on snowy cloths. Black hats bobbed as the women talked in Welsh and flannel skirts were tucked around black-booted feet, for sometimes the weather turned chill.

'*Duw*, look at those plump cockles, man!' David said,

grinning. 'What I couldn't do to a plate of those fried with bacon and lavabread!'

'Me too,' Morgan agreed as he pushed his cap back from his eyes, 'but we're here to sell, remember?'

David swung his chair to the ground and nimbly edged himself into it. 'I'm getting really good at handling this damn chair,' he said easily and Morgan glanced at him, admiring the man's spirit.

'We've got to get across to those other stalls over by the side of the market, man,' David said. 'We need to find a stallholder who doesn't farm his own produce — it used to be easy, but by God it's getting more difficult now, which is one reason why I persuaded Catherine not to put down too many vegetables.'

Morgan stepped back as David propelled his chair towards one of the stalls and watched as he bargained with the man who seemed reluctant to buy. After a short argument, he agreed to take one of the sacks and Morgan hurriedly took it down from the cart.

'Robbing myself I am, mind,' the man said, his voice surly.

Morgan looked at him levelly. 'Got the best country potatoes here, man, what are you on about?' His voice was even, but the man backed away from him.

'Well, don't come back with no more, right?' he said once he was safely behind his stall. 'I got plenty of people wants to sell to me and civil they are to. I don't know what this country is coming to — the young people haven't got no manners these days.'

'Perhaps it's because we've been over in France killing Germans to keep people like you safe!' David's voice rose angrily and Morgan touched his shoulder.

'Take no notice of this skinflint,' he said evenly. 'He'd wet himself if he even saw a German, let alone have to shoot one!'

David had lost his easy good-natured mood of earlier that morning and slumped in his chair, his eyes downcast. 'You'd better try your hand at selling boyo,' he said to

77

Morgan, 'for I'm sick to my guts of it.'

Morgan paused and looked around him carefully, sizing up the situation, noticing which stalls were running short of supplies. 'Wait by here, you, man,' he said to David. 'I'll be back in a tick.'

It took him almost two hours, but at last Morgan cleared the cart of all the potatoes. 'That's the last sackful,' he said, dusting his hands and smiling at David. 'Had to let them go at thirteen pounds for a shilling — less than we'd agreed but lucky to get it, if you ask me.'

'Aye, you're right. Let's go and have a pint of beer for God's sake, I'm parched.' David wheeled his chair forward and Morgan followed him more slowly, leading Sheena who stepped out more jauntily now that she was relieved of her burden.

They sat outside the Lamb and Flag, Morgan crouched on the pavement beside David. '*Duw*, this is a good pint mind,' David said as he emptied his glass. 'Like to fetch me another one?'

'I'll tell you what,' Morgan said, 'Why don't you stay here while I go up to the Hafod to get that superphosphate we need? I don't see any point in us both getting sick to the stomach with the smell from the works. In any case. it'll be quicker for me to ride up on the cart.'

'Aye, go on you,' David said, smiling. 'I won't find it any hardship to spend my time drinking, don't you worry!'

It was strange riding along the old familiar road out of town and as he moved higher up the hill, the sky seemed suddenly overcast, though Morgan knew it was simply the effect of the copper dust that spilled from the chimneys of the works.

Vivian's Superphosphate Works was on the banks of the river and Morgan reined Sheena to a halt as he neared the gates. 'I've come to collect some manure,' he said and the man on the gate opened it for him.

The smell was overpowering and Morgan tried not to breathe in too deeply. If anything, the superphosphate stank worse than the copper. He guided Sheena down towards the river, where he saw the women bagging the manure and loading it on to the waiting ship. A little downstream was the ferry which carried passengers over to Foxhole on the other side of the river and Morgan waved to the owner, for Siona Llewelyn was a well-known figure in Sweyn's Eye.

Morgan bought his supplies as quickly as he could and Sheena moved impatiently as yet another load was placed on the back of the cart.

'I know, girl,' Morgan said soothingly, 'it's a tough life for an old lady, all right!'

When he had paid for the manure, it seemed as though most of the profit made on the potatoes had been lost. Yet the ground needed to be well prepared, Morgan had enough sense to see that, although he was beginning to believe that he would not even recoup the money he had invested in Ram's Tor the way things were going.

By the time he got back to the Lamb and Flag David was well away with a pint in his hand, telling ribald jokes to anyone who would listen. Goodnaturedly, Morgan helped him up on to the cart.

'You're going to stink to high heaven, man, by the time we get home,' he said, but David lifted his glass and drained it in one swallow, quite unconcerned that he was surrounded by the evil-smelling bags of superphosphate.

'Come on then, boyo,' he said cheerfully, 'get me back home so that I can sleep it all off. God, Catherine will kill me — never seen me pissed, she hasn't.'

Morgan flicked the reins and Sheena began to walk at a steady pace away from the crowded streets of town and towards the broad roadway that led back home.

*　　*　　*

Catherine woke slowly, stretching like a cat curled before a warm fire. She felt refreshed and ready for anything, which was just as well for when she returned to the farmhouse it was to find David rolling drunk accompanied by a sheepish-looking Morgan.

'Sorry about this, Mrs Preece.' He had placed David's chair near the doorway. 'I know we both smell like a sewer and that David's had a bit too much to drink, but at least we sold the potatoes.'

'And bought the manure, I see!' Catherine wrinkled her nose. 'Well then, perhaps you'd better help me get David washed and into bed.'

They worked together unselfconsciously and while Catherine washed David, Morgan took his clothes outside and hung them over the fence. She glanced up at Morgan; he wasn't so bad, she thought — at least he had remained sober.

When David was in bed, she returned to the kitchen to find it empty. Outside, the pump seemed to be working overtime and Catherine smiled. Morgan could not stand the smell of superphosphate any more than she could.

He returned to the kitchen after a time and Catherine looked up at him from her chair. 'How much did you get for the potatoes?' she asked without preamble and he shook his head.

'Not as much as we'd hoped — only one shilling per thirteen pounds and lucky to sell at that.'

'Well, it seems that David was right to cut down on the ground given over to root crops then. All we have to hope for now is that the corn harvest is good, otherwise we're going to take a hiding.'

She stared across at Morgan, expecting perhaps horror at her pessimism but his expression did not change. But then he was a 'townie' after all and he didn't know farming in all its varied moods. At least he was still here though — she had expected him to turn tail at the first sign of difficulty and vanish back into the busy streets of Sweyn's Eye.

'Why are you staring at me like that?' Morgan asked, his eyebrows lifting. 'Have I suddenly grown two heads or something?'

'No,' Catherine smiled, 'I was just thinking that you're not so bad. In fact, I do believe I'm growing to like you, Morgan Lloyd.'

CHAPTER EIGHT

The summer came in hot and fine with the fruits growing in abundance. Blackberry bushes flowered and when the blossom faded the fruits stood proud and green, wanting only the continued sun to bring them into ripeness. And in the fields in Ram's Tor the corn was unbowed, for there had been no wind nor rain to damage the crop.

David Preece sat outside the white stone house, staring across the land. It had been his since birth, passed on from generations of farmers to sons who would perpetuate the old ways. But he was a cripple and would have no sons.

He signed heavily, for he was weary of his degenerating state and of his dependence on others, especially his wife. Each morning Catherine would help him from his bed and that simple-sounding task was a trial for both of them. Catherine would put both her arms around him and he would cling infant-like to her neck; then there would follow a series of movements whilst she edged him forward until his useless legs dangled to the floor. The effort of transferring his weight from the bed to the chair invariably left him panting and Catherine flushed with exertion.

And how he hated the ride along the garden path to the privy. He had no sensation in his lower limbs or in his gut and it was a good day if he performed his bodily functions in the appointed place. On those days he would start the morning with a feeling of relief and a sense of having kept some shreds of dignity.

Catherine was a wonderful and loyal wife to him and it seemed ironic that he had not loved her when he had taken her as a bride — rather he had been in love with the

81

might leave him the richness of his farmlands near Port Eynon. But now, God help him, he cared for her deeply; her touch pleased him, her soft hair was like a caress against his skin and at such times when she was clasped close to him, he felt remembered passions burn uselessly in his belly.

Now he became aware of figures on the horizon and put his hand to his eyes, straining to see into the distance. His heart warmed a little as he recognised the dumpy form of his mother and at her side young William, taller than her in spite of being in his green years.

David had been surprised and not a little shocked when his mother had remarried fourteen years earlier. Small of stature, with a cheerful but unexceptional appearance, she had seemed to him then to be an old woman. But he had wished her well and had been quietly pleased when William was born, for the boy could be a pleasure to him without becoming a threat. Ram's Tor belonged to the Preece family and William most certainly was not a Preece and never could be.

David had little to do with his stepfather, but none the less he was saddened when Joe Richards died. Since that time he had endeavoured to be a father as well as a brother to William and had been rewarded by a touching hero-worship which was enhanced rather than dimmed when David returned from the war severely wounded.

'Hey there, David!' William came towards him, covering the uneven ground with easy strides of his long thin legs. 'There's lovely weather — when are you going to bring home the harvest, boyo?'

He drew to a stop, his eyes shining and his skin gleaming with health. He was a fine boy, David thought — not for the first time — and with his own lack of sons he could do worse than to will the farmlands to his half-brother, for there would be no Preece now to work the land.

'Oh, we'll give it a few more weeks,' David said evenly, not recognising the fact that he was asserting his authority, making decisions in an effort to prove that he was still of some use.

82

'Hello there, *cariad*, there's well you're looking.' His mother rested her arms on his shoulders, kissing his cheek gently, her love enveloping him warmly like a comforting blanket. He smiled up at her in gratitude, for she asked nothing of him except that he would receive her love.

'Make us a cup of tea, there's a good girl,' he said, holding on to her hand and squeezing it gently, the gesture saying what he could not put into words. She beamed at him, glad to be allowed to do something to help, however small.

'There's brown as a berry you are, my love, your hair's streaked with lights and although I'm your mam, I will have it that you're the most handsome man for miles around. Wheel your brother into the kitchen, now, William and get me some water for the kettle, is it?'

William did as he was bid and leaned over his brother's shoulder, so close that the young clean scent of him bathed David in a feeling of nostalgia for his own youth — everything was so simple then.

'Can I come up to the farm to help with the harvest?' William sounded eager and David laughed shortly.

'Can't wait to get off school can you, boyo? Well, all right, you can come and stay if Mam's willing.'

'Me, Glady's Richards, willing?' His mother aimed a playful blow at him. 'I'm coming up here too, my boy, not leaving me out of the harvest fun you're not, oh no!'

David smiled. 'All right, all right, I can take a hint when it's thrown at me like a brick! You can both come up here for the harvest — now can I have that cup of tea?'

They were laughing together when Catherine and Morgan Lloyd entered the farmhouse and David felt a contraction of pain in his belly. She looked so glowingly alive as though she had absorbed the sun — it was in her hair, in the shine of sunburn on her cheeks and in the sparkle of her eyes. He had never seen her look so beautiful.

'Cup of tea, Catherine?' Glady's got to her feet at once and moved to kiss her daughter-in-law's cheek. 'Just brewed one, I did, you must have smelled the pot?'

Catherine smiled warmly and David knew there was a

genuine liking between his wife and his mother. Doubtless they both spent time grieving over his injuries, talking together about how best to handle the invalid. He knew he was being unfair, self-pitying even, but somehow the sight of Morgan Lloyd standing tall and strong at Catherine's side had struck a painful chord of memory in him for the days when he himself was young and whole with the world before him.

'Corn is almost ready for harvesting now, David.' Morgan sat beside him talking quietly, the set of his hunched shoulders excluding the women from the conversation. 'I think we could start in about two days' time if that's all right by you?'

Anger caught at David and he mentally shook himself. It was his own fault that Morgan was working here on Ram's Tor and he had no right to be churlish. Yet it stuck in his craw that a 'townie' like Morgan should be trying to tell him his business.

'We'll wait a while until I think the time's right,' he said, his tone brooking no argument.

Catherine looked at him anxiously, the cup half-way to her lips. 'But David, the corn is almost ripe — why wait and risk a change in the weather?' She spoke softly — her eyes imploring him to be reasonable — and anger shook him.

'Everyone's an expert farmer now.' He raised his hands in mock despair. 'I'm telling you that we've got plenty of time, woman — or do you think that Morgan here is so well-versed in the ways of the land that he can make all the decisions alone?'

Catherine subsided into her chair, though not before David had seen the flash of anger in her eyes. She was quiet because she pitied him and he knew it. Had he been whole she would have shouted back at him, told him that she knew as much about farming as he did. And so she did — he admitted it, but only to himself. The corn could be cut very soon, it was tall and strong and almost ripe . . . and he was a fool perhaps to delay.

He was about to concede that she was right when Morgan

rose to his feet, standing there, young, handsome and confident. His face was sunburned to a golden brown, his hair streaked with lights.

'Won't you reconsider, David? The corn will be ready soon — I give you my word.' Morgan spoke evenly, his attitude suggesting that he made no allowances for a man's bodily disability; he was appealing to David's common sense and it irked.

'We'll cut the corn when I say and not before. For heaven's sake, do people think I'm out of my mind all of a sudden? Allow me to know my own land, will you.'

Gladys made a great show of warming the pot and making fresh tea and the only sound to break the silence was of the coals shifting in the grate. David looked down at his hands; they were strong, square, farmer's hands and if only he had been able to move he could have harvested the corn with more skill than any farmer in the district.

'There, *cariad*, have another nice hot cup of tea,' his mother said softly, the gentle pressure of her hand on his shoulder indicating where her loyalties lay. He looked up at her gratefully, dimly comprehending the selflessness of her love.

William got to his feet and stared out into the sunshine. 'I think I'll go for a walk.' His lean young face was troubled and David cursed himself for a bad-tempered lout.

'Aye, go on, boy *bach*, it's too nice to stay indoors.' Now why did that have to sound self-pitying, damn it! William gave him a quick look and David smiled reassuringly. 'Mind you keep away from Ram's Tor, do you hear me? The silly sheep are always pushing the wall down there and the cliffs are dangerous.'

'I'll be careful, David, don't you worry about me.' William flung to the door with the quick, supple energy of the very young and hurtled along the path, his cheerful whistle hanging sweetly on the still air.

'Well, *merchi*, if you'll excuse me taking over your kitchen, I'll cut some bread and cheese for a snack,' Gladys smiled, her round face flushed from the heat of the fire, and Catherine nodded her head.

'You make yourself at home, Mam, you know there's no need to ask.' She seemed suddenly pale as though the sunshine had drained from her. The golden hair that a few moments before had shimmered and gleamed in the sunlight now lay like dark honey on her bowed shoulders. God, what was he doing to his wife? She looked into his face suddenly as though sensing his thoughts and he smiled — which was a rare enough occurrence these days he told himself.

She came and sat near him, resting her hand on his arm and he looked down at her fingers, roughened with work. The nails, though delicately shaped, were cut short as was practical for a girl who worked the land.

Suddenly he was overwhelmed by love for her, cursing himself for being so short-sighted in the past when he could have wooed her, taught her about loving instead of taking her as his right. He had been little better than a rutting boar, showing no sensitivity, making no allowances for her virgin state . . . and now it was too late.

'I don't want anything to eat — think I'll go and have a lie-down.' He spoke softly and Catherine turned to him anxiously.

'You're not feeling sick, are you, David?' The words were almost a whisper and he shook his head, smiling reassuringly.

'I've had about enough tea to sink a ship and I'm worn out with women's talk — you know what I mean, don't you, Morgan?'

He saw the younger man raise his head; his eyes were guarded and though there was a smile on his lips, it was difficult to know what he was thinking.

'Aye, I know exactly what you mean.' Morgan rose to his feet. 'I think I'll go down into town for an hour and have a pint of ale with the men at Maggie Dick's — it's a long time since I've seen my mates.'

David might have been mistaken, but he thought that Catherine tensed at his side. He glanced toward her but her head was lowered and there was no sign of any response to what Morgan had said.

'Shall I wheel you in then, David?' She spoke without looking at him and David patted her hand.

'No, love, let Mam do it for a change, is it?' Gladys was only too willing to be with her son and she beamed broadly as she turned the chair with ease, propelling it along the passageway to the room at the back of the house.

'So long, David, see you later!' Morgan's voice called and David felt a certain satisfaction in hearing the outer door close. At least Morgan was not alone with Catherine, he thought, though why that situation should suddenly worry him he had no idea.

'Let's get your shoes off then, boy.' Gladys bent over him panting a little, her corsets creaking, David smiled.

'Mind you don't bust you whalebone. Mam, — we'll have an avalanche by here if your fat escapes.'

'Cheeky monkey!' Gladys smacked him playfully on the hand. Nothing ruffled her good nature and it was a relief to have her around.

'Listen, Mam, I meant it about you coming up to stay at harvest time; we could do with you and it'll be good for me to have you shouting your head off at me whenever I get too gloomy.'

As Gladys put her arms around him and hugged him, he closed his eyes, wishing he was a boy again with the faith that mam could make him better.

'Oh, I love you, David, *bach*,' she said as she kissed the top of his head, 'and I feel your pain as if it was my own — you know that don't you?'

'Aye, Mam, I know,' he said gently. It was good to be with her, for she took him as he was and he didn't need to pretend to be strong; he could indulge in his bouts of anger and still Gladys would love him . . . but then she was not a wife.

A wife expected a man to shoulder the load and expected a lot more into the bargain. Catherine might pretend that she did not miss bodily love and perhaps now she even meant it, but one day someone would come along, some man who would reach out to her and stir her into life.

He might already be here beneath David's own roof.

'Do you want the privy David, before I get you into bed?' Gladys asked matter-of-factly and he nodded. Better for mam to witness his indignity than Catherine, who should be learning the strengths of a man and not his weaknesses.

At last, he was alone. He lay silent in his bed and it was here in the small room at the back of the farmhouse, with the cattle making soft noises outside in the shed, that he felt more at peace with himself. Here he could pretend that his body was not shattered and here, miraculously, the pain seemed to ease. Perhaps he should spend his life lying flat and then he would be spared the agony of moving.

He sighed in relief and reached out for a Woodbine and as he watched the smoke curl upwards, he knew there was still a great deal in life he could be grateful for. But perhaps it was not the bed or the Woodbine which gave him his feeling of euphoria — might it not be the medication that old Doctor Bryn Thomas had prescribed for him and which Gladys had just doled out with a liberal hand? Well, whatever it was, he was grateful and soon he would put out his cigarette and sleep.

He heard the cheerful sounds from the kitchen, cups chinking against saucers, the murmur of the women's voices, soft and lilting and he felt cocooned and safe. How foolish was that moment's unease when he saw Catherine and Morgan together; Morgan was his friend, they had shared their experiences of the war. At last he closed his eyes and allowed sleep to claim him.

*   *   *

Suddenly he was awake. It was dark and he had no idea how long he had been asleep or what it was that had disturbed him; then he heard it and his heart sank.

'It's raining! Damn and blast, it's *raining*!' He thumped his fist against the bed and felt the taste of despair in his mouth. He had been wrong to delay and though it was true that a little more sun would have benefited the crop, it would have been far better not to take the risk. Standing corn could be cut swiftly and efficiently and would store well. But corn battered and buffeted by wind and rain presented twice the problems — took longer to cut and would moulder away if not continually being moved so that it could dry out.

Why had he not listened to them? Catherine and Morgan had wanted the harvesting started almost at once and he had ignored them. His stupid pride had stood in the way of his common sense.

If the bad weather continued, he might lose his entire crop, for the wind would snap the neck of the straw and the grain would fall to the ground. Retrieving the seed would be a long hard struggle followed by the necessity to dry it out — what a damn fool he had been not to bring in the harvest while he could.

He became aware that there was silence in the house, that everyone must be in bed. He heard the night sounds — the creak of the boards, the tap of the trees against his windows, all seemed to echo in his head. Mam and William would have gone home long ago, he reasoned, while Morgan would be in his room over the stables. Should he call Catherine, have her make him a cup of hot milk? He felt suddenly that the bed was damp, the sheets pressed in sodden ridges against his spine. He turned his face into the pillow and softly he wept.

* * *

Catherine awoke to the sound of the wind howling against the house. Rain dripped mercilessly against the window and quickly, she rose from her bed and stood on the rag mat, staring out into the greyness. Her hands were pressed to her mouth as she saw the cruel bending of the branches of the trees in the garden. A flurry of leaves was driven against the glass, pasted there as though with glue.

'Oh, no!' She washed quickly in the cold water from the jug on the table and pulled on her calico skirt and blouse and a thick knitted sweater. Twisting her hair into a knot, she pinned it with fierce, impatient jabs.

Downstairs, she put a light to the fire she had set before going to bed and was relieved to see the flames lick upwards as the sticks began to catch.

'David, you're awake.' He was lying against the pillows, his face pale and a growth of stubble making him appear unclean. His eyes were red-rimmed and at his side, the table was littered with Woodbine stubs. Her eyes were drawn to the floor where an untidy heap of sheets lay damply and she felt pity trickle along her spine.

'Let's get you up and into the warm kitchen!' She spoke cheerfully — what was the point in talking about the crop? David knew the fact as well as she did.

She boiled water and washed him with gentle hands and he simply sat slumped in his chair without any expression in his eyes.

'Will you shave yourself, *bach*?' she asked softly. 'And I'll bring you clean clothes.'

She stared around her, wondering what to do first. There was breakfast to cook and the bedding to soak, never mind about the cows crying mournfully in the shed. Several of them had calves and would be content to suckle, but the rest needed relief from overfull udders.

The door opened and Morgan looked into the room, taking in the scene at a glance. David was still bare-chested, holding his open razor in his hand, his shoulders slumped in an attitude of defeat.

'I'll see to the milking,' Morgan said, his eyes briefly meeting Catherine's. She nodded gratefully.

'Aye, well, breakfast will be ready in about half an hour, all right?' She pushed the kettle on the flames, longing for a cup of tea for her throat was dry with apprehension — what if the crop was ruined? How would they feed the stock . . . and themselves come to that?

'It's been raining all night,' David said abruptly as though reading her thoughts. 'I should have listened to you, Catherine. *Daro*, I should have told you to get started

90

on the harvesting before this. I'm a damn fool.'

Catherine put her arms around his shoulders and rested her cheek against his. 'There's no need to take all the blame on yourself. If I'd taken you out to see the crop then you'd have known for yourself that the corn had not run as I'd feared, but was in good ear and ripe for cutting.'

'Well I'll have to take a look later on and see how bad it is. You'll have to get me on to the cart Catherine — and in the meantime pray that it stops raining.'

Breakfast was a silent affair and Catherine was aware that each of them was avoiding the others' eyes. Morgan chewed stolidly as though making up for David who hardly ate a thing; he was slumped in his chair, his big strong hands resting on the table, tensely curled into fists as though fighting an inner anger.

Catherine was pouring the tea and watching it run fragrant and golden into the cups when suddenly she lifted her head and listened.

'It's stopped!' She put down the heavy pot and moved quickly to the door, flinging it wide. The greyness of the morning was gradually warming into light as a weak-faced sun peered in surly reluctance through the clouds. 'It has, it's stopped raining! There's glad I am. David, perhaps things won't be too bad after all.'

He looked up, unaffected by her relief. 'Maybe they will, maybe they won't.' He manoeuvred his chair towards the door and stared out at the dripping landscape. 'Aye, it looks as though it might clear up, but the corn will be bowed by the wind and rain of the night — we'll still have the devil's own job to cut it.'

'Morgan, David wants to go look at the fields; you'll help, won't you?' Catherine asked swiftly. 'I'll go and harness Sheena and bring the cart round the front.'

The ground was sodden beneath her boots, but Catherine was looking joyfully up into the sky where the sun was gaining strength, banishing the rain-clouds. It would be all right, everything would be just fine, it had to be.

She worked swiftly and surely, for Catherine was used

to animals and as far back as she could remember had been set to work cleaning out stables. She knew how to soften leather reins and saddles with dubbin and shine brass with a mixture of ash and water. Her father might have sired only girls, but he had made sure they worked as hard as any boy.

Morgan was waiting for her at the door and he smiled briefly before wheeling David out into the open. He lifted him easily into the cart and there was no trace of embarrassment on his face as he tucked a coat round David's shoulders. Catherine wondered how many bruised and sick soldiers had Morgan seen to make him so used to suffering.

'Ride to the top field,' David said gruffly. 'That's where the most damage will have been done because it's exposed to the sea wind and the rain.' He sighed softly, so softly that Catherine only just heard him.

'The fields on the lower ground are more sheltered, we can only hope they've not been too badly affected.'

Catherine found herself walking behind the cart. Morgan was leading Sheena and the horse moved forward obediently, indifferent to the mud sucking at her shoes and matting the hair on her fetlocks. But then Sheena was an old farmhorse and used to the elements. She worked in snow and hail and rain, pulled the plough with patience and with the same equilibrium took the loaded cart to town, unafraid of the new-fangled motor cars which threatened to replace her.

The top field was in sight now and Catherine's breath was like a long sigh. The straw was bent like so many old men but had not snapped. Her heart lifted with hope — the work of bringing in the corn would be difficult but not impossible.

'The crop will be saved then?' Morgan asked, his voice curiously strong compared with David's.

'Aye, with a bit of luck,' David replied, 'but then the corn will have to be dried, mind — moved about, turned over — it's a tiresome job and not for those who can't take hours of backbreaking toil.' He laughed shortly; 'I forget I'm talking about myself here.'

'David, you can help — of course you can,' Catherine found herself saying breathlessly. She was about to continue when he turned and looked at her with such anger that she fell silent.

'Doing what — making the ruddy tea, is it?' he said through his teeth. Catherine looked down at the muddy path beneath her feet and searched her mind for something to say, but it was Morgan who salvaged something from the moment.

'I don't see why you can't do some of the turning and moving of the corn that you talked about,' he spoke easily. '*Duw*, I've not seen such powerful arms and shoulders on any man in a long while.'

David's tension seemed to ease. 'Aye, you're right, boyo, take no notice of me; I'm a right grouse sometimes and poor old Catherine takes the brunt of it.'

Morgan smiled. 'What if I get in some bottles of ale for us tonight? That taste of it I had down at Maggie Dick's has given me a thirst for the stuff!'

'Good idea, Morgan, go get some ale — and no need to go in so far as Sweyn's Eye, plenty of good beer to be had in Oystermouth, man. Now that's settled, let's go and look at the rest of the fields. We've seen the worst, so what's to come can't be so bad!'

Catherine was mentally thanking Morgan for his intervention; he seemed to have cheered David and given him other things to think about and she was grateful.

The rest of the fields on Ram's Tor were hardly affected by the rain and wind, lying as they did on the softly sheltered slopes that caught the afternoon and evening sun. It appeared now as though a haze was rising up from the ground so that the patchwork-shaped land hemmed in by walls took on a mystical quality.

'*Duw*! I never realised how beautiful the country was,' Morgan said softly. 'Spent most of my life in a mining valley and then in a small house in Green Hill where the vegetation was ruined by copper smoke. It's difficult to believe that we're only a few miles from the town, isn't it?'

His question needed no answer but Catherine was warmed by his praise; it was almost as though he had paid her a personal compliment. She looked towards him and their eyes met and held. She felt unable to breathe and tried to turn away, but could not. As the silence stretched around them, the misty haze seemed in Catherine's mind now and she was frightened.

'Let's get on home then, is it?' David's voice shattered the illusion and Catherine closed her eyes, feeling strangely unreal, hearing as though from a distance Morgan urge Sheena onward. She felt the horse jerk into motion and she held on to the warm wood of the cart as though seeking support.

What a fool she was . . . of course Morgan was only being polite.

And yet, in spite of herself, her eyes were drawn not to the figure of her husband seated in the cart but to Morgan who strode forward over the uneven ground, head high as though if he so wished he could conquer all before him. Suddenly Catherine was afraid.

CHAPTER NINE

Sweyn's Eye was shrouded in a mist that snaked between the hills and lay flat over the river, with the effect of containing the green copper smoke so that a choking stench enveloped the town.

The streets that housed the shops were busy in spite of the inclemency of the day, for a post-war boom had filled the pockets of the people of Sweyn's Eye and the false prosperity seemed real enough.

Mary Sutton's emporium was the fashionable place to sit and take tea, for the soft green carpet and the tastefully arranged furniture gave an air of luxury to what was, after all, only a glorified shopping arcade. And yet the innovation of elegant tea-rooms where shoppers could pause and consider what purchases to make whilst exchanging the latest snippets of gossip had pleased the women of Sweyn's Eye greatly. And the latest news bandied around the damask-covered table-tops was that Mary Sutton herself had been involved in a motoring accident and with the little boy she had borne during the war years.

In the big silent house up on the hill away from the copper smoke and just out of reach of the swirling mists, Mary was coming awake, finding herself in bed staring up at the ceiling, her head aching still and her arm bruised and painful.

A sharp rapping on the door seemed to echo inside her brain and then Greenie was smiling down at her.

'The doctor's here, Mary.' Greenie's voice was shaky and Mary realised quite suddenly that she was getting old. Mrs Greenaway and she had worked together for many years and yet Mary had seen no change in her — not until now.

'I'm sorry I frightened you,' Mary said weakly, 'but I'm all right; no need of a doctor. How did I get home, Greenie? The last thing I remember is falling from the motor car.'

A feeling of dread encompassed her. 'Stephan! Is he all right?' She tried to sit up, but the pain in her head intensified. Greenie put a hand on her shoulder and gently pushed her back against the pillow.

'There's a daft question! Would I be standing here all calm-like if there was anything wrong with our boy? He's right as ninepence and to answer your question, it was your brother-in-law Mr Dean Sutton who found you. Now I'm going to bring the doctor in so that he can take a look at you.'

Mary sighed with relief. Nothing mattered except that her son was safe and well. 'All right, Greenie, tell Bryn I'll be glad to have him take a look at me.'

But it was not Bryn Thomas who entered the bedroom. Paul Soames was advancing towards her, smiling shyly; the way his knuckles gleamed white around the handle of his leather bag told Mary that he was making an effort to conceal his nervousness.

'It's been a long time, Mary,' he said softly, aware of Greenie standing in the background with hands folded over her spotless apron.

Mary closed her eyes briefly, unable to help remembering that she had lain in this man's arms. It had only been the once and it was grief which drove her to find comfort with him. It had been an act of desperation on her part, yet the repercussions had changed her life.

'That's a nasty contusion.' Paul was speaking in a professional manner, but examining the wound on her head with hands that shook. Pity for him dissolved her own embarrassment and she managed to smile up at him.

'I'm lucky that's all I got,' she said lightly. 'The front wheels of the Austin caught a tree stump and the motor car bucked like a mad horse, throwing me forward.'

'Well, you're likely to have headaches for a time.' Paul Soames said carefully. 'I'll give you something to take to ease the pain. Any feelings of nausea or sleepiness?'

'She was out for the count for hours, doctor!' Greenie's voice came from the background. 'That's why I sent for you; there's worried I was with her looking so pale and ill.'

'I'll have to keep an eye on you then, Mrs Sutton,' Paul smiled and the warmth in his eyes forced Mary to look away. There was no point in encouraging him; her lapse had been unforgivable and it would never happen again.

'Do you think you could look at my son?' she asked slowly and painfully, knowing that for a time both she and Paul Soames had believed the child to be his.

'Greenie, take the doctor to the nursery, will you please?' Mary asked and at once the woman swung open the door. Her face was inscrutable, but there was no pulling the wool over Greenie's eyes for she was a bright and intelligent woman.

Paul hesitated. 'Would you go on up, Mrs Greenaway?' he said firmly. 'I'll join you in just a moment.'

Greenie pursed her lips and for a moment it seemed she might refuse, but with a quick glance towards Mary — who allowed herself a slight nod — she left the room.

'Mary, I've longed to see you again and you've kept me at a distance for more than two years, do you realise that? I've had to be satisfied with a glimpse of you in the store now and then. I've been like a silly schoolboy, worshipping from afar; why won't you let me at least be friends?'

Mary shook her head, staring up into his face and seeing that he was thinner than she had remembered and there were small lines around his eyes. How far-reaching was that one act of weakness; it had devastated three lives, she thought dismally.

'How can two people who were once lovers ever be friends?' Mary asked gently. 'You know that it wouldn't be enough for you, Paul. There's no point in talking about it,' she added quickly as he made to speak. 'I was wrong, so terribly wrong to come to you and I've paid dearly for it — we all have. Even my son, who is the innocent one in all this, he's been deprived of his father's love.'

'I could be a father to him, Mary,' Paul said earnestly. 'Why not? You can't spend the rest of your life alone, can you?'

Mary put her hand to her aching head. There was a great deal of truth in what Paul was saying. Brandon was lost to her for ever, returning to America with Mary Anne Bloomfield, so why should she remain a woman alone?

'Let me be for now, Paul,' she said at last. 'I promise I'll think about what you've said — I can't be fairer than that, can I. Now go and see to Stephan, I want to be quite sure that he's come to no harm.'

Mary watched as Paul left the room — he was a fine man and a good doctor and he loved her. She sank back against the pillows and though her eyes were hot and dry, she felt she was shedding bitter tears. Deep within her, she knew that Brandon was the only man she could ever love and while he was alive she could not give up hope that he would some day return to her.

It was almost a week before Mary was able to leave her bed and during that time Paul Soames had called almost every day, much to Greenie's disapproval.

'Give me old Bryn Thomas any day,' she said, as she closed the door behind the young doctor. 'There's a to-do, coming here so often — get folks' tongues wagging, he will.'

'Well, that was his last visit so let's not hear any more about it.' Mary spoke more sharply than she had intended and Greenie folded her arms across her thin chest, a mutinous expression on her face.

'There's a lot of people love a good gossip, mind,' she said at last, 'and no need to give them cause, is there?'

Mary sighed. 'I know you mean well, Greenie, but I've needed to see the doctor and as Bryn Thomas was too sick to call, I had no choice but to see Doctor Soames.'

Greenie's disdainful sniff spoke volumes. 'Well, I've said my piece and I can do no more. Now what are you going to have for tea? You haven't forgotten that Mrs Richardson is coming to see you, I hope?'

A warmth swept through Mary and she smiled in pleasure. 'Yes, I had forgotten, what with you telling me off about the doctor! I must get up, Greenie; I don't want Mali to think I'm ill.'

'All right, you can get up,' Greenie conceded, 'but don't you go overdoing things, mind.' She put her hands on her hips. 'How about if I make you a nice *tiesen lap* with plenty of fruit and sugar and a touch of spice?'

Mary laughed. 'There's a woman you are, one minute scolding me as though I was a little girl and then tempting me with your lovely plate cake.'

A smile twitched the corners of Greenie's mouth. 'Well, you're nothing but a little child to me. I shall never forget seeing you in Dean Sutton's shop and you all keen and eager to make a go of the job. Rousted us you did — me and Nerys and Joanie — right afraid of you we were!' Greenie paused. 'I knew even then that you had the star of good fortune over you.'

'Good fortune?' Mary echoed the words. 'Hard work has got me where I am, nothing to do with fortune.'

Greenie moved to the door. 'Yes, you've worked hard, I'll give credit where it's due.' She smiled gently. 'Aye, even then you were modest and didn't realise that Dean Sutton was after you.'

Mary shook her head at the memory, for it was true that Dean Sutton had his own reasons for giving her the job in his store; he wanted her in his bed as his mistress. But all that was past and done with, she had loved and married Brandon Sutton and then had lost him through her own foolishness. But it did not do to dwell on things which could not be altered.

A little later she was greeting Mali Richardson, hugging her friend with warmth.

'Sorry to entertain you in my bedroom, but the fire is nice and comforting in this miserable rainy weather — it looks as though our summer has gone. Anyway, I might just as well admit at once that Greenie insists I'm not well enough to manage the stairs.'

'Mary, you're looking so pale! There's sorry I am not to have come sooner.' Mali seated herself on the opposite side of the glowing fire, drawing off her gloves. '*Duw*, the weather's turned cold and spiteful all right and what will it be like when the winter comes?'

Mary smiled. 'You always were a freezer — thin blood you've got, Mali Llewelyn!'

Mali leaned forward and sighed softly, 'I suppose I'll never be Mrs Richardson to my friends and, truth to tell, I can't think of you as anything else but Mary Jenkins.'

Mary studied her friend, thinking she looked well and happy and probably was still just as much in love with Sterling as when they first got married. Mary had secretly envied Mali — oh, she'd not had it easy, not by any means, but she had been loved all her life and who could ask more than that? Perhaps Mali and Sterling Richardson had disagreements but if they did, it didn't show. The only emotion Mali revealed in her face was one of happiness.

'I've come to be a cat and tell you all the latest gossip,' Mali said confidently, edging forward in her seat as though in fear of being overheard.

Mary laughed. 'You couldn't be a cat if you tried, but go on — I'm dying to hear what's been happening in Sweyn's Eye this past week.'

'Well, they say that Bryn Thomas is thinking of retiring to the country. He's had enough of doctoring, so it seems, and by all accounts his wife is none too pleased about it.' Mali smiled wickedly. 'Can you imagine Marion Thomas buried somewhere in the country, with no one to lash with that tongue of hers?'

Mary was uneasy, hoping Mali was not going to mention Paul. She had tried her best to bring Mary and Brandon together and would not understand how Mary could have been driven into another man's arms.

'Oh . . . and then there's talk about Delmai Richardson. My dear sister-in-law is having yet another baby, so they say, and she with two sons already.' Mali's eyes were dark. 'I never could understand how she came to give up her daughter, not even for Rickie's sake. Pretty child Cerianne's turned out to be, bless her!'

Mary leaned back in her chair. 'The urges of the flesh have a great deal to answer for, but then perhaps you wouldn't know anything about that?'

'There's soft you are, Mary — do you think I've been a nun or something all my life? Didn't I go to bed with Sterling and us not married? Having his child I was, don't you remember?'

'Oh dear' Mary smiled. 'I suppose there *is* a lot I've forgotten, Mali. I'm conceited enough to think that I'm the only one in the whole world to have sinned.'

There was a tap on the door and Greenie entered the room, carrying a tray which wobbled as it rested on her thin arm. The appetising aroma of fresh-baked cake permeated the air and Greenie smiled as Mali sniffed appreciatively.

'There's a treat!' Mali leaned forward, watching as Mrs Greenaway cut the flat fruit cake into thin slices. 'Takes me back to when I was a little girl.'

Greenie snorted inelegantly. 'Not much more than a babba now, are you?' she said disparagingly. 'You wait until you reach my age, my girl, then you'll know what life's all about.'

Mary smiled and winked at Mali. 'Tut, tut, Greenie, you're only a spring chicken yourself, mind.'

'For that,' Greenie said graciously, 'you can have two pieces of cake!'

As the days went by Mary was happy to see that Stephan appeared to suffer no ill-effects from the accident. His knee had been grazed and his fine worsted trousers torn, but the small boy showed no fear when Mary led him outside and lifted him into the Austin motor car.

'There's soft you are, going driving in that contraption again so soon after you hurt yourself.' Greenie was behind Mary, fussing around and almost wringing her hands with anxiety. 'I'll not have a minute's peace until you come safely back home again.'

'Don't be silly, Greenie,' Mary said amiably. 'I could have fared worse being thrown from a horse. I'll be all right, I promise you, but I must get out into the fresh air for the house is stifling me. You can see for yourself that the sun

101

has come out again and I'm determined to make the most of it.'

Greenie was still agitated. 'It's still cold, mind, not like summer at all - and the weather can turn awkward in a minute, bringing back the rain. *Duw*, there was even a shower of hailstones this morning, so watch out. And don't drive that monster too fast, mind!'

Mary started the engine of the Austin and shook her head, sighing in resignation. 'I'll never convince you that the motor car is safe, will I?'

'No, you will *not!*' Greenie folded her arms and stared mutinously at the gleaming bodywork as though the force of her thoughts could silence the rumble of the engine.

'I'm only going as far as Spinners' Wharf,' Mary said reasonably, 'and I promise I'll be back early before it gets dark — there, how's that?'

Greenie mumbled something with her head bent so that Mary didn't catch her words — and perhaps it was just as well, Mary thought with a trace of humour.

'Now go indoors and don't worry.' She slipped off the brake and pulled away down the drive knowing that behind her, Greenie would doubtless be muttering oaths in her native Welsh damning the motor car to hellfire.

The air was sweet as wine, fresh after the rain and fragrant with the scent of berries ripening in the hedges. Apple trees hung low under the burden of rosy-cheeked fruit, windfalls lying plentiful in the grass. There had been several days of grey rain which heralded the end of the summer weather but now the sun had come again, lightening the earth.

As Mary neared the town, the all-pervading stench from the copper works replaced the freshness of the western side of Sweyn's Eye and as always, the smell evoked memories of her childhood. She could see again the hovel in which she and her brother Heath had lived, could almost taste the dirt, feel the bite of the fleas that were a constant trial.

But that was all behind her, for she had made a success of her life. She had fought her way up from the slum in which she was born to the position of a woman who owed no one a penny.

Mary concentrated on guiding the car through the busy streets, yet her mind was occupied with thoughts of business. After the initial shock the war had brought a boom to the town, but now it had been over for more than six months she felt in her bones that the good times were coming to an end. The country had given not only of its young men but of its resources, sacrificing everything to the jaws of the conflict. It was time for changes to be made and Mary knew exactly what she was going to do.

Selling the emporium would send shock waves reverberating through Sweyn's Eye and there would be no shortage of buyers for that was a thriving concern. But the store dealt mostly with clothing — and clothing for the rich at that. It was all a far cry from the days when Mary had travelled the valleys selling from a van, each single sale and achievement to be savoured. But the stylish fashions she displayed at the emporium these days were a luxury, not a necessity, and when the spiral turned downwards as Mary believed it must, such stock would be the most difficult to clear. So she intended to go back to the beginning, selling shawls and good tough flannel clothing. And she would open up a small food store with some of the money from the sale and the rest . . . well that would be put into property: small coal pits and perhaps workers' cottages on which she could collect rents and a van — motorised instead of horse-drawn — in which to tour the valleys. However poor the workers, they would always need food and clothing.

She drew the car to a stop outside the long low buildings of Spinners' Wharf and looked down at the stream running red as though with blood. In the past Rhian Gray, as she had been then, had been grateful to sell her good woollen products to Mary Sutton. Since then Rhian had married and Mansel Jack had bought the mill, but doubtless they could still do business together.

Rhian was pleased to see her and as Mary was drawn

into the warmth of the kitchen, she noticed how beautiful Rhian had become. She was a woman now, slim and small, yet with a quality of determination that shone from her clear eyes. Her hair, dark red, was neatly pinned in a quaint old-fashioned style which none the less suited her.

'I've come to see you on business as well as pleasure,' Mary said as she held Stephan on her knee. The small boy wriggled, wanting to be free to play on the floor with the other children.

Rhian's niece was prettily plump, with more of her father in her than her mother. But that was only to the good, for Delmai Richardson had enjoyed a brief fling with Billy Gray, borne him a daughter and then returned to her husband Rickie as if nothing had happened.

The other child, a boy, was Gina Sinman's son and Dewi was growing up in the likeness of his Austrian father. The boy had the same broadness, the large head and the charming amiable smile which had stamped Heinz Sinman when he was alive.

'There's a good boy,' Mary patted Stephan's plump backside. 'Go and play then, but don't get yourself all grubby, you've got your best clothes on.'

'*Duw*, Mary, I never thought I'd hear you being such a fussy mammy to your boy — let him be, he needs a bit of fun in his life.'

'I suppose so.' Mary stared at Rhian in surprise. 'Yes, perhaps I am getting over-fussy.'

'You need another one to keep him company,' Gina Sinman said softly and then the rich colour flooded her cheeks as she realised Mary was no longer with her husband. 'I'm sorry, there's thoughtless of me to say a thing like that!'

Gina's embarrassment was painful to see and Mary smiled, trying to set her at ease. 'You're probably quite right, mind. If I'm not careful Stephan will be growing up to be a mammy's boy.'

'That's not likely,' Rhian said firmly. 'Now come on, Mary, don't keep me in suspense; what business have you come to talk over with me?'

104

'It's about the wool, of course.' Mary leaned forward eagerly. 'I want to put in an order for a good stock of Welsh wool blankets and a batch of shawls too.'

'Aye, I suppose they'll sell well in your store what with winter coming nearer, but I thought you'd given up buying that sort of stock in favour of the latest fashions in silks and satins and such.'

Mary smiled. 'Well, I've different plans which I won't speak of now — only to say there's a job going for a man who can drive a motorised van. What about your Billy — would it suit him?'

Rhian nodded. 'He's been looking for a job that will take him outdoors, says he couldn't abide to be shut in a factory now.' She turned to Gina. 'What do you think, would Billy like a driving job?'

Gina smiled softly, her eyes glowing. 'Yes I know he would. *Duw*, he'd be that thrilled because he'd be his own boss then, wouldn't he?'

'Virtually,' Mary said quickly. 'He'd have to keep a stock record and tally of the takings, but apart from that he could go where he wanted to and do what he liked.'

'I'd keep the stock record and count up the money for him.' Gina said eagerly. 'I used to do all that for Heinz. . .'

Her voice trailed away and Rhian broke in quickly: 'I know, let's all celebrate with a nice cup of tea! I'll make it and I can take one up to Carrie then — she'll be just bursting to know who's come to call on us.'

'Oh, I forgot to ask, how is Carrie?' Mary asked quickly. She felt guiltily that she should have enquired sooner for Carrie had once been very close to Heath. 'You know how fond of her my brother was,' she added softly.

For a moment Mary glimpsed a sudden pain in Rhian's eyes, but then she thought she must have imagined it for Rhian was smiling.

'She gets tired easily these days and her arthritis plays her up a bit, but apart from that she's not too bad.'

'Let me take her tea up,' Mary said on impulse. 'I'd like to have a bit of a chat with her.'

Rhian seemed almost reluctant to agree, but after a moment she shrugged. 'All right then, Mary, it might do Carrie good to see a different face.'

When Mary entered the darkened room with the tray in her hands, she almost dropped it, so shocked was she at Carrie's appearance. The woman seemed to have shrunk into herself and her face was lined like a folded parchment. Mary sat down on the edge of the bed and stared into Carrie's eyes.

'Don't lie to me, Carrie,' she said gently. 'There's no need, *cariad*.' She felt tears burn her eyes, but knew that Carrie would hate to see them fall.

'It's bad.' Carrie's voice was dry, an autumn leaf whispering in the wind. 'Rhian knows, but I don't want no one else to learn the truth.'

'Oh Carrie, they love you — and Gina is such a gentle girl, she would want to wait on you hand and foot.'

'I know, I know, but I won't put the burden of knowing on anyone else's shoulders. It's bad enough that Rhian's got to carry the load. Perhaps it's just as well you coming along now, because you can help the girl.'

'She's a fine woman, Carrie, and most of the credit for that goes to you. I think you can be proud of Rhian Gray.'

A thin smile lit Carrie's face and it was like a candle placed within a mask at Hallowe'en, Mary thought, pity tugging at her heart.

'My Rhian won't thank you for forgetting she's no longer called Gray — a married woman she is now, mind.'

Mary sat with Carrie for a long time after the tea had cooled unnoticed and when at last she rose to leave, she put her hand gently on Carrie's thin shoulder.

'Goodbye, Carrie, my dear, I don't know what else I can say.'

'Nothing else to say, *cariad*. Go on, now — no mourning for me and not a word to Gina, mind.'

Mary drove home slowly through the streets which were less busy now. Her mind was calmer, her thoughts clear. Life was too short for silly quarrelling; she would get in touch with Brandon, ask her husband — no, beg him — to come back to her. What was her pride compared with a lifetime alone with only regrets at the end? At her side, her son slept softly and as she looked down at him, so like his father, she felt love tighten like fingers around her heart.

'You'll have your daddy soon, boy *bach*, if I've got anything to do with it!' she whispered.

CHAPTER TEN

Mumbles Head jutted out into the wash of the Bristol Channel, a grey promontory composed of a large headland of rock and two separate islands between which the seas could roar or murmur according to the prevailing winds. Beyond the outer island lay the Mixon Shoal, where ships had foundered ever since man had taken to the waters and where heroism was an accepted facet of life.

Morgan Lloyd stared down from the cliff where he stood with hands thrust into his pockets, trying to come to terms with the fact that the harvest corn would be poor because of renewed bad weather. He had stood in the field beside Catherine and watched as she tugged at the stalks and twisted them until water ran between her fingers. She had avoided his eyes and turning, had made her way silently back to the farmhouse. Morgan had no way of knowing how bad matters were, but of one thing he was sure — he would not go down without a fight, it was not in his nature.

It was a relief to get away from the farm, if only for a little while; as Morgan stood watching the launch of the *Charlie Medland*, he was grateful for the diversion. The lifeboat was almost thirteen years old, but still sailing like a witch as close to the winds as it was possible for any vessel to do. Her grace enchanted Morgan, who had known nothing of the sea until now for he had lived most of his life in the blackness of a coal-mining valley. He had only moved to Sweyn's Eye when his father was too sick to work any longer and was weary of breathing in coal dust. At least Dad had seen something other than a pit before he died, though that was little enough comfort, Morgan thought ruefully.

He crouched down on his hunkers, eyes narrowed as he watched the thirteen-man crew handle the boat with a skill and an ease of familiarity that he envied. The *Charlie Medland*, a graceful forty-seven-foot-long vessel, had cheated the sea of its prey many times.

He must try to join the crew, Morgan thought with mounting enthusiasm. Farming was all well and good; it was a new way of life and one he was growing to love, yet his four years in the Army had given him a taste for adventure that made settling down a difficult task.

Impatient with his thoughts, he made his way down the hill towards the pier, wanting to watch the exercise of launching the lifeboat at closer quarters. There was no emergency, the seas lay soft and calm licking with tongues of foam the grey rocks of the Mumbles Head. But practice was essential; there was need for the coxwain to know his men were trained and ready.

The crew were mostly local fishermen, well-used to the sea in all her moods. But the *Charlie Medland* needed to be launched in boiling seas when any sensible fisherman would leave his boat on dry land.

Watching, Morgan saw the oars dip into the water with precise movements: white oars on the starboard side, blue on the port. The men were garbed in oilskins and appeared unwieldy and misshapen in cumbersome life-jackets.

The coxswain went forrard, negotiating his way through what seemed to Morgan to be a veritable chandler's shop. Masts, spars, sails, ropes and oars sprouted from the vessel, so that the effect was a scene of chaos. But as the *Charlie Medland* moved through the water, it was clear that the crew knew exactly what they were about.

And they worked with zeal for, contrary to what Morgan expected the crew were paid comparatively well for their services, making in one night what amounted to a third of their week's takings as fishermen.

When the boat returned to the slipway, Morgan went forward to help tow the vessel in from the sea. He was surprised at the suck of the ocean which looked so calm and innocent to the untrained eye.

'*Daro*! Useful you being on the spot at the right moment. Morgan Lloyd isn't it?' The man was huge, appearing even larger in his oilskins and with his cumbersome life-jacket.

'Aye, that's right. I'm working up on Ram's Tor, farming with the Preece family.'

The man held out his hand. 'I'm Bill Owen, coxswain. I've heard all about you from Gladys Richards — her second husband used to be one of the crew, rest his soul.'

'I didn't know, but then David Preece doesn't talk over-much about his stepfather,' Morgan replied.

'No, I suppose not.' Bill pushed back his sou'wester and scratched his head. 'From farming stock is David. It's the young'un, William, who has the sea singing in his blood.'

'I'm beginning to think I have too,' Morgan smiled. 'It's exciting to watch you work at any rate.' He looked at the coxswain levelly. 'Could you find a place for me in your crew?'

'*Daro*! You're a landlubber, man — no offence mind you.' Bill Owen began to undo his life-jacket. 'Wouldn't know the first thing about the sea, you boyo, takes a lot of respecting she does.'

'I could learn,' Morgan persisted. 'And I'm young and strong, used to hardship.'

'You'd need to be, it's enough to freeze off a man's privates out there sometimes.'

'You must have men going sick,' Morgan insisted. 'I could come and practise with you and if ever you're a man short, I could fill in.'

'Aye, all right. If you're that eager, come down next week and we'll see what your sea-legs are like. I'm not promising anything, mind,' Bill finished dryly.

'I can see that.' Morgan grinned as he retraced his steps up towards Ram's Tor. It seemed as though he had won over the tough old man; at least he would be given a trial run, which was no mean concession to a man not even from the village. He stood for a long time looking down at the sea rushing between the islands off the Mumbles Head and felt exhilarated by it.

His life seemed to have turned completely about and it was almost as though since the war he had become a different man. Memories were still there, but they no longer had the power to hurt him. And here in the peaceful surroundings of Ram's Tor, he felt cleansed and renewed.

The church bells began to ring out on the quiet air, reminding him that it was Sunday evening. Catherine would have donned her best clothes: neat worsted coat, long skirt and buttoned boots polished lovingly.

Her hat would be of velvet — unfashionable, even shabby, for Catherine did not believe in spending good money on herself. And yet as a farmer and a hard-headed business-woman, she took some beating. He had watched her work for hours over the accounts, planning costs and profits down to the last farthing, and he could not help but admire her diligence.

He moved towards the road and, picking a piece of tough grass, chewed it thoughtfully. He was reluctant to return home, since he would have to face David's anguish over the poor crop for it was his silly pride which had made them delay too long.

For a time Morgan watched the fishermen, sitting on the foreshore mending their nets with skilful hands browned and toughened by the weather. What a far cry was the village of Mumbles from the stink and fumes of Sweyn's Eye! And then he heard a voice rise on the evening breeze and turning, he saw Catherine at the same moment as she saw him. She lifted her hand and waved, nudging Gladys Richards who was puffing along at her side. Young William was running ahead, darting back impatient looks at the two women.

'Morgan, what are you doing here? Not coming with us to church, are you, boyo?' Gladys paused, thankful for the respite and clung to his arm. He smiled, his eyes on Catherine, trying to gauge her mood; was she despairing or hopeful? There was no way of knowing, for she kept her thoughts very secret.

'No, not right now, Gladys — not dressed for it, am I?' He looked down, surprised to see the bottoms of his

111

trousers were soaked with sea-water; he had not noticed the coldness of the cloth against his legs. 'Been down with the crew of the *Charlie Medland*,' he said by way of explanation and Gladys clutched his arm more eagerly.

'My husband was a crewman, you know,' she said quickly, her words coming out in short spurts as she tried to draw air into her lungs. 'Not David's dad of course — my second husband, young William's father.'

'Yes, so I heard,' Morgan smiled, he liked Gladys, she was blunt and honest and a little woolly-headed, but she gave of her love generously not only to her sons but to Catherine, too.

'We'd better go or we'll be late.' Catherine's eyes meeting Morgan's were soft gold in the evening light.

'Aye, don't let me stand in your way.' He moved back a pace and Gladys released his arm reluctantly.

'Pity you're not coming to church, boy *bach*,' she said, a frown creasing the plump folds of her forehead. 'Catherine will have to walk back up the new cut road on her own and I'm that nervous for her.'

'I could meet you,' Morgan said slowly, but Catherine shook her head.

'There's no need, I've walked alone for years without coming to any harm.'

'Aye, but only the other day a young woman was attacked right by here, mind. Funny people are about since the war, I'll have you know,' Gladys said dubiously.

'Don't worry, I'll be outside the church.' Morgan's tone brooked no refusal and Catherine bowed her head, staring down at the black shiny cover of the bible clutched between her hands.

'There, isn't that better than you going home by yourself, *merchi*?' Gladys said in satisfaction.

As the two women resumed their journey, making an effort to catch up with William, Morgan frowned impatiently. It was true that he had no intention of returning to the farm just yet, but on the other hand he had no wish to be tied to an arrangement which had been more or less foisted on him.

He decided he would sit on the bank near the boats and look at the water. The sea lapped the shores gently, softly spitting foam against the rocks. Boats dipped and rose on the tide like a group of fussy women at a dance and the sea wind carried a chill in its teeth.

The waiting seemed endless, but at last he stood outside the imposing arched doorway of the church with the sea behind him flat and grey in the twilight. The doors were opened and the soft light spilled out on to the pavement, dazzling Morgan's eyes for a moment so that he did not see Catherine coming towards him until she was so close he could smell the clean scent of her.

'Gladys is still inside, talking as usual,' Catherine said and her voice was amused, without censure. 'There's a woman, talk the hind leg off a donkey she would!'

They walked away from the church together and Morgan was wryly conscious of the good Christian people watching them who must be curious to see Morgan Lloyd walking Catherine Preece home.

'It was kind of you to wait,' Catherine said, her tone impersonal as though he were nothing but a stranger, 'but I'm well used to these roads — I should be, I walked them alone for all the years of the war.'

Morgan searched for something to say to break down the barrier she was erecting between them. But then he imagined Catherine would be uncomfortable away from the farm, where their only contact was the business of her teaching him the ways of the land.

'I'm sorry about the corn,' he said. 'I realise what a blow it must be.'

She paused and stared at the sea which was lying now below them whispering darkly against the shore. 'Do you?' she sounded doubtful. 'Well, somehow we have to harvest what we can and clear the land of the rest; we might be able to dry the straw and use that.' She sighed. 'But it's no good going on about it — crying over spilt milk, I suppose.' She had taken a deep breath before speaking and the words came out in a rush. He stood close to her, forcing her to face him.

113

'Tell me the worst, Catherine — just how bad is it?' He watched the changing expression cross her face and wanted to shake her for her slowness in replying.

'All right, if you must know, it's very bad indeed, Morgan — and as I said, there's no point in me lying to you. At worst we could lose the farm and everything.' She gave him a quick look before turning away. 'And at the very least we'll need to sell some of the stock; your prize bull will be the first to go, sorry.' Her tone was clipped and abrupt and he felt anger rise within him.

'Well, I must say you farm people give in very easily — don't you know how to fight round here?'

As she began to walk up the hill, the click-clack of her heels beat within him like a pulse of anger at her indifference. He caught up with her easily and walked by her side, trying to think rationally.

She was silent, her face hidden from him and Morgan realised he had been unjust, cruel even.

'I'm sorry, Catherine.' He spoke quietly and when she did not look at him, he caught her arm.

'I'm sorry and I won't say it again.' His voice was hard and she glanced at him giving a slight nod of her head.

'All right, apology accepted.' She looked quickly away from him and sighed heavily.

'Couldn't we just lease out the bull to the other farmers?' he asked and when Catherine immediately shook her head, Morgan felt as though he was a stupid child.

Catherine looked up at him. 'The animal isn't mature enough and we don't know what he'll breed like. No, it's the market for him and for some of my best calves too.'

Her words were a reproach because he had dared to question her and Morgan fell silent. He must bow to Catherine's better judgement, he decided, for she had farmed the land all her life.

'Perhaps I could earn some money,' he said suddenly. 'If Bill Owen would take me on as a crew man, at least I'd be bringing something in.'

Catherine paused and stared back down the hill towards

the little village of Oystermouth. 'But you're from the town, I don't think the villagers would accept you; they're very clannish round here, mind.'

'You let *me* worry about that,' Morgan said, smiling. 'I've already convinced Bill that he should let me help out at practice.'

Catherine shrugged and moved forward again. 'I see.' Her back was stiff, her shoulders upright and Morgan wondered what he had said wrong this time. She really was a difficult and exasperating woman.

'Got any objections, then?' He knew his voice was hard, but he was angry at her attitude. She looked at him, her eyes guarded.

'You just bumble into everything headlong without thinking!' she said quickly. 'The land, the sea — you think you can conquer it all without any trouble, but the elements have a way of doing their worst to the ignorant.'

They walked on in silence until the farmhouse came into sight as they rounded the bend of the road. It lay flat and pale beneath the moon, insubstantial and shadowy, the window downstairs glowing faintly with the light from the oil-lamp.

Catherine paused and took a deep breath and it appeared to Morgan that she was drawing on her resources of strength and patience, ready for the moment when she would step inside the house and face her husband.

He put his hand on her shoulder without speaking and it was not a caress, simply a gesture of understanding.

She smiled up at him shyly. 'There's more to you than meets the eye, Morgan Lloyd.' Her shoulders were straight now, her profile pure in the moonlight. Seeing her lashes brush the fine bone structure of her face, he realised quite suddenly that she was beautiful. He had grown used to seeing her as a farmer, wearing muddy boots and thick knitted woollens which gave her figure a shapeless, indistinct appearance. He blinked rapidly and as she opened the door and the light spilled over her, she was once more Catherine Preece, hard-working but ordinary.

*　　*　　*

David Preece had been asleep in his chair. Tired of waiting for Catherine to return home from church, he had closed his eyes and drifted off into a dream of times past when he could move like any normal man, run across his fields, stare down from the hills into the blue depths of the sea and watch the sunshine and shadow make patterns on the water. And most painful of all, he had dreamed that he was lying in bed with Catherine, holding her soft womanly body close.

He became aware that his neck was aching where he had slept awkwardly and his mouth was as dry as an old bone which had been buried for months. Where the hell was Catherine? A quick glance at the clock showed him that she should have been home from church at least ten minutes ago.

And then he heard the unmistakable click-clack of her heels on the path and warmth surged through him. He realised that he was often hard on her, making her life difficult, but it was only because he loved her so much and detested the way she had to minister to him as though he was a child.

She came into the room carrying the scents of the night and he could smell the grass, the soft sea breezes. Her hair beneath the old-fashioned velvet hat was the colour of ripe corn; her eyes were luminous woodland pools, green and yellow and mysterious. Behind her was Morgan Lloyd, dwarfing her with his size . . . and David felt as though a knife had been thrust into his gut.

'You're late.' His voice was heavy, falling into the silence of the room like a rock thrown into the sea. 'The fire's almost gone out and it's getting chilly in by here.'

He hated himself for the whine of self-pity in his tone and hated even more the way Morgan moved forward and with quick deft movements, raked out the fire and threw on more coal.

'The fire's soon mended.' Morgan was straining to be

116

pleasant, but David could hear the edge of impatience in his voice. Why was he with Catherine anyway — how dare he walk through the darkness with her?

'Your mam insisted on Morgan coming up the road with me,' Catherine said, knowing with some unfailing feminine instinct just what he was thinking.

'I told her not to be so soft,' she went on. 'I said I've walked that way for years on my own, but she would have it and there's no arguing with her when she sets her mind on something.'

'It's all right,' Morgan said cheerfully. 'I was in Oystermouth anyway, so no hardship to wait for the women to come out of church.'

I'll bet it wasn't! David would have liked to give voice to his thoughts, but he was too tired for an argument and anyway, he knew he was being unreasonable.

'Get the kettle on, *cariad*,' he said more softly, his eyes on Catherine's pale face. 'I'm that thirsty I could drink the sea dry.'

She smiled and pushed the kettle on to the coals and then moved around him, resting her hand on his shoulder, leaning over him from behind with her hair swinging against his cheek.

'The kettle's nearly boiling, David, it's been on the hob for ages — you'll soon have that cup of tea.' She paused. 'Tomorrow, I'm going to try to salvage what I can of the corn; it's got to be taken up off the land one way or another.'

He twisted round, trying to see her, feeling the bite of impatience that his wife was doing what should be his job. She shook her head and the golden tresses brushed like silk against his face.

'Most farmers have done their harvesting early, so perhaps we'll get some help from Gethin-the-Stack and a few of the other men.'

As she made the tea, David watched her, noticing there was a glow in her which was reflected in Morgan Lloyd's face. Nothing he could pin down, but he wondered suddenly if there was something between this man and

Catherine. Anger exploded within him and he wanted to lunge forward and thrust a fist into Morgan's handsome face.

God! Why couldn't he do the decent thing and go out into the barn and shoot himself, David thought angrily. He was a burden to everyone, especially to his wife. And she was a good woman, he knew her faithfulness in the very sinews of his being; her morals were beyond reproach and whatever her feelings for Morgan might be, she would never give in to them. Yet the urge to taunt her was difficult to suppress.

'I suppose you're blaming me for losing most of the corn, aren't you?' He did not wait for a reply. 'Why did you listen to an old cripple, why not follow your own judgement? A farmer's daughter, aren't you?'

Catherine gave him a long look, very much on her dignity, but her face was pale and suddenly David subsided in his chair, his anger spent.

'I'll be going to bed shortly.' He spoke abruptly, wanting Morgan to leave so that he would not witness the indignities David suffered every night before he retired. How he dreaded the journey along the back path to the privy and the subsequent efforts to move from his wheel-chair on to the bench seat inside the roughly erected lavatory building.

He hated being washed by Catherine, revealing to her his scarred back and useless limbs. And then to be settled beneath the blankets like a babba, left in the darkness with only his bitter thoughts for company. *Daro!* A man would be better off dead. Why hadn't a bullet struck him clean and honest, sending him into oblivion?

Morgan stared at him levelly. 'Can I be of help?' He didn't smile but stood poised and at ease, waiting for a civil answer to his question. David forced himself to smile.

'*Duw!* Don't you bother, you get off to your bed — we'll have a tough day tomorrow if the harvest's to be brought in. Anyway, Catherine looks after me just fine!' He could not say more plainly what his feelings were and it was a relief when he saw Morgan move to the door. '*Nos da*, Morgan.' David made himself speak cheerfully but once the door closed behind the younger man, he slumped back in his chair.

'I'm tired, Catherine,' he said quietly, 'tired in the very core of me.'

Sighing softly, she moved towards him and knelt at his feet, putting her head on his knee. He could not feel anything, not the soft weight of her, nor the press of her breasts against his legs, but at least he could touch the glory of her hair.

'I know it's hard for you, *cariad*,' she said gently. 'I only wish there was more I could do for you.'

'I know,' David sighed. 'Well, tomorrow I shall come out to the fields with you.' He forced himself to speak cheerfully. 'Morgan can help me up on to the cart and then I can watch you all working like slaves while I sit back like a sultan.' And if he could gather together his courage, he would throw himself from Ram's Tor, which was something he should have done a long time ago.

'That's easy enough to arrange,' Catherine said brightly. 'And I've asked your mam to come up and William, too — they both want to do as much as they can for us.'

'I don't want them here!' David said hoarsely and Catherine looked at him in surprise.

'But David, you know how your mam loves to make Welsh cakes and brew tea, it makes her feel needed.'

His anger was dissipated at once by Catherine's gentle reasoning and he smoothed her hair, letting the silk of it fall between his fingers. What if mam was up at Ram's Tor when he went over the edge of the cliff — wouldn't his death appear even more of an accident? He wanted no blame attached to anyone, he just wanted an end to the pain and indignity of his life. And yet he trembled; would he have the courage when the moment actually came?

'Come on then David, *bach*, let's get you ready for bed, is it? We'll all be too tired to get up in the morning otherwise.'

'Aye, but make me another cup of tea first, love. I don't feel ready for sleep yet.' Nor ready to lie in the darkness of his solitary room, trying to look into the face of death without flinching. He wanted to hold this moment close, savour the nearness of the wife who had never loved him but had given him all of herself with unfailing generosity and loyalty.

'I love you, Catherine.' The words were low and he felt foolish saying them, but it was only right to tell her. 'You have been wonderful to me ever since I came home from the front . . . like this.' He swung his hand in an arc over his legs. The eyes that returned his gaze were luminously golden as Catherine reached out and touched his cheek.

'There's soft you are, I'm only doing what any wife would do — nothing wonderful in that is there?'

He took her hand and kissed the palm and both of them were silent for a long moment with the only sound the ticking of the clock and the fall of the coals in the grate.

'Right then,' he said briskly at last. 'Let's get going then, is it?'

As she rose to her feet and moved behind him to man-oeuvre his chair out into the darkness for the nightly journey to the privy, he felt the heat of pain sweep over him at the thought of her distress. But she would soon get over the horror of what everyone would conclude was an accident and then she could make a new life for herself in whatever way she wished.

He looked up at the stars, clean and bright and large in the softness of the sky, tinglingly aware that this might be the last time he would ever see them. Panic as blind and fearful as anything he had experienced in battle possessed him and he gripped the sides of his chair tightly as though he was already about to fall into the washing seas at the foot of Ram's Tor . . . then suddenly he was crying, silent tears which rolled along the furrow of pain in his cheeks and fell salt on to his lips.

But when he awoke in the early hours of the morning to hear heavy rain falling once more, and knew he would not be able to go to Ram's Tor that day, his despair was too black for tears.

CHAPTER ELEVEN

The wet roadway shone as though polished in the light shed from the street-lamps. The stream rushing beside the long low building of the mill house greedily sucked in the moisture which made no ripple on the foaming surface of the water. Boulders stood proud, breaking up the reddish flow, but the rush and thunder of the stream was drowned by the louder rumble of an engine.

The van was bright and splendid, with carbide lights set in gleaming brass. It was a triumphant, proud vehicle which would serve well, taking woollen stock from Spinners' Wharf into the surrounding valleys. And it would also give a vocation to Billy Gray who had been looking for work.

Rhian stood in the window of the mill house, smiling as she saw the van come to a shuddering stop outside. She flung open the door and looked warmly up at her brother, who stared down at her from the grandeur of his seat, his face alight with joy.

'Round the back with her, Billy Gray, if you please. I don't want oil on my front step!'

Billy grimaced ruefully and then guided the van around the corner before hurrying to the door.

'Got her beat, I have!' He swung Rhian off her feet, holding her up above him and laughing into her face. 'The very devil to drive, she is, but I kept on at her until she broke.'

'It's not a horse, mind.' Rhian struggled out of his arms but was affected by his enthiusiasm. 'It's a motor van with steel and wood and an unfeeling engine that makes a dreadful noise.'

'Don't you believe it!' Billy said. 'She's a monster who thinks for herself — now come on in and let a man have something to eat, will you? I'm starving!'

As they entered the kitchen arm-in-arm, Rhian was aware of Gina who looked up from her baking with an air of studied indifference. There was a streak of flour across her cheek, but the glow in her eyes was unmistakable and it was for Billy alone.

He stared at her across the scrubbed table, watching in delight as her deft fingers pressed the rim of a cup into the rolled-out pastry that was rich with fruit and sugar.

'Making Welsh cakes then, is it? Knew I was coming, did you, *merchi*?' he said, suddenly quiet as though all his enthusiasm and energy was being contained. He did not reach out and touch Gina but his admiration was plain to see as he looked into her flushed face. 'You're a good woman, Gina,' he said quietly. 'I'm a fool not to have taken you up the aisle before now.'

'*Duw*! I think I've become invisible,' Rhian said softly. She pushed her brother towards the big armchair. 'Sit down for heaven's sake, you're making the place look untidy!'

'Where are the children?' Billy asked, doing as he was bid and stretching his long legs towards the fire. Rhian pushed the kettle on to the flames.

'Went for tea with Doris,' she said. 'Don't worry — both Cerianne and Dewi will be spoiled to bits, for they always seem to get exactly what they want out of the poor girl. You'd never believe she's the same Doris who could carry coal like a man in the Canal Street Laundry — she's so gentle with them.'

As she warmed the tea-pot, watching the swirling water and tinglingly aware of the warmth in the room generated by Billy's and Gina's regard for each other, she was suddenly more lonely than ever for Mansel Jack.

'It's a pity that Doris can't work for us any more,' she forced herself to say brightly. 'A good help she was to us, mind. But now she's a respectable married woman, she has her own house to look after.' She smiled. 'Thrilled as a young bride with her little cottage — you wouldn't know she had two big boys growing up around her.'

Billy was silent for a moment, seeming absorbed in the flames which rose and fell, spluttering behind the black-leaded bars of the grate.

'And how's Carrie?' His quick glance towards Rhian and the expression in his eyes told her that he had dreaded asking the question for fear of what her answer might be. It was Gina who replied.

'Well, there's bad she's looking, Billy, but she won't have it — says she's getting better . . . and who would dare argue with Carrie?'

Billy pushed himself upright and stood tall and loose-limbed, his arms hanging at his sides.

'I suppose I'd better go up and see her.' There was a world of reluctance in his voice and Rhian marvelled at the way even brave men could be cowards when faced with sickness.

'I'll come with you,' she volunteered quickly and Billy's relief was evident by the way his tense shoulders relaxed a little. He smiled and opened the door leading to the stairway, indicating with a sweep of his hand that Rhian should go first.

She felt the grip of the old familiar apprehension which was her constant companion these days. Each time she went into Carrie's room, she was frightened of what she might find. Carrie was eating less and less as time went by and drinking only in small quantities. Her will to live was being sapped by the pain that was her constant companion. Rhian sometimes wondered why a human being was left to suffer when an animal would be put out of its misery.

Carrie looked pale and shadowy against the softness of the pillows. Rhian heard the quick intake of Billy's breath and squeezed his hand warningly.

'There's our Billy to see you!' She moved forward and picked up the small clock from the mantelpiece. 'It's almost time to take your medicine, Carrie — I'll fetch a clean spoon.'

Billy had seated himself carefully at the side of the bed

and he was making a manful effort to appear casual, but his hands were clenched together so tightly that his knuckles gleamed white.

'Well, there's a lazy girl staying in bed like this, though I don't blame you, mind — it's been raining off and on these past few days and bed's the best place if you ask me.'

'*Duw*, Billy, there's a Job's comforter you are — and me thinking of getting up and doing a bit in the garden.'

Rhian, pausing in the doorway, marvelled at the courage of the older woman. Carrie hid her pain well and was even managing a smile, but she could not disguise the weariness in her voice.

'I won't be long.' Rhian hurried down the stairs, brushing aside the tears from her eyes; it was becoming a strain to conceal her fears from Gina.

As she opened the drawer of the dresser and took out a spoon, Rhian heard the sound of Billy's footsteps on the stairs. He entered the kitchen and leaned against the door with his head back, his eyes tightly closed.

'*Daro*! Why did no one warn me? God, that's not the Carrie I knew up there in that bed, it's a poor dying beast who should be put out of her misery.'

'Hush!' Rhian said sharply, her eyes moving to where Gina was leaning over the table, her head bowed. She looked up and met Rhian's gaze.

'I've known for a long time,' she said softly, 'but I know you were trying to spare me.'

Rhian sank into a chair, her hands trembling. 'Thank God!' Her voice was trembling too and the tears which she had tried so long to suppress rolled unchecked down her cheeks. 'Thank God I don't have to carry the burden alone any more.'

'Oh, Rhian, love, there's soft you are!' Gina hugged her, regardless that she was streaking flour over Rhian's neat blouse. 'You're not alone, never would be — not while I'm here. Now I'll take up the spoon and give Carrie her medicine while you have a quiet cup of tea.'

Carrie had always been like a mother to Rhian and it

was right that she should end her days under Rhian's care, but though her duty was crystal clear, watching a loved one die was clouded with fears and doubts and not least an impotent anger.

More than once Rhian had longed to make up a potion of lethal herbs and administer it to the suffering woman upstairs. But she held back, less from fear for herself than from the hope that the doctor might be wrong and that Carrie would be well again. But these last few days, it had been increasingly obvious that no miracle was about to happen.

She became aware of Billy leaning over her. 'Rhian, don't take it so hard. Carrie must have been getting worse for some time now and you wouldn't want her to linger now, would you?' His hand pressed into her shoulder and she looked up at him gratefully.

'I know, but it frightens me to think of life without Carrie.'

Billy sighed heavily. 'I've seen men die, young men who have had no chance of life. Some died screaming for their mam, others cursing God, but when it comes it's just like going to sleep.'

Rhian shuddered. She knew Billy was trying to comfort her, but his words were only making a reality of her fears. Carrie had been a pillar, a familiar rock to which Rhian could cling, but now it was Carrie who must do the clinging and that did not seem right.

Suddenly the door flew open and the flushed, triumphant face of Dewi Sinman beamed in at her. Rhian sat herself straighter in her chair, squared her shoulders and forced a smile.

'I won, Auntie Rhian, I beat Cerianne and Doris — I'm too fast for them!' He flung himself into Rhian's arms and lay with his face against her breast. She removed his cap and pushed back the hair from his hot face.

'*Duw*, there's a noise you're making, boy, *bach* — come like yourself and not like a herd of cattle!'

Dewi smiled, not at all insulted by her words for he knew that he was loved. He turned to Billy as to a fellow man and struggled away from Rhian's grip.

125

'Boys are supposed to run faster than girls, aren't they, Uncle Billy?' He expected support and Billy did not disappoint him.

'Of course they are, we men have to stick together.' He ruffled the boy's hair and smiled down at him with warmth in his eyes. Dewi could almost be Billy's son, Rhian thought as she watched them together, for he gave the boy as much of his time as he did Cerianne who was his own flesh and blood.

Doris came panting to the door, clutching Cerianne's hand. 'God 'elp us — there you are, you little beast!' She aimed a playful slap at Dewi's ear and he sidestepped her hand easily.

'If I 'ad my time again, I'd make sure I gave birth only to girls.' Doris seated herself in a chair, placing her legs apart in order to support her belly which had grown large with too much eating. 'This boy here, he's just as bad as my own two — little monsters they are!' She drew Cerianne close to her. 'But this sweet little girl now, I could take her home and eat her for tea!'

Cerianne smiled, knowing there was no threat in Doris's words. She moved to her father and leaned against him with an easiness of manner that revealed her love for the big man who had gone away to something called the war and had then come back to her. She loved him best in all the world — after Gina that was, for Gina was the mainstay of her life.

'Take off your coat,' Billy said gently, 'and put it away carefully, for you're a big girl now and must help about the house as much as you can.'

'I do help!' Cerianne's face was hot with indignation as she turned to her aunt looking for confirmation and Rhian nodded.

'Of course you do, there's no room in the mill house for slackers, everyone does a share including Dewi.' But the boy wasn't listening; he was staring out of the window at the motor van standing in the yard.

'Is that your van, Uncle Billy?' The awe in his voice made the adults smile and Billy nodded.

'Aye, you could say that. Really speaking it belongs to Mrs Sutton, but I'm to drive it round the valleys so it will be more mine than anybody else's, I suppose.'

'Can I come with you sometimes?' Dewi's face was lit with envy. The gleaming machine seemed to beckon to him with glittering charm and at last, unable to resist, he opened the door and went outside to lovingly touch the shiny painted side of the van.

'It looks as though we may have another driver in the family,' Billy said wryly. 'I'll have to look to my laurels, or I can see myself being out of a job in a few years' time!'

Rhian hardly heard the boy's chatter for she had suddenly become aware that Gina was taking an inordinately long time to give Carrie her medicine. A prickling sensation began in the pit of her stomach and rose to her temples, bringing her to her feet. Without a word to anyone she hurried upstairs and into the bedroom and heard at once the sound of Gina sobbing softly.

Slowly now, she moved across the room. It seemed to have grown to the proportions of a cathedral and the floor shivered and moved beneath her feet. But at last she reached the bed and stared down at the face of her beloved Carrie, peaceful now in death. Carrie who had been everything to her would suffer no more, but in that instant Rhian felt she would have given anything to have her back just for a few moments to say goodbye. She felt robbed . . . cheated. She who had loved Carrie, had nursed her and shared her secret, had not been there at the end.

Gina's sobbing intruded on her own grief and she turned to see her holding an empty medicine bottle in her hands, staring at it as though bemused. Rhian drew in a deep shuddering breath and slowly, reluctantly, Gina met her eyes.

'She begged me to give it all to her. I couldn't bear to see her so racked with pain!' She dropped the bottle and as it fell to the floor with a soft thud Gina put her hands over her eyes. 'She took all the medicine, Rhian — oh, my poor Carrie!'

And then Rhian saw that she was needed by the living. She could no longer do anything to help Carrie, who was past all pain, but Gina — brave, meek Gina — was crying out for reassurance.

'There, cry it all out, *cariad*.' She stood beside the stooped, grieving woman and held Gina close to her, as a mother comforts a child.

'Be proud, for our Carrie ended her life with a bit of dignity.' He voice broke and she closed her eyes tightly against burning lids. The two women stood in silence for a moment and then Rhian sighed heavily.

'We'd best tell our Billy,' she said, her tone subdued. 'And the sooner the better, for he'll have to fetch the doctor.'

Rhian took a deep breath — one thing was sure, Carrie would go to her resting place in *Dan y Craig* cemetery with a show that would dazzle the town. Rhian could afford to have a good pine coffin made and employ the services of the shiny hearse drawn by fine horses. It was all she could do for Carrie now.

Billy's face was pale as they came down the stairs, his eyes drawn to Gina's blotched and tearstained face. He gazed from her to Rhian, who nodded her head slightly and sighed a long sigh before sitting down in the chair near the fire. Doris has long since left and the children were playing outside, which was a relief.

'It's over, Carrie's gone.' The words fell into the silence of the kitchen and it seemed strange to Rhian that the clock continued to tick and the flames rose bright as ever behind the blackleaded bars of the fire-grate — somehow she felt that the entire world should have come to a stop.

Billy shook his head and unconsciously clung to Gina's hand, rubbing the small wrist in a a gentle rhythm which eased some of the strain from Gina's white face.

Watching, Rhian felt very alone, longing for Mansel Jack's strong presence, a comforting shoulder to lean on.

'I will see to everything,' Billy said, as though sensing something of Rhian's feelings. 'There's no need to worry about the funeral arrangements and all that.'

Gina lifted her head and there was a white line around her mouth.

'Yes, but first we will have to call in the doctor and then Mrs Benson,' she said softly. 'Carrie must be put tidy-like.'

Rhian shivered and Billy rose to his feet, relieved to have something practical to do. 'I'll go and see to it all now.' He looked through the window to where the two children were admiring the van. 'I'll take them both with me out of the way.'

The silence stretched long and empty and Rhian felt that even her pulse could be heard for her heart was beating unevenly. She knew she must do something to remove the empty expression from Gina's eyes.

'Make us a cup of tea, there's a good girl!' She spoke loudly and Gina started to her feet, her instincts to serve and succour rising to the surface. It was as if in the last few months Gina had donned the cloak worn by Carrie.

The clink of cups and saucers and the grating of the blackened kettle being drawn from the flames were familiar and soothing sounds. Rhian found the tension easing from her limbs and quite suddenly she leaned forward and put her head on the scrubbed surface of the table that smelled of carbolic soap, giving way to the tears which had been choking her.

'That's right, my lamb, about time you had a good cry,' Gina said in her soft gentle voice. 'But now you must start to think about yourself.' She placed the cup on the table and smoothed Rhian's dark red hair.

'You need your man and he needs you, so it's off to Yorkshire with you tomorrow, right? You've done more than your share by here.'

Rhian stopped crying and rubbed at her face with a handkerchief which was just a foolish scrap of lace.

'I do want to be with him, but it would be disloyal to Carrie to rush away before she's settled in her resting place. I must stay for the funeral.'

'There's a soft way to talk now — as if you haven't done enough.' Gina handed her a good plain square of linen. 'Have a proper hankie — you're making your face all red with that silly bit of a thing you're using.'

129

She paused. 'Well, promise me that you'll be away to Yorkshire as soon as the funeral's over, then?'

Rhian nodded. 'You'll be all right when I've gone?' she asked and Gina smiled the gentle smile which lit up her face.

'*Duw*, there's a thing to ask, of course I'll be all right! I'll find someone to help in the house and then I'll be down in the mill working the looms, which I love to do as you well know.' She seated herself across the table, her hands clasped round the cup as though to warm them.

'The spinning is in my blood, so it'll be no hardship for me to make wool in the mill and the babbas are growing up now.' She paused. 'And there's Billy . . . he hasn't said anything, mind, but we've got an understanding.'

'I know.' Rhian smiled and reached across the table to take Gina's hand. 'I think you both deserve a bit of happiness.'

Rhian saw clearly in her mind's eye the figure of Heinz Sinman, tall and genial, his hair and beard always coated in fluff from the wool he worked with such skill. He had been taken away from his home to an internment camp at Camberley during the war where he had died of a heart attack.

Time had eased the pain for Gina and now she was ready to fall in love again — and who better than Rhian's brother?

'You've been like a mother to Cerianne,' Rhian said quietly. 'At least you won't have any problems with our Billy's daughter.'

Gina smiled gently. 'No, there's nothing of the wicked stepmother about me.' Her smile suddenly vanished. 'I love her as my own child, but do you know what my nightmare is?' She glanced at Rhian and then looked quickly away, an embarrassed flush rising in her cheeks.

'Come on, tell me,' Rhian said. Please talk, her mind begged, say anything that will stop me thinking of Carrie lying dead upstairs.

'Well, I dream sometimes that Delmai Richardson is coming to take Cerianne away. Cerianne is that woman's only daughter, for I hear she has three sons now.'

Rhian bit her lip thoughtfully. It was so long now since

Delmai and Billy had shocked the town of Sweyn's Eye by running off together — a woman of the gentry and a man from the mean streets of the town . . . and one who had been convicted of murder at that.

The gossip had been a nine days' wonder and the resulting ripples had spread out to encompass all who had any connection with Billy Gray.

Rhian had visited them in the small coal-mining town where the couple had fled from the sharp tongues of Sweyn's Eye women. She had found them living in poverty with Delmai, gently raised, unable or unwilling to run the house properly; she dismally failed to eke out the small wage Billy earned in the pit on food and supplies.

And finally the inevitable had happened and Delmai returned to her life of luxury, to the husband who forgave her sins in order to inherit his father-in-law's wealth.

'No, Delmai Richardson wouldn't dare to anger her husband by bringing Billy's child into the house; it's said he made that a condition of taking her back. In any case, she's too selfish a woman to even think of reclaiming her daughter, I bet my last penny that her sons are being brought up by some nurse or other.'

The two women fell into silence once more, each locked into their own thoughts. Rhian was still trying to push from her mind the picture of Carrie's face, devoid of life, the bright eyes closed for ever. The kettle at the side of the hob hissed and spat out water which fell sizzling on to the black bars of the fire.

'More tea?' Gina asked as though eager to be doing something and Rhian nodded absently. She blinked rapidly and tried to concentrate on Gina, who was emptying the tea-pot outside on the garden; when she returned to the kitchen her hair was bedecked with light drizzle.

'Billy's coming,' she said, relief evident in every line of her body as she washed the brown tea-pot in hot water, spilling medallions of dampness on the floor.

Mrs Benson and Doctor Soames arrived together and vanished upstairs and Rhian could hear them talking in low

131

voices. Then Mrs Benson returned to the kitchen and smiled sympathetically at Rhian.

'Been sick for some time, has Carrie,' she said, tying a crisp apron around her ample waist. 'Didn't expect her to last this long, truth to tell.' Mrs Benson rubbed her hands together as though to warm them. 'Doctor says it was a merciful release, so don't you girls go grieving too much now.' The nurse moved towards the stairs again, carrying a bag in her hand.

'No need for you to come with me, lovey,' she advised as Rhian hesitated behind her. 'These things can bring distress to friends and relatives and you're best out of it.' She paused and turned to smile at Rhian again. 'Though I do remember you were a good little midwife when Gina Sinman was giving birth — saved her boy's life, you did. But go back down, *merchi*, I'd sooner work alone.'

Reluctantly, Rhian returned to the kitchen; there was nothing she could do without making a fuss and drawing Mrs Benson's attention to things best left alone. As her eyes met Gina's she saw the anxious question which could not be spoken and shrugged almost imperceptibly.

Paul Soames left as quickly as he had come, nodding to Billy who was seated in the chair before the fire.

'Thank you, doctor,' Billy said automatically as he opened the kitchen door. Then he returned to his seat and as Rhian saw him frown and chew his lip she wondered if he too felt the pain of Carrie's loss as she did.

'Where are the children?' she asked softly and Billy's mouth stretched into a smile that did not reach his eyes.

'I let them stay with Doris in Canal Street. She saw me going to Mrs Benson's — she couldn't fail to, living almost next door — and knew something must be wrong.'

After that there seemed nothing more to say. Rhian sat listening to the sounds of Mrs Benson's footsteps moving overhead and her imagination veered away from the pictures that were forming in her mind.

It seemed an age, though it was probably only little more than half an hour later, when Mrs Benson entered the room, her round face flushed from her exertions.

'Could somebody put out a bowl of hot water for me to wash?' she asked and Gina was on her feet almost before the words were spoken.

'I found this.' Mrs Benson dipped into the deep pocket of her apron and brought out the empty bottle. Rhian's mouth was dry and Gina seemed to be frozen to the spot, half-way to the sink, her mouth open.

'I think we'd better get rid of it,' the nurse said lightly though her eyes were shrewd. 'We don't want those lovely little babbas of your playing with dangerous medicine bottles, do we?'

It was Billy who took it from her hand and disappeared outside, closing the door quietly behind him. And afterwards, though Rhian wondered if Billy guessed as Mrs Benson obviously did the significance of the empty bottle, the subject was not spoken of again.

CHAPTER TWELVE

The heavy spiteful rain which had continued for several days, clouding Ram's Tor and blocking out the sunlight, disappeared as suddenly as it had come. The skies grew clear and the curving bays of Bracelet and Limeslade seemed bathed in a crystal light which intensified the shape of the rocks and softened the contours of ochre sands.

David drew a shuddering sigh and as he dragged himself upright in his bed he could vividly imagine the pity of the neighbouring farmers for the poor war-torn cripple up on the hill who had lost most of his crop. Even Catherine's father would come from Port Eynon, for he was a better farmer than he was a man and loathed to see good lands ruined.

He peered through the chink in the curtains, trying to see more of the morning. At least for the present the weather was fine, which would give him the best part of the day to put his plan into action.

Then Catherine entered the room, her smile warm but not reaching her eyes. He knew she was waiting in apprehension to see which way he would turn, for sometimes he vented his pain and frustration on her, striking out at what was most dear to him.

'Is William about?' he asked evenly and the tenseness of her shoulders relaxed a little as she nodded.

'There's a good boy he is — up early and had the fire lit for me, so as soon as you like you can shave and then I'll make you a nice cup of tea, is it?'

He had no need to shave, for no one would care about his stubble when he was lying at the bottom of Ram's Tor.

'I'll have the tea now, *merchi*,' he said and tried to ignore

134

the flicker of surprise in her eyes at the gentleness of his tone.

It was William who brought him the cup of steaming tea and set it down on the side table, grinning from ear to ear.

'What are you so happy about?' David asked easily and William leaned forward, his eyes warm.

'Just glad to get away from the women for a bit, they seem so grumpy today. I know the rain's been bad but . . .' he paused, lifting his head in an attitude of listening. 'Aw heck! Here it comes again.'

Well today was the day whatever else happened, David thought savagely. Morgan would be well out of the way, leaving early to visit the O'Connor family before accompanying them to Katie Murphy's wedding. And Gladys would be going off with him, as she wanted to attend to a few things at her home. He would persuade William to hitch up the horse and then somehow he must dredge up his courage to do what he should have done long ago.

'Perhaps we can do some work on our own then,' David said softly, his breathing ragged and fear boiling within him. 'You and I will see how the crop is standing up to this weather — but it's our secret, remember!'

William nodded. 'Yes but David, the crop is beaten down — I can tell you that now — some of the corn has fallen to the ground and turned a funny colour.'

'I'd like to see it for myself.' David's voice was sharp and William drew back a little, his mouth pressed into a stubborn line. David reached out a hand and clasped his young brother's thin fingers.

'Sorry, boyo, don't take any notice of me.' He smiled, the knowledge that he must use William to carry out his plan weighing heavily on him. But he must not think like that or his resolve would waver. He drank his tea and set down the cup.

'Come on then, William, help me out of this damn bed,' he said, his voice loud with forced cheerfulness. It hurt him to see the way William responded so readily, his

135

hands gentle, pleased to be of service to his brother.

The kitchen was empty when David wheeled himself on to the stone flags of the floor. The silence hummed around him and the warmth of the fire fell upon his face, but his useless legs could feel none of it. His heart was beating rapidly as he pushed open the door and peered out into the rainy misted day. The greyness of the cloud reflected his mood; even the fields looked grey and David wondered briefly how Catherine would manage if the crop was a complete failure.

But then she had managed very well during all the years of the war and had attained a strength and independence that he admired. And at least without him she would have one mouth less to feed. He stared down at his hands, wishing he could hold his wife close one more time, kiss the softness of her mouth and smooth back the lovely sun-touched hair.

The clatter of hooves on the path outside brought his thoughts up sharply — self-pity, he was wallowing in it more and more each day. If he lived he would become un-bearable even to himself . . . with the thought, a surge of energy and determination brought his shoulders erect and his chin jutting forward.

'There's a good boyo you are, William.' He smiled and was rewarded by the warmth that crept into his young brother's face. Knowing that the boy loved him unreservedly, asking nothing in return, guilt rose painfully in his throat along with unwanted tears.

'Are we taking your chair, David?' William asked and David pursed his lips consideringly. Would the chair be of any use on the rutted paths that wove around the fields? On the other hand, he would be immobilised totally if he did not take the chair.

'Aye, take it, might as well.' He manoeuvred himself as near to the cart as he could and then pressed his arms against the wooden sides, heaving his leaden body upwards. As the blood pounded in his ears and sweat beaded his forehead, he thought for a moment that he would not be able to conquer the first hurdle. Then William came and pushed from behind and David found the strength to pull even harder with his big arms. At last he lay gasping against the wooden planking, staring up at the sky, feeling the rain like a woman's tears on his face.

'Are you all right?' William's anxious voice reached him and David dragged himself into a sitting position, knowing that he must make a move quickly before Catherine returned from the shed and insisted on accompanying him.

'Course I am — get up into the driving seat and let's get on with it,' he said cheerfully. He felt the cart dip as William climbed aboard and then the jolt of movement and the clip-clop of hooves that became muffled as the animal trod the grasslands outside the farm.

'Go up to Ram's Tor, Willie; I might as well see what the worst of the fields are like first.' The Tor faced the might of the rain and the strong winds coming in off the sea and there the grain would most probably be lost; the straw would have snapped off at the neck and the harvest would be impossible to reap.

'Keep to the edge of the fields, so that the wheels won't get bogged down in the mud,' David called and William shouted back at him through the rising wind.

'All right, David, I won't let you down, don't worry!' William pulled his cap down on his head to shield his face from the rain and David smiled.

'We'll make a farmer's boy out of you yet! Used to all this you'll have to be — out in all weathers, rain, shine and wind.'

William turned in his seat. 'I'm not soft, mind, I've gone sailing with my father in terrible storms and the sea is more dangerous than the land.'

'Don't you believe it,' David said more to himself than to his brother. The land could sap the strength, the wind push a man to the limits of his endurance. The cruel rocky face of the Tor took the foolish sheep and cast them down into the sea to drown, which was why the Tor beckoned with such fascination.

The ground was becoming uneven, the rutted pathways

were heavy with mud. The wheels of the cart turned reluctantly and David peered ahead, praying that nothing would happen to prevent him from reaching his destination. How exactly he would accomplish his goal, he wasn't yet sure, but he would bide his time and wait for the right moment and then he would plunge down into the arms of the sea.

The journey was slower than he had expected and the weak sun which had shone briefly that morning had vanished entirely. The sky was heavy with rain, the clouds grey and scudding ominously over the headland. The horse was plunging forward gamely but finding the going heavy.

David leaned back in the cart, closing his eyes, the rain coating his lashes so that he seemed to be crying. But the time was past for shedding tears. The war had toughened him, made him impervious to the sound of men dying, yet the love of his family had made him soft again . . . for a time, but he was over that now.

There was a sudden cry and the cart lurched drunkenly. David sat up, straining to see over his shoulder.

'William, what's happened?' He saw his brother leap from the driving seat and bend down in the mud; it seemed an eternity before he replied.

'Duw, I think poor Sheena has broken her leg! Come on, David, I'll help you down and you can take a look; I might be wrong.' But it was clear from his tone that the hope was a faint one and David felt his spirits plummet.

He lowered his wheel-chair first and then swung himself from the cart. It was easier to get down than it had been climbing aboard and he was hardly out of breath as he settled himself into the chair. He saw at once that William's summing up of the situation was correct, that the animal's fetlock was swollen and the joint misshapen. Anger pure and hot poured through his veins. But this was only a setback, he told himself — he would get to Ram's Tor if he had to drag himself all the way on his belly. He sighed heavily and patted the horse's heaving flank.

'Unhitch her,' he said sternly and William, uncomprehending, obeyed. David stared at the beast for a long time and the large eyes seemed to gently rebuke him. If only he had a gun he could put the creature out of its misery, but as it was . . .

'What's to become of her?' William's voice sounded far away and David looked up, meeting the boy's eyes unflinchingly. What was the point of trying to shield his brother? Farm life was hard and he must learn that as soon as possible if he was to survive.

'She'll need to be shot,' he said more gently and William's head drooped in acknowledgement. His young face was pale, but then he could not expect to hide from the cruelties of life; he would be a man soon and would need to act like one.

'Come on,' he said, 'leave her be — we'll send someone out to her later.' He met the sudden flare of enquiry in William's eyes without flinching. 'I might as well do what I came to do, otherwise all our efforts are wasted.'

'But couldn't I run back to the farm?' William suggested. 'I could fetch Morgan, he'd know what we should do.'

His brother's faith in the man irked and David stifled his anger, taking deep breaths and trying to control his voice.

'You know as well as I do that Morgan's off to Katie Murphy's wedding today. And do you want to let Catherine deal with the beast? You know she loves that horse!'

William swallowed hard. 'I could do it,' he said, his voice faraway. David leaned forward and grasped his arm, realising that his brother was more of a man than he had given him credit for — it seemed that Gladys's well-meaning attentions had not softened the boy.

'Well, I'm going back to find help anyway,' William said firmly, his hands twisting his cap out of recognition.

'All right then, bugger off!' Angrily, David pushed at the rims of the wheels, forcing the chair forward over the uneven ground, but even with the great strength of his arms and shoulders the task was almost impossible. His face grew flushed and the veins stood out on his forehead, but determinedly he pushed on, aware of William standing uncertainly behind him. He did not look back and with the slope of the land now in his favour, made his way more easily to the wall that separated the fields from the sheer rock of the Tor.

He had no need to take a second glance at the crop, for most of it on the seaward side was ruined. Some fields in the softer areas nearer the sun might be saved, but the harvest would be a poor one. Not that he need concern himself with it any longer — if Morgan Lloyd wanted to be a farmer, then he could take on the problems right from the start.

The bitter taste of fear and anger made him retch and fiercely he forced the chair towards the place in the wall where badly placed stones had given way in the rain. He tried to ram his way through the gap, but there was little chance of moving the larger lower boulders and all he succeeded in doing was sapping his strength.

He paused for a moment, marshalling his thoughts, telling himself that he must take things slowly and not panic. He took a deep breath and, looking over his shoulder, saw William bending over the horse's swollen limb.

'She's trying to get back home, David,' he said. 'Sheena's trying to get back home, did you hear me?'

Anger shook David and he wanted to tear and rend. 'Forget the blasted animal!' he called, his voice little more than a croak — why couldn't William go away and leave well alone?

David slumped over in his chair with his head on his knees, praying for strength — not that he believed in any deity; the only thing a man had going for him was his own will.

He lifted his head and reaching forward as far as he could, began to try to roll the boulders aside, cursing under his breath as his hand slipped on the mud.

'I must go back for help, David,' William called. 'You just stay where you are — I won't be long.'

David was no longer listening; everything was drowned out by the rush of the tide as the seas washed against the rocks below. The ocean seemed to call to him like the stories he had heard of sirens drawing sailors to a dark death beneath the water. It would be cold and perhaps painful at first, but his leaden limbs would not matter for the sea would suck him into its depths and there would be an end to it all.

With a superhuman effort, he pushed a boulder aside and attempted to force his chair through the space. The wheel caught and held and, cursing, David thumped one fist into the other. Painfully he backed away and with an effort leaned forward again, his useless lower half obstructing him. His hands slithered in the dirt and he uttered an oath, staring up in anger at the glowering skies.

David sighed and leaned forward once more, moving another stone with such effort that his vision blurred and his head swam, but he *would* get through, damn it! The earth clung to his hands, heavy with rain, and he stared at the bright run of blood which suddenly welled up between his fingers. He was reminded of the war, mud and rain and cold . . . and blood. He could hear the cries of men dying around him and his own hoarse voice pleading for someone to come and take the weight of the gun from his twisted body.

But when at last the shattered metal was pulled away, there was no sensation of relief — only the gnawing bite of pain through his upper back. It was only later, in the field hospital where sweet French nurses ministered to him, that he realised the truth that he would never walk again. And that was only the beginning . . . there was so many truths to face, the worst of all being that he was no longer a man, not in the sense of the word, for he had cried himself to sleep whispering the name of his wife . . .

At last the gap was big enough for the chair to move through and David hardly felt the sweat that ran down his collar, misting his eyes. He was exultant and at the same time afraid, for the moment had come and could not be put off any longer.

Ram's Tor was a high peak which overlooked the head

141

of Mumbles and the two small beaches curving shyly inwards. It was the top of the world — or so he used to think when he first came here and stood looking out to sea. His father had given him a good beating for being alone in such a dangerous spot, but afterwards David went there often to think his own thoughts.

When his father had died, he had felt grief but not an unbearable sense of loss, for the land gave a man the feeling of continuity. Things died and then grew again — that was the way of it.

He had loved Ram's Tor more than anything, more than his mother or even his small half-brother William — and certainly more than the wife he had taken because it suited him to do so. When had that changed? It was difficult for him to tell.

He rolled the wheels of the chair towards the great edge of the cliff, knowing that before him there was nothing but rocks and sea and wild wind and the ragged cries of the gulls swooping overhead. Just one strong push, he told himself, then he would be over the edge and there would be no turning back.

He put his hands on the wheels and spun them as hard as he could and the chair jerked forward. Hearing a thin cry, at first he thought it was one of the gulls coming too close to the cliff-top and then he realised that it was William's voice and the boy was calling to him frantically.

David twisted the wheels again, leaning forward and jerking the chair into swifter motion. He could no longer think of William's pain, only his own.

And then, just as the cliff edge came nauseatingly close, he felt a great force push against his side and then he and William were rolling in the rain-soaked grass. David shook himself free and turned over on his face, his hand reaching . . . straining. But slowly, before his horrified gaze, William was disappearing over the cliff.

'Jesus help me!' David's hands dug into the earth and painfully he dragged himself forward until he could peer over the clumps of grass to the rock falling away in the distance.

'David, help me, can you reach me?' Miraculously William was alive, clinging desperately to the dying limb of a tree, his white face staring upwards.

'Don't worry, I'll get you.' David moved closer, his dead limbs hampering him, but at last he was able to reach out and catch his brother's thin arm.

'Come on, now,' he gasped. 'Give me your other hand — easy does it, now . . . carefully.'

The branch cracked suddenly, the roots tearing a black hole in the soil. William shouted out and hung by one arm, his feet searching for purchase on a small ledge, and it took all David's strength to hold him.

'Come on, boyo, use your other arm to reach up and grasp my hand — there's a good man.' David tried to speak calmly, but the pain in his shoulder was almost too much to bear.

William stretched upwards in a desperate jerky movement and as David clutched his wrist, gave a thin cry.

'My arm, David, I think I've broken it! Oh help me, I can't hold on!' His voice was faint and his head was lolling back on his shoulders and all David knew was that, whatever pain it cost either of them, he must not relinquish his hold on William or he would plunge to his death in the stormy seas.

David gasped, lowering his hot face into the grass. He could feel the wetness of it through his shirt and his body suddenly began to tremble. He closed his eyes and tried to think — perhaps he could edge backwards and gradually draw his brother to safety. But when he tried to move, he knew it was useless; without the strength of his arms and shoulders, he had nothing to aid him. All he could do was to lie still and hope that they would be found.

It was a slim chance, but perhaps the horse would make its way back to the farmhouse. Catherine would send for help straight away; she had her head screwed on right way, did the girl he had married.

William began to moan and David lifted his head. 'Boyo, are you all right, can you hear me?'

'Yes, David.' The voice was weak with pain and it was like a knife shafting through David's gut.

'Try to find a foothold, boyo; rest on that narrow ledge there and ease the weight on your arms. Perhaps if you take time to rest, you can climb up by here with me.'

William made a manful attempt to do what he was told, but his strength was not equal to the task. Pain sapped him, took away his sense as he lapsed into unconsciousness once more.

David felt tears trickle from beneath his closed eyelashes as silently he cursed himself for a fool. He had wanted to take his own life, uncaring of how his goal was attained and now, by his sheer thoughtlessness, it seemed as though he would be responsible for his brother's death instead of his own.

He tightened his hold and below him, heard William moan. Gritting his teeth, he lifted his head and shouted to the racing clouds.

'You're not going to get him, do you hear, you up there? I'll save him if I have to hang on here all day.'

His head sank on to the wet earth, he smelled the scent of the land he loved and his heart was heavy. 'I'm sorry, William,' he said hoarsely, 'I'm sorry, my little brother.' And then he wept, not silent tears as becomes a man but great, rending sobs which tore at muscles in his chest and gurgled in his throat. And the heavens looked down and great gusts of rain washed over the land that lay soft upon Ram's Tor.

CHAPTER THIRTEEN

The air was heavy, the haze of sunshine shafting through mean courts where children played barefoot in the cobbled roadways. The stench of the works lying along the river banks permeated the air and the abrasive flecks of golden brilliance which were copper dust scored and scratched at small panes of glass in the windows covered by discoloured lace curtains.

In Market Street, the all-pervading smell of fish from Murphy's Fresh Fish Shop which blanketed even the sulphurous fumes of the copper works went unnoticed for Katie Murphy, only daughter of Tom and Jessie, was about to be married, And not before time was the general consensus of opinion, for Katie was fast reaching the age when a girl became an old maid; would never see twenty-five again, some said, and those who were disdainful of the Murphy family uncharitably mentioned the fact that thirty was nearer the mark.

In fact Katie was twenty-six, though she confessed to feeling much older especially when she remembered her first love. William Owen had charmed her into a passion found in the sweet grass on top of the hillside and Katie had given of herself freely, for she had believed theirs was a romance that would last for ever. But William, had been killed when he jumped from Sterling Richardson's car in an effort to avoid being injured at the time of the Kilvey Deep disaster; ironically, he himself had set the explosive at the instigation of others, all motivated by hate of Sterling. Yet even before his death Katie had known him for a villain, a selfish man who would do anything to further his own ends.

And now she had been given a second chance of happiness for Mark was everything that William was not — he was strong and honest and he loved her. The war had prevented the marriage taking place sooner, but now there was nothing to stand in the way of their union and indeed, Katie's father had been vociferous in his requests that the ceremony take place as soon as possible.

'You'll go bringing trouble home to us if you're not properly wedded as well as bedded!' Tom Murphy, his ginger hair thinning into tufts across a shiny pate, had not mellowed over the years. 'Get that man to make an honest woman of you, Katie, or it's out of my house for sure, with my boot behind you!'

In fact the arrangements had been going ahead already although Katie, smiling to herself, thought it did no harm to let her father believe he was the instigator of all the plans.

Now, as her mother placed on her head the small cap of cream flowers which picked out the embroidery on her gown, Katie felt happiness surge through her. On an impulse she hugged her mother who smelled of gin as always, kissing her cheek soundly.

'I love you Mammy, you know that, don't you? And I won't be far away. I'll only be living over on the slopes of Mount Pleasant, not a long ride in the car.'

'Stop your nonsense now, girl, for to be sure you'll have your ould ma crying in a minute.' Jessie spoke in a hard voice but her eyes were moist, for Katie was her eldest child and her only girl and though they had never been close, it had been good to have another woman in the house. And Katie had always been able to manage Tom; even when he was in his cups, he would lavish his love on his only daughter, though it would injure his pride to mention it.

'Well, I'd better get off down to St Joseph's, it wouldn't do to keep the holy father waiting.' Jessie stood for a moment in silence, knowing that certain things should be said to a daughter on her wedding morn but at a loss as to how she should frame the words.

'I know Mammy,' Katie said softly, her eyes luminous.

146

'You don't need to say anything; I'm a big girl now, not a sweet young maiden.'

Her mother tutted and turned away, but there was a thin smile curving her mouth. 'See that you make your man a good wife, now, Katie — don't turn him away from your bed or you'll find him going into another.' She would have said more, but Katie held up her hand.

'I told you there's no need to give me advice, Mammy. Now go on with you or you'll be arriving at the altar at the same time as me!'

It had begun to rain, a soft gentle drizzle which laid the dust and coated the cobbles with a fine mist so that they looked as though they had been lovingly polished.

'Come on then, girl!' Tom held out his arm and as Katie took it, father and daughter smiled into each other's eyes. 'This is it then, my colleen, your wedding day — and it's so proud I am that you're marrying well.'

'I'm marrying happy, Daddy, and that's what's important.' Katie stepped outside to the accompaniment of sighs from the women waiting for a glimpse of the bride.

'God be with you, Katie Murphy!' Dai-End-House called loudly and began to play on his accordion; his fingers were gnarled now but still able to bring forth music from the instrument that was older even than he.

Tears burned and trembled but through them, Katie smiled. She was leaving Green Hill, the place of her birth; the street which had seen her struggles and pain were swiftly rolling past and even though she would return everything would be different for then she would be Mark's wife.

* * *

The Central Hotel in Oystermouth was filled with revellers and the large rooms that usually echoed with discreetly played violins now rang with the toe-tapping music of the fiddle. Gin bottles lay empty beside glossy aspidistra plants and in one corner Tom Murphy, father of the bride, lay slumped against the wall, his high collar open, his tie askew.

147

Katie shook her head and smiled at Mark, who leaned close to whisper in her ear. 'I'll be glad when I can take my new wife away from this crowd; it sounds like bedlam in here!'

Katie brushed his cheek with her lips. 'So will I but be a bit patient and let them all enjoy the merrymaking — they get little enough of it, God knows.' She paused, her eyes searching the room. 'Look, there's Stella O'Connor coming to pay her respects with all her little girls trailing behind her.' She sighed. 'And each one of them the image of poor Honey who died in the munitions factory.'

'Now no sadness today, I won't have it.' Mark slipped his arm around Katie's shoulder. 'Who's that man with the O'Connors? His face looks familiar, but I can't quite place him?'

'It's Morgan Lloyd. He used to lodge with Stella and was in love with Honey, poor man — see how much older he's grown since he came home from the war.'

Morgan was aware of the scrutiny of the bride and groom and wondered not for the first time how he had allowed Stella to talk him into coming to a wedding where most of the people were virtually strangers to him. When he had visited her in Emerald Court she had told him he was becoming glum and far too serious and a good shindig would do him good.

In the face of continuing bad weather and the resulting atmosphere at Ram's Tor Farm, Morgan could not help but agree with her.

Returning Morgan's smile, Katie held out her arms as Stella stepped forward. 'Sure 'tis good to see you so happy, Katie Murphy!' Stella said. Then Morgan was taking Katie's hand, his head bent politely towards her. She could see the lines that should not be present on such a young face and yet there was a glow about him somehow — perhaps he had found another love?

But then she was being a romantic, she told herself, wanting happiness for everyone just because she had found it with Mark.

148

'Tis good to see you at my wedding celebration, Morgan,' she said lightly. 'You look sun-tanned and very well indeed; you're no longer in the copper, then?'

Morgan shook his head. 'I'm up at Ram's Tor, working the farm, but the weather is doing its best to defeat me!'

Katie smiled warmly. 'Well, at least the rain brings you to my wedding.' Morgan's smile did not quite reach his eyes, but he made a polite and appropriate reply.

Suddenly there was a stir in the doorway and Katie stared in open-mouthed amazement at the girl who was standing before her, gripping Morgan's arm fiercely. She was rain-soaked, her golden hair lying darkened and glued together with wetness, but she was Honey O'Connor reborn and Katie felt herself sway against Mark's strong arm.

Stella O'Connor was staring at the girl too, as though she couldn't believe her eyes; her face had grown deathly pale and her eyes started from her head. Almost she reached out a hand but then let it fall to her side, shivering convulsively.

'Morgan!' The girl spoke and her voice was soft with the Welsh lilt, not at all like Honey O'Connor who had caught the Irish from her mother and father. 'I'm sorry to barge in like this, but David and William have gone out some-where and I can't find them — you must come and help me look.' Seeming to become aware of her surroundings, she glanced apologetically towards Katie.

'There's sorry I am to interrupt your wedding party, but it's my husband — he's not well, you see, and he shouldn't be out in this bad weather.'

Morgan took over with a smoothness and efficiency which made the incident seem insignificant; he apologised swiftly and then ushered Catherine from the room. In the sudden silence, Stella seemed to diminish in stature as slowly she sank into a chair.

'That girl is Brendan's love-child, 'tis as plain as the nose on my face — and me not knowing all these years that she's living just a few miles away!' She stared up at Katie, who was bending over her solicitously.

149

'I knew he had someone else, a long time ago, a girl from Port Eynon, but I never dreamed he'd given her a baby — and her so like my lovely Honey that I can't bear it.'

'Hush now, people are listening,' Katie said softly and Stella sat upright, brushing back a wisp of hair and trying to regain her composure.

'I must go, take my little girls home — he can come later or not just as he likes,' she said with a disdainful nod towards the figure of her husband lying in the corner. 'Good day to you, Katie, and God's love bless your marriage!'

Katie watched her hurry to the doorway of the hotel with her children flocking after her and turned to Mark, her eyes worried.

'Do you think she'll be all right? Should I go after her?' she asked, clinging to his arm.

He shook his head. 'No,' he said firmly, 'you'll only draw more attention to her and that's not what she wants. It's time we went and you must forget other folks' problems, right?' He put his hand beneath her chin and Katie smiled.

'What about our guests, we can't just leave them without a word, can we?'

Mark nodded. 'The guests can get on with the festivities if they like, but I want to be alone with my wife.'

Katie shook her head at him. 'But Mark, we're only going up the stairs to our room — it's not exactly as if we're going away on honeymoon, is it?'

He kissed the tip of her nose. 'It's exactly as if we're going away on honeymoon — come on, let's get out of here.'

When he led her to the stairs there were a few cheers from the merrymakers, but most of them were too affected by drink to take any notice.

'I must confess it *is* nice to be alone.' Katie leaned against the closed door and stared around the room. There was a festive air about it and she could not be sure if it was the flowers which graced the mantelpiece or the decorated silk of the curtains and bedspread that lent the room charm, but contentedly she smiled.

'Is it wrong of me to be so happy when others are

150

miserable?' she asked as she slipped the flowered cap from her head and shook free the softness of her red-gold hair.

'If you can't be happy on your wedding day, then when can you be?' Mark asked as he took her in his arms. 'Now forget everyone else — there's you and me to think of now and this is our moment, so don't spoil it, right?'

He kissed her gently and his fingers were firm as they undid the buttons of her gown. She nestled close to him smiling up into his eyes.

'Well, I'd say you've done this sort of thing before — for shame and you a new husband!' Her teasing voice was silenced by his kiss and she stretched on tip-toe to press herself close to him. She knew that he was right, that she must savour this moment for such joy might never come again.

*   *   *

The rain washed down against Morgan's face as he led Catherine from the hotel and into the street. On the opposite side of the road the sea sang against the shore, clattering against the belt of pebbles on the ebb.

'Now, Catherine, tell me exactly what's happened.' He looked down at her, painfully aware that he longed to take her in his arms and erase the crushing weight of worry from her.

'I think David must have got our Will to harness Sheena, but I don't know where they've gone. I waited until dinner-time had come and gone, then I went out to look but there's no sign of them. I suppose they might have gone into town for supplies but it's funny they should go so early and not tell me.' She paused. 'I don't know why, Morgan, but I've got a terrible feeling in the pit of my stomach.'

'Well, I'm sure there's no need to worry overmuch. Could they have gone visiting perhaps?'

'No, I don't think so somehow. I can't imagine David doing anything like that.'

'We'll go to see Gladys, she might know what both her

sons are up to. Now don't look so frightened, Catherine, we'll find them.'

'The two of them must have gone when I was doing the chores.' Catherine's voice had a brooding note in it and Morgan felt her guilt as though it was a tangible thing. 'Left the house early they did, whatever.'

'David is a grown man,' he chided gently. 'You can't be watching him every minute of the day and if you could, he would hate it.' Even as he spoke, he felt the pain of knowing that Catherine was bound to David, that she was his wife and her first concern must be with his well-being. He saw the dark mass of Mumbles Head come into view and over it, storm clouds gathering; was there never going to be a break in the weather?

He held Catherine's arm as they crossed the road. On his left was the plethora of boats and ketches lying darkly against the shoreline. A small rowing-boat drifted free on the incoming tide, lifting and turning on the boisterous waves.

'They can't have come to Gladys's, for I can't see any sign of the horse and cart,' Catherine said in a breathless voice, the rising wind carrying her words away.

'Come on, we'll do no good standing here.' Morgan hurried her along the street to where the hill rose sharply at right angles from the main thoroughfare, the steep steps leading to a row of fishermen's cottages.

Gladys was open-mouthed with surprise when she saw them standing on her step. Her head was swathed in a white cloth and in her plump hand she held a tin of lavender polish.

'*Duw*, there's a surprise — what are you doing here, Catherine? Nothing wrong is there?' She didn't wait for a reply but rushed on, her words tumbling out, revealing her fear. 'If that rip of mine has got into a scrape in the short time I've been down by here doing my cleaning, I'll box his ears, that's what I'll do!'

Morgan stepped into the warm spotless kitchen and placed a hand on Gladys's shoulder. 'Nothing to be alarmed about — it's just that David and William seem to have gone out somewhere and Catherine wondered if they'd come here.'

Gladys pulled her cloth from her head and her hair hung in wisps over her face. 'Now that's a funny thing.' Her voice shook a little, her hand rubbed against her skirt as though wiping away her worries and suddenly she smiled.

'Gone to look at the fields, they have, I'll bet! Our William probably agreed to hitch up the horse so that David could see the crop for himself, find out how bad it was beaten by the wind. They'll be back at the farmhouse wanting their tea, that's what I think.' In her anxiety, she was babbling and Catherine put a steadying hand on her arm.

'Let's get back home,' Catherine said, her troubled eyes meeting Morgan's. She didn't believe that David would be so stupid as to go out into the fields in such weather, but there was little point in worrying Gladys further.

'I'm coming too,' Gladys said at once, frowning uneasily. 'I'll just fetch my coat.'

The journey to the farm along the winding road cut from the rock seemed endless. The rain sent jagged rivulets of water running down the slopes and Morgan longed to run ahead of the women, for Gladys walked slowly on her plump legs. She paused to draw a breath every few minutes, her eyes wide and apologetic. But at last the low white-washed building came into view and he saw at once that there was no light shining from the windows.

'The cows have come down to be milked,' Catherine said softly. 'Poor beasts, I expect they're full and heavy and wondering what's happened to me.'

'You and Gladys can see to the animals,' Morgan said decisively. 'I'll search for David and William.'

'But where can they have got to?' Gladys said in hushed tones. 'I can't see them staying out in this bad weather, it's raining so hard.'

'Don't start panicking,' Morgan said quickly. 'There could be all sorts of reasons why they are out . . .' Though if challenged he knew he'd not be able to think of a single one.

153

The fire had gone out long since and the kitchen was unusually cold. Morgan watched as Catherine lit the lamps. 'I'll fetch some coal,' he said, but she shook her head.

'No, go you to find the boys. Gladys and me will see to everything else.' Her eyes met his and in the lamplight they were beautiful, golden and filled with fire. Morgan wanted to take her in his arms, hold her close and promise her that everything would be all right, but after a moment he turned to the door and left the farmhouse without a word.

The rain ceased to fall as he skirted the fields but darkness was closing in and the sky was patterned with scudding dark clouds blown by the wind coming in off the sea. The corn was battered, bowed as though giving up the fight for survival. Had he lost all he had invested in Ram's Tor in one disastrous week of rain and winds?

He moved on past the sty where the boar stared at him with fevered angry eyes, rather like David Preece himself — but then both animal and man were prisoners each in a different way.

Morgan had no idea where he was going to search. With the darkness came a keening wind and if David and his young brother were not under shelter of some sort, their plight would be a sorry one.

Then he paused, his soldier's instincts suddenly alerted by a sound. It was no more than a breathing somewhere to his left, beyond the boundary wall of the farm. He moved forward cautiously, his head held at an angle as he listened intently.

There was a movement again, the noise louder this time and as he stared into the darkness, Morgan made out the shape of an animal dark against the night sky; it was Sheena. Making soothing noises, he clambered over the wall and smoothed the animal's flanks.

'Why didn't you come home, then, girl?' He spoke gently and the creature raised a drooping head and stared at Morgan with mournful eyes.

'Let's have a look at you — hold still, I'm not going to hurt you.' Morgan was no veterinary surgeon, but it didn't take him long to realise that the animal had broken a fetlock. He frowned angrily into the darkness. The horse would have to be put down and that would be a loss to the farm as well as to Catherine, who loved the creature.

'You'll have to wait by here, Sheena,' Morgan said softly. 'I can't stay with you — I've got even more reason to search now, you see.'

But when he moved away the horse tried to follow and Morgan paused, knowing that he must put the animal out of its misery. He turned and ran back to the farm, his eyes — grown used to the dimness — picking out the pitfalls so that his progress was swift.

'What is it?' Catherine's face was pale as she came out of the shed, alerted by his approach.

'I've found Sheena but the animal is hurt. I'll have to get David's gun. I'm sorry, Catherine.'

She made a soft muffled sound in the darkness as he stood before her, his arms hanging helplessly to his sides.

'I must hurry. David and William are out there somewhere, but I couldn't leave the poor beast to suffer. Get me the gun quickly, Catherine.'

Morgan stared up at the clouds and the moon struggling to shine through the darkness, wondering that he who had killed men almost thoughtlessly in the war was so distressed at having to shoot a helpless animal.

Catherine returned more quickly than he had expected; she had a shawl pulled over her head and round her shoulders and her beautiful hair was hidden away from the moonlight.

'I'll do it,' she said decisively. 'You must find David and William — they could be lying injured as you yourself said, so let there be no arguments, is it?'

Morgan wanted to chase the pain from her eyes but said 'Good girl,' as he turned and hurried away from her, his footsteps echoing over the cobbled yard before fading into silence in the mud of the pathway. He made his way back to the edge of the cliff, where below him the sea washed against the rocks in cruel little gusts. His straining eyes saw what appeared to be pieces of planking that rose and fell to dash against the rocks and splinter into small pieces and then he recognised with a thrill of horror one of the wheels from David's chair.

Behind him he heard a shot ring out in the silence of the night and he stiffened, picturing Catherine crying over the body of her beloved horse. But there might be worse sorrows for her to face. He sighed softly and rubbed his hand through the tangles of his hair; he thought he had come home to peace, but it was only to find that he must fight another kind of war.

* * *

In the darkness it was difficult for Catherine to find Sheena. She stood and listened and at last heard the softness of the animal's breathing close to the fence near the farmhouse.

'There's a good girl, quiet now.' Catherine felt the heaving flank beneath her hand, saw the eyes roll piteously and for a moment, leaned weakly against Sheena's warmth.

'I'm sorry, girl.' Catherine's finger tightened on the trigger, the sound of the shot reverberated through the silence of the night and then Sheena was a silent shadow on the ground.

CHAPTER FOURTEEN

The silver ocean seemed far away, the waves washing at the rocks sucking backwards, receding like an opponent gathering strength for the kill. Clouds were scudding across the night sky intent on obscuring the moon. The rain had stopped but dampness hung in the air, moisture dripped from the leaves of the trees and the sodden earth lay cold.

Morgan shivered and turned up the collar of his coat. He had been searching for what seemed an eternity and hope of finding either William or David alive was fading. He had moved slowly along the perimeter of the land, trying to gauge the direction of the seas. His blood had chilled when he had spotted the debris of David's wheelchair some time before; he searched now for signs of the crippled man's survival, but knew he was working on instinct rather than knowledge.

He paused, lifting his head like a hunter sensing his prey. From the dark mass of Ram's Tor, he heard a cry so faint that he could not tell if it was human or not. It came again and Morgan began to run, stumbling in his haste over the pitted land.

He found them more dead than alive: David Preece was lying prone against the ground, the only sign of life in his eyes as the whites gleamed in the moonlight. Morgan quickly assessed the position — it was clear that William was injured, lying limply on a small shelf of rock while David, clinging to the boy's hand, was near to exhaustion.

Morgan leaned over the rock and below him the sea hissed inwards, rearing up over black rocks — a monster waiting with an open greedy mouth.

He edged forward and encircled William's rain-soaked body with his arm, hauling the boy upwards. William was a dead weight, surprisingly heavy for so thin a boy. Gasping, Morgan laid him on the grass, then paused and bent his head, trying to draw breath into his lungs.

'Take him to the farmhouse.' David's voice was edged with weariness and something that sounded like despair and Morgan looked at him sharply, correctly assessing the significance of the situation.

Quickly, he replaced the stones, making an effective barrier between David and the sea. Not a word was spoken but the angle of David's head, slumped on his chest, was enough to convince Morgan that he would not have the strength to move even if he wished to.

'Poor sod!' His voice was carried away into the wind as he gently lifted William on to his shoulder and began the return journey to the farmhouse. Sometimes stumbling over the dark patches that hid hollows in the land, Morgan at last reached the beckoning light from the window.

Gladys came forwards and took her son in her arms, rocking him as though he was a baby. Morgan stared levelly at Catherine, reading the unspoken question in her eyes.

'David's alive,' Morgan said, 'but I'll need help to get him back to the farmhouse — can you call someone?'

'There's no one, not at this time of night — and in any case, it would take too long. I must come with you.'

After a moment, Morgan nodded. 'Aye, *merchi*, I suppose you must.' He stared impatiently around the room. 'I'll need a makeshift stretcher and blankets too, Catherine.'

She moved into the back room and he heard her opening cupboard doors. When she returned, she handed him some thick woollen shawls.

'We can take the sled,' she said softly. 'It's out in the back; we use it to take fodder to the animals in the snows. It's not ideal, but it will be easier than trying to carry David between us.'

'Good! Come on, we daren't waste any time.' He refrained from saying that David might even now be moving the stones from the wall and repeating what had obviously been an attempt to end his own life.

The sled bounced and cracked against the cobbled yard as Morgan moved forward harnessed like a horse, his legs and shoulders aching with fatigue already. How much harder it would be on the return journey with the weight of a man to pull, but he would do it — he was determined to for within him was a grudging admiration for David Preece.

At his side, Catherine hurried to keep pace with him. Her breathing was ragged but she made no complaint and he sensed she feared she might be impeding him. He glanced at her face, small and pinched with worry, and the overwhelming, unexpected urge to protect her swept over him.

'We're nearly there — to your left, see, near the break in the wall just by Ram's Tor.' He changed direction slightly and the sled bucked and lifted, dragging at his shoulders. Morgan muttered an oath under his breath as he watched Catherine run the last few yards to the huddled figure lying against the stone wall.

'Oh, David *cariad*, what's happened to you then?' She didn't wait for an answer. 'Just look how you are shivering!' She took the shawls from the sled as Morgan drew near. 'Come on, boyo, let's get these around you.'

Morgan moved forward, 'Catherine, you take his legs while I lift him on to the sled.' He gasped as David's weight strained his arms until they felt as though they were being pulled from their sockets. 'Lift now!' he said urgently.

David lay back on the sled like a dead man, his eyes closed, his hair clinging wetly to his face. There were great dark hollows in his cheeks and his jaw seemed skull-like and sunken, though it might all be a trick of the light.

As Morgan began to drag the ropes the blood started pounding in his head with the effort. The ground was sodden and clung to the wooden struts of the sled, hampering its progress.

'I must pull with you.' Catherine took the rope and stood beside Morgan determinedly. 'Get your arm around my waist and let me loop the rope over my shoulder.'

Yoked together, they began the journey back from Ram's Tor in silence. Morgan was acutely aware of Catherine's softness and the slenderness of her waist and the rain-washed scent of her hair. He was aware too of his own hard breathing and the ache in his muscles as they stood proud with the effort of pulling the sled. He glanced down at her, but her head was bent as she strained against the rope and he could not help but admire her strength of will.

David bore the jolting of the sled in silence. Indeed, glancing back at him Morgan saw that he had not stirred; he might be a dead thing lying there in the darkness. He was a man of character — there was no doubt about that — and even his flashes of foul temper were understandable for he had come home to a woman to whom he could no longer be a husband.

Catherine stumbled and fell to her knees in the mud and without a word, Morgan lifted her to her feet. She leaned against him for a moment as though drawing strength from him and then she looked up into his face. Her lips were trembling and her eyes were filled with tears she was too proud to shed.

In harness once more, she leaned forward and began to pull on the rope and Morgan tried to take the greater burden of weight by stepping a little ahead of her. The paths that skirted the fields of beaten corn were rutted and the rain had unearthed stones which seemed to rise up spitefully to strike the underside of the sled.

Catherine stumbled again and Morgan paused, standing upright, his head tipped back as he took lungfuls of air, attempting to gather his strength for the next onslaught on the unfriendly land.

'Leave me.' David's voice was weak and faint. 'You'll do yourselves harm; get help, for God's sake.'

Ignoring him, Morgan squared his shoulders. 'Ready?' he asked, for there was no question of leaving David, not for either of them.

'Yes, I'm ready.' Catherine moved forward once more and he could feel her body trembling with fatigue. He clenched his teeth together and pulled with all his might, straining forward, almost bent double with the effort.

'Look,' Catherine said eagerly, 'the lights of the farmhouse! Not far now, David, we're nearly home.'

Gladys had the door open and she ran forward anxiously, adding her considerable weight to the rope so that the sled moved the last few hundred feet almost with ease.

'There's hot water on the fire,' Gladys said quickly. 'We'll get David stripped off and wash him down, he's shivering like an aspen leaf. Come on, my son, into the bedroom with you.'

David said nothing; his eyes were closed wearily and huge blue shadows circled them. Morgan watched Catherine disappear from his sight with a feeling of helplessness — there was still so much for her to do.

Exhausted, he dozed by the fire and woke with a start when Gladys bustled back into the kitchen.

'I know you're dead beat, boyo, but I need your help, see.' She paused, shaking her head so that her plump chins trembled. 'I don't know what to do about my young one. William is in such pain with his arm and I can't help him.'

'Where is he?' Morgan asked wearily. It seemed there was more he must do before he could fall into bed and seek the sleep which seemed the most desirable thing in the world just now.

'I've lit the fire up in Catherine's bedroom — he's in there. *Duw*, he's that pinched and pale, he looks like death.'

'Fetch me some sticks, good stout ones,' Morgan said, 'and strips of linen or some bandage — anything will do.'

He mounted the stairs quickly, aware of the muscles in his legs protesting at every move. There was a fire in his shoulders and his back felt broken in two. How much worse must Catherine be feeling — she was smaller and weaker than he was.

William was wide awake, staring up at the shadows on the ceiling cast by the flickering glow from the oil-lamp. He looked sharply at Morgan, his head lifting from the pillow though it was clear that even such a small movement caused him pain.

161

'Our David, is he all right?' His voice was hoarse with dread and Morgan smiled at him encouragingly.

'He'll be a new man when your mother and Catherine have finished with him. He's got a soaking and perhaps sore muscles, but nothing serious.' He looked down at the boy's arm. 'You now are another matter — you have a broken bone there and I'm going to have to set it as best I can.'

'Will it hurt?' William asked and Morgan nodded. 'Aye, it will hurt, boyo, I won't tell you any lies on that score, but when I've finished, you'll feel much easier.'

'There's courage you showed, Morgan, out there on Ram's Tor. You risked falling into the sea to save me, but then I expect you learnt to be brave in the war, did you?'

Morgan sighed. 'I don't know. I think bravery is in us all, for you saved your brother's life, didn't you?'

William looked surprised. 'I didn't think David would say anything about that. Going over the cliff, he was; his chair ran away with him, see? I threw myself at him just to stop him, but then we got all tangled up and I was hanging on to a dead stump of tree.'

Morgan smiled dryly. 'And I suppose the stones in the wall moved themselves just enough so that the wheel-chair could get through!' He ruffled the boy's damp hair and put his finger to his lips as he heard Gladys labouring up the stairs.

'Will these, do, Morgan?' Triumphantly she held up two stout pieces of timber and a long length of cloth and Morgan nodded.

'They will do fine. Now get out of here, Gladys, it will be better for all of us.'

She stood indecisively, looking first at Morgan and then at her son. William smiled cheerfully and nodded his head.

'You go, Mam, I know it's going to hurt me but it's for my own good.' With a small sound of distress, Gladys obediently left the room.

'Now then, let's see what we've got here.' Morgan took his knife and cut carefully through the sleeve of William's

162

jacket. The arm was swollen and blue just below the elbow and he took a deep hissing breath.

'You must have been in agonies with this, boyo, — talk about bravery, you've got enough for a whole battalion!'

As he spoke, he grasped the arm and pulled, drawing the broken telescoped bones apart and then allowing them to meet. William growled low in his throat, his face patchily white, his teeth clenched tightly together. Quickly now, Morgan placed the splint and wrapped the sheeting around the lengths of timber in neat folds.

'Done that a dozen or more times, William,' he said softly. 'It always gives pain at first, but it allows the bones to knit together properly — don't want a funny bent arm, do you?'

Some of the colour was coming back into the boy's face as William sighed heavily and relaxed against the pillow.

'I'll get your mam to make up some potion that will help you to sleep,' Morgan said, rising to his feet. He glanced round the room, seeing the little womanly touches, revealing touches which told him more about Catherine than he had learned since arriving at the farm.

On the polished chest of drawers rested a mirror in a plain wood frame and before it lay a hairbrush and some coloured ribbons. He had never seen Catherine in ribbons and only rarely had he seen her garbed in anything other than her working clothes.

Over a chair was placed a stiff clean cotton nightgown with buttons that fastened to the throat and sleeves so long they must cover her small hands.

The neck was frilled with white lace, the only concession to prettiness on a gown which would have been more suited to a nun than a young woman.

Two pairs of shoes with crumpled newspaper inside stood in an orderly file beneath the chest of drawers and a long cardigan, much darned, hung behind the door. Catherine Preece had very few worldly goods, he thought with sudden insight; she was a woman who lived for the land, pouring into the fields of Ram's Tor the pent-up frustrations of her life with David Preece . . .

163

'Morgan?' William's voice, though weak, was questioning. 'What do you think happened to our David out there on Ram's Tor — did he really want to kill himself, do you think?'

Looking into the boy's clear eyes, Morgan decided against dissimulation. William was too intelligent, too honest, he deserved the truth. Morgan was silent a moment, considering the best way of answering the question.

'That's most probably what he intended; I can't see the point of him taking you all that way out otherwise.' Morgan moved closer and thrust his hands into his pockets. 'Though you more than anybody must know the truth — you were with him, after all.'

'Aye, well, he told me he wanted to see the fields for himself though I thought that a bit of a waste of time, mind, but it seemed best to humour him.' William closed his eyes briefly. 'He was acting so strange and when Sheena broke her leg, it didn't occur to him to do something about the poor beast. He just kept going towards the edge of the Tor, pushing his chair with all his might.'

Morgan sighed. 'Well, boy, *bach*, I think you'd better forget it. Get some rest now, otherwise I'll have your mam up here after me.' He smiled encouragingly. 'Try to sleep . . . and William, don't mention what you saw out there on the Tor — don't want to upset Gladys or Catherine, right?'

Downstairs, Catherine and Gladys were huddled over the fire, both women showing signs of strain. Catherine looked up and there were shadows beneath her clear eyes.

'How is David?' Morgan asked, standing before the fire, realising suddenly that his clothes were chill and damp.

It was Gladys who answered. 'Don't like the look of him, Morgan, there's something about the way of him I can't put my finger on but it bodes ill, I feel it here.' She pressed a plump hand to her large bosom and if she had not been so serious, she would have struck a comic figure.

Catherine rose to her feet and stared at Morgan. 'Sleep down by here in the kitchen, you.' She avoided his eyes. 'It's no good going back to your room with no fire in it — you must dry your clothes.'

Gladys nodded her approval as she rose from her chair with an effort and moved along the passage, her shoes slapping loosely against her feet. A door closed and then there was silence in the kitchen and Morgan stared at Catherine, not knowing what to say to her now they were alone.

'Have a hot drink, Morgan?' she asked, but without waiting for an answer she was pushing the kettle on to the flames and stirring the coals with the poker. He watched as she went about the everyday task of making tea with such grace of movement that he was fascinated. Her slender hand swung the shiny tea-pot in a circular motion, warming the china as though it was the most important thing in the world.

'Sheena's out of her misery,' she said without looking at Morgan, but suddenly her hands were still. 'David wanted an end to it all, I just know it and who can blame him?' She did not require a reply. 'I know it's supposed to be a sin to do away with yourself, but how can anyone understand the workings of a man's mind when he's crippled and sick?'

Morgan sat down and removed his jacket, steam rising from the coarse cloth as he placed it over the back of a chair. He could not keep his eyes from Catherine who was leaning forward now, tipping the huge, blackened kettle while the steam turned her hair into little ringlets of gold.

He was silent, not knowing what she wanted from him — absolution for David, perhaps, but then he was the wrong one to ask because he had few religious beliefs. Oh, he had prayed with the best of them when he lay in the mud of the trenches bombarded with shells which exploded into a fury of death all around him. But it had been an act of superstition more than faith, an involuntary reflex of the mind.

She handed him the tea and as he took it their fingers touched; she looked up at him quickly and then away again, seating herself on the far side of the fire and curling her feet under her for warmth.

'I think the weather will change tomorrow,' she said lightly. 'If it's fine and sunny, we'd best try to harvest what's left of the crop.'

'How can you possibly know the weather will change?' he asked, leaning forward in his chair.

Catherine smiled, unaware how wistful and appealing she looked with the neat collar of her cotton dress ruffled and her hair hanging loose.

'*Duw*, I've lived on a farm all my life,' she answered quietly. 'My father was disappointed when I was born because I was another girl. His only interest in life was to get us married off as soon as possible.' She glanced down into her tea as though pretending indifference, but he could see the remembered hurt reflected in her face as she went on:

'My eldest sister Connie, she did well, married a rich farmer whose land lies beside Dad's in Port Eynon — at least *she* pleased him! I was the last in line and I think my father was growing desperate because he gave me to the first man who asked.' It was the most she had told him about herself since they met.

'*Gave* you?' Morgan echoed the word in disbelief. 'God, that's barbaric! I thought women were free to choose their husbands these days.'

'Well, maybe in the town they are, but the old ways seem to stick in the country. I could have refused David, I suppose, but I was young and frightened that my father meant what he said when he told me it was marriage or the streets. You can't blame him too much; it's the old ways that he's used to and he thought he was doing well for me getting me a man who had his own farm, even though it was a small one.'

She had never loved David Preece, he understood that. He understood too the rigid principles which would keep her true to her husband. Morgan stared at her wonderingly.

'What about you, Morgan? You don't talk about yourself much, do you?' She half smiled. 'Tell me to shut up if I'm prying, mind!'

Morgan held on to his cup even though he had emptied it. He was interested in learning more about her life and he felt that once the excuse for staying with her was no longer valid, she would rise and go to her bed — and strangely, he wanted to talk, to remain in her company.

'Not much to tell,' he said as he looked into her eyes. 'I nursed my dad until he died. Stayed over at Mrs O'Connor's house, we did — and a fine family they are too, especially Stella. Do you know that you are the image of their daughter Honey?'

Her eyes were questioning as she shook her head. 'Honey? No, I didn't know — it's just a coincidence I suppose.'

'She died in the war,' Morgan continued. 'She worked at the munitions factory and there was an explosion . . . she was very young.'

'And you cared for her.' It was not a question. 'I'm sorry.' She put down her cup and placed her small bare feet on the flagstone floor. 'There's soft we are, sitting up here until midnight and plenty of work to do tomorrow.'

'Catherine,' he took her hand and held it fast, 'you did remind me of her at first, there's little point in me denying that, but I've grown to know you now and I like you for yourself.' He could have told her that he desired her and would like to take her to his bed, but he imagined she would shy away like a startled filly.

She drew her hand from his as though she had been stung and he cursed himself for a clumsy fool; his words had sounded patronising, not at all what he intended. As she rose to her feet, she said, 'I'll just say this — thank you for what you did tonight, I'll always be in your debt.'

Then she went slowly along the passage and he could hear her light footsteps on the stairs. He sighed heavily and sank back into the chair, closing his eyes, suddenly aware how very weary he was; his back ached and the muscles in his arms were painfully stiff. He tried to clear his mind of all thoughts of Catherine, but it was a long time before he fell asleep.

*   *   *

In the morning, the sun was streaming through the window and Morgan, rising from the chair stiff and uncomfortable, acknowledged that Catherine was right about the weather.

Gladys was kneeling before the fire which was already glowing behind the freshly blackleaded bars and she winked at him as he sat up. 'Mornin', boyo, and a fine one it is too!'

'Morning, Gladys. Yes, it seems to be a good day for us to bring in the corn, wouldn't you say?'

'Don't go asking me such daft questions, boyo. I'm no farmer, I leave that sort of thing to those who know better. Here, drink this tea, it's hot and sweet and just been brewed.'

He drank thirstily; his throat was dry and he savoured every mouthful. 'You make a beautiful cup of tea, Gladys, fair play.' Morgan brushed back his hair, feeling as though he could do with a good scrub-down in hot water to ease the aches in his bones.

'Aye, *chware teg*, I'm the best tea-maker for miles around — everyone tells me that.' Gladys grinned good-naturedly. 'Not good for much else these days, mind, been a widow woman too long I suppose.'

'Now Gladys, don't be wicked or the devil will come and carry you off to hellfire and damnation — isn't that what they teach you in that Methodist church you go to?'

'No, it isn't then, and you just watch your tongue or I might wash your mouth out with soap — you're not too big, mind!' She gave him a coy look. 'Too young for me though, worse luck.' She moved stiffly on her swollen legs. 'Well, I'd better go in to David. The poor boy had a restless night and there was nothing I could do to ease him. There, hear him coughing now — caught a chill he has, if you ask me.'

Morgan, listening to David's harsh racking cough, realised that he needed a doctor — he must have been lying for hours in the rain-sodden grass before Morgan found him.

Catherine came into the kitchen, her hair tied back from a face which was pale and drawn.

'Our William moaned in his sleep so much that I was afraid to close my eyes,' she said softly. 'We'd best get a doctor up here to see him and David too, for he's been coughing for hours. Will you go and fetch Bryn Thomas,

Gladys, for I'll need to see to the harvesting?'

'There's not much hope of old Bryn coming right up here,' Gladys said dryly, 'but I expect I can get that new doctor to call — needs the money, does Doctor Soames.'

'Look, wouldn't it be better if I went into town for the doctor?' Morgan suggested quickly as Gladys picked up her coat. 'Otherwise your sons will be left on their own.'

'No!' Catherine's voice intruded sharply. 'David will understand the need for us to be out in the fields. I can spare Gladys, I can't spare you.' She looked at him with a silent plea for his cooperation; when he made no answer, she shrugged her shoulders and turned away from him.

'If we don't salvage at least some of the corn we're liable to face ruin — there now, I can't put it more bluntly than that! As it is we'll need fresh seed. I think we'll try Rivetts; it's slow growing and might well suit the land better, but what about fodder for the animals and corn for our own need? We could never afford to buy in such quantities, can't you see that?'

When he remained silent she looked at him in exasperation. 'Anyway, understand or not, you must do as I say. Get a good breakfast inside you and then go out to the fields on the southern slopes — that's where we'll salvage most of the grain.'

Morgan felt a momentary sense of outrage at being ordered around by the slim young woman standing before him. She sensed his feelings and looked at him, not softly as she had done in the dark hours of the night but with a determined set about her features which brooked no argument. At last he turned and went outside, feeling the heat of the sun as it washed down on his shoulders.

He strode angrily towards the fields that took the most sunshine; there the corn was dryer and sweeter and not bent too badly by the wind and rain. Aware of footsteps at his back, he turned to watch Catherine cross the fields behind him. Wordlessly she handed him a scythe and bent in a swooping gesture to slice the corn in swathes as effortlessly as though she was picking daisies.

'Like that, see? You cut and I'll come behind you to put the stooks ready for drying.'

When he took the scythe, he found to his astonishment that he was clumsy and slow. He paused to watch the twist of her wrist and the stoop of her body and tried again, but he was awkward in comparison with Catherine and realised that there was a great deal he needed to learn.

The sun had moved higher in the heavens when he stopped and rubbed at his back with his finger-tips. Catherine finished her task of putting the corn together with heads within the stooks and took out a cloth from the deep pocket in her apron.

'Have something to eat and then you'll feel better.' She did not look at him and her voice was impersonal as she offered him a hunk of bread and a piece of cold bacon. 'When you cut the corn, bend into the scythe and not against it,' she said slowly, 'and don't hold your arm so stiff; try to be fluid, like a flowing river, otherwise you'll strain your muscles.'

'I think your advice comes a little too late,' he said, smiling; she didn't respond but continued to eat stolidly, her eyes roving over the skies as though assessing how many hours of daylight there would be.

'When the ground is cleared,' Catherine said, 'we'll give it a dressing of fertilizer.' She paused, carefully folding the cloth containing the cheese. 'One hundredweight of sulphate of ammonia to four bushels of that superphosphate you brought from town should do an acre.'

'What will be the effect of that?' Morgan, asked anticipating the hard work the laying of the manure would mean.

Catherine looked at him levelly. 'The manure encourages growth and brings the seed to maturity much more quickly,' she said as she rose to her feet. 'Don't worry, you'll soon know all there is to know about farming.'

He smiled at her wryly; the one thing he was sure of as the sun began to crawl across the sky was that never in all his life had he worked so hard. His muscles screamed and his bones felt torn apart, but looking across to where Catherine still laboured as fiercely as any man, he could not give in; he would work until he dropped, he decided, as once more his arm swung out and severed swatches of corn.

It was almost dark when Catherine called a halt and by that time, Morgan was past feeling the pain of his rebelling muscles. He stood staring up at the sky, shaking with fatigue, but in his heart was pride for he had mastered the scythe . . . and looking into Catherine's eyes, he knew with a sense of achievement that he had earned the respect with which she was regarding him.

CHAPTER FIFTEEN

The wind was sharp and the swollen sea rolled heavily against the sides of the ship that dipped and bowed, seeming to make no headway on its journey from France to the shores of England.

In the saloon, Margaret Francis sat on the dusty plush seat, a little withdrawn from the other passengers as she rocked her young son in her arms. He was almost asleep; his blue eyes were closed, the gold-tipped lashes resting on round cheeks, and looking down at him she smiled.

At first, when she had discovered she was going to have a child, she had been incredulous. After all, she was a woman rising thirty-seven, no mean age for mothering a first-born. And furthermore, she had no husband to work and care for her.

There had been a war raging around her home on the outskirts of Mametz Wood and no way of knowing who would win. The British soldiers had driven the enemy away from the perimeter of the tract of land, but in the foolish ways of war — where men fought hard and long for a mere patch of ground — Mametz Wood might be recaptured at any time. And yet, as the months crept on and the new life inside her began to grow, Margaret had felt herself blossom with a feeling of happiness.

She had no doubts whatsoever about the paternity of her child: Heath Jenkins was the only man she had lain with in years. She had taken him in and nursed him and eventually shared her bed, for it was a long time since the death of her husband.

It was true that a pig of a German had attempted to rape

her, but the act was never complete for Heath had defended her at the risk of his own life, fighting like a man possessed. More of the British had come then and taken Heath back to his regiment and that was the last she had ever seen of him.

When the war had ended, Margaret felt a growing urge to return home. She had realised very soon after Heath had gone how much she loved him and though she was no dreamer and guessed he would have a woman waiting for him, she felt that she must at least make an attempt to find him and acquaint him of the fact that he had a son.

When the boy had been born, Margaret's French neighbours had assumed that he was the result of the attack on her by the enemy and it had suited her to let the story stand that way. Jonathan was accepted as the innocent victim of the war.

Her mouth curved into a smile now as she stared down at her son — he was so like Heath that it touched her heart with joy to watch him. Would he be a ram the way his father was, she wondered in amusement — if so the women could look out, for none would be safe from him!

The ship heaved and she held Jonathan close, enjoying the feel of his soft skin against her cheek. He would be four years old come winter and already he was a fine lad, strong of limb and with a quick intelligence that delighted her.

Margaret had decided to travel to Sweyn's Eye before making her way back to her native Yorkshire. There she would see Heath and introduce him to his son, that was only fair and right. There was the possibility that Heath would want to provide for the boy, even if by now he had married. But within her heart, she knew she wanted Heath for herself and that all her reasonable arguments about his being free to do what he liked were generated by her mind and not her heart. And once he set eyes on Jonathan, how could Heath bear to turn his boy away?

Some of the passengers were rousing in their seats, picking up hat-boxes, drawing on gloves. The journey across the Channel had been much shorter than she had anticipated and now the coast of England was in sight.

'Come on, Johnnie, your mother can't carry you — not with my bags an' all. Wake up, sweetie!'

Jonathan opened his blue eyes and smiled happily, clambering from his seat and standing with plump legs astride on the swaying ship. Maragaret pulled on his hat and buttoned his coat around him, excitement making her hands tremble.

'We'll sleep the night in England, then tomorrow we'll catch a train to Cardiff and from there it's only a short distance to Sweyn's Eye. We'll see your daddy then — what do you think of that, Johnnie?'

'I want to see my daddy,' he said solemnly and laughing, she hugged him close, kissing his cheek.

'Now hold my hand, we're getting off this ship as fast as we can, I never did like the sea.'

The dockside was noisy and smelly and foreigners seemed to abound. And yet as Margaret stood staring up at the gentle skies she was washed with a feeling of wonder that she was actually home in England.

She found lodgings in a small guest-house near the shore and sat in the window staring out at the night, feeling a longing for Heath Jenkins which would not be pushed into the back of her mind however hard she tried. She spent a restless night, hardly sleeping at all but continuing to gaze out between the curtains at the stars and the soft silver of the moon. Soon, perhaps, she would be with Heath and he would take her in his arms and love her as he had done before. In the darkness, she could tell herself that of course he would not have found himself a wife yet — he was a young man and full of adventure, he would be reluctant to settle down. She pushed away the thought of the name he had called out in the night — Rhian — a strange-sounding name and not easily forgotten. But the chances were that this Rhian would have married someone else — and good riddance to her!

At last, Margaret forced herself to climb into bed beside her son and close her eyes. She must try to get some sleep, or she would arrive in Sweyn's Eye looking like a hag. But even as sleep came to her, her mouth curved into a smile as she dreamed of Heath holding out his arms ready to embrace her.

The journey to Cardiff next day seemed endless and even Jonathan, usually so good-natured, began to grumble. 'There, there, not long now, my son — see the great train puffing out smoke? You go to sleep and soon the train will be bringing us into the town.' She sat back in the dusty seat and hugged the boy close and after a time her own eyelids began to droop.

The Metropole Hotel was quite elegant and comfortable, especially after the cramped room of the guest-house where she had spent the previous night. Once Jonathan was tucked up in bed, Margaret made her way to the dining-room and seated herself unobtrusively at a corner table. The sounds of lilting Welsh voices were all around her, reminding her of Heath, so that she felt exhilarated.

A very tall lady entered the room and so stunning was she that Margaret hardly noticed the man with her. The couple sat at the next table and on closer inspection, she looked amazingly like Heath Jenkins. But that was silly, Margaret told herself, she must be imagining things — yet she felt compelled to watch the woman as she talked animatedly to her companion. Having finished her meal, she decided to retire early so as to be fresh when she arrived in Sweyn's Eye.

But the reality was very different from her imaginings. As she alighted from the train Margaret wrinkled her nose at the sulphurous smell and tried to tell herself that she was seeing the worst face of Sweyn's Eye — for hadn't Heath described the beautiful curving bay and the soft mountains to her in glowing terms?

'Excuse me,' she stopped a woman who was carrying a basket on her head and hoped that Jonathan would not speak up in his disconcerting way and make some observation which would offend.

'I'm looking for Heath Jenkin's home — do you know it?' She spoke slowly and was relieved when the woman smiled at her, but then Margaret realised there was something besides curiosity in the woman's expression.

'*Duw*, I think it best if you go to see his sister — Mary Jenkins as was, she's Mary Sutton now of course.'

A feeling of coldness crept over Margaret's heart and she bit her lip, knowing that the woman's words could mean only one thing.

The woman seemed flustered. 'There's sorry I am, *merchi*!' She leaned forward. 'Take my advice, go and see Mary, she's got a big shop just along the road there and you can't miss it.'

Margaret watched as the woman walked away, back straight, made graceful by the burden she carried on her head. She tried not to think, she looked at the unfamiliar streets and tears burned in her eyes; had she come all this way in vain?

She found herself walking in the direction the woman had indicated — she at least would see this Mary, Heath's sister, and perhaps find a bed for the night, for her small supply of money was running out more swiftly than she had anticipated.

The shop was indeed big, it was so grand that Margaret found herself hesitating to walk across the red plush carpet. At her side Jonathan was beginning to grizzle; he was tired and too little to walk very far.

An elderly woman came towards her, smiling politely but with an air of authority as if questioning Margaret's right to be there.

'Good day, I'm Mrs Greenaway — is there something I can do to help you? If it's the tea-room you want, it's not open just yet.'

Margaret shook her head. 'No, it's not the tea-room, I need to see Mary Jenkins.'

The woman stared at her askance and then her eyes widened as she saw Jonathan clearly for the first time.

'*Duw*, you'd best come upstairs with me then. I'm sure Mrs Sutton will want to see you, though she's just returned home from Cardiff this very minute.

Margaret followed Mrs Greenaway in her slow progress up the wide staircase, the bag in her hand seeming to grow heavier with each step. What if this Mary should be hostile, think of her as a loose woman and turn her out without a hearing? Margaret didn't think she could bear it if that happened.

Mary Sutton was tall and elegant, with swept-back hair touched with grey. She was the woman Margaret had seen at the Metropole Hotel.

'Please can I sit down?' Margaret sank into a chair and dropped her bag to the carpet, drawing Jonathan closer. 'I'm sorry to barge in like this,' she said, her voice beginning to tremble. 'I thought I would find Heath here in Sweyn's Eye.'

To her chagrin, she began to cry and Jonathan, frightened by his mother's emotion, burrowed his head under her chin. Mary gave some orders to Mrs Greenaway in a soft voice and Margaret understood with gratitude that she was at least to be given a cup of tea.

'I think you'd better tell me all about it; I'm not an ogre, mind,' Mary said with a hint of reproach in her voice. 'I can tell you're not from Sweyn's Eye by your voice, so where was it you met my brother then?'

'In France,' Margaret replied. 'I lived there with my husband and then he died and the war was on and I just stayed.' She knew she was babbling and made an effort to think rationally.

'I found Heath wounded, badly wounded — and took him to my cottage to care for him and . . .' she pointed to Jonathan, 'he's the result.' She wiped at her eyes. 'I didn't know if I'd find Heath married or what, I asked some woman in the street about him and she told me to come to you. Then I realised the truth that he hadn't come home from the war and I don't think I can bear it!'

'I'm sorry,' Mary spoke gently. 'I know how you must feel, coming all this way and then learning the truth about my brother. I'm surprised you left it so long.' She tipped up Jonathan's chin and looked into his eyes. 'But there's no mistaking that this is Heath's son; he's the spit out of his mouth.'

Margaret warmed to the tall, serene woman who was Heath's sister; she did not ask questions or condemn, she simply accepted.

'You must stay with me for the time being; there's plenty of room for you and your son and I'd like to get to know him — I am his auntie, after all.'

Mrs Greenaway arrived with the tray and set it down on the shiny surface of the desk and Margaret leaned back in her chair, feeling a little comforted.

She felt a warm rush of gratitude as she sipped her tea and regarded Mary, liking her smooth face and clear eyes, feeling that here at least was some kin of Heath's and a little piece of him.

'When we've finished our tea, we'll go up to the house and settle you in, then you must stay just as long as you want to. No need to make any decisions now, you're too tired to think straight — anyone could see that.'

Margaret nodded. 'I've travelled for days, I am very tired and thank you for your hospitality which I accept gratefully.'

When Mary smiled, she was so like Heath that pain tugged at Margaret's heart; there was the pain of loss in Mary's eyes too, which spoke of the love she had had for her brother. It consoled Margaret to know she was not the only one to grieve for Heath Jenkins.

When Mary spoke, it was as though she had picked up Margaret's thoughts.

'I brought him up, you know,' she said softly. 'Heath and me were always close, for our mam was . . . well, she was not very strong. Closer we were than most brothers and sisters because we had to fight to live, you see. So poor we were that sometimes we went hungry.'

Margaret glanced round at the plush, richly furnished room and then gave Mary a shrewd look. 'You are a remarkable woman, then, to have got all this for yourself, Mrs . . .?'

'*Duw*, you must call me Mary, for we are family and you have Heath's son.' She smiled suddenly. 'And I wonder if he'll be wicked like his daddy, for our Heath had girls from one end of the valley to the other. In his younger days of course,' she added hastily and Margaret nodded ruefully.

'Ah, well, he hadn't changed when I knew him, then, though he did call out one name — Rhian, was it?'

Mary's brow was furrowed. 'He was courting Rhian Gray for years really. In the beginning he didn't take her seriously and then, when he did, she fell in love and married a Yorkshireman.'

Margaret stared at Mary in surprise. 'Well, I don't know how anyone could prefer another man to Heath. Even a Yorkshireman! Did he know anything of the marriage?' she went on quickly, 'I mean, did he die thinking that Rhian was still his?' In a way she hoped so, because she could not bear to imagine him going into battle angry and embittered.

Mary sighed heavily. 'He knew. Rhian wrote to him as soon as she could; she felt it was the only honest thing to do.'

Margaret bit her lip and stared down at the carpet without really seeing it. Honesty was all fine and good provided it didn't hurt anyone; it would have been far better if Rhian had kept her feelings to herself for the duration of the war. But she did not voice her thoughts out loud, for it didn't do to run people down.

Mary got up from her chair and smiled at Jonathan. 'I think it's time I took you home to meet your cousin, don't you?' She held out her hand and when the boy grasped it readily Margaret felt a lump rise to her throat. She had not found Heath, but at least she had found her son a family.

*　　　*　　　*

Mary sat in her bedroom, staring out of the window, listening with a smile curving her lips to the sounds of the children playing out in the garden. To say she had been surprised to learn of the existence of Margaret Francis and her son was an understatement, but the more she thought

179

about it the more natural it seemed for Heath to have found his pleasures wherever he was. She well remembered scolding him for going up into the mountains 'tom-catting' with some young girl or other and how worried she had been when he had fallen sick with the lung fever, but even that had not curtailed his activities for very long.

She wondered if she had allowed her bitterness to show when talking to Margaret about Rhian Gray. Many times she had tried to talk herself out of her foolishness, but the feeling persisted that Rhian had let Heath down badly. She was fond of Rhian, yet there was a small part of her that could not forgive.

But that was hypocrisy of the worst kind, for she herself was no saint as she reminded herself sternly. She had had more than one man in her life, for first there had been Billy Gray — the sweetheart of her youth, the romantic dream which had quickly vanished when she had recognised that he was no god but a mortal man with feet of clay.

She had found real love when she married Brandon and their life had been idyllic until the war had come to plunder and destroy. She still remembered the shock which had paralysed her when the news had come that her husband was missing. What happened then she was to regret ever after, for she had fallen into the arms of Paul Soames.

At least she had one crumb of comfort. Paul had never thought of her as a bad woman, he loved her and had continued to love her even though she had kept him at a distance.

And she had her son to shower her love upon, she mused, watching Stephan now as he ran and played with Jonathan, the cousin he had not known he had until a few days ago.

Mary moved away from the window, feeling restless. She had taken several days off work in order to spend time with Margaret and her son, but now she needed to be back in control, organising her business affairs. There was a buyer for her store — the man from Cardiff who so far had haggled over the price she was asking. She would need to see him again, convince him that he was getting a bargain.

Greenie entered the room carrying a tray and Mary smiled gratefully. 'There's a good girl, you must be a mind-reader; a cup of tea is just what I need.'

The older woman laughed shortly, 'I may be a mind-reader but I'm certainly no "girl", I'm practically in my dotage.'

Mary stared at her questioningly. 'What do you think of her — Margaret I mean?' She took the cup and seated herself in the chair near the window once more. 'Not Heath's usual type, is she?'

Greenie shook her head. 'No, but then I expect he was grateful to her for looking after him and that. She's quite pretty, really, though a bit old for the likes of Heath.'

'Do you know, Greenie, this is the most we've talked about him since he died? I suppose that's a sign that we're coming to terms with losing Heath, isn't it?'

'Aye, *merchi*, it's the truth that time is a great healer — not that he'll ever be forgotten, mind, especially now there's the little *bachgen* looking so much like him!'

Mary continued to watch the children playing until Margaret, weary of the game, brought them indoors. Stephan's face was flushed and he had a huge smile as he manfully held the hand of his cousin.

'It's good of you to spend time entertaining the children,' Mary greeted Margaret in the hallway. 'There's tea in the pot — I'm sure you could do with something to revive you.'

Margaret smiled as she took the children's coats. 'Yes, indeed, they've fair worn me out, have these two little lads.' She smiled at them fondly. 'But it's so good to see them making friends with each other — you don't know what it means to me.'

Mary smiled. 'I think I do.' She paused, watching the boys for a moment as they pushed and jostled each other play-fully. 'I hope you won't think me rude, Margaret, but I've got some business that just won't wait. I'll have to leave you alone for a bit, can you manage?'

'Yes, of course, I don't want to be in your way at all — indeed I'd like to help.'

Mary smiled warmly. 'Then you can. I must return to Cardiff for a day or two and I'd be grateful if you could keep an extra sharp eye on Stephan for me.' She shrugged deprecatingly. 'I suppose I'm being an old fusspot, but Nerys — who usually looks after him — is off visiting her family just now.'

Mary looked down at her hands, noting how tense they were. 'Stephan was involved in a car accident a while ago; not serious, mind, but I don't think he's quite picked up properly since then.'

'Don't you worry, lass, I'd be very pleased to look after him,' Margaret said quickly, her face flushed with pleasure. 'He's such an amenable little boy, too, very much the same temperament as my Jonathan.'

Mary sighed with relief. 'Then that's settled, isn't it? I can leave him with an easy conscience. Greenie's getting too old for coping with children; she fares better in the tea-rooms where all she needs to do is supervise.'

Margaret nodded in agreement. 'You go off on your business trip and don't worry at all about your lad, I'll take good care of him.'

Mary decided to leave early the next morning, making her way down into the driveway where the car was standing ready. Jim, who had once been her driver, sat next to her sulking a little because he was just a passenger. Retired now, Jim still sometimes enjoyed working up at the big house but at the moment he was impatient, waiting for the return journey when he would have complete charge of the gleaming Austin.

Mary smiled to herself, sensing his mood. 'You'd better do the driving, Jim, I feel a bit tired.' With a sigh, she settled back to enjoy the journey to the station, looking around her at the familiar sights of the town, so familiar that she had ceased to really see them. It was only when she tried to imagine how Margaret must feel coming as a stranger to Sweyn's Eye that she realised how much had changed since the war ended.

Now some of the small shops which had been a feature

of the town had closed their doors and sad whitewashed windows looked blankly into the streets. Most families had suffered losses of husbands, sons and fathers and the effect of the death of menfolk was reflected in the disappearance of small trades.

The saddler's shop in Canal Street was no longer occupied and folk were forced to walk further up into Green Hill to have saddles made or reins restored. And the baker's shops once to be seen on almost every street corner were now few, with bread prices inevitably rising because in its turn corn was dearer, coming from farms where there had been only old men and young boys to harvest the crops.

So much had been changed by the war, Mary mused, not least her own circumstances, but it would not do to dwell on the past — she had done enough of that to last her a lifetime.

She thanked Jim as she climbed from the car and he smiled at her, his face wizened now by age and etched with lines of pain. Her heart contracted with pity, for during the war, Jim had lost three of his four sons. He touched his cap to Mary before driving back the way he had come and she watched him for a moment, conscious of the way his shoulders were bowed and of the thinness of his neck above the clean collar.

The train was waiting, hissing and puffing, spitting sparks into the air, vibrating as though with a life of its own. She climbed on board and seated herself near the window, where she could look out on to the valleys and to the mountains beyond as the train moved away from the town.

The train ride to Cardiff took a little under two hours and during that time, Mary busied herself writing figures into a book. At last, satisfied, she closed it knowing she could afford to lower her price for the store — by just a little, but enough to sway the deal in her favour.

As she stepped from the train she saw Paul Soames was waiting on the platform and bit her lip as she recalled mentioning her trip to him when they had met at the hotel.

'You'll have people talking about us,' she said quietly and

183

not without a little anger. 'First the dinner at the Metropole and now this! I thought you'd have returned home by now — surely your conference has ended?'

'It's taken longer than I thought,' Paul said quickly. 'In any case, Mary, I wanted to see you again.'

'Look, I know I allowed you to join me at the Metropole the other night and I admit I was glad to see a friendly face in an unfamiliar town, but please Paul, don't go making anything of it. I think between us we have made enough of a mess of my life as it is.'

'That hurt,' Paul said softly and Mary looked at him. knowing it was wrong of her to continue to blame him for something which was not his fault. Once his arms had provided comfort and solace when she had needed them most, yet since then she had treated him very badly.

'I'm sorry, that was unfair of me — let's have supper together, shall we?' She spoke in defiance of her own feelings and when Paul's face lit up she once more felt guilty and uneasy.

The streets of Cardiff were just as dirty and begrimed as the industrial side of Sweyn's Eye, Mary decided as she left the station. They took a cab to the hotel and, making her excuses, she swiftly went to her room, thankful to be alone. She took off her coat and hung it in the cupboard, then stared round the impersonal room realising that she didn't know what to do with herself. Her meeting with Frank Raynor was not until the next day and suddenly she was glad she had arranged to have supper with Paul. It was exactly the same situation that had occurred a few days ago when she had been surprised to see him in Cardiff and had wondered for a moment if he had been deliberately following her, but almost at once had dismissed the idea as absurd.

She sat in an uncomfortable hide chair, aware that already she was missing Stephan. Each evening, however busy she was, she made a point of kissing him as she tucked him into bed. Sometimes she would tell him stories about his daddy fighting in the war. She very much wanted

Stephan to have a sense of identity, although she knew the time would inevitably come when he would begin to question her as to the whereabouts of this marvellous hero figure who was his father.

Mary moved to the dressing-table and unpinned her hair, rubbing her fingers against her scalp. She felt tense, uneasy and lonely in the strange surroundings of the hotel.

'Fool!' Her voice hung on the silence in the room and she felt even more alone. She was Mary Sutton, business-woman, hard-headed and shrewd, so why was she sitting feeling sorry for herself instead of thinking of her meeting tomorrow, planning what she would say to this man who wanted to buy her store but at a bargain price?

If she traced the time of the change within her, she knew it dated back to the time when her son was born. Becoming a mother had transformed her, made her ambition burn less brightly, for he was so much more important to her than any business could be. And where had gone her joy in the independence she had earned for herself? She rose restlessly from the stool and welcomed the sound of knocking on her door, even though she knew it was bound to be Paul.

'Come in,' she said, moving back for him to enter balancing a tray which held a bottle of wine and two glasses.

'I thought it would be nice if we had a little drink before supper?' He smiled disarmingly and she sighed in mock resignation.

'All right, Paul, we'll have a drink together but I hope you realise that you are ruining my reputation!'

He placed the tray on the table and turned to her earnestly. 'Oh, I shouldn't think anyone here would know us, do you?'

Mary shook her head. 'I was only joking Paul — what on earth's happened to your sense of humour?' She sank into a chair and stared up at him, unaware of her hair tangled becomingly around her face.

He handed her some wine and then sank on to the bed, twisting the stem of his glass between his fingers.

'I honestly don't know, Mary.' His voice was low. 'I think

I lost it when I fell in love with you.' He held up his hand when she would have stopped him talking. 'No, I must speak. I love you, Mary, and even though I realise that you don't love me, why not think of the future? I would be a good father to Stephan.' She was grateful that he did not refer to the fact that for a time they had both believed him to be the boy's father.

'No, Paul, I don't think it would work. I'll tell you something I wouldn't admit to anyone else, even though I know it's going to hurt you. I still haven't given up hope that Brandon might one day forgive me and come home.'

'All right.' He squared his shoulders and forced a smile, though he was suddenly pale. 'Well, for now, let's just enjoy each other's company, shall we? I'll wine and dine you and then go to my solitary bed. I promise I won't suggest anything more intimate if you'll only relax and stop being on the defensive with me.'

Mary raised her glass. 'Here's to friendship, Paul!' She took a sip of the wine, feeling much better now that she knew he would make no impossible demands on her. 'And here's to a happy conclusion to our business meetings for both of us.'

And happy she was with the result of her meeting with Mr Frank Raynor the next day, for once he had seen her revised figures he made her a firm offer for the business. Now she was free to put her new plans into action and for the first time in years she felt the thrill and the tingle of the challenge before her.

*   *   *

In the big house on the hill overlooking the sea Margaret Francis sat on the window seat staring out into the night sky. Her feelings of gratitude to Mary were beginning to fade. Why should Mary and her son Stephan have all this luxury surrounding them, whilst her own boy was penniless? Surely if Heath had lived, a portion of the wealth would have been his and in that case, Jonathan had a right to some of that fortune.

It was quite disgusting the way Mary had sailed off and left her in charge of the boy without a qualm. What was she to be — a nursery-maid to the young lad and an unpaid one at that? Well. Mary would have to think again for no one put upon Margaret Francis!

Oh, she had put a good face on holding out a welcome when all the time she must have been planning her little trip away. Margaret's coming must have been like a gift from heaven and one of which Mary had made full use. If Margaret wasn't careful, her own boy would be waiting on Stephan hand and foot — a little playmate to be put away like a discarded toy when no longer required. Well, if Mary thought she had found a fool, she could just think again. Margaret flounced away from the window and pulled back the silk cover from the bed, telling herself to be calm; she had a good home here for as long as she needed it and at the moment, she needed a place very badly. If she bided her time and kept her eyes and ears open, she might just learn something to her advantage.

CHAPTER SIXTEEN

The chill of the misty day seemed to lay a pall over the fields which straddled Ram's Tor and settled a quiet hand on the pewter seas that licked delicately at the dun-coloured rocks. Sheep, ghostly grey shapes, moved silently over the land and ate of the coarse grass beyond the boundary walls of the Tor. And the fields lay desolate beneath the overcast skies, for the harvest was lost.

Within the whitewashed farmhouse, the greyness of the season seemed to penetrate the rooms; dampness and mud begrimed the floors and not even the cheerful fire glowing in the grate could dispel the gloom.

'*Duw*, where's that doctor? Why isn't he here?' Gladys sat at the table, her plump elbows resting on the scrubbed wooden surface, her face twisted with fear. She glanced towards Morgan who was pulling on his boots and he met her eyes briefly before concentrating once more on his task.

Morgan was bone-weary for since what Gladys euphemistically called 'the accident' on Ram's Tor, he had been responsible for most of the work on the farm. In the first few days, he had not been aware just how many of the tasks Catherine had taken upon herself. And now he was without her, he realised that she had worked as hard as any man. He tugged at his laces, thinking that the top field had to be spread with lime to sweeten the earth for the root crop he intended to put down. The poor corn harvest was a plague and it had taken him days of ploughing to rid the land of the unwanted germinating seeds. Some of the other fields would go to grass and the stock grazing them would restore fertility to the earth.

He could do with some help, Morgan mused, but much of Catherine's time now was taken up with nursing David, for his condition had steadily worsened and the rattle of his cough could be heard throughout the farmhouse. At last, and with reluctance, Catherine had decided she must call out the doctor even though payment for his fees must come from the money she had got from the sale of the prize bull and some of the younger milch cows.

Morgan rose to his feet. 'I'll have a look down the hill, see if there's any sign of Bryn Thomas, but he's an old man and bound to be slow.' He rested his hand for a moment on Gladys's shoulder. 'Don't worry, I'm sure he'll come in an emergency.'

Gladys stared up at him, her usually cheerful face morose. 'I don't know about that, boyo, it's a long way to Ram's Tor, mind — perhaps he don't feel like making the journey. What a shame we couldn't get hold of that nice young Soames — rather have him, I would, he's not so toffee-nosed.'

Catherine entered the kitchen and placed a large enamel bowl on the table, her shoulders bowed with fatigue. 'There's no response from him,' she said as she sank into a chair and stared first at Gladys and then at Morgan. 'I've tried to ease his chest with steaming water and I've given him a mustard poultice, but none of it does any good.'

'There, there, girl,' Gladys said with rough kindness. 'Leave it to the doctor, he'll be here any minute now.' She glanced up at Morgan as if to dare him to mention the fact that only a few moments before she had been cursing the doctor's lateness.

Catherine looked washed out, he thought, pity shafting through him. Her lovely hair was pulled back severely from her face and tied tightly with a grimy ribbon. Her face was so white that her eyes glowed over-brightly and there was an attitude of despair in the way her shoulders drooped.

Angrily Morgan let himself out into the cool of the evening, though he could not say exactly where his anger was directed. He heard the mournful sounds of the cows anxious to be relieved of their burden of milk and shook his head; they would just have to wait a little longer. He strode up the sloping ground and when he was high enough, stared down the winding road which led to Oystermouth village. It was empty — there was no horse and carriage, nothing to indicate that the doctor was on his way.

'Damn and blast!' He felt anger well up afresh within him, wanting to run to the town and take the doctor by the scruff of his neck and drag him to the farm. But slowly he returned to the shed and set about the milking, relieved to have something to do even though tiredness dragged at him and blurred his vision.

Later, when he returned to the kitchen, it was to find the room empty. He heard a woman's cry from the back of the house where David lay sick and without pausing to take off his mud-caked boots, he hurried along the passageway and threw open the door.

Gladys was standing huddled against the wall with eyes tightly closed, her cries muted by the hands clasped to her lips. Her body trembled and even as he watched, her knees sagged and she fell to the floor. Catherine was simply standing staring down at the bed. She neither moved nor looked up when Morgan came to her side.

He saw at once by the pallor and the gaping mouth that David Preece was dead. Morgan had seen death before, but none like this with the skin shrunken to the skull and the open eyes wide and staring as though in hate.

He deliberately drew the blanket over the dead man's face and took Catherine by the arm.

'Come away into the kitchen. There's nothing more you can do here now, girl.'

She looked up at him then, her eyes brilliant with pain. 'He didn't want to get better,' she said as though explaining a difficult problem to a child. 'Lost his will to live, he did.'

She seemed to be dazed, and Morgan took both her hands in his. They were cold and lifeless and she simply stared at him as though waiting for him to make a decision. He glanced down at Gladys.

'For God's sake, woman, pull yourself together!' He spoke with deliberate harshness and as he had intended, Gladys was shocked out of her misery. 'Help me to get Catherine out of here and then you'd better go up and see young William — he'll be worried sick with all this palaver going on.'

Gladys rose to her feet at once and took Catherine's arm, calm now although her mouth trembled. 'Come on, my chick,' she said, 'let's go and sit by the warm fire, shall we?' She drew in a harsh breath as she stared at the figure under the blanket and then led Catherine out into the passageway.

'There are things to be done,' Gladys said as she pushed the kettle on to the fire.

'Go you into the village, Morgan, and fetch someone to lay my boy out proper like.' She gulped and rubbed at her eyes. 'Why didn't the doctor come, Morgan?'

He shook his head. 'I don't know, Gladys, but I don't think there would have been anything more he could have done; you and Catherine have nursed David so well.'

She took a little comfort from his words and gave him a grateful glance. 'Will you go fetch the laying-out nurse, then?'

Catherine moved abruptly and shook her head. 'I'll lay him out,' she said and began to roll up her sleeves. Gladys bit her lip and her eyes brimmed with tears once more.

'But, *cariad*, can you bear to see him like that, won't the sight haunt you for ever more?'

'He's my husband,' Catherine said simply. She was about to leave the kitchen when there was a loud imperious rapping on the door. It was Morgan who moved to open it and Bryn Thomas entered the kitchen, his face drawn and pale.

'I would have been here sooner — I do apologise — but there was a mishap in town when a wheel came off the trap and I had to find someone to help me repair the damage. It's so unfortunate that young Soames is away just now.'

'It's too late,' Catherine said tonelessly, 'but there's no blame attached to you, doctor, don't think that.'

'Oh, dear, I am sorry.' Bryn Thomas stared miserably round the kitchen, uncertain what to do next. His grey hair was sparse and thin beneath his hat, his shoulders were bowed and Morgan realised he was nothing more than a tired old man.

'Perhaps you could help Catherine?' He gestured towards the back room and after a moment Bryn Thomas nodded.

'Not my job usually, you understand, but in the circumstances it's the least I can do.'

Gladys rose to her feet. 'Go up to see my William, Morgan, there's a good man. I'll stay down by here and give a hand.'

Morgan was reluctant to be the one to break the news to William, but there was no one else. He moved to the stairs, kicking off his muddy boots and hurrying towards the bedroom in his stockinged feet. He searched in his mind for the right words to say . . . but how could death ever be made easy or even acceptable?

William was just waking from sleep. His hair was tousled over his forehead and he smiled at Morgan in recognition, sighing a little as he moved to ease his aching arm.

Morgan approached the bed and sat down, not meeting William's eyes. The boy slipped his fingers into the other's large hand and fear darkened his features.

'What's wrong?' he asked in a small voice. Morgan looked at him then and cursed the fates which had put him in such an invidious position. There were no comforting words, no easy way to break the news.

'It's David, he's dead.' Morgan spoke gently, his heart gripped with pain as he felt the boy cling convulsively to him.

'But how can that be, he wasn't hurt or anything in the accident? Is it my fault, Morgan?' William's voice was filled with pain and guilt and Morgan shook his head sharply.

'Of course it wasn't your fault, you must never think that. If it hadn't been for you, David would have been smashed against the rocks beneath Ram's Tor, we all know that.'

William's screwed-up face seemed to relax a little, though his hand still trembled in Morgan's. He was making a brave effort not to cry — and what was so wrong in a man showing his grief? And William had become a man since he had taken the decision to save David's life up there on the Tor and keep silent about the real facts of the matter.

'What happened then?' William asked. 'Tell me everything, Morgan, please.'

Morgan shook his head; he knew very little, for he had not once been into the sick-room to see David. For one thing, he had been working like a dog these past days and apart from that, there was nothing he could contribute; the women had seen to it all.

'A lung infection, I'd say at a guess, I used to hear him coughing a lot . . . but then I'm no doctor. Perhaps David's injuries finally caught up with him.' He paused and tried to think of something else he could say, for William was waiting anxiously.

'When a man's spine is crushed there are other things that happen; for instance, the work of the kidneys can be hampered and the blood flow round the body can't be so efficient — do you see, William? Your brother could have caught a chill just being out of doors and he had not the strength to fight such things off as a healthy man would.' He knew he was searching in the dark, pulling thoughts out of the air, but the boy seemed satisfied.

William sighed heavily. 'And what will we do now, will Catherine have to sell the farm?'

The question brought a cold chill to Morgan's heart. Of course everything would be altered now and even though he himself had a financial interest in the farm, he was not experienced enough to run it alone. The question mark hung in his mind — would Catherine wish to keep working the land? The poor harvest had been a disaster and soon it would be time to sow the seeds for the new crop of grain, yet he knew only too well how short the money was.

He became aware of William's silence and attempted to smile reassuringly at him. 'I expect everything will go on in the same old way but whatever happens, you and your mam have got your little house in Oystermouth to go home to and you'll be all right.'

Morgan heard sounds from the kitchen. Gladys was poking the fire with great fuss and noise and he guessed she would be making one of her endless cups of tea. Tea, it seemed, was the panacea for all ills.

'I think I'll just ask the doctor to look at your arm while he's here — let him do something for his money, right boyo?'

As William turned his head into the pillow, the soft hair stuck out in spikes against his thin neck. Morgan rested his hand on the boy's shoulder.

'Nothing wrong in tears, mind. I've seen grown men crying for their mams, so don't you hold back now, let it all come out.'

He left William then, allowing the boy to be alone with his pain, and hurried down the stairs into the warmth of the kitchen. Gladys, though red-eyed, seemed to be in possession of herself. She had cups set out on the table and as he had guessed was busy brewing the tea.

'Doctor said it's a miracle David lasted so long.' Her tone was deceptively calm. 'His injuries from the war being so bad and all.' The thought seemed to bring her a measure of comfort, as though responsibility of her son's death was attributed to a larger fate than she was capable of controlling.

'That's more or less what I've been telling William. He's taking it hard, but then youngsters are resilient and he'll come to terms with his grief in his own time.'

Gladys sat down suddenly, the china tea-pot banging against the wooden table, tea tipping from the spout and lid on to the white boards and running in small rivulets into the grooves. She put her hands to her face and began to cry, softly and bitterly, her shoulders heaving.

Catherine returned to the kitchen, the old doctor in her wake. She looked with compassion at the older woman and quite naturally folded her in an embrace.

'Hush now, there's no more left to do, it's all finished and David looks so peaceful. Be glad for him that he's out of his pain.'

'Have you put pennies over his eyes?' Gladys asked almost fearfully. 'Those eyes, staring upwards as though

194

hating God and all the world! I just couldn't bear to see him like that.'

'It's all right, no need for pennies, the doctor has seen to that. He's beautiful now, your son is, just like he was before the war.'

Suddenly Morgan knew he had to get outside into the cold freshness of the open land and sky. He felt he had had a surfeit of grief and suffering and although David's death did not touch him with a heavy hand, witnessing others' pain was not something he relished.

It was cold on Ram's Tor and the sea below was loud and angry, crashing against rocks that jutted from the foam like rotten teeth. He sucked air into his lungs as he stared up at the darkening skies and an early moon struggling for supremacy over the rushing clouds.

A measure of peace came upon him as he stood facing the elements of sea and wind and his strength seemed to burgeon and grow. He would wrest a living from the farm, he would *not* be beaten by the harshness of life on Ram's Tor. And somehow, he would convince Catherine Preece that whatever the difficulties, together they could make the farm into a thriving business.

*   *   *

The air was still, the skies grey and clouded, but there was no rain falling on the fields of Ram's Tor. Within the farmhouse the niceties of the burial ceremony were being observed as the minister of the Methodist church conducted a brief service in the overcrowded parlour.

Catherine's shrewd eyes missed nothing as she watched the neighbours who had come to mourn for David Preece, those whom he had turned away from his doors in bitterness and injured pride. Denny-the-Stack was standing sheepishly near the window, trying to make himself invisible. Gethin-Sheep-shearer was an old man but strong still and willing to help, though David would have none of it. Her glance moved to her relatives, those who would do

195

nothing for David in his lifetime but now came to mourn his death.

Her father stood stiff and pompous in his best worsted suit, his watch-chain hanging from his pocket, his head unbending, for being a stout supporter of the Church of England he did not hold with nonconformist ways.

And thronging round him were his daughters, good obedient girls who had married well and produced fine grandsons. His gaze met Catherine's briefly and she read the disapproval there in his eyes. It was true that Catherine had run the farm like a man during the war, but she had not given him grandchildren and perhaps now she never would for who would want a penniless widow woman and a clutch of in-laws to support? She shivered, feeling the old sense of being unwanted, unloved and worthless.

Though she did not turn round Catherine was aware of Morgan standing behind her and she no longer felt alone. At her side sat Gladys, wearing her only good coat which was grey rather than black but had to suffice, for there was no money to be wasted on buying new coats.

William stood, one of the men, looking tall and thin in one of David's cut-down suits. His arm was still giving him pain, Catherine could tell by the small lines under his eyes where he wanted to screw them up tightly. But he nobly stood without flinching, his gaze resting on the minister rather than on the coffin resting on a trestle in the corner of the room. One thing she could thank David Preece for was the love given to her so freely by his family.

While the men walked behind the coffin to the graveyard in the village, the womenfolk remained in the farmhouse making tea and putting out thick succulent ham on good china plates. Catherine moved as though pulled by unseen strings, her feelings numbed.

'There's sorry I am, Catherine.' Her sister Connie stood beside her with a look of genuine pain on her face. 'It's sad to lose your man this way; for him to come through the war and then die of the lung sickness is so cruel!'

Catherine nodded, unable to blurt out the truth of her

feelings — that to her mind, David had been given a blessed release. With her rich, handsome husband and brood of children, how much could Connie know of the sufferings of David Preece with his strong mind trapped in a useless, twisted body? Had she come even once from Port Eynon to offer help and sympathy, Catherine would have warmed to her sister — perhaps told her a little of the difficulties she had faced alone on Ram's Tor during the war years.

But she could not blame Connie, whose husband had been needed on the farm and who had stayed at home on the land so that their way of life had changed very little. She put out her hand and forced a smile.

'Thank you, Connie, I appreciate the thought.' The sisters touched hands and Catherine felt a sudden pain within her. They should have been a close and loving family, all of them being girls, but their father with his sternness and unswerving principles had separated them, bundling each daughter into marriage as soon as she became of age.

'We had some good times at home, didn't we, Connie?' Catherine said softly. 'Remember that time when you made us rag dolls for Christmas and how disapproving Father was?'

Connie smiled reminiscently. 'Aye, it wasn't so bad especially when Mam was there, but once she died it was as though Father just wanted rid of us too. The responsibility was too great for him, I suppose. Can't blame him really, can we?'

Catherine was silent. She could and did blame her father for thrusting her into marriage with scant consideration for a young girl's feelings. As she stared at her sister, fifteen years her senior, she wondered if she knew love for her man. She would have liked to ask, but how could she put such thoughts into words?'

'Are you . . . content?' she asked at last and Connie's eyes were suddenly clear and blue as they rested upon her.

'Things have a way of working out right,' she said hesitantly. 'My husband is good and honest; I know I couldn't have found better anywhere in the world.'

'You are happy then?' Catherine found herself saying,

though she would not have been surprised if Connie had told her to mind her own business.

Connie sighed softly. 'It's like you said, Catherine, I am content.' The two girls looked at each other and on an impulse Connie leaned forward and hugged her; as Catherine smelled the apple scent of her sister, she felt closer to her than she had ever done before.

'But what's to become of you now?' Connie continued. 'You can scarcely live here alone, it wouldn't be right.'

Catherine felt only surprise. 'Why on earth not? I did it in the war, worked the farm with help from only the old men and the wounded. I'll manage, don't you worry about me.'

Connie frowned and looked down at her hands. 'You know as well as I do that things were different in the war. And as I understand it, that young man Morgan Lloyd lives here, so there would be talk.'

Catherine felt a knot of apprehension tighten within her. Morgan was part of the fabric of her life here on Ram's Tor; he worked like a slave in the fields and in any case, he had put his money into the land. Yet she could see that Connie had a point: there was bound to be gossip if he stayed.

'He doesn't live in the farmhouse, mind,' she said quickly. 'His room is over the stable. In any case, there's David's mam as well as young William, they will look after me and help me.' But that was no answer and Catherine knew it even as she spoke.

Connie sighed, 'You always were strange and wild, the one father took the strap to for disobedience. If you can't see how tongues would wag, then there's nothing more I can say to you.'

Catherine twisted her hands together as though they were physically hurting her. She tried to clear her mind to see matters as Connie did, but the land of Ram's Tor needed farming and Morgan had become part of that land as surely as if he had been born on it.

'But I couldn't tell Morgan to go if I wanted to — he's put his savings into the farm.'

Connie shrugged, suddenly impatient. 'Look, *merchi*, it's not my place to solve your problems. I've got my own to tend to.' She sank down on to a chair and brushed back a stray hair. 'There's my son wanting to go away and be a soldier in the regular Army, while both my daughters are plain as milk and spineless as kittens!' She spread her hands wide in despair. 'Tell me why should I take on the worry of you too — you who have been a married woman for long enough and should know better?'

The sound of the tea-cups tinkling against saucers penetrated the haze of Catherine's bewilderment. She had experienced a transient feeling of being close to her sister, but seemingly it had been nothing more than an illusion. Connie was wrapped up in her own little world and had no patience to spare a thought for her youngest sister; indeed she had added to Catherine's burden, for now she must face the harsh fact that Morgan could not stay at Ram's Tor Farm.

'Excuse me, Connie,' she said quickly. 'I'd better go and help Gladys in the kitchen; her legs are bad — playing her up they are — and she's naturally grieving because she's lost a son.'

Catherine made her way through the press of women into the comparative quietness of the kitchen. Gladys was seated on one of the wooden chairs, her legs spread to contain her plumpness, her head bowed.

'There's a noise in the parlour,' Catherine said with a catch in her voice. 'Let's you and me sit in by here on our own for a while.' She busied herself with the fire, stoking it up, placing coals carefully on the chilling embers; she felt affection for Gladys, who was honest and kind and was grieving alone in a press of strangers.

'There's glad I'll be when it's all over.' The older woman's voice was low. 'Like vultures, some of them in there are.' She jerked her head towards the neat parlour. 'Not that I'm insulting your kin, mind,' she added hastily and Catherine put a hand on her shoulder.

'Don't worry, Gladys. I know exactly what you mean.'

Catherine sank into a chair gratefully; the kitchen was an oasis, a retreat from the opinions of others, particularly of Connie. Why did her sister have to speak, to send shudders of doubt reverberating through her mind? Catherine did not want to think of the problems of her life ahead, not just now; it was all she could do to come to terms with the swiftness with which the pattern of her days was changing.

'You look all in, *cariad*,' Gladys said softly. 'This has been no picnic for you either, has it?'

Catherine shook her head. 'No picnic for any of us.' It occurred to her then how closely interwoven her life had become with these people who were not of her blood: Gladys, with her unstinting kindness; William, the younger brother she had never had; and Morgan. But her mind shied away from examining thoughts which might be uncomfortable; today, with the sharpness and finality of death brought terrifyingly to her consciousness, her nerve-endings were raw and painful.

Gladys sighed and pushed her bulk up from the chair. 'The menfolk will be returning any minute now and I'd best cut some bread for more sandwiches.'

Catherine fetched the butter from the cool marble slab in the pantry and placed it on the table.

'You cut the bread and I'll see to the ham.' It was a small unimportant task, but one which would occupy her hands if not her thoughts. Catherine sat opposite Gladys watching as she skilfully wielded the knife, feeling in the quiet of the kitchen a sense of peace which lasted only until the men returned from the cemetery.

It was her father who broached the subject of her future and from the set of his thin lips, Catherine knew she was to be given a lecture on the observing of the proprieties. He clutched his bible against his waistcoat and stared down at her from his great height, disdainfully ignoring the fact that the other men were drinking home-made ale.

'Now, Catherine, I would like to know what you intend to do with your life.' His voice was hard and the words fell like flintstones into the babble of voices which were suddenly quiet. Unperturbed, he continued:

'I think it might be just as well if I take over the running of Ram's Tor in future.'

'But, Dad, I wouldn't think of putting you to any trouble and I did manage on my own in the war, mind.'

Phillip Carver looked down his long nose and beneath bushy grey brows, his eyes were cold as ice.

'That was when you had a husband serving in the Sweyn's Eye battalion and expected home when the war was at an end. Matters are very different now.'

Catherine was aware of Morgan suddenly at her shoulder; he smiled easily at Phillip Carver and leaned forward confidingly, his voice lowered.

'You need have no fears about Ram's Tor, or about your daughter, Mr Carver.' He spoke firmly, as a man used to getting his own way. 'I've put money into the farm and signed the papers with David Preece some months ago, so there is no question of anyone other than myself running the farm.'

Carver's eyes were fixed on Morgan with something close to hate in the pale depths. He held his bible closer as if to protect himself from evil and spoke in the manner of a preacher giving a sermon to the heathen.

'My dear young man, you know nothing of farming.' His thin mouth moved into what might have been a smile. 'I shall give you the benefit of the doubt and assume that you mean well — and of course if it's a matter of compensation, I would be more than willing— '

'No!' Morgan's tone was still pleasant, but the underlying threat was unmistakable. 'It's not a matter of anything except you going your own way back to Port Eynon where you belong. Ram's Tor is my concern.'

Phillip Carver was not used to being gainsaid; his face became a dull red and the eyes so piercing were almost closed.

'Very well, but do not call on me for help at harvest, or at any other time come to that.'

'That's understood,' Morgan said almost affably. Cheated

of triumph, Carver turned his wrath upon his youngest daughter.

'And if you remain under this roof with him — you a widow woman with no husband to protect you — you will be little more than a harlot.'

Catherine lifted her chin proudly. 'I'm no harlot, Father, and you have no charity in you, for all your bible-punching. Thought you would take over my life again, did you? Well, I'm a different person now from the meek and mild daughter I was five years ago.'

Phillip Carver put on his hat and like sheep his daughters gathered around him, glancing fearfully towards Catherine as though she would be struck dead for her impudence. Abruptly Phillip Carver left the house and Connie, with a last despairing glance at Catherine, followed him.

The sound of horse and trap rolling away echoed for a moment in the hushed room and then suddenly, as though with the turning on of a tap, the remaining visitors began to talk.

'You've made an enemy,' Catherine stated as she looked at Morgan for the first time. 'And though he lives some miles down the coast, my father has a great deal of influence.'

'To hell with him!' Morgan's eyes were clear as they looked into hers. 'We must do what suits us, no one else need have any say in the matter.'

But he was wrong, Catherine thought miserably and she was too much of a coward to lay herself open to unpleasant gossip. Morgan would have to move away from Ram's Tor. She looked at him and was riveted by his eyes, so clear and direct . . . and quite suddenly, she knew without doubt that she loved Morgan Lloyd. And yet she knew too that nothing must come of her feelings; they must be buried away, for otherwise she would prove her father's words to be right and she would be nothing more than a harlot. She turned and left the room and even though she stood alone in the emptiness of her bedroom under the blackened beams, she felt Morgan's presence as though he stood beside her.

CHAPTER SEVENTEEN

Margaret Francis sat in the nursery, her head bent over the small garment she was sewing. Indignation burned within her and her hands shook as she jabbed the needle into the fine cotton. Oh, it was nothing but the best for young master Stephan — no coarse calico would be allowed to touch *his* pink flesh! He was spoiled beyond belief, given everything under the sun while her dear boy Jonathan had nothing.

Nerys came into the room with her cheeks aglow, her hair under the pulled-down hat curling and windswept. The young nurse had taken advantage yet again and left Margaret in charge of the boy on the merest pretext of having shopping to do. And yet Margaret revealed nothing of her feelings as she smiled pleasantly; her position in the household was a precarious one and as yet she had neither plans nor the means to move out.

'Cold out by the look of it, lass,' she said, putting down the finished garment. Nerys shrugged out of her good wool coat and nodded emphatically.

'I'll say it's cold, let's get by the lovely warm fire for a bit and thaw out.' She smiled. 'I wouldn't say no to a cup of tea, mind!'

Margaret rose to her feet at once. In spite of everything, she liked Nerys, there was no side to her and she never pretended to be anything but a paid servant in the richness of the Sutton household. It was Mary who put her back up with the constant comings and goings, off to this town or that, riding in her gleaming car . . . with never a word about some sort of settlement for Jonathan.

Nerys took a paper bag from her basket and smiled mischievously. 'Got us some hot buns — just smell them, aren't they enough to make your mouth water?'

They ate in companionable silence, for both Jonathan and Stephan were asleep on their small beds in the next room. Mary insisted that her son took an afternoon rest and it suited Margaret to ensure that Jonathan slept too; at least it gave her a short time to herself each day.

'What if I do the shopping tomorrow?' she asked pleasantly, 'I'd like to see a bit of the town while I'm here.'

'Well, there's soft of me!' Nerys looked at her in surprise. 'It didn't occur to me that you'd want to go down into town, there's selfish of me.'

Margaret warmed to the young girl. She was sweet and generous and it was not Nerys's fault if her employer was a hard-bitten businesswoman.

'Look,' Nerys said quickly, 'I did forget to bring more soap for the nursery — how would you like to go into Sweyn's Eye this afternoon and fetch some for us?'

Margaret smiled. 'I'd like that very much, but you'll have two energetic boys on your hands — can you manage?'

Nerys sank back in her chair and made a rueful face. 'They'll be a handful, I'm not denying that, but I'll take them over to Cwmdonkin Park for an hour and let them play on the swings.'

'Right then, I'll accept your offer gladly.' Margaret picked up the shirt she had been sewing and held it up. 'I've finished the mending, thank goodness, I don't think my eyes are what they used to be.'

Nerys was looking at her strangely and Margaret could almost read her thoughts. 'You're wondering what Heath Jenkins ever saw in someone like me, aren't you?' she smiled as Nerys, blushing, shook her head. 'Well, don't worry, I've asked myself the same question time and time again and there's no answer!' Her face softened. 'All I'll say is this, lass — if you find a love the like of that I had with Heath, then hold on to it tightly for it only comes to a woman once and then only if she's very fortunate.'

Nerys sighed. 'I've never been in love. I've fancied men,

of course, but only from a distance. Don't get much chance to meet anyone, stuck in the house the way I am.'

'Well then, why not change your situation? I'm sure a pretty girl like you could get work anywhere.'

'Oh, no, I couldn't leave Mary!' Nerys was shocked. 'Known her since I was sixteen, I have; we worked in Mr Sutton's shop together, Greenie as well. Old friends we all are and loyal to Mary to the death.'

'I'm sure you are, lass,' Margaret spoke slowly, 'but she wouldn't want you to give up everything in caring for her son, would she now?'

Nerys seemed uneasy at the turn the conversation had taken and smoothly, Margaret changed the subject.

'How much soap shall I get, Nerys?' she asked. 'I'm as excited as a little girl on an outing at the thought of going into town.'

The tension in Nerys shoulders eased. 'Oh, a few pounds will be enough. I don't like to have too much of a stock as it only dries up and cracks if it's kept too long.' She rose to her feet. 'I'll go down to the kitchen and find out when lunch will be ready. The boys will be awake and moaning about how hungry they are before long.'

When Nerys had gone, Margaret sat in the silence of the room and her thoughts were dark. What was it about Mary Sutton that instilled such loyalty in her staff that they were on the defensive at any hint of criticism?

From the next room, she heard the sound of small voices followed by a giggle and sighed. Nerys had been right — the boys were awake. She pushed her hair into place and rose to her feet, smoothing out the creases in her skirts and smiling a little to herself.

'Come on then, boys, out of bed with you — I'm ready for the fray!' In moments, the silence of the nursery was shattered as the two boys burst into the room.

Later, as Margaret made her way into town, she found herself enchanted by the liveliness of the streets. It was a strange sight to see women carrying baskets on their heads and to hear the raucous cry of 'Cockles!' as they passed her, straight-backed and graceful.

There were many shops with closed doors and faded posters still hanging in begrimed windows, yet there was an air of prosperity about the shops which were still open — especially the emporium that belonged to Mary Sutton.

She was glancing through the entrance when with a start she realised that a thin dark man was standing before her, studying her expression. He smiled and Margaret stepped back a pace, somewhat repelled by his appearance.

'Are you looking for Mary Sutton?' He lifted his hat politely as she shook her head.

'No, I'm not — though what it's got to do with you I don't know.' Margaret retreated a little, her eyes curious.

'I know Mrs Sutton, you see, and I thought I could be of help if you wished to ascertain her whereabouts.'

Margaret was irritated by the man's pompous voice, yet something told her that this man was no friend of Mary's.

'I'm staying at her house and I know exactly where to find her, so that's all right isn't it?' She would have walked away but his soft insidious voice stopped her.

'Relative, are you?' he asked. 'If so, you're fortunate to belong to such an influential family.'

'No, I am not a relative!' She saw his smile widen and knew that her tone had given her away.

'I'm a friend and she's shown me great hospitality — I'm very grateful to Mary Sutton.' But she was blustering and they both knew it.

'Not very enamoured of her though — not by the sound of your voice — and no one knows better than I what a difficult woman she can be,' Phillpot said gently. Inwardly he was congratulating himself; he had hoped to make an ally of Margaret Francis, but not this easily. Like everyone else in town, he had heard the story of how the woman had come over from France with Heath Jenkins' bastard child. Mary Sutton had taken them into her home but human nature being what it was, Alfred had deduced that soon the woman would tire of being the poor relation and come to resent Mary.

'I still don't know what it has to do with you,' Margaret

stiffly, not sure what the man expected of her. He shrugged and made to move away but on an impulse, she reached out to stop him. 'Wait, tell me exactly what you meant.'

'Let us take tea together,' he smiled. 'Now then, there's no harm can come to you sitting in a crowded tea-room, is there, my dear lady? And you never know, we might be of service to each other.'

Margaret followed him almost against her will and, as he held the chair for her, took her seat still wondering why she was bothering with this evil-looking little man.

'Now then,' he said smiling, 'let me introduce myself. I am Alfred Phillpot from the Cooperative Movement.'

* * *

The afternoon seemed to stretch out long and empty and Nerys realised that she was missing Margaret's company. She had grown used to having the Yorkshirewoman in the nursery and was grateful for her help. Once Greenie would have been her right hand, helping with the mending or taking Stephan for his walk, but now Greenie was getting old she was no longer able to cope with the child's boisterous behaviour. Supervising in the tea-rooms was all that Greenie attempted these days, apart from generally helping with lighter tasks around the house.

At last, bored with the boys' constant bickering over toys, Nerys called them to her side.

'What do you boys think about a run in the park?' she asked and immediately Stephan threw his arms around her and kissed her cheek. 'Righto, then, fetch me your caps and coats — and scarves too, mind, for the wind is blowing cold today.'

She noticed with dismay that Jonathan's coat was thin and so darned that it would not protect the boy from the cold at all. Rummaging in the cupboard, she found an overcoat belonging to Stephan. True it was a bit on the small side and it was a job to fasten the buttons, but at least it was made of good strong Melton and would keep the boy warm.

In the park the trees bowed in the wind and with a shriek

Jonathan let his cap soar away from him. It landed in the small pond and at once the boy attempted to retrieve it, his face pinched with worry.

'Let it be, boyo!' Nerys said urgently. 'I don't want you getting a ducking, the weather's too cold for that. Don't fret, I'll find you another cap — no harm done, I promise you.'

She tried in vain to coax him out of his gloom, but his small face was drawn and his ears were growing red from the cold and at last Nerys turned towards home, clutching the boys by the hand.

'Mama will be cross,' Jonathan said in his strangely stilted English. 'She not like me to lose my clothes.'

Nerys patted his head. 'Don't worry, it's not your fault. I'll tell your mam that I forgot your cap.'

Poor little boy, she thought, he must feel strange being uprooted from his home in France and brought to Sweyn's Eye where he knew no one. And he was a sweet child, good-natured and willing always to let the more boisterous Stephan have his own way. And just lately Stephan had been more irritable than usual, though Nerys felt sure that his moods had nothing to do with the appearance of his cousin because they had started before Jonathan's arrival.

They had almost reached the gates of the house when Nerys saw Margaret toiling up the hill with a basket over her arm, her skirts whipped around her ankles by the spiteful wind that came in from the sea.

Together they entered the house and with a sigh of relief, Margaret closed the door against the cold.

Mary was standing in the doorway of the sitting-room with a cheerful fire ablaze behind her. She smiled and held out her hand to Stephan and when he ran into her arms, she hugged him against her.

'*Duw*, there's cold your face is boyo! Come in and have a warm.' Mary led the way towards the fire with the two boys behind her. Her face stormy, Margaret Francis put down the basket and hurried into the sitting-room.

'Look at *my* son!' she said, her voice high-pitched and almost hysterical. 'Just look at him, will you?'

Mary turned in surprise and Nerys, standing in the doorway, saw the bewilderment on her face.

'What's wrong, Margaret, why are you shouting?' Mary asked, her hand rubbing at her skirt which was a sure sign that she was agitated.

'It's a wonder you aren't ashamed!' Margaret continued. 'There's your boy all done up like a dog's dinner — nice coat and cap and a warm scarf — and there beside him stands Heath's son, your own brother's son, but just look at that coat! See how the buttons will hardly do up around the boy's chest — and where is his cap, I ask you, what sort of monster would send a child outdoors in this weather without a hat to cover his head?'

Nerys moved forward. 'If you'll let me explain . . .' she began, but Margaret brushed her aside.

'Oh, I know you'll stand up for your mistress, you always do, but I shall have my say.' She put her hands on her hips and faced Mary squarely. 'You ruin your boy, he's selfish and mean and takes away any toy that Jonathan wants to play with.' She turned to Nerys. 'Now deny *that* if you can!'

'Is this true?' Mary asked in a calm voice and Nerys held out her hands in despair.

'Well, it is in a way, but poor Stephan has not been too well lately, — it's not like him to be nasty.'

'There!' Margaret said in triumph. 'I've kept silent, thinking things would change, but now seeing how my boy is allowed to go outdoors dressed like a beggar, I can realise we're not welcome here.'

'The coat is my fault,' Nerys interrupted quickly. 'Jonathan's coat was so thin that I couldn't take him out in it. I just found one of Stephan's that was thick and warm, I didn't mean any harm. And as for the cap— ' In full sentence, Nerys stopped speaking for she had promised Jonathan that she would not let on he had lost it.

'Yes?' Margaret said quickly. 'What lies are you going to make up about that?'

'I just forgot to put one on him,' Nerys said lamely and Margaret snorted in anger and disbelief.

'Forgot — that's not very likely, is it?' She took her son's hand and led him out of the room, pausing at the door. 'I shall make other arrangements as soon as possible, I shan't stay where I'm not wanted!'

'But this is silly,' Mary began. 'I don't know where you get the idea that you're not wanted — have I said anything to offend you?'

'That's just it,' Margaret said. 'You've hardly said two words to me since I got here, I sew for you, do the shopping, look after your son — I'm little better than an unpaid servant.'

'I'm sorry, I didn't realise how you felt. It's just that I've been busy lately and I've had a great deal on my mind.'

Margaret gave her a quick look and then without another word went up the stairs, her son hurrying to keep pace with her.

Mary sighed. 'Have I really been so neglectful?' She sank into a chair and Nerys moved to sit opposite her.

'Of course you haven't. I don't know what's got into that Margaret — only this morning she was practically begging me to let her do a bit of shopping. There's no pleasing some people. Take no notice, you've done all you could be expected to do and more.'

Mary's shoulders slumped. 'I don't know, perhaps I should have taken more time off to get to know her and Jonathan. Of course she's right in one respect, I should have at least made sure that he had warm clothing. Go out tomorrow and buy him everything he needs, will you, Nerys? I might feel a bit better about things then.'

Nerys got to her feet and moved to the doorway. 'It's strange,' she said, 'but I've got a funny feeling about Margaret and I don't think anything you did would please her now.'

As Nerys made her way upstairs she wondered what sort of mood Margaret would be in, but she need not have worried. It was as if the quarrel downstairs had never occurred, for Margaret was playing on the rug before the fire and amusing the two boys just as though nothing had happened. And yet, Nerys's uneasy feeling that all was not well persisted, even though she told herself repeatedly that she was simply being foolish.

CHAPTER EIGHTEEN

Winter laid cold hands upon the sleeping earth and early morning frosts made mirrors of ice upon the mud of the farmyard. But Catherine noticed none of this as she left the fire in the kitchen, on her way to the shed where the cattle made mournful sounds as they waited to be milked.

Her days were still full of work, for no farmer was idle even in the winter, yet there was an emptiness and a strangeness about her life because she no longer had David to care for. She wondered now how she had borne the difficulties with such fortitude.

And yet she missed him. The husband she had never loved had carved for himself an unmistakable niche in her life. He had shown great courage in the face of pain, a courage which had been underlined when he saved his brother from the seas below Ram's Tor. David had the strength of character which had earned him Catherine's admiration, but she must never forget the outbursts of cruelty caused by anger and despair because it did not do to put a dead husband on a pedestal.

She leaned herself against the warm flank of the animal she was milking, drawing comfort from the task. The strangest part of being a widow was the lack of touching, the lack of ordinary everyday contact. Catherine was not naturally an outgoing person, but she had tended David's most intimate needs. She had cut his hair and washed his body and now there was no closeness any more.

'There, there, be quiet now, Sal,' she said softly to the animal, her words making small puffs of breath on the cold air. 'I'm nearly finished with the milking.'

She heard the sound of clanking milk churns and the rumble of cartwheels and sighed heavily. 'There we are, Sal.' She patted the animal's side. 'There's Betty-the-Milk come now and me not ready!'

But Betty was always a one for the gossiping and didn't mind the delay as she dipped into the canvas bag beneath her apron and counted out the payment for the week's milk.

'Going to have two helpers,' she said in her soft voice. 'My brother Siona Llewelyn has seven sons, see, and don't know what to put them into.' She paused, rattling the money in the bag. 'So I said I'd take the twins on with me, need someone young with the round I do now. Good boys they are, too, Alexander and Hector — there's names for you now.' She smiled. 'Heroes' names, so their mam informs me, but I'd rather a good Welsh name any day.'

'Sorry to keep you waiting, Betty,' Catherine said breathlessly and the older woman smiled.

'No need to rush, see, rushing gives you indigestion!' Catherine watched as Betty drove the horse and cart out of the yard and then returned to the kitchen to stoke up the fire. In the silence, the ticking of the clock was abnormally loud. It seemed odd to think that never more would she hear the creaking of David's chair along the stone passageway. But she was allowing herself to be maudlin and she must stop it at once for that part of her life was over and done and she was a widow woman with the heavy burden of responsibility for Ram's Tor. She tried not to think of the desperate situation she was in; stores of flour were getting low and she was forced to make meals of potatoes without bread.

Into the silence of the kitchen came Morgan Lloyd, his hair curling around his face, his eyes very blue against his tanned skin. He looked every inch a farmer and it was difficult to believe that he had not lived all his life on the land. And soon she must tell him to leave Ram's Tor.

'I've mended the wall above the Tor yet again,' he said, sinking into a chair. 'There's daft those sheep are, falling to their death and all to satisfy their curiosity. I'll have to put up a proper fence, when I've got time.'

Catherine pushed the kettle on to the flames. 'The food will be ready in a few minutes,' she said, wrapping an apron around her thin waist. 'Baked potatoes and a bit of mutton to go with it. Eat hearty, mind, for there's a long time it will be before we'll next eat.'

'Why, what's to be done next?' Morgan brushed back his hair and smiled at her and quickly Catherine averted her eyes.

'Fodder to be taken up to the animals — they must eat too, mind.' She bent over the oven, drawing out a tray of potatoes that were splitting open and smelling rich as the butter she spread on them liquefied.

'*Duw*, I'm as hungry as a horse,' Morgan said, 'and it only seems just now that we had our breakfast.' He leaned forward with elbows on the snowy-white cloth and stared at her intently. 'There's something bothering you, isn't there?' He spoke softly and she glanced at him, her large eyes golden-flecked with bronze and green and wild with something akin to fear.

'I'm lately widowed, isn't that enough to be going on with?' She sat opposite him and looked down at her plate, feeling she had been unfair to him.

'But there's something more,' he persisted, 'you've been very quiet and withdrawn since the funeral. What is it, Catherine, isn't it about time you were honest with me?'

The silence lengthened and at last she put down her fork. 'All right, if you must know, you will have to get out of here. Folks will gossip otherwise. It's not proper for us to be up here alone, you must see that.'

Catherine felt Morgan's anger and was frightened to look at him. She pushed away her plate, no longer hungry. 'It's all right,' she said quickly, 'you needn't go right away, take a bit of time to find a place. I've asked if William can come and stay so that things will be respectable.'

I don't believe I can be hearing this!' Morgan said in a hard voice. 'You don't seriously expect me to journey to work here every morning and then go away again at night, do you?'

Rising from the table, she drew on a shabby woollen coat and tied a scarf around her head; she must look most dowdy and plain, she thought ruefully, but the winds on Ram's Tor could be fierce and cold. 'I said there's no need to rush into anything, but you can't stay here indefinitely, understand that. Now let's take the fodder to the animals, is it?'

It was Catherine who drove the cart, pulling on the reins of the new young pony bought to replace Sheena. Still owed for the beast, they did and Catherine felt a heaviness of spirit descend on her. She wondered if they would even manage to get through the winter on the small supply of fodder in the barn.

The cattle in the top field chewed at the sparse stunted grass rimed with frost with a stolid determination that touched Catherine's heart. Was she a fool to try to continue farming Ram's Tor, she wondered uneasily?

As Morgan began to fork the fodder out of the cart, the wind sang through the trees, rippling the straw and distributing it with more efficiency than a man's hand could do. Catherine faced the wildness of the sea, her eyes staring out into the distance seeing not the seething waters but the innermost thoughts that she had held at bay for so long.

She was in love with Morgan Lloyd — no, not in love, the description was too facile; she loved him with her entire being and she was ashamed, for her husband was not yet cold in his grave.

'Catherine?' Morgan's voice was stern. 'There is a solution — we could be married.' He stared down at her but she avoided his eyes; how could he know that he was speaking words she longed to hear but there was no love in his voice — he was just being sensible.

He came to her and put his hands on her shoulders. 'I'm sure we could make it work, we're no longer strangers — indeed, there's a lot we have in common.'

'No!' The word was dragged from her lips and she felt tears burn her eyes but was too proud to shed them. 'No,' she said more calmly. 'I must have a time of mourning.'

Morgan's hands dropped to his sides. 'All right, Catherine, I'll respect your wishes even if I don't understand them. Let us get on with the work then, is it?'

Later as Catherine cooked the supper, she felt a softness within her as she thought of Morgan's hands upon her shoulders. He was a strong handsome man and he could have any of the village girls if he so chose, for she had not been unaware of the stir he made when last they had gone into town to buy provisions. But he had offered her marriage and not love, she reminded herself sternly.

She stirred the pot and the aroma of mutton stew rose temptingly, filling the small kitchen. Quickly Catherine spread the cloth and put out the dishes, glancing at the clock and wondering how much longer Morgan would be.

It was his habit to go to his room over the stable and bath himself, for he was very fussy about his person. Clean and sweet-smelling he would come to the supper table, his hair still damp with drops like dew shimmering on his brow.

She had studied him so many times that she felt she knew every line of his face, from the clear-cut jaw to the small creases around his eyes. She knew his moods too, for sometimes there was a melancholy in him that told her he was thinking sad thoughts about his past. And at first she had been afraid to recognise the softness in her for him, the warm glow that took her whenever he was near, for she had never known love before Morgan Lloyd came into her life.

The hands of the clock moved very slowly, the ticking growing loud and somehow menacing in the emptiness of the kitchen. Where was Morgan, why had he not come in for his food? She moved to the door and stared out into the darkness of the night. Rain was washing downwards and the cobbled pathway gleamed golden in the light from the open door.

Catherine stared across to the stables as though by the force of her will she could draw him forth. Had he taken sick? she wondered desperately and took a step forward before her natural reticence stopped her going any further. How could she invade Morgan's privacy? The room above the stables was his house and she had no right there.

In the kitchen she took the pot from the coals and the rapidly cooling stew formed a rim of fat even as she watched. She crouched before the fire, staring into the flames, not understanding the pain that was gnawing at her.

She tried to eat, but the food tasted like sawdust in her mouth for the stew had lost its savour. Instead, she made herself some hot strong tea and sat in the lamplight drinking it, her hands curved around the cup for warmth.

At last she realised he was not going to come and rose to her feet anxiously. She knew she could not go to her bed without first seeing if Morgan was all right; this was the first time he had not come over for his meal and worry for his wellbeing tore at her.

The rain was blown into her face by the wind as she made her way across the cobbled yard to the stables. From inside came the soft snorting of the young pony and Catherine paused for a moment, uttering softly-spoken words of comfort.

'There, there, boyo, you're all right — it's only Catherine.'
The stairs at the side of the building rose sharply and she stared upwards, her heart beating swiftly. She held the lamp higher and mounted the stairs cautiously, for they gleamed wetly under the glow.

Her loud knocking on the door produced no results and she stood uncertainly, wondering what she should do next. If she went away now, she would be imagining him lying ill in his bed. With determination she lifted the latch and went into the small room, seeing at once that it was empty. The bed was neatly made with the patchwork quilt drawn into place; over a chair hung Morgan's working clothes, the only sign of his occupation of the room.

Slowly she moved forward, lifting the sleeve of his jacket, holding the roughness against her cheek and breathing in the scent of him. She felt unbearably lonely and fear knotted within her as she wondered where he could be.

She moved towards the door and let herself out into the rainswept night, retracing her steps across the yard and shutting herself into the warmth of the kitchen, pushing home the bolt with a flash of anger. If he came to her table now, he would find he was too late and if he went to his bed hungry, he had no one to blame but himself.

She raked out the fire, watching the ashes fall and turn from red-gold to lifeless grey. Tears blurred her vision and she felt somehow betrayed. Morgan should have told her he was going out — had he no thought for her feelings at all?

Later as she pulled the cold of her cotton nightgown over her head, she found that her anger had evaporated and turned to a deadly fear. Perhaps Morgan would never come back to the farm? So far the only return he had had for his investment was hard backbreaking work and the daily worry that Ram's Tor might not survive the winter.

Her bed was cold and tired though she was, Catherine could not sleep. She tossed and turned, trying to find ease, but her thoughts would not let her be. Her ears seemed to be straining for any sound in the night, but there was only the wash of the rain and the sound of the wind sighing through the bare branches of the trees.

*   *   *

Morgan had left his room in a mood of restlessness, having felt the warmth of Catherine's shoulders beneath his touch and sensed her withdrawal from him. He could understand her reluctance to commit herself to another man so soon after her husband's death, yet what was the alternative? That he move out of the farm and find himself lodgings in the village? Such an arrangement would be absurd, for how would he manage the new cut road between the cliffs if there was a heavy fall of snow? Didn't she realise she might be alone for days on end in winter time?

And so in a mood of impatience, he had washed and dressed and left his room, clattering down the steps and feeling by the breeze sweeping across the Tor that rain was on the way. He had paused for a moment, staring at the

217

small squat farmhouse and picturing the warmth within, wanting to be part of it.

Perhaps he should at least tell Catherine that he was on his way to town? But no, he was not bound by any ties whatsoever and he would not act like a bull led around by a ring in the nose. He glanced back briefly at the lighted window of the farmhouse and imagined Catherine inside preparing supper for him. She would be absorbed in her task, self-sufficient, needing no one for she had grown used to taking charge of the farm and of her own life.

He strode away from the farm quickly, heading for the new cut road and the bright lights of the town beyond. He needed diversion, for he was becoming too immersed in the farm and in Catherine Preece. And on reflection she was nothing to him, they just had a business to run together. Beyond that, he owed her damn all!

The town was crowded and noisy in contrast to the quietness of the hills of Ram's Tor. Morgan felt a lightening of his spirits, a release from the ever-present threat of disaster that accompanied his work on the farm. Had he been a fool to plough his money into the land and was he becoming introspective, losing his sense of fun?

The Dublin Arms nestling in the hollow beneath Green Hill was swept with the sound of Irish voices singing lustily of the Emerald Isle and Morgan was drawn into the vortex of sound by Brendan O'Connor, who reached out a thin arm to clasp his shoulder.

'Morgan, my boy, 'tis a long time since I saw you! At the wedding of Katie Murphy, to be sure?' He appeared a little embarrassed. 'And wasn't there some kind of accident up on the Tor that night?'

'Aye, that's right,' Morgan said easily. 'There's been a lot of old water under the bridge since then. How is Stella keeping, well enough I hope?'

'Sure, she's foine, the girls too, growing up apace they are — lovely and golden, but none to compare with my Honey.'

Morgan felt a flash of surprise. He had not thought of her in a long time and it was strange how the image of

Catherine Preece came into his mind when he tried to recapture memories of Honey.

'Have a pint of ale, my boy.' Brendan handed him a foaming tankard and Morgan smiled his thanks. The ale tasted strange and bitter, yet slipped down the throat as easily as milk. Morgan began to relax, looking around him at the mingling of Welshmen small and dark and the Irish with fair skins and red in the hair. It was good to be with men again, men whole and strong without the stink of sickness about them.

'There's a night for rain,' Brendan said. 'Will you not bide along with us until morning?'

'Aye, I'd like that.' He thought briefly of Catherine alone on the farm, but pushed his guilt away. He gave of his blood to Ram's Tor and man deserved a rest from grafting; it was only right.

The clatter and noise of the room drifted into silence as Dai-End-House rose to his feet beside the piano. He was bowed now with age and his thin hair was frosting on his shiny pate.

But his voice was clear and true as he began to sing of David of the White Rock, *Dafydd-y Gareg-Wen*. The sound brought the hairs rising on the back of Morgan's neck and he supped more of his ale, feeling stupid tears in his eyes.

'I don't know what those Welsh words mean, but they are lovely and touch the heart of me,' Brendan said softly.

'They tell of a dying man giving his birthright to his son,' Morgan explained and Brendan sighed.

'An' that's something I've never had, a boy to follow me. Girls in plenty — even my by-blow was a little girl, which is hard on a man's pride.' Brendan's glance flickered towards Morgan. 'Not that it would be wise to say such things before Stella O'Connor, boy!'

'No,' Morgan smiled reassuringly, 'but then I never heard a word you said, man — listening to the singing I was and Dai-End-House is in full voice, good and loud for all that he's getting old.'

219

'Old enough he is,' Brendan agreed. 'Lived on the corner of Market Street and Copperman's Row for as long as I can remember. Cleaned chimneys all his life and his lungs not touched by soot, strange so it is.'

Morgan felt the ale cling to his throat; it was good and strong and his spirits were lifted by the effects of it. Not a man for drinking, Morgan knew that he was quickly becoming intoxicated, but it didn't seem to matter.

The door opened and a gust of rain accompanied the two women who entered the bar, glancing round quickly and assessing the men. The heavy perfume they both wore outdid even the tobacco smoke and Morgan looked at them without interest, knowing at once what they were about.

'You don't want nothing to do with those two,' Brendan said in his ear. 'Been rutted by all the men for miles around, so they have. See that one there? She's Rosa; used to be courting with David Llewelyn, rest his soul — ran off with his money, so 'tis said.'

Morgan saw that Rosa was eyeing him hopefully. She could not have been more than about thirty perhaps, but her face was heavily lined and her eyes appeared to have seen the world in all its hardness and found it wanting.

'Got a few shillings for a good time tonight, boyo?' she said, leaning against him. Smiling, he put her away from him.

'Not tonight, lovey. I've seen better flossies on the battle-fields of France and they came cheaper too.'

'Huh, lost your balls in the war, did you boyo? Got nothing to give a girl a good time with, is it?'

Morgan simply smiled. 'Let's put it like this, *merchi* — it would take more than you've got on offer to make me feel it's worth-while.'

The girl standing at Rosa's side stared at him through strangely pale blue eyes, her brows lifting in surprise.

'Don't you feel like coming out the back for a shilling standup, then?' she asked in a quiet voice and Morgan, laughing, shook his head.

Cursing, the girl slapped at his hand. 'There's no call for making a show of me, mind,' she said. 'I'm just doing a job to earn some money to keep my babba.'

'Well, fancy that — only one baby, there's a bit of luck for you.' He didn't know why he was baiting the girl for she was nothing to him, but the pent-up ill-humour of the past weeks seemed to need release. 'Anyway, love, the day I've got to pay for it, I'll hang up my boots.'

'Come on, Doffie,' Rosa said angrily. 'Let's get away from these louts, is it, not a real man among the lot of them.'

They left to a roar of laughter and Brendan was busy slapping Morgan on the shoulder.

'Sure an' didn't you send the pair of them off with a flea in their ear? Needed putting down — getting to think that they're offering gold to a man, not just a roll in the hay and away as quick as greased lightning!'

Morgan took a deep draught of ale but his high spirits were evaporating. He had not lain with a woman for a long time, far too long — he was allowing himself to get as dried up as old Dai-End-House.

'Let's have another drink, Brendan,' he said and reached in his pocket for some pennies, but his probing fingers encountered only emptiness.

'*Daro*! One of them flossies has robbed me. Wait by here, Brendan, I'll be back.'

The rain had ceased and the wind came sharply from the docks, carrying with it the stink of the fish market. And he would break the neck of the flossie who had robbed him, Morgan thought with anger burning in his belly, for that money was hard-earned.

He glanced quickly round him — which way would the flossies take? The wide road into town was well-lit, but the back streets, now they were a different matter.

Like a cat, using all the instincts of chase learned in the war, he scouted the courts and alleyways. The darkness was no obstacle, for Morgan's hearing was acute and he could place a sound and identify it within seconds. It was Rosa's coarse laugh which was her undoing; hearing it, Morgan slowly made his way towards the lighted window of a small hump-backed cottage The roof was about to give up the effort of remaining straight and the whitewash was flaking from the walls, but the sound of merriment lent an air of festivity to the shabby dwelling.

Morgan opened the door and went inside. Rosa stared open-mouthed at him, one bare shoulder revealed by her sagging dressing-gown. A man, obviously a customer about to be served, was hanging on to her, his feet slipping from under him.

'Out with you, boyo!' Morgan spoke in a low voice, but with such venom that the man blinked, quickly did up his trews and shuffled from the room with head bent.

'And what do you mean by busting into my home like this? Sorry you'll be when I call the constable!' Rosa blustered. Nevertheless she stepped back quickly as Morgan advanced towards her.

'My money, I want it now or this place will look like a slag-tip by the time I've finished with it!'

'What money? You never paid us nothing! I don't know what you're talking about. Get out of here or I'll scream for someone to get the bobby, so I will.'

'Carry on.' Morgan folded his arms across his chest and leaned against the sideboard which rocked precariously, having one foot missing. 'I'd be most interested to speak to the bobby myself.'

Rosa's eyes flickered away from him. 'I got no money,' she said, her voice sullen. 'Only what I've earned tonight.' She glanced up at him, smiling suddenly. 'But I could give you a good time, boyo — worth it, I'll bet you!'

Morgan sighed. 'Unfortunately, Rosa, you are not my sort of woman. In any case, no one is worth the shillings you took from my pocket and I sweat hard for my money, so cough up unless you want a black eye.'

'You wouldn't hit a woman, you sewer rat, you!' She backed further away from him, her eyes large, spiky lashes sticking together and untidy hair hanging in fronds over her face.

'I wouldn't hesitate, *merchi*, so don't push your luck!' When he thrust himself away from the sideboard and moved a step towards her, Rosa's mouth folded like an empty purse.

'All right then, you swine, I'll get the money. Wait by here.' She left the room and Morgan heard her raised voice and then the sounds of crying from an upstairs room. He took the stairs two at a time and was just in time to see Rosa raise her hand to the girl on the bed.

'You fool, Doffie! If only you'd earned us a bit more tonight we wouldn't have had to steal — not much good at the job, are you? The men don't like a girl with no spirit, I've told you that before. It's no good just lying there like a rag doll, you have to pretend to like what they do — it makes them generous, see.'

The girl on the bed looked small and defenceless, her eyes red with weeping. 'I'll try to do better tomorrow night.' She raised her arm as Rosa's hand swept downwards, protecting her face from the onslaught.

'That's enough!' Morgan took some of the money from Rosa's open handbag and placed it in his pocket. 'Now leave this girl alone, is it, you can see she's had enough for one night.'

'Leave her alone? I'll flay her alive,' Rosa shouted, staring furiously at Morgan. 'I gets all the dirty old men while she has the young ones, but no more will Rosa make a show of herself, oh, no — it's Old Tom Murphy for you next time he comes into town, my girl!'

Doffie's eyes filled with tears once more and on an impulse Morgan caught her hand. 'Come on, get dressed, I'm getting you out of this. There's other work a girl can do besides lying down for a man.'

He had no idea where he was going to take her and as they stood in the dampness of the street some minutes later, he stared around him uncertainly. Brendan O'Connor had offered him a bed for the night, but he could not inflict a flossie on the household; Stella would have a fit.

'Well, girl,' he said, staring down at her. 'It's a long walk to Ram's Tor, so I hope you're stronger than you look.'

She made no reply and he had to take her hand and draw her along the streets towards the town. She clung to him with touching faith and he smiled at her reassuringly.

'I don't know what I'm going to do with you, Doffie, but sure as soap goes with water, I couldn't leave you with that old harridan.'

She scarcely came up to his shoulder and her face, now washed free of paint, was round and childlike. Her soft, dark hair was loose around her shoulders and she carried a small bag that appeared to contain all her wordly goods. Pity washed over him and he held her hand more tightly.

'How old are you, Doffie?' he asked and she stared up at him, her chin held defiantly high.

'I'm sixteen, mister — nearly seventeen, see.' Her eyes blinked and she looked away from his sceptical expression.

'If you're sixteen, then I'm a Dutchman — more like fifteen if you ask me. Now come on, let's get going before I change my mind.'

They walked silently in the rainswept night and Doffie grumbled incessantly. She was just like a little child, unable to hide her feelings.

At last they reached the Tor and then the farm. Morgan sighed with relief as he led her up to his room.

'Here, give me your coat and then you can get your head down on the couch by there. I'm for the bed; there's a lot of hard work waiting for me come morning and you can sleep the day away if you like.'

'But what am I going to do, mister? I can't sit around here all the rest of my life, can I now?'

'No, quite right, you can't, Doffie, and what's more I shan't allow it. As soon as I can find you a position in the town, then it's away with you into a respectable life, right?'

'Well, aren't you going to ask me how I got into all this?' Doffie sat on the bed, her hands hanging limply on her thin knees.

'I know you haven't got a baby to keep — that was a lie for a start.' Morgan smiled and shrugged off his coat. 'No mother of a young baby is as small in the breast as you.'

Doffie blushed and looked mortified. 'I'm not that small, look at me!' She drew open her blouse to reveal touchingly

224

thin ribs with breasts as yet undeveloped, the nipples innocent and pink.

'Come on, boyo.' Her voice had softened and she looked up at him with all the knowing of a woman twice her age. 'Come on, you don't have to pay for it — not with Doffie, you don't.'

Morgan moved over to her and caught the edges of her bodice, drawing them together.

'Button yourself up, girl — and get on that couch before I change my mind and throw you out into the rain!'

'Don't you like me then, mister? Aren't I pretty enough for you? Rosa keeps telling me a man needs to be pleased and I am trying to please, really I am.'

Morgan took her hands. 'Stop calling me "mister" for heaven's sake; my name is Morgan. And Doffie, listen to me, I want you to forget about pleasing men — keep that for when you have an honest husband. You don't want to end up bedraggled and old before your time, like Rosa, do you?'

She shook her head, her eyes large, then after a moment, she rose from the bed and made her way to the couch, curling up there like a small animal. In a few minutes she was asleep and with a smile, Morgan covered her with a woollen blanket.

'Sleep well, *merchi*.' She did not hear him and he climbed into his bed suddenly overcome with weariness. Closing his eyes in the darkness, he thought of Catherine and laughed dryly. It seemed he had solved the problem of any impropriety taking place at Ram's Tor Farm, for he had found them a chaperone.

CHAPTER NINETEEN

The dark skeletal branches of the trees waved eerily against the cold night sky. On the western slopes of Sweyn's Eye the gracious solid houses stood staunch against the wind that swept in from the Bristol Channel and lights glowing in windows offered a spurious warmth to the man huddled in the leather seat of a car.

Paul Soames was unaware that he was shivering. His thoughts were darker than the night sky and a turmoil of emotions welled within him. All he knew was that he must see Mary Sutton, talk to her, find a solution to his dilemma. For the deacons of Zoar Chapel had called him before the *Set Fawr* and accused him of fornication with a married woman in an hotel in Cardiff.

At last he moved stiffly from the seat of the Morris and walked up the driveway beneath moaning swaying trees to the door of Mary's house. He pressed the bell, hearing the mournful ring of it through the hallway and waiting impatiently for an answer.

Mrs Greenaway was not pleased to see him. Paul knew she disapproved of him and although she could know nothing for certain, her instincts were to mistrust his motives. In fact, she was only too correct.

'You'd better come in out of that old wind,' she said grudgingly and Paul took off his hat as he entered the warmth of the hallway. He sighed heavily as the old woman moved off awkwardly towards the sitting-room; her gait was stiff — probably inflammation around the joints, he diagnosed absently.

Mary looked beautiful. Her hair was loose and she was

dressed in a warm woollen gown; obviously she had been preparing for bed.

'I shan't keep you long,' he said, glancing meaningfully towards Mrs Greenaway, 'but I must talk to you.'

Even after the door closed and he was alone with Mary, he found it difficult to speak.

'What's wrong, Paul?' she asked, breaking the silence. 'You look so pale.'

'I don't know how to tell you this, Mary,' he began, rubbing at his hair impatiently. 'We were seen together at the Metropole in Cardiff and whoever it was spied on us has informed the deacons of my parish.'

Mary sighed softly and sat back in her chair. 'Oh, Paul, is that so bad? We did nothing wrong at the Metropole and I'd be only too willing to tell the deacons so to their faces! In any case, why should a few chapel people worry you? I didn't know you were all that religious?'

'It's not that.' Paul sat down, wondering how he could explain his fears to Mary without sounding like a ten-year-old whining about his lot. 'You see, Mary, a doctor has to take an oath and must abide by certain principles. If he does not, then he faces severe reprimand and even perhaps the loss of his livelihood. If the deacons proved some misdemeanour against me, then I could be reported to the British Medical Association.'

'*Duw*, I see only too clearly.' Mary stared at him with wide eyes and even now, he knew he would give up everything if she would be his.

'But I repeat that we did nothing wrong, Paul — and I'm willing to go before anyone and swear to that.'

Paul sighed. 'It may well come to that and could you really bear it? There would be a scandal, no doubt about it, and you know the old saying that mud sticks even to the innocent.'

The door opened and Mrs Greenaway entered the room with a tray balanced in her hands. The china was fine and delicate, Paul noticed, and the tea service was silver. What he earned on his doctor's salary would not be enough to keep Mary in incidentals, he thought ruefully.

Mary seemed to read his thoughts, for her fine dark eyes rested on him and a smile curved her generous mouth. 'There's soft you are sometimes, Paul,' she said gently and he didn't even consider asking her what she meant — he knew well enough.

'Aye, soft over you, Mary. I love you and there isn't a thing I can do about it. Is there any chance at all for me?' He paused as she shook her head and took the cup of tea she offered him. 'No, of course not, forget I spoke.'

A few moments passed in silence as they drank their tea. Then Mary leaned forward. 'Now listen to me, Paul, I'll stand by you. Don't forget you're the only doctor we have in the area now Bryn Thomas has retired. Fight for what you know is right and don't give in so easily.' She reached over and took the empty cup from him and as their hands touched briefly, he felt her strength flow into him.

He smiled suddenly. 'You are right, Mary, as always; what harm can idle gossip do me?' He rose reluctantly to his feet and stared down at her, longing to take her in his arms. He could remember even now the feel of her body close to his, the warmth of her arms and the tenderness of her touch. He knew that he had stolen a few hours of pleasure with a desperate woman, but it had been more than that and he must have loved her even then.

He turned and left the room, unable to speak for fear of falling to his knees and begging for her love. Mary Sutton was a proud woman and she would despise a man who was weak. But he was weak, there was a core of softness within him even if only where Mary was concerned.

He climbed into the Morris and as the seat cracked coldly beneath him, Paul Soames stared up into the darkness of the skies and told himself that he was a fool. He had possessed Mary once and then had allowed her to slip away. He sat for a long time, staring at the house until one by one the lights were extinguished and the windows became dark, gaping mouths. It was time he went home, he told himself, as reluctantly he climbed from the automobile and cranked the engine into life.

*   *   *

Mary had worried about Paul's visit for days and so when the letter came, she opened it warily. The paper crackled between her fingers and as she read the carefully penned words her heart beat a little more swiftly. A formal complaint was to be made concerning the unprofessional conduct of Paul Soames with Mary Sutton. She would be called upon to state her side of the case to the elders of the chapel if she so wished.

She sat at the dining table, her breakfast untouched as she stared at the sheet of paper. Vaguely from upstairs, she heard the sound of the boys arguing and then Margaret's voice raised in anger.

'Anything wrong, Mary?' Greenie placed a plate of succulent bacon on the table and sat down, staring at her anxiously. Mary shrugged and passed the letter over.

'I suppose it will be all over Sweyn's Eye before long, so you may as well know about it right now.'

Greenie read quickly and sniffed derisively. 'There's a nerve! Not going to turn up are you, *merchi*? I don't see why you should put yourself to all that trouble and upset.'

For a moment Mary was tempted to take the line of least resistance; Greenie was right, she was not bound to subject herself to what would be some sort of trial. Then as she thought of Paul's eyes, worried and tired, she knew she could not let him down.

'I'll not give in to this sort of thing, Greenie,' she said firmly. 'Paul and I did stay at the Metropole Hotel in Cardiff on two occasions, but it was nothing more than a coincidence. And nothing improper took place — I can swear that under oath.'

Greenie sighed. 'Then you must do what you think best, Mary. There never were any half measures with you.'

As the sounds of Margaret's voice rose, Mary left the breakfast table and hurried up the stairs, her nerve-ends tingling.

'What on earth's going on here?' she asked as she saw her son kneeling in the corner, clutching his favourite tin soldier close to his body. He scrambled to his feet and came towards Mary and she saw with concern that his face was white and drawn.

'Stephan is being a naughty boy,' Margaret spoke more softly. 'He will not share his toys and I think it's in his own interests to have him learn a little generosity.'

'Well, leave it to me now, would you?' Mary said acidly, rather tired of Margaret's increasingly reproachful attitude. 'Come along, Stephan, it's time for breakfast.'

Later, as she re-read the letter, Mary felt a prickling of apprehension. She wished now that she had never set eyes on Paul Soames; since he had come into her life, he had meant nothing but heartache and trouble.

The door opened quietly and Margaret Francis entered the room, her face flushed. 'I'm sorry for that scene before breakfast, but that boy of mine kept me awake all night and I suppose I was a little irritable.'

She did not quite meet Mary's eyes, but settled herself at the far end of the sitting-room. 'Oh, by the way, I've found rooms at a little house on the outskirts of the town, so I shan't be troubling you much longer.'

Mary looked up sharply. 'No trouble, Margaret — you know you're welcome to stay here as long as you like.'

'No, it's best to be independent.' The words had an edge to them and Mary glanced quickly at Margaret, wondering if she had failed her. She tried to imagine her lying with Heath, giving him of her passion, but the rather staid appearance of Margaret Francis belied the fact that she had conceived a son in a moment of illicit love.

Mary had seen definite changes in Margaret's attitude over the last few days. When she had first arrived from France with her son, who was so like Heath, she had been soft and gentle and grateful for the least kindness. But of late she had seemed to resent her position in the household and the last thing Mary wanted was to put upon her.

'Well, you must suit yourself of course. Where are the boys?' Mary spoke evenly and Margaret glanced up at her.

'Nerys is playing games with them and later she means to take them both to the park — that's if it's all right by you.'

Mary forced a smile. 'Of course, why shouldn't it be?' She rose to her feet. 'If you'll excuse me, I must get down to the store, there's lots of clearing up to be done there.'

'Clearing up?' Margaret's eyes were large and curious and Mary felt a tingling of unease, which was foolish for what harm could Margaret do her or indeed wish to do her?

'Yes, I've sold the shop.' Immediately the words were spoken Mary regretted them. 'But for the moment, I don't want anyone else to know about the sale.'

'I see.' Margaret looked down at her hands. 'Well, I won't say anything.'

Mary sat down again and leaned her chin on her hands. 'Margaret, I'm sorry if I've offended you.'

The other woman flushed hotly and shook her head. She didn't speak, but carefully began to pluck at a thread of cotton hanging from her hem as though the task was of the utmost importance to her.

'You can talk to me, you know,' Mary continued. 'I just feel there is a wall between us somehow.'

'Well, we're not exactly blood relatives, are we?' Margaret responded. 'Not friends, either. We owe each other nothing.'

Mary did not blurt out the angry words which rose to her lips, words which would have told Margaret that not everyone would take in a woman who had borne a byblow, or accept that the child was her nephew. Without another word, she turned and left the room.

Hopefully Margaret would move out during the day and then Mary would see no more of her. And yet it rankled that the woman who had been eager to accept her help had now somehow turned against her.

Mrs Greenaway was waiting in the hall for Mary and

held her coat ready. 'You must wrap up warm, *cariad*, it's blowing a gale out there.'

'Are you sure you want to go in to the store today, Greenie? I wouldn't mind if you stayed at home.'

Mrs Greenaway shook her head fiercely. 'I love it in the tea-rooms, Mary. I feel like cock of the walk when I'm showing the rich folks to their tables.'

Mary sighed. 'All right, get into the car then, while I crank the starter.' She drove away from the drive and down the hill towards the town. Spread out below was the panorama of the bay and the dark cliffs shelving away in the distance.

'I've sold the emporium, Greenie,' Mary said quickly. 'I've been made a fair offer which I've accepted.'

'*Duw*! And why have you done that, Mary girl?' Greenie sounded shaken to her boots and Mary smiled.

'Now don't you go worrying, I know what I'm doing. Fine stores are going to be difficult to finance, for bad times are coming, Greenie — I feel it in my bones.'

Mrs Greenaway was silent for a long moment and then she pulled her shawl closer round her head and turned to Mary.

'Then if it's what you want, you're right, for you have a business head on you that would do any man proud.'

'Thank you for your confidence in me, Greenie,' Mary said. 'You know I've bought a van and that Billy Gray is going round the valleys selling woollen goods for me? Well, it's paying off and that's where my bread and butter will be when the rich folks start salting away their fortunes in foreign banks and such.'

'You are the businesswoman, not me,' Greenie said softly, 'but I'll miss that shop I will — loved it all from the smell of the polish to the lovely fresh scent of the bales of cloth.'

'I know, Greenie; but satins and velvets are luxuries, you see, and I want to be selling food and basic clothing — things that are always needed.'

'But if times are bad, then the poor won't be able to afford those things, will they?'

'Perhaps not,' Mary said gently, 'but I'll put my money

into a variety of small undertakings instead of risking that one big holding; my emporium might go bust.'

Mary drove in silence for a time and the question of Margaret Francis's strange attitude nagged at her mind.

'By the way, Greenie, Margaret has found herself some rooms so we'll be losing our guest.'

'And good riddance to her, I say! She was lovely at first, wasn't she, but then she began to be waspish to young Stephan, taking away his toys to give her own boy. Jealous she was of all you had to give your son, while she had nothing.'

'If that's true, then I can understand her attitude a little,' Mary said thoughtfully. 'I suppose I should make an allowance for her son, he is my brother's child after all.'

'Nonsense! You owe those two nothing. Who provided for you and Heath when you were young, tell me that? And why should this foreigner come and expect a handout from you?'

Mary concealed a smile. 'She's not a foreigner, Greenie, she's from Yorkshire.'

'Aye, well, she can't be too fussy for didn't she marry a Frenchman?' Greenie folded her arms in an attitude of disapproval. 'I wouldn't worry about the likes of her; let her go her own road to hell, that's what I think.'

The streets of the town were busy, the shops were thronged with people and for a moment Mary wondered if she was wrong to believe there would be a slump in trade. Perhaps she had been too hasty selling off the emporium, but it was too late to change her mind now.

'Come on, Greenie,' she said as she drew the Austin to a halt. 'Out you get, we've got work to do!'

The hum of activity in the large store was familiar and still exciting and from the tea-room came the clink of china as the tables were set for morning coffee and as she turned towards the stairs that led to her office, there was a hard lump in her throat.

*　　*　　*

Margaret Francis felt sick inside as she stood in the clean well-appointed nursery waiting for Nerys to dress Jonathan. She could not help but feel a traitor, for Mary Sutton had shown her nothing but kindness and had seemed genuinely distressed about her leaving.

And yet, shouldn't some of the wealth surrounding her belong to Heath's only living child? Nothing had been offered by Mary, no plans that would assure Jonathan's future security, so a mother must fight for her child in whatever way she could.

She recalled her suspicions when first the little man in the dark suit approached her. She had looked anxiously around her and been reassured by the crowds of shoppers peering into windows.

When he suggested they might have interests in common she had been intrigued and thought there could be no harm in accepting his invitation to take tea with him. Then, after he had introduced himself as Alfred Phillpot, representative of the Cooperative Movement, he had also told her that he was a deacon of the chapel.

Margaret could not say she liked him even then, for he had narrow eyes and a thin mouth, but his offer to help her find not only a respectable home but also a position in one of the Cooperative stores was too good to turn down and so she had listened to what he had to say.

'All I need in return is a little information,' he said unctuously. 'You said you are at present staying with Mary Sutton?'

Margaret had withdrawn a little. 'Yes, I am, but she's been very kind to me,' she said defensively.

'Of course,' Alfred Phillpot said quickly, 'although I'm quite sure that you are more than repaying any hospitality shown you by Mrs Sutton. But rest assured, my enquiries concern one Paul Soames, a doctor, and I would be pleased if you could inform me of any visits he pays to Mrs Sutton.'

'What's wrong with him visiting? He's a doctor, after all, and the two of them are friends.'

'Ah, I see, that's all right then.' The narrow eyes became

slits. 'Are you sure they're friends? It wouldn't do to be mistaken.'

'Of course I'm sure, didn't I see the two of them at the Metropole Hotel in Cardiff? That was before I knew who Mary was, of course. And yet the likeness was there — her resemblance to Heath, I mean. It struck me straight away and I couldn't keep my eyes off her.'

'The Metropole Hotel in Cardiff?' He coughed. 'Now I'm sure you must be mistaken.' He had carefully looked down at the hat held fast between his fingers and Margaret had been annoyed with the silly little man — what did he take her for, a fool?

'It was just a week or two ago and I am *quite* sure about it. Check at the hotel if you don't believe me.'

'I will, my dear.' He rose to his feet. 'You have been very helpful indeed and all I shall require is for you to repeat what you have just told me before a meeting of the elders of the church.'

'Oh, I don't know about that.' Margaret had suddenly been uneasy. 'It might bring harm to Mary — Mrs Sutton — and I wouldn't like to do that.'

Alfred Phillpot brushed an imaginary fleck of dust from his hat and glanced towards her. 'How on earth could Mrs Sutton be harmed by the truth my dear lady? No, it's the doctor I am interested in. Now about those rooms — I can promise you it's a lovely little house right near the docks. You'll be very comfortable there and all your expenses will be met until you begin work.'

And the house to which he had taken her had indeed been comfortable. Not palatial in the way that Mary Sutton's house was but neat and clean and with the waters of the sea lapping almost to the doorway. Jonathan had clapped his hands with delight and in that moment, Margaret knew that as far as she was concerned the die was cast.

*   *   *

It was a cold day when the rain fell in spiteful spikes,

spitting up from the cobbles and dripping from the leaves of the overhanging trees. Mary had wrapped up warmly and huddled into her Austin, driving down the hill from her house almost in a daze of apprehension. She was to go before a meeting of the elders of Zoar Chapel for a preliminary hearing on the conduct of Paul Soames. And there it would end, Mary was certain of it, for once she had had her say there could be no doubt of Paul's innocence.

She guided the car through the busy streets of the town and was unnerved at the number of beggars sitting in shop doorways or simply crouched at the side of the roadway, holding out cold hands in supplication. The war had a lot to answer for, she thought bitterly.

The chapel hall was chill and unprepossessing, smelling of old books and dampness. The deacons sat waiting in their fine suits as though sitting in judgement, and as Mary's eyes roved over them she felt a sense of fear which was quite irrational. And then she saw him, his thin mouth stretched into a grimace.

'Alfred Phillpot! I might have known you were behind all this — what are you up to now?'

He held out his hand as if to silence her and gestured that she take a seat at the centre of the room. Mary felt anger rise within her; why was she allowing herself to be treated this way? She had done nothing wrong.

'Before I sit down, I want an explanation,' she stated firmly. 'Where is Paul Soames?'

Alfred Phillpot gestured towards the door. 'Here he comes now. Please have patience, Mrs Sutton, anger and ill-will are not going to help matters.'

He spoke with a false kindness which angered Mary. She placed her hands upon her hips and stared at him fiercely.

'There's a fine one to talk you are!' She heard her voice rising, but was powerless to control her sense of outrage. 'You who tried to ruin my business, who would have seen me in the gutter, who are you to sit in judgement on me?'

The other deacons were moving restlessly and Mary realised that she was causing some embarrassment. She sat down quickly, hating the self-satisfied smile that appeared in Alfred Phillpot's face. He glanced around him as though to ask what could one do with a woman of this sort.

'Perhaps we will find the doctor more reasonable,' he said slowly. 'Please be seated; we have only a few questions to ask of you then you will be free to go.'

Paul glanced at Mary in swift apology and she pressed her lips together to prevent the angry words from spilling forth. She leaned closer to him and whispered her protest.

'I don't think we should put up with this nonsense — what can these men do to you anyway?' She watched him bite his lip and waited impatiently for his reply.

'You don't understand, Mary,' he said desperately. 'If I can satisfy this hearing, then the matter will not be taken any further. I'd rather not have any of this brought before the Association.'

'Perhaps we should proceed,' one of the elders said, nodding to Alfred Phillpot. 'We're all busy people and don't want to delay any more than necessary.'

'Just a few minutes, if you please,' Phillpot said quickly. 'I'm waiting for a witness to put in an appearance.'

Mary clasped her hands together in her lap. Witnesses, indeed! She had thought this was a chapel, not a court of law. She heard the door open and stared up in amazement as Margaret Francis entered the hall. She was neatly dressed in a high-necked blouse and dark coat and she appeared very different from the woman who had come to Mary seeking help.

'This is going to be quite informal.' Alfred Phillpot smiled thinly and Mary glared back at him, making no attempt to hide her contempt.

'Now, doctor, there are two complaints against you. The first is that you failed to turn out to an urgent call to go to Ram's Tor and Bryn Thomas had to go in spite of his age and infirmity. In the event the patient, David Preece, expired, sad to say.'

Paul looked at the man in surprise and Mary could see him floundering, unable to marshal his thoughts. She stared

237

at him, urging him silently to deny this man's absurd accusation, but when Paul spoke his voice was quiet.

'I was away at the time, on business.' His voice lacked conviction and Alfred Phillpot almost visibly rubbed his hands together.

'Ah, yes, at the Metropole Hotel in Cardiff, I believe?' Phillpot leaned forward and Mary was reminded of a bird of prey as she stared at the man's scrawny neck jutting from the dark collar of his coat. 'And by some strange coincidence, Mrs Mary Sutton was there too — isn't that correct?'

Paul spoke quickly. 'I can't be sure of that, I was there to attend a conference. Anyone can confirm I was at the conference; you have only to ask my colleagues.'

Mary sat back in her chair, fear grasping at her. She saw now which way Phillpot was manoeuvring the questioning and yet she was powerless to stop it. She knew too what role Margaret Francis was to play — she had seen Paul and Mary dine together and apparently would not hesitate to say so.

'What about you, Mrs Sutton? Is your memory better than the doctor's? He may be trying to protect someone, attempting to be gallant.'

As Mary stared at the man, bitterness at all the old injustices rose to the surface. 'You sly creature!' She heard the hysteria in her voice and tried to calm herself. 'You've always hated me, haven't you?' she continued more quietly. 'You always wanted to see me ruined. Well, you can't prove anything, do you understand? For there is nothing to prove.'

Alfred Phillpot moved closer to her. 'There is nothing personal in this, Mrs Sutton, I do assure you — and you may leave at any time if you feel so inclined. I simply thought that your presence here might help the doctor.'

'You would not want to help a beggar in a snowstorm, there's false you are and you a deacon of the chapel!' She heard the rhythm of the Welsh lilt come into her voice, as it always did when she was distressed. 'But you are wrong this time — *wrong*, do you understand? I will swear on the holy bible that I did nothing to be ashamed of that night!'

'My dear lady, just one simple question: did you see this man and this woman together in the Metropole Hotel in Cardiff?'

Margaret looked at Mary and then turned quickly away. 'Yes, but only in the dining-room; they were not alone.'

Mary saw the embarrassment on Margaret's face and knew that she had been taken in by the cunning Alfred Phillpot. She meant no harm, she was simply a tool to be manipulated and Mary almost felt sorry for her.

'I see. They had company at the table with them, did they?' Phillpot said mildy and Margaret's colour rose.

'Well, no, but . . .' She stopped speaking as the man waved his hand towards her, indicating that she might go. Mary sighed heavily and leaned forward in her chair.

'May I speak?' She saw the deacons confer with each other and then, before anyone could stop her, Mary was on her feet.

'If to be seen in a dining-room of an hotel is a sin, then most of your wives have committed the same sin in my tea-rooms.' She smiled disarmingly. 'There I see men and ladies talking and taking tea together every day and no one thinks any wrong of it, for there is no wrong.'

There was a muttering of assent and Mary smiled warmly at Paul, trying to infuse a little of her strength into him for he seemed to be struck dumb by the fervour of Phillpot's attack.

Mary began to draw on her gloves and stood for a moment staring down at the odious little man who seemed intent on interfering in her life. Well, she had won again and he could go to hell!

'Just one minute, Mrs Sutton. I have only one further question to put to you.' Handing her a shiny black bible, he stared into her face intently and suddenly her elation vanished.

'Now, think carefully before you speak, Mrs Sutton, for we are all waiting to hear your reply.' He stood back and paused, his thumbs in his waistcoat pockets, his slit eyes shining with triumph.

'Can you truthfully say, here in this house of the Lord and before his deacons with his good book in your hands, can you *truthfully* say that you have never been the doctor's mistress?'

Mary felt as though the dark suits of the deacons had turned into feathers and a horde of black birds was waiting to descend upon her, waiting to rend her to pieces. She glanced at Paul: seeing his bowed head she felt pity and then hot impotent anger welled up within her. She swallowed hard and looked at the book in her hands and knew that she could not lie.

'On the night at the Metropole Hotel there was no impropriety.' Her voice was a thin whisper and Alfred Phillpot smiled, knowing he had her beaten.

'Ah, but that is not the question I asked — now is it, Mrs Sutton? *Have you ever been this man's mistress? We are all waiting for an answer.*'

Mary stared down at the floorboards worn by the passage of many feet. 'Yes!' The word fell softly into the silence like a stone in a small pool which sent ripples racing towards the shore. And still Alfred Phillpot was not content.

'I don't think we all heard you, Mrs Sutton. Do you think you could speak up a little? After all, this is very important, isn't it?'

Mary lifted her head and stared directly at him. 'I said yes, I have been the doctor's mistress, if you can call it that. Just let me explain . . .' But her words were lost in a buzz of voices as Phillpot turned to the deacons.

Mary glanced towards Paul, who smiled at her encouragingly. 'Don't worry,' he said softly 'there was nothing else you could say. It's the truth and I'm proud of it — perhaps it's just as well it's all out in the open.'

'But your job, you won't be able to work any more. Oh, Paul, I'm so sorry!'

Alfred Phillpot turned to Mary and his expression was one of scorn. 'You may leave this sacred place, Mrs Sutton,' he said abruptly. 'There is no room in God's house for harlots.'

Margaret Francis gave a small cry and rushed forward.

240

'How dare you speak to her like that, you monster! If I'd known what you intended to do, I would never have helped you.' She drew herself up to her full height. 'What has happened to charity, I ask you that?'

Phillpot ignored her. Her usefulness to him was over and she was not important.

'Come along, Margaret.' Mary caught her arm. 'If we stay here, we may do the old goat an injury!'

Paul picked up his hat and stick and there was a look of relief on his face as he stared around him.

'Do your worst, Phillpot, old boy,' he said cheerfully. 'But if any of you or your family take sick, don't ask for me, will you?'

Outside Mary took great gulps of fresh air, trying to free herself from the bitterness that held her in its grip. Phillpot was a tyrant, a little tin god who surely could have no power over Paul's future. In any case, she intended to fight him as she had always done and she would get her story over to the medical board before he could.

'I'm not beaten yet,' she said, her voice strong and vibrant. 'I'll get my own back on Alfred Phillpot if it's the last thing I do!'

*   *   *

It was a few days later when Mary sat in the large sitting-room and stared into the wise face of Bryn Thomas. He had listened to her story with silent but sympathetic interest and when she had finished, he put his hand on her shoulder.

'My dear, there is nothing for you to worry about.' He took out his pipe and lit it, puffing with enjoyment, his eyes twinkling.

'I don't understand,' Mary said, shaking her head. 'As I've told you, the deacons mean to take the matter to the British Medical Association and it could ruin Paul's practice.'

'Nonsense!' Bryn's smile widened. 'There's no fear of that, Mary, my dear, for you were *my* patient up until the time

241

I retired. Your name was on *my* list, not that of young Paul — don't you see?'

Mary sank back into her chair, still not quite understanding what Bryn was getting at. He leaned forward, his arms resting on the shiny cloth of his trousers.

'What a doctor does in his spare time is his own concern so long as the lady in question isn't his patient, do you see?'

'Ah!' Mary smiled in understanding and leaned back in her chair, relief flooding through her.

'You just leave the deacons of Zoar Chapel to me, my dear. I don't think they will want to pursue the matter once I have had a word with them.'

'Thank you!' Mary got to her feet, aware that Marian Thomas was peering round the door, her long nose scenting scandal. 'I'd better be on my way, I've taken up enough of your time as it is.'

'Anything wrong, dear?' Marian's voice was honeyed. 'I thought you were looking rather pale when you came in.'

'Mary is just fine, Marian, and there's nothing for you to concern yourself over,' Bryn interrupted dryly. 'Now come again any time you like, Mary; I'm always glad of a chat, life is so dull since I've retired.'

He saw her to the door and Mary waved to him before she drove away. She sighed in satisfaction. Paul was no longer in any danger from the deacons or the British Medical Association. But for all that, Alfred Phillpot would not be allowed to get away with his deviousness, she would see to it.

CHAPTER TWENTY

Snow lay as a frosting of white over the softly folding hills, icing the stark branches of the trees, beautifying the barren hill of Kilvey which lay to the east of Sweyn's Eye. The small whitewashed cottage blended into the background with only the light from the windows and the spiral of smoke rising from the chimney to identify where it stood.

Within the warmth of the kitchen, Katie Murphy was ladling hot rabbit stew into blue and white dishes, an apron around her slim waist, her red-gold hair hanging free.

'There's a sight to warm any man's heart.' The door had opened and her husband stepped into the room in a flurry of snow. His face as he pressed it against hers was cold, his eyebrows whitened as though he had suddenly become an old man.

Katie rubbed her apron across his brow, brushing away the snow; she smiled up at him as he leaned forward once more and this time kissed her lips.

'Get those wet clothes off you, my lad, or you'll be catching your death of cold! And hurry, for the food is ready and waiting and I'm starving, so I am.'

Mark hurried upstairs, returning after a few minutes wearing a thick flannel shirt and a clean pair of trousers.

'Well, that's better. I can't allow my new husband to catch cold.' Katie put her arms around his broad shoulders, hugging him to her.

'Eat now, talk later, you look as though you could do with a good meal.' Katie sat at the table and held out a wooden bowl containing thick slices of freshly baked bread.

'*Duw*, it's good to be home.' Mark brushed back the

243

damp hair that curled around his face. 'I still can't believe my luck when I look at you — why did you marry a failure like me? Tell me, Katie girl.'

'Hush now.' Katie felt a mingling of anger and pain within her as she looked into his eyes. 'It wasn't your fault that Mr Sutton decided to return to America, now was it?'

'No,' Mark dipped a crust of bread into the stew, 'but it is my fault that I can't find another job. What's gone wrong Katie? Once I thought I had the whole world at my feet. Remember when I helped Brandon Sutton to bring out the handbook for tinplate workers? Life was good then, full of promise, yet now there isn't a job of work for me in the whole of Sweyn's Eye. Have to go down the pits, I will, by the look of it.'

'Not on your life, Mark, my lad! We'll move away from here first.' She pushed aside her dish. 'No man of mine is going to give his blood for the coal, I've seen enough of that. What if I ask Dad to help us?'

Mark shook his head thoughtfully. 'No good, love, everybody is finding the going tough right now. We thought that the war would solve everything, didn't we, but it seems to have brought us a whole heap of fresh trouble.'

There was silence for a moment in the small kitchen and then Katie smiled, determined to be cheerful.

'Guess what?' She didn't wait for a reply. 'There's a woman come over from France to stay with Mary Sutton — well, she did at first anyway, then there was some sort of row.' Katie left the table to pour water from the kettle into the china tea-pot. 'Well, it seems this Margaret has got a son by Heath Jenkins, the image of Heath the boy is. Anyway, that's not the end of the story, for this Margaret was travelling to Sweyn's Eye when she stopped off at the Metropole Hotel in Cardiff — and who should be there but Mary and the young doctor!'

Mark's eyebrows lifted. 'Well, I shouldn't think Mary Sutton would have much in common with Paul Soames — just a coincidence it was, if you ask me.'

'Yes, perhaps so, but you see Mark . . . I know something

you don't.' She poured the tea and then sat at the table once more, leaning her elbows on the white cloth. 'Mary's son Stephan — well, she didn't know who the father was; it might have been her husband or it could have been the doctor. A right dilemma she was in and me not very sympathetic. But I've never told anyone about it and wouldn't, not if hell had my tongue — got a loyalty to Mary, sure I have.'

'Well, remember that and keep your lip buttoned, *merchi*; you don't want to cause any more trouble. Mary's alone now, got no man at all — had enough of punishment, I'd say, without adding to it.'

'You're right enough, Mark. I'm sorry for Mary, for she took Margaret Francis into her house and then the woman seemed to turn against her.'

'How did you come to be speaking to this Margaret, then?' Mark took another piece of the crusty bread, crumbling it in his fingers. He sounded disapproving and Katie glanced at him quickly.

'It was down in the market, I don't honestly think she meant any harm to Mary, for Alfred Phillpot was behind the whole thing, you see.'

'Well, I suggest that we forget all about it — right? I don't know why we're even discussing it!' Mark spoke impatiently and Katie made a rueful face at him.

'I only brought it up because Margaret was talking about France as though it was the land of milk and honey — said she wished she'd never left there. Plenty of work for a young strong man, she claims.' Katie paused. 'And rather than see you go down the pit, I'd move away to France like a shot.'

Mark leaned back in his chair with a flicker of interest in his eyes. 'Well, now that is something worth hearing, Katie love.' He rose from his chair and walked around the table, staring restlessly out into the night. 'A new start in a new land — it sounds very attractive. I must speak with this woman — invite her here for tea and then I can ask her a few questions.'

245

Katie had spoken bravely of moving from Sweyn's Eye, but when she lay beside her husband in the double bed beneath the sloping roof of the cottage, she was not sure that she could bear to leave behind everything familiar. Her family were here — come from Ireland many decades ago, settled into the community like threads of different coloured wool bound together to form a pattern. Her father's fish shop in Market Street was the place where the Irish met to talk, not always to buy the Tom's fresh fish but welcome anyway.

And yet to see Mark go underground was unthinkable. She would do anything rather than have him become a miner, digging in the bowels of the earth for the coal that killed without discrimination.

And so it was that the next day Katie sought out Margaret Francis. She had just taken up lodgings in a small house near the docks in comfortably furnished rooms and she was pleased to have a visitor.

'Come on in, lass.' She smiled a welcome. 'It seems a very long time since anyone's spoken to me. I'm being blamed for the scandal about the doctor and Mary Sutton, you see.'

'Well, we all know who was behind that, pushing you,' Katie said quickly. 'I doubt if even Mary herself blames you; that Phillpot is an old enemy.'

'I don't know about that . . . but sit down and have a warm, the fire's just been mended.'

'What I want to see you about is work for my husband. You were saying that France is a good place for employment, is that right?'

Margaret leaned forward eagerly. 'Yes, there's farm work aplenty and jobs in the clothing factories — it all depends on what parts you want to travel to.' She pushed back a stray wisp of hair. 'Is your husband thinking of going overseas then, lass?'

'Yes, sure he's thinking about it but what he'll decide in the end I don't know.' Katie smiled ruefully. 'I expect I'll have to stay here and keep the home going, just in case there's nothing in France for him.'

'I've been seriously thinking of going back,' Margaret said

slowly.' I've cooked my goose here in Sweyn's Eye and even if I go up to Yorkshire, I expect things will have changed beyond belief. And strangely enough I miss my little home beside Mametz Wood. Perhaps your husband and I could travel at the same time? I might be able to help him out with a few introductions and that sort of thing.'

'That's very good of you.' Even as Katie spoke she felt a pang of fear; events were moving much too swiftly and what had been only an idea to play with had suddenly become a reality.

'Mark would like you to come up to our house for tea one day when you can spare the time — he'd be only too glad to hear what you say about France, sure enough.'

Margaret smiled in relief. 'Well, I'll be delighted to tell him everything I know. The truth is I can't stay here, not with all the hostility I've met, and I've been so lonely since I left Mary's house. Serves me right, I suppose. Didn't really mean harm to Mary, her being Heath's sister an' all, and I was foolish to be taken in by that awful Mr Phillpot.' She shrugged her shoulders. 'Any road, what's done is done and there's nowt I can do to change things.'

Katie rose to her feet and moved towards the door. 'What about tomorrow then, is that all right?'

Margaret nodded. 'Yes, that will suit me very well. My landlady will look after my boy for me and Jonathan's very amenable, just like his father.' She sounded wistful and Katie glimpsed the sadness behind the woman's bright appearance.

'See you tomorrow, then.' She spoke warmly and took the hand Margaret extended towards her. 'You'll be very welcome.'

She left the small neat house and moved towards the town, deciding that she might just as well go home to see her family now that she was out and about and in any case a walk would do her good. She crossed the busy streets cautiously, the snow having turned to treacherous slush which coated her boots and pierced the leather with chill fingers.

Green Hill was away uphill from the town and the streets were rimmed still with crisp snow. Katie hugged her coat closer and wished she had covered her head with a warm shawl, for there was comfort in the Welsh wool.

The smell of the fish shop greeted her as she turned into Market Street and memories swamped her as Dai-End-House began playing on his accordion. The tune was a lilting Irish ballad and Katie waved her hand to him through the window, knowing that the old man had spotted her.

'Katie, my girl — sure 'tis fine it is to see you!' Her mother reached out thin arms and hugged her only daughter with more warmth than she had ever shown when Katie was a girl. 'Your daddy's out with the cart and your brothers with him, so there's a bit o' peace in the house today. Come on, I'll give you a hot dish of soup — a body needs warming in this cold weather.'

The kitchen these days was both comfortable and respectable, unlike the times when Katie was small and her younger brothers played in an old pram on rag mats. There was a good carpet covering the stone floor and the furniture had been changed and was polished to a shine that Katie could see her face in.

'Are things still going well with the shop, Mammy?' Katie asked softly as she settled into an armchair.

'Sure they're fine, folks are always needin' good cheap cuts of cod and some tasty smoked haddock. And your dad's not gone mad buying new-fangled motor vans either — same old horse Big Jim and the old cart that's done us right proud all these years. Bad times are comin' though, I can feel it in my bones, Katie. You and Mark look to your own selves.'

'We'll be all right, Mammy. Don't you go fretting about us, do you hear?' Katie concealed her uneasiness, knowing it best not to confide in her mother; there was no point in stirring up a hornets' nest before anything was properly arranged.

Mrs Murphy was busy pouring a generous measure of gin into a glass; she had always liked her drop of spirits

248

and even now, old though she was, she seemed not to have suffered any ill-effects.

'No liquor for you, my girl — mother's ruin so 'tis,' Mrs Murphy said complacently, 'and I want some fine spanking grandchildren from you some day soon.'

The bell on the shop door tinkled and with a sigh, Mrs Murphy put down her glass, looking martyred. Katie rose to her feet, holding out her hand.

'There, Mammy, stay where you are and I'll see to the customers,' she offered cheerfully. She moved quickly into the shop, where the slab of marble sloping into the window displayed fish of all kinds. Played the devil with the hands, did the fish, especially the spines which were as sharp as razors.

'Mali Llewelyn!' Katie's voice echoed her pleasure as she skirted the counter and hugged her friend. 'Well, an' isn't it funny to see you here in my daddy's old shop, then?'

'Not funny at all, Katie Murphy. Don't I always buy my fresh fish here then, would I go anywhere else?'

Their laughter brought Mrs Murphy from the back room. 'Well, Mrs Richardson, 'tis nice to see you've called for your order; I thought the cold might have kept you away. Come through to the back and have a little chat with my girl then — 'tis a while since you two have been together.'

'Too long,' Mali said, hugging Katie's arm. As they moved into the kitchen the shop bell rang once more and Mrs Murphy left the girls alone; Katie felt a sense of being taken back into the past when she and Mali were girls together.

'Well, it's an old married woman I am now, Mali, though I thought I was going to end up an old maid.'

'You an old maid, fiddlesticks!' Mali laughed, tucking her small feet up beneath her skirts for warmth.

'It seems only the other day we were living next door to each other,' Katie remarked. 'Then you went and married the copper boss and were the talk of Sweyn's Eye. And I can see you're as happy now as you were then — meant for each other, you and Sterling were.'

Mali nodded her head. 'Aye, a lot has happened since

then, what with the war and everything. And you are happy now, *cariad*, I can see it in your eyes.'

'Oh yes,' Katie spoke quickly. 'Me and Mark have got a lot to be thankful for, he's a wonderful husband and the more I learn about him, the more I want to learn. Do you think we ever know the depths of our menfolk, Mali?'

'*Duw*, that's a hard question. I feel I know Sterling, of course but then everyone has a bit of private self that they hide from others, I suppose.'

'Sure 'tis wise you've become, Mali! All grown-up and mature, you're the same as the girl I once knew and yet different, too.'

Mali nodded. 'I know what you mean, motherhood changes women and makes us more vulnerable. I suppose it's because there's another life to be responsible for. Anyway, I thought I was going to be offered a cup of tea? I'm getting all daft here! Like an old woman chewing her gums and offering unwanted advice. I've not come here to lecture, have I, but you started it, Katie Murphy!'

'And so what if I did? If I can't talk to my old friend, then who can I talk with?' Katie felt suddenly lighthearted, for being with Mali had infused her with optimism. She had her family and her friends and she and Mark would come through the troubled times together.

* * *

The winter skies were swept with grey, the clouds heavy with unfallen snow. Mary held Stephan's hand firmly as she led him into the house where Paul Soames had his surgery. She well remembered the old hide couch and the skeleton hanging in the corner and the ever-present smell of wintergreen oil. But her memories were of the past and nothing she could do would change what had happened, so she might as well put aside the unhappy thoughts.

'Mary, I've wanted to talk to you so badly, yet I was afraid that a visit to your house would only confirm the stories put around by Alfred Phillpot.'

'I've talked to Bryn Thomas and it seems everything is all right because I wasn't officially *your* patient at that time . . .' She paused. 'In any case, I have every faith in you as a doctor, Paul,' she smiled, 'and it's as a doctor I've come to see you. It's Stephan, I'm worried about him,' she sighed as she gently pushed her son forward. 'He's been complaining of pains in his head.'

'Well now, old man, let's have a look at you.' Paul became at once the professional man as he held Stephan's hand, drawing him closer. 'I'll just look into your eyes with this little light — it won't hurt at all, so don't worry.'

Paul's examination was thorough and Mary felt a new respect for him; he was a good doctor and it would have been so wrong if he had been deprived of his livelihood. She watched his hands as they gently tilted Stephan's head. Paul was wearing a bland expression that she could not read — an expression calculated to shut her out, a professional barrier between a doctor and his patient.

'Can you find anything wrong, Paul?' Her voice trembled as he reached out to take her hand at once.

'I would like Stephan to see Bryn Thomas. I know he's supposed to be retired but I still consult him on occasions as he's much more experienced than I am.'

'What is it then, what do you think?' Mary asked urgently.

Paul shook his head. 'There could be a slight problem with Stephan's eyes. But you're not to worry, I'm sure it's nothing that can't be corrected.'

Mary felt an icy chill sweep over her. Paul was being too reasonable, too reassuring and she sensed there was something he was not telling her. She glanced down at her hands as they lay clasped together in her lap, fighting her tears.

'Is it the after-effects of the car accident, Paul?' she asked fearfully, remembering her own pain and the voice of her son calling into the darkness in which her world had been immersed.

'I shouldn't think so, not for one minute. Now please don't jump to any conclusions, Mary; you're a sensible woman and you must act like one.'

She relaxed a little. 'All right, Paul, thank you for seeing us and please arrange for Bryn to examine Stephan as soon as possible.' She took a deep breath. 'And Paul, take your own advice and don't worry about that fool Phillpot — he doesn't know what he's let himself in for, yet!'

When she took Stephan home, Nerys was waiting anxiously in the hallway. She gathered the boy into her arms and kissed him soundly in spite of his protests.

'There, let me take you coat off you now before you get it dirty, then.' She glanced up at Mary, waiting anxiously for her to speak.

'The doctor thinks there may be something wrong with Stephan's eyes,' she said, 'but we're not to worry, mind.' Her calm tone concealed her own mixed emotions, yet she recognised the sense of Paul's words — what was the point in becoming agitated?

Mary did not bother to remove her coat, as there was something she must attend to and at once. Her worry over Stephan had pushed the matter of Alfred Phillpot out of her mind but now she must act, find a way of putting the evil little man in his place.

Margaret Francis had insisted on leaving the house more from a sense of guilt rather than anger. Mary believed, when she took the rooms down by the docks which Alfred Phillpot had found for her. She drove her car into town with an air of quiet determination, knowing she must speak to Margaret.

As she pulled up outside the neat little house, she heard the hoot of a tug in the harbour with unusual clarity. She glanced up at the overcast skies and wondered if there was more snow on the way.

Margaret was suprised to see her and smiled uncertainly as she led the way into her rooms.

'Goodness me, I'm having so many visitors these days I don't know if I'm coming or going!' She spoke quickly so as to cover her nervousness and Mary touched her arm reassuringly.

'There's no need to be alarmed, I haven't come here to

give you a ticking off or anything. I know that man Phillpot and how sneakily he works, so I don't blame you for what happened — I've told you that more than once.'

Margaret pulled a chair nearer to the fire. 'Sit down, Mary, I'll be glad to have a talk with you. I've been wrong and I know it — jealous of you I was, lass, knowing that you could give your son everything while I . . .' She shrugged her shoulders expressively.

'Forget all that and just tell me what Phillpot did and said — he arranged this for you, didn't he?' Mary gestured round the room and Margaret nodded.

'Yes, he promised me a job too, but so far that's not been forthcoming. What's more, he'll no longer pay my rent and now there seems nothing left for me but to go back to France.' She sighed. 'It's what I want, lass, to be back in familiar fields again. I miss my home so badly.'

Glancing at Mary, she paused and then went on. 'I got talking to a nice young lady — Katie, her name is, I expect you know her. Asking about work in France for her husband she was, poor dear.' Margaret moved towards the window and stood staring out into the cold of the day. 'I thought I'd find Heath, but without him there's little point in me staying.' She hesitated. 'I hope I'm not upsetting you, reminding you of Heath this way, Mary — I know how close you two were.'

Mary shook her head. 'It's good to know that Heath has a son, it's as if there's a tiny piece of him here with us and I'll be sorry if you do return to France, Margaret, in spite of everything.'

'I've made up my mind to go,' Margaret said quietly. 'I'd forgotten how cold and rainy it is here; the sunshine in France seems so much brighter. I suppose it's because I miss them so much, my neighbours in the village. Far-flung we all were and yet close, like a family. France is my home now, though it's taken me long enough to realise it.'

'Well, we'll talk about that later,' Mary said. 'For now, I want to know all about that little weasel Phillpot — I must find a way of stopping him. Tell me exactly what the arrangements were.'

Margaret frowned. 'Well, I don't know that I can be of much help. He just told me he'd find me these nice little rooms and you can see that everything here is clean and respectable just like he promised.'

'Have you ever paid the rent?' Mary asked carefully and Margaret shook her head positively.

'Oh, no, any money that's exchanged hands has come to my landlady straight from Mr Phillpot's own pocket.'

'That's very interesting,' Mary smiled. 'I must have a word with . . . what is your landlady's name?'

'Mrs Fraser, but I doubt she'll help you. She must be a friend of Mr Phillpot's, mustn't she?'

'We'll see about that.' Mary moved towards the door and stood looking around her, listening for sounds of movement. She made her way along the dim linoleum-lined passage and let herself into the warmth and steam of the spotless kitchen.

'Mrs Fraser, please forgive me for intruding.' Mary spoke in the voice usually reserved for customers in her emporium. 'I would very much like some information, if you please.'

Mrs Fraser was a stern woman wearing a crisp white apron tied over a blue serge dress, her lace collar neat and flat. This was a no-nonsense kind of woman, not one easily frightened, hence Mary decided she must use guile.

'I'd like to know how much rent Mrs Francis owes you?' She smiled graciously, but there was no answering smile on the other woman's face.

'Why, what business is it of yours?' The voice was cold and flat and it took great effort of will for Mary to remain pleasant.

'I'm prepared to settle the outstanding balance Mrs Fraser, if that meets with your approval.'

The woman studied her at great length and Mary returned the cold stare without flinching.

'All right then.' Mrs Fraser looked pointedly at Mary's

bag. 'I believe the amount to be above fourteen shillings.'

Mary smiled. 'Of course you have proof of this sum? Not that I disbelieve you, of course, but I'm a businesswoman and I like to see things in writing. Not an unreasonable request, as I'm sure you'll agree?'

The woman lifted her head like a horse sensing danger and Mary quickly opened her bag and drew out some coins, rattling them enticingly in her palm. 'Best take the money now, it won't be offered again, Mrs Fraser.'

'Very well.' The landlady went to the drawer and took out a grey book, opening it and flicking through the pages. 'There!' She spoke triumphantly. 'See for yourself.'

Mary took the book and saw that it had been signed by Mrs Fraser. 'I see you received from Councillor Alfred Phillpot the sum of thirty shillings. How long a period of time did that cover?'

'Let me see now . . . it's twelve shillings a week for the room and three shillings extra for food; that's a period of two weeks paid for.'

'And how long overdue is the rent?' Mary smiled without humour. 'Just the one week, wouldn't you say, which makes the sum due thirteen shillings and not fourteen as you mentioned just now.'

'There are extras, mind, like laundry — and if I say the amount owing is fourteen shillings, so it is.'

Mary handed her two guineas and while the woman was counting the money, tore out the relevant pages from the book and put them in her bag. She moved to the door then and turned back for a moment.'

'Mrs Francis will be staying until it's convenient for her to move. The money I've given you more than covers her for some time yet. Thank you for your cooperation, Mrs Fraser, I'm very grateful.'

Margaret was waiting for her in the doorway and it was clear from her expression that she had heard everything. She bit her lip against the tears that formed in her throat and speechlessly held out her hand towards Mary.

'Just let me know the exact date you're leaving,' Mary

said quickly, 'I'll come to see you off at the station. Now don't worry about Jonathan's future — I'll help all I can, I promise. Let me know as soon as you are settled in and then I can write to you.'

Mary left the house with a feeling of satisfaction and did not look back as she set the Austin into motion. She drove through the town and took the coast road towards Ram's Tor, thinking it might be just as well to check whether or not a complaint had been made against Paul.

*   *   *

Catherine Preece was a beautiful young woman with rich shining hair and large eyes. She appeared gentle and reserved as she admitted Mary into the neat farmhouse, yet there was a quality of strength about her that was impressive.

'I realise I'm intruding into your busy routine and I'm sorry,' Mary said quickly, 'but it is important.'

Catherine sat calmly with her hands folded in her lap, quite in control of the situation as she waited for Mary to speak.

'I know you lost your husband some time ago and I'm sorry.' Mary felt out of her depth, she was usually so good with words, but in the face of Catherine's dignified manner she felt awkward and blundering.

'I'll come straight to the point,' she went on. 'A friend of mine, Doctor Paul Soames, has been accused among other things of being neglectful of his duty — slow to come to Ram's Tor when your husband was sick. Did you make any complaint?'

'There was no complaint.' Catherine's eyes were calm and level. 'I understood the doctor was away on business and so he could hardly come up to Ram's Tor. In any case, Bryn Thomas said there would have been nothing anyone could do for David and I accepted his word.'

Mary rose to her feet. 'Thank you, Mrs Preece. I'd be grateful if you could put that in writing.'

A fleeting expression of doubt crossed Catherine's face

and Mary understood the other woman's reluctance to get involved in a situation which after all was not her problem.

'Please help,' Mary urged. 'Paul's professional reputation is at stake, you see.' After a moment, Catherine went to the drawer, took out a piece of paper and began to write.

When Mary left the farmhouse, she stared around the fields of Ram's Tor and breathed in the fragrant air with a feeling of satisfaction. Now she had a meeting to arrange with Mr Alfred Phillpot and the rest of the deacons who had stood in judgement over Paul Soames.

* * *

The chapel was cold, for there had been no time to light the boilers. The deacons in their best dark suits with high collars and neat ties stared down at Mary as though she had taken leave of her senses, calling them suddenly from their homes.

'I take it this is important, Mrs Sutton?' It was Alfred Phillpot who spoke, his eyes narrowed and his thin nose twitching. He was just like a rat sensing a trap and Mary returned his gaze with haughty dignity.

'Yes, I have something here which I think the deacons should see. First of all, a letter from Mrs Catherine Preece of Ram's Tor Farm absolving Paul Soames of any blame connected with her husband's death. Indeed, she states that Bryn Thomas — a doctor of long standing in the community who came in his stead — told her that nothing could have been done for her husband even if Paul Soames had been there.'

She paused to let her words sink in. 'And then there are these,' she added, producing the pages torn from the rent book and holding them out. 'Please pass them round.' She spoke quietly. 'I think this will prove coercion on the part of Councillor Phillpot and that he had a private spite against myself and the doctor.'

There was a murmur of voices as the entries in the rent book were read aloud and Phillpot turned a dull red as he listened.

257

'I was just doing the lady a kindness,' he blustered. 'Turned away by Mrs Sutton, the woman had nowhere to lay her head and it was only my Christian duty to find her respectable rooms.'

'And to pay the rent, Alfred?' one of the deacons asked in a low voice. There was a slight titter of laughter, quickly subdued.

'It doesn't alter the facts.' Phillpot said sourly, 'that a doctor — a member of this church — had knowledge of a woman who was not his wife, who indeed was another man's wife.'

'And all that happened several years ago during the war,' Mary put in quickly. 'I wasn't even his patient then. And if he leaves town, who then is going to minister to the sick in Sweyn's Eye, tell me that?'

'Go you home now, Mrs Sutton,' the spokesman for the deacons advised. 'This is a matter for discussion amongst ourselves, isn't it?'

Mary nodded, knowing she could do nothing more. Leaving the chapel, she felt the evening air cold on her face as she walked towards the Austin. If nothing else, she had had the satisfaction of putting Alfred Phillpot in his place! Above her the moon slid out from behind a cloud, pale and silver and shining like a circle of ice in a velvet sky.

CHAPTER TWENTY-ONE

An easterly wind threw the spikes of bare branches on the sycamore tree against the window panes in a fierce tattoo. The whitewashed farmhouse appeared to cower close to the land, the wisps of smoke from the chimney diffused by the force of the gale.

Within the kitchen Catherine was bent over the fire, her eyes hot and dry, for she had had little sleep that night or any night since Morgan had brought a loose woman to the farm. She moved the big black kettle, impatient for the water to boil for her throat was dry and her whole being ached as if in the grip of one great pain.

She told herself to be calm. Morgan Lloyd was a free man, answerable to no one, yet within her there was a sense of outrage that he had dared flaunt a flossie before her so casually.

She tensed as the door opened and Morgan stamped into the warmth of the kitchen, his hair flung over his forehead by the cold wind. His cheeks were red and he stared at her with eyes that openly appraised, so that she quickly looked away from him in anger.

'Anyone would think that it's me's done something wrong!' The words spilled forth before she could stop them and Morgan looked at her across the room, his face expressionless.

'Wrong, who's talking about *wrong*, then? Who do you think you are, Catherine — a Sunday school teacher, is it?'

Catherine had never known such rage, it was composed of anger and pain and a mixture of emotions she could not understand.

'She may be a young girl but she's a flossie, isn't she, a harlot who sells herself for money? And you've had her hidden in your room for days!' The picture conjured up in her mind of the two of them together brought a renewed sense of outrage.

Morgan's eyes were alight with humour as they looked into hers. 'I've not hidden her, Catherine. You would have seen her much sooner if you'd cared to come over to my rooms. What's really eating you, is it jealousy?'

She moved away from him and sank into a chair staring up at him, seeing the truth she had sought to hide from herself — that he was right and she was jealous.

Morgan sat beside her and stretched out his long legs to the warm blaze of the fire, his smiling eyes looking into hers. 'Have you no answer, then? I've never known you to be lost for words.'

'All I'll say is this,' her voice was low, 'you can't keep her up in your room for ever, Morgan.'

Morgan sighed heavily. 'Full of good intentions, I am, Catherine — saving this young girl from a life of sin and all that and providing you with a chaperone into the bargain! Wasn't that what you wanted?'

'Fine chaperone and her come in off the streets!' Catherine heard the hardness in her voice and bit her lip. 'I doubt she'll want to help me with the scrubbing or anything else for that matter — girls like her do not like hard work.'

Morgan laughed in amusement. 'And what would Catherine Preece know about girls like Doffie? Never been near a whore 'till now, have you?'

'I'm not stupid, mind,' Catherine said, offended. 'I may have been brought up strict, but I don't go round with my eyes shut and flossies are flossies wherever men may be found to pay them.'

She sighed heavily. 'But one thing is certain, she'll not stay on Ram's Tor for long. Anyway, there's no time for talking about her any more — someone's got to give the animals fodder, though this wind is going to play the devil with the straw — cast it to the end of the earth it will.'

Morgan was on his feet in an easy movement. 'You stay here, I'll see to the animals.' He smiled at her and her mouth was suddenly dry; she longed to lay her head on his shoulder, but knew that there she would be playing with fire.

He had been gone only a few minutes when the door opened and a small timid face looked in at Catherine. She felt herself grow tense, picturing again the scene when at last she had gone to Morgan's room searching for him. The girl had been sitting on the couch, her bare feet blue with the cold. But it was not pity Catherine had felt, it was the pure primitive emotion of jealousy.

'Come on in then if you must, it's freezing with that door open,' Catherine said flatly.

'*Duw*, there's sorry I am to cause a row between you and Morgan.' Doffie sidled up to the fire like a kitten seeking warmth.

'Not daft, are you?' Catherine said grudgingly. 'Getting a fine fellow like him to bring you home! But remember, this is my farm and I have the final say on who stays here and who doesn't.'

'You needn't worry — he wouldn't do nothing with me, mind,' Doffie said, her eyes wide. 'Said he's never paid for it and not going to start now!'

Catherine put a cup of tea on the table, indicating with a sweep of her hand that Doffie should take it. The girl's words rang true, there was no denying that and she felt a bubble of laughter well up within her as she imagined the scene with Morgan impervious to the girl's charms.

'Offended, I was,' Doffie continued. 'Offered it for nothing, but he still didn't want me. Now I can see why, of course.'

Catherine felt the colour run into her cheeks. 'And what is it you can see then?'

'Oh, no offence meant, just that it's as plain as the nose on my face that you two got something special. Envies you I do, wish I'd met a fine man like Morgan before I went on the streets. All that Rosa's fault it is — told me it was money for old rope, but it isn't, believe you me.' Doffie took a sip of tea. 'Letting a man have you when you don't care for him at all is not nice.'

Catherine smiled at the understatement, but there was a sadness in her as she remembered the times when she had lain rigid beneath David Preece, gritting her teeth and praying he would get the business over quickly. How much worse for a girl to go with men she did not even know! For the first time, as she stared at Doffie with her young face puffy and lined and the brave red bangle on her small wrist, she felt compassion.

'I'll help you to get a job if you like,' she offered and the girl looked up at her warily.

'What sort of job?' Doffie pulled her skirts down over her feet as though to protect herself and Catherine became impatient.

'Can you be choosy then, miss?' she asked sharply. 'How do I know what sort of job? In a house perhaps, cleaning, or maybe in one of the shops in Sweyn's Eye — or isn't that good enough for you, then?'

Doffie made a rueful grimace and pushed back her long tangled hair. 'I'm not very strong,' she said pathetically and Catherine laughed in her face.

'Nonsense! You're as strong as a mule and just as stubborn. Right then, *merchi*, if you don't want to work it's out on the streets with you again, for I'm not keeping you.'

'I didn't say I *won't* work,' Doffie smiled engagingly. 'It's just that I don't want to do nothing hard, like — not cut out for it.'

'For now,' Catherine said, 'you can wash up the dishes and be thankful I'm not sending you out to the chicken coop to collect the eggs!'

She drew on her coat, watching Doffie stare around her as though expecting the dishes to come to her of their own accord. Catherine smiled and pulled on a scarf. 'I shan't be long, so get on with it!'

The force of the wind came as a surprise, nearly sweeping Catherine off her feet as she leaned into the gale, slipping on the icy ground as she made for the hen-house.

The birds fluttered uneasily as the wind accompanied Catherine inside and then settled back on to the straw, beady eyes alert, heads turning sharply from one side to the other as though constantly searching for something unseen.

Catherine felt a primitive joy in gathering in the eggs, plunging her hand beneath the warm body of the bird and bringing forth sustenance in the form of brown-shelled eggs. And yet she recognised, uneasily, that the store of chicken meal like everything else was getting low. Outside the wind whined and cried, snapping branches from stark winter trees, punishing the sleeping earth.

The return journey to the farmhouse was difficult, for now she carried a basket of fragile eggs. She forced her way forward step by step, buffeted and bruised, her scarf flying away like a bird suddenly released. She felt her strength beginning to ebb and stumbled, almost falling to her knees. Her hair flew wildly and whipped around her face so that she could no longer see where she was going and for a moment she felt panic claw at her.

Then she felt an arm around her and Morgan's strong body at her side, drawing her onwards and nearer the farmhouse. She clung to him with her free hand and he dragged her towards the door that opened like welcoming arms.

The kitchen was a sudden welcome harbour and Catherine put the eggs on the table before sinking into a chair and pushing the hair away from her eyes. She stared up at Morgan and he shook his head.

'There'll be more than a few sheep lost over the Tor today,' he said in a hard voice. 'The wall is down again, blast it! Why didn't I get on with that fence I was going to build?'

Catherine shrugged her arms free of her coat. Her body ached, she felt as though she had been kicked and bruised, her legs were trembling with weariness and her eyes were red-rimmed and sore

'*Duw*!' Doffie broke the silence. 'Did you ever see such a storm, for I never did. Is the weather always this spiteful out here on the farm?'

No one answered her question and with an indifferent

shrug, Doffie settled herself into her chair.

Catherine looked at Morgan anxiously. 'Is the pony safe and the cattle — are they in the shed?'

Morgan nodded. 'Aye, but the sow's broken loose from the sty and I couldn't see where the silly animal was heading. Damn this gale, it's going to cost us a fortune in lost livestock!'

Catherine felt weary and dispirited; she seemed to be facing one crisis after another.

A sudden sound rent the air, sharp and short, exploding through the force of the gale. Catherine's eyes met Morgan's and held.

'It's the lifeboat,' she spoke in a low voice. 'There's a ship aground somewhere out in the bay. Where are you going, Morgan? They won't let you help — you're not experienced enough.'

But he was already shrugging into his coat and pulling a cap down on to his head. He stared at her briefly and then smiled, his eyes alight with excitement. 'In this storm, they'll need anyone they can get!'

She knew there was nothing she could say that would stop him. 'Go with God, then,' she said and then he was making eagerly for the door and she was forgotten as he let himself out into the wailing wind.

'*Duw*, he must be mad going out in this,' Doffie said in awe. 'Wouldn't catch me going near the sea, not in such a storm.' She paused, looking at Catherine searchingly. 'Shall I make you something nice and hot to drink? she asked coaxingly. 'There's pale and tired you look, *merchi*, but don't you go worrying now, for Morgan is a boy that nothing will beat, you'll see!'

But Catherine was drawing on her coat, hardly listening to Doffie, 'I've got to try and find the sow,' she said flatly. 'Can't afford to lose her, good for breeding she is.' She stared at the girl. 'There's a lot Morgan still doesn't understand about farmers — we don't give up on our animals that easily.'

'I'll come with you,' Doffie offered quickly. 'Anything's better than staying in by here on my own.'

Catherine would never have believed she could feel gratitude towards a flossie, but as she handed the girl a thick warm coat and watched her draw it on over thin shoulders, she smiled grudgingly. 'You're not so bad, are you?'

Outside, the wind was howling like a live creature as Catherine made her way towards the sty. The boar grunted — eyes red and angry, snout twitching in fear — but there was no sign of the sow and the fence was down, flattened against the land.

Doffie clung to Catherine's coat with head bent, following blindly. The ground was a mire that sucked and pulled at Catherine's feet as she struggled forward.

'Over there!' Doffie's thin voice was just audible and Catherine looked where the girl was pointing. The sow was lying against the ground and as Catherine approached, the animal began to squeal with fright.

'There's wire twisted round the sow's trotter,' Catherine shouted. 'I'll need the axe. It's by the pile of logs just outside the farm door — can you get it for me, do you think?'

Doffie was already moving away, a strangely eerie figure in the coat that was too big for her and with her hair streaming upwards from her head as it was whipped by the wind.

'You'll be all right now, girl,' Catherine said softly to the terrified animal. 'I'll soon have you free.'

It seemed an age before Doffie returned and the girl was bent almost double as she laboured through the rising wind. Catherine took the axe and grasped it firmly.

The wire was more difficult to cut than she would believe possible and the frantic squealing of the sow jarred on her. 'Keep quiet, you stupid animal!' Her shoulder ached with each blow she struck and then Doffie was tugging at her arm excitedly, indicating that she take a turn. The girl wielded the axe with more strength than Catherine would have given her credit for and at last, the wire broke.

'Get her back to the sty!' Catherine called. 'Don't let her wander away.' But the animal was limping badly and with a sinking heart Catherine realised there was a circle of wire biting into the sow's leg.

The sow ran for home instinctively and burrowed into the straw of the sty. Catherine tried to raise the fence and push the wooden stakes back into the ground, but the force of the wind was against her and at last she had to admit defeat.

Doffie pulled at her sleeve and clinging together, the two of them struggled back to the farmhouse. Catherine shut the door with a sigh of relief and sank into a chair.

'Come on, get out of them wet things,' Doffie said quickly, shrugging off her own coat and pushing the kettle on to the fire. 'Need something hot, we do now.'

They sat together drinking tea and Catherine felt bone-weary as she stared at Doffie. 'I couldn't have done it without you,' she said slowly. 'If we hadn't released the sow she would have died out there; I owe you my thanks.'

Doffie grinned, but there were shadows beneath her eyes and she trembled with weariness. 'Think nothing of it. Will that poor animal be all right now?'

Catherine rubbed a hand over her eyes. 'I hope so — at least she's in no immediate danger and when Morgan returns he can probably remove the rest of the wire from her leg.'

After a time, the warmth of the kitchen was too much for Doffie and she fell asleep suddenly just like a child. Catherine fetched a blanket and placed it over her, then she stood for a moment, trying to see out of the window which was running with rain. Tired though she was, she could not sleep, not until Morgan was safely back on Ram's Tor.

*　　*　　*

The gale was increasing in ferocity, roaring between the cliffs and tossing the waves into a frenzy. Morgan made his way cautiously to the lifeboat station, seeing through the wooden slats of the pier the waves suck and recede beneath him. The seas around the Mumbles Head had appeared to be gentle and docile and seldom had he seen them so angry.

Morgan hurried along the arm of the pier and saw to his disappointment that the lifeboat had already been launched. He stood above the slipway, peering out into the trough of the seas trying to assess what was happening.

Out beyond the Mumbles Head was a crippled French schooner with masts broken and twisted like matchwood. Making difficult headway towards her in the fierce seas was the *Charlie Medland.*

Morgan crouched on his heels, waiting, reflecting that at least he would be on hand to help bring the men ashore from the wrecked schooner. His muscles were tense, and even as the wind roared in his ears he heard the sudden shout from the *Charlie Medland.*

Straining his eyes, he saw that there was a man overboard, washed towards the shore by huge rolling waves. He sensed the dilemma facing the coxswain — should he turn back for his own man or go on towards the stranded ship?

The lifeboat was turning back and Morgan, concentrating his gaze on the darkness of the man's head, covered sometimes by water, shouted directions to the coxswain. It seemed as though the boat made one move forward and two back, battling against the onrush of waves. As the man was being washed inshore towards the slipway, Morgan saw his chance and waded into the freezing seas, grasping the unconscious crewman by his shoulders and dragging him upwards on to safe ground.

Bill Owen put ashore another of the crew who immediately bent over the man lying on the slipway, pressing on his chest to expel the water from his lungs. The coxswain waved his arm towards Morgan. 'Come on, boyo, there's no time to waste!'

Then Morgan was on board the lifeboat crouching between the other men, his legs swamped with water. His heart was beating swiftly as the boat pulled out from the shore into heavier seas.

Morgan focused his eyes on the small figures of the survivors on the sloping deck of the schooner and felt a sense of exhilaration at the thought of rescuing them from the mighty sea.

There was a sharp retort as a rocket soared into the air

in the direction of the schooner. Morgan thought it must fall short, but a second thrust carried it on course towards the crippled vessel.

The *Charlie Medland* was taken as near to the schooner as possible in the heavy swell and the few men aboard began to scramble down the rope into the well of the lifeboat.

'Let's get going, boys!' Bill Owen shouted into the teeth of the wind. 'We don't want to go down with the schooner, do we?'

The boat seemed to sway and roll and drift dangerously close to the rocky promontory of the Mumbles Head.

'Keep her steady, boys, pull on those damned oars!'

Morgan turned to watch the broken ship sink without trace, the sea rolling over the last of the pointing masts like a giant bird swallowing its prey.

'Keep your mind on your job, Morgan Lloyd, or you'll be overboard, man!'

Morgan was not used to rowing; he tried to match his movements to those of the other men, but he knew he was making very little headway and for sure there was no time for any lessons.

One of the crew from the schooner leaned over the side, his face pallid as he vomited. He slumped downwards on to Morgan's leg and with a curse Morgan attempted to lift him away.

'We're too near the rocks, pull to port!' Bill Owen's voice was the last sound Morgan heard, for suddenly it was as though a great tongue had reached out for him and he was being drawn into a gaping black hole beneath Mumbles Head.

*   *   *

Catherine was just raking out the ashes in the fire-grate when she heard running footsteps approaching along the cobbled yard. The door burst open and William stood gaping in the sudden light.

'There's been a disaster, Catherine — the lifeboat's overturned and one of the crewmen said that Morgan was on board!'

Catherine straightened, telling herself not to give in to the fear which numbed her limbs. She put down the poker and stared at William, shaking her head.

'No, there's some mistake, *bachgen*, Bill Owen wouldn't let a green-stick like Morgan anywhere near the lifeboat.'

'But it's true, Catherine. Some sort of accident happened when the *Charlie Medland* was first launched and the crew were short-handed by two men. Bill had to take a chance on Morgan.'

'I'll get my coat,' Catherine said tonelessly and as she was pulling on her boots, Doffie came down the stairs already dressed.

'I heard what the boy said,' she explained quickly. 'Lend me an overcoat, Catherine, and I'll come with you.'

The fury of the gale had abated a little, but on the heights of Ram's Tor the trees still bowed and moaned overhead as though in mourning. The rain was coming down in spiteful darts that stung the face and burned the eyes.

'Mammy sent me to fetch you just as soon as we knew,' William said, his long legs covering the ground easily. 'Watching through our window, we were, saw the ship break up and the lifeboat struggling to get to her. Then when the Frenchies were picked up, the *Charlie Medland* seemed to rush in against the rocks at The Head and suddenly the boat was empty.'

Catherine gripped his arm. 'How do you know that Morgan was aboard, William?' Her last hope died when her brother-in-law caught her hand in his.

'There are survivors being brought ashore all the time, Catherine. The coxswain was uninjured though he'd drunk a fair amount of sea water, mind. Gave a list of the men aboard when he came to a bit and that's when Mammy sent me up for you.'

Catherine heard the sound of excited voices before she reached the rocky basin of Bracelet Bay. There was the *Charlie Medland* intact, resting on the rocks as neatly as though a giant hand had placed her there. Pieces of the wrecked schooner were being washed ashore and even as Catherine scrambled over the rocks, a cry went up as a survivor was spotted.

A human chain was formed at once, with the men waist-deep in water reaching out for the dark shape that was a man. Catherine hugged her coat around her shivering body and tried to see who it was.

'Willie-Lobster-Pot, pass it on,' a voice called and a woman beside Catherine began to sob in relief and was comforted by a friend.

'There, there, *merchi*, it's your man! He's all right, thank the good Lord, and you with five babbas to feed — 'tis a blessing.'

One by one the men were brought ashore, some unconscious while others were past help. As the hours dragged by Catherine began to feel afraid, but she refused to leave the bay. It seemed to her that while she kept vigil, there was still hope of Morgan being found alive.

Dawn was piercing the sky with rosy fingers and the wind had blown itself out when the search was abandoned. Bill Owen, his face grey with fatigue, touched Catherine's arm.

'Go on home, *merchi* there's no point in waiting by here any longer. He's gone, swept down the coast perhaps — we'd have found him by now if he was alive.'

Catherine looked up at him dully. 'Of course he's still alive, I feel it inside me. I'd know if Morgan was dead.'

The coxswain turned to Gladys Richards for help. 'Take the girl away indoors and give her something to warm her up; she looks that pale and pinched, poor thing.'

'Come on, *cariad*,' Gladys said softly. 'William, take her other arm and help me lift her to her feet.'

'No!' Catherine shook her head stubbornly. 'I'm not coming with you, I have to wait here. Please believe me, Morgan's alive — I know he is!'

'Right then,' Gladys said firmly. 'William, you go and bring blankets, we'll wait here with Catherine all day if need be.' She turned to Doffie, who was staring unhappily at

270

a sea still surging forward in gusts as the wind drove against the shore.

'Why don't you go home?' Gladys suggested. 'There's nothing more you can do by here. We're family, see, and Catherine is our concern.'

'Got no home,' Doffie said shortly. 'I'll stay with Catherine if you don't mind.'

Gladys sighed. 'It will be like a Sunday school picnic down here in the bay — there's soft we'll all look, just watching the water.'

'I'll be all right by myself,' Catherine said loudly. 'Just leave me, will you? I want to be alone.'

'Right you are,' Gladys said. 'When Will comes back with a warm blanket we'll all go back in the house — won't be far if you need us.'

Catherine sighed, closing her eyes as if shutting everyone out. She leaned her head on her hands and tried not to take any notice when someone draped a blanket round her shoulders.

'I'll stay if you like,' said Doffie softly, but Catherine shook her head without replying and after a moment she heard footsteps clambering over the rocks.

There was silence then but for the calling of the birds up above the beach and the lap of the waves against the rocks. Catherine felt alone in the world, locked in with her emotions for she could not — dare not — think.

The hours passed, how many hours she did not know, and it was only when she heard hard, masculine voices that she opened her eyes. The coxswain was ordering the men to right the beached lifeboat; with ropes and pulley and brute strength, the wood grinding against the rock, the *Charlie Medland* was brought on to the sand.

'She'll need some repairs,' Bill Owen was saying and suddenly Catherine lifted her head, hearing another voice. She rose to her feet and began to walk across the bay.

The jutting headlands of the Mumbles stood separated by a stretch of water, but the tide was receding and Catherine managed to cross the centre island without difficulty. Behind her she heard the coxswain calling and was dimly aware of the men, clambering over the rocks and urging her to turn back.

One of the younger crewmen caught up with her and grasped her arm, but she shook him off angrily.

'He's out there, Morgan is out there, I tell you!' She spoke firmly, but he shook his head. Then Bill Owen came panting to her side, his eyes anxiously searching her face.

'She couldn't have heard anything from the shore,' the younger man said gently, but Bill shook his head.

'*Duw*, a woman is a funny thing. Like the sea she has her moods and it pays to listen to her, boyo. Go on, girl, we're with you.'

Catherine was already walking ahead, sure-footed on the wet rocks. She passed the squat middle rock and continued walking out to the furthest point with Bill scrambling behind her.

Beyond the point of Mumbles Head, beneath the jutting rock of the headland lay a cave. The mouth gaped wide, thinning away at an upward slant to a small aperture in the heart of the rock. The sea still lapped at the opening, but Catherine walked through the waves uncaring. In a bed of tiny pebbles too high for the tide to reach lay a still figure — unerringly, Catherine went towards Morgan Lloyd for she knew it was him.

She cradled his head in her lap while Bill felt for his pulse and listened to his heart. But Catherine did not need to be told he was alive.

'Nasty knock on the head, he's had, but he'll survive — a strong boyo, this,' Bill said, his voice subdued as he stared at Catherine wonderingly. 'Faith as small as a grain of mustard seed will move mountains,' he said softly, but Catherine didn't hear him. She was looking into Morgan's clear eyes and her own were filled with tears.

CHAPTER TWENTY-TWO

The small cottage nestling in the folds of Kilvey Hill was ablaze with lights. Smoke curled upwards from the chimney into a pale evening sky and the soft wind coming in over the docks from the open sea shook the leafless trees so that they trembled like skeletal fingers.

Within the cottage Katie was packing clothes into a bag, tears threatening as she placed a shirt neatly on the top of the pile. Mark was actually leaving, starting the journey to France early in the morning, and Katie dreaded the separation for they had not been apart since their wedding.

'Nearly finished?' Mark came behind her and put his arms around her waist, lifting the loose mass of her hair, kissing the back of her neck. She turned into his arms and their lips met urgently.

'Leave the packing,' he whispered softly against her mouth. 'I want to give my wife some loving before I go!'

He took her hand and together they extinguished the lamp. In the darkness he reached for her again, holding her close, his hands warm on her back and his mouth searching.

'*Duw*, there's a woman I've got myself,' he said as he led her up the narrow staircase. 'The most beautiful woman I've ever seen!'

Katie clung to him, holding him so close that he had difficulty opening the buttons of her blouse.

'Let me touch my lovely girl properly,' he said, his fingers gentle against the proudness of her breasts. She sighed softly and kissed his eyelids, his cheeks and lastly his mouth — wanting to drink him in and hold the memory of this moment like a precious gem. She knew it was foolish of her, but it seemed as though he was leaving her for ever and not just going across the waters to search for employment. He sensed her feeling and as he laid her on the bed, he leaned on his elbow trying to read her expression in the moonlight that slanted in through the window.

'We won't be parted for long for as soon as I find a job and a place for us to live, I'll send for you, Katie — you know that.'

She reached up and wound her arms around his neck, drawing him close to her. 'Sure and don't you talk too much, love!' As she felt his lips on hers, passion flared within her; she wanted him so much, wanted to be part of him, united so that they were one flesh.

He was tender, containing his fervour out of love for her and Katie responded to him as she always did, but now her emotions were heightened by the knowledge of their parting. She moaned beneath him, loving him, savouring him until the explosion of joy that began deep within her expanded like ripples in a pond, encompassing her. Yet even in the height of her passion there was pain, for he was going away from her.

Afterwards he cradled her gently in his arms, smoothing the hair from her hot face, his touch tender. She snuggled into the circle of his arms, breathing in the aura of him.

'I'm a lucky woman, sure enough,' she whispered in his ear. 'You're a stud of a man and you love me — what more could I want?'

He twisted a ringlet of her hair in his fingers. 'And you know how to make me feel ten feet tall, don't you Katie Murphy?'

She stretched luxuriously beside him. 'Not Katie Murphy, you're forgetting I'm a respectable married woman now!'

He hugged her to him. 'No, I'm not forgetting anything, *merchi*. I'm trying to remember every little thing about you — the touch of your hands, the scent of your skin, the silky feel of your hair . . . everything.'

So he felt the same as she did about being parted! Katie didn't know why she should be pleased and surprised, for

Mark was a sensitive intelligent man. But his strength of will was impressive and she had not expected him to need her as much as she needed him.

'Go to sleep now, there's a lovely girl,' he said softly. 'You don't want to have shadows under those beautiful eyes of yours, do you?'

But it was a long time before sleep came and even then, Katie dreamed that Mark was being dragged forcibly away from her and woke to find that she was weeping.

* * *

The station was full of people arriving and departing, carrying cases and bags, immersed in their own problems.

Katie stood beside Mark studying the folk around her, giving her mind something to do so that she would not dwell on the moment when he would climb aboard the train and leave her.

And then Margaret Francis arrived in a bustle of activity, bags hanging from her arms and her son dragging behind her.

'I'm sorry I'm late,' she said breathlessly, 'but I had trouble with my little lad.' At her side her son grizzled impatiently, wanting to enter the puffing dragon that spat sparks and cinders.

'Of course I will be going straight home,' Margaret continued. 'I shan't go into Paris at all and in any case I hate towns. But the addresses I gave you . . . they'll be useful, I hope.'

'I'm sure they will and it's very kind of you to bother.' Mark spoke lightly, but his hand searched for Katie's and their fingers met warmly, curling into a handclasp.

'Katie, what are you doing here?' The voice was light and warm and familiar and she turned with a smile.

'I might ask you the same, Rhian.' Katie felt surrounded by people when what she most wanted was to be alone with Mark.

Rhian put down her bag thankfully. 'I'm returning to Yorkshire, I've just been on a visit to see our Billy — and

275

Gina and the children of course. But I can't wait to be back with my husband.' Her smile was brilliant and Katie envied her.

'Mark's off to France to try and find a job,' she explained. 'I'll be out there with him once he's settled.'

'I know how you must be feeling then.' Rhian's voice was gentle and Katie found her eyes misting with tears.

'How is Billy?' she asked quickly. 'Driving a van for Mary, isn't he?' She brushed her hand against her lids impatiently.

'Aye and enjoying it too. He goes into the valleys, selling clothing and pots and pans and such. He's his own man for Mary leaves everything to him, fair play.' Rhian's smile faded. 'The sad part about living away now is that I have to leave my family and friends behind. Little Cerianne cried her eyes out; I can still see her little face all blotchy and her eyes red, but there's soft I am going on like this — I'll have us all in tears in a minute!'

Mark was drawing Katie closer as the doors of the train began to slam. Katie's heart was beating so fast she thought everyone on the platform must hear it.

Rhian leaned forward quickly and kissed Katie's cheek. 'I'll say my goodbyes now and leave you two in peace.'

As Rhian climbed on board the train Margaret took the hint and followed her, admonishing Jonathan to mind where he put his feet. The train seemed to vibrate with a life of its own and then Katie was in Mark's arms, clinging to him desperately.

'Don't worry, love, it won't be for long,' he said gently. 'As soon as I'm fixed up, I'll be back for you, so no weeping now, is it?'

She kissed him fighting back the tears, swallowing the lump in her throat. And then he was gone from her arms and she stood there bereft.

The big wheels of the train began to move, chugging away at the silver rails, gathering momentum. Katie waved her hand frantically, unable to see through the tears that burned her eyes. She watched until the train disappeared round the curve of the hill and then turned back towards her home.

The house was empty and silent without him; even the clock had wound down and was no longer ticking. Katie sat in her chair staring at the dying fire, knowing she should save it while there was still some flame alive in the grate, yet her limbs felt numbed and heavy.

'This is no way to live your life for the next few weeks!' she told herself as she pushed up from the softness of the chair and mended the fire, placing coals carefully on to the embers and blowing puffs of breath through the blackleaded bars until at last the flames were fanned back into life.

'Now come on, girl, make yourself a bite to eat and then it's off out with you — anywhere you like, just out.'

* * *

It was a fine afternoon and even though the air was still cold a weak sun was shining, so that the waters in the bay were crystal clear and the sand appeared fresh-washed and golden. Soon winter would fade into spring, the blossoms would be appearing on the trees and surely by then Mark would be home again?

Katie hugged her coat close around her shoulders as she made her way towards the shops in the *Stryd Fawr*, determined to be cheerful. She passed the big emporium, staring in at the splendid elegant gown on display and wondering if she could call to see Mary. Yet somehow there had been a wedge driven between them and Katie knew it had existed ever since she had rounded on Mary, calling her a fool to go to the arms of another man.

Inside the store, everything was different. The small elegant chairs which had stood beside bales of linen were gone and even the tea-room was altered — had become more functional and less luxurious. Katie looked around for a familiar face and saw none. A tall nattily-dressed man appeared from nowhere and the smile vanished from his face when he saw her plain dress.

'Can I help you?' He appeared to tilt his nose just as if there was an evil smell under it and Katie frowned at him angrily.

'Mary Sutton — is she here? She's a friend of mine,' Katie said sharply, but the man's expression did not change.

'Well in that case, I'm surprised your *friend* didn't inform you that she was selling the emporium! The fact is that Mary Sutton is no longer the owner.'

Katie turned on her heel and made her way back into the street. Her cheeks were hot; she had been made a fool of and she did not like the feeling. Beneath her chagrin though, she felt a sense of fear; everything was changing and she was powerless to do anything about it.

She caught a tram at the bottom on the hill and as she seated herself, wondered what sort of reception she would have from Mary. Perhaps she wouldn't even want to see her? But the idea of talking to Mary and trying to mend the breach was fixed in Katie's head and she would not rest until at least she had tried.

Mrs Greenaway opened the door, looking distinctly agitated. 'Oh, Katie Murphy! I'm sorry — we were expecting the doctor — but come in, I'm sure Mary will want to see you.'

'What's wrong?' Katie hesitated on the step. 'I don't want to be in the way.'

'No, no, come on in, there's a good girl. It's little Stephan, see, he's not very well just now.'

Mary came hurrying down the stairs, her skirts flapping around her ankles, her normally calm face blotched with tears.

'Katie, come in by here and talk to me while I wait for the doctor, Greenie, will you go help Nerys see to Stephan?'

Katie followed Mary into the drawing-room and caught her arm anxiously. 'Mary, is it something serious — you look so worried.'

'I don't know, Katie, I might be making a fuss about nothing but I'll be glad when Paul gets here to take a look at my son.' She sank into a chair, her hands clasped tightly together.

'I had this car accident, some time ago it was,' she began. 'I didn't think Stephan had been hurt at all, it was me that got the bumps. But since then he's had these headaches, you see.

'Bryn Thomas examined him and didn't think there was much wrong — said just give it time — but Stephan woke up this morning real feverish, telling me his head hurt and his eyes were feeling bad. Oh, Katie, I'm so worried, what if he goes blind?' Mary . . . calm unflappable Mary . . . began to cry and impulsively, Katie put her arms round her friend's bowed shoulders.

'It's a punishment for the bad things I've done — I know it is — but why is it my little boy has to suffer?'

'Hush now, that's just silly talk,' Katie said quickly. 'Do you think you're so wicked then? Why Mary, there's people around more wicked than you could ever be and flourishing they are too — you've only got to look at your old enemy Alfred Phillpot to see that. Going to be mayor of Sweyn's Eye, he is!'

Mary squeezed Katie's hand in gratitude and at that moment there was a loud knocking on the door. Mary got to her feet immediately and hurried out into the big hallway.

'Paul, thank goodness you've come!' Mary's voice carried strongly to where Katie stood uncertainly in the drawing-room. She couldn't just leave, she decided as she heard footsteps on the stairs; she would wait and see what the doctor had to say.

It was probably just a feverish cold, Katie told herself; her own brothers had been sick more than once. One minute children were very bad and then they would recover as though nothing was wrong — that was the way with them.

It seemed an age before anything happened and Katie sat in the chair staring around her at the luxurious carpets and hangings, wondering what it must be like to live in a house of this sort. But she knew she wouldn't change her own little cottage for anything.

'Can I get you some tea or something, Katie?' Mrs Greenaway looked into the room, her lined face anxious.

Katie shook her head. 'No, thank you. Have you heard anything yet, from the doctor I mean? He seems to have been up there an awfully long time.'

Mrs Greenaway shook her head. 'No, not a peep out of either of them — I can't help feeling it must be bad.' She bit her lip and stared at Katie anxiously. 'The boy's father should be here now — that's what I think — but I haven't got the courage to suggest it to Mary.'

The door on the landing at the top of the stairs opened and Paul came down alone. Mrs Greenaway moved towards him.

'How is he, doctor? Is it something bad?' She stood directly in front of him so that he was obliged to reply and he rested his hand on her shoulder.

'It's not good, Mrs Greenaway. I think he should go into the infirmary at once. Now, please,' he added as the older woman gave a little cry of distress. 'Please don't make a fuss — you must do all you can to support Mary.'

'I know, doctor, but I love that little boy as if I'd given birth to him myself,' Mrs Greenaway said in a low voice. 'Oh, God be good to him and let him be all right!'

'Come on, Greenie,' Katie said quickly. 'Let us make a nice hot strong cup of tea for everyone.' She guided the woman into the kitchen and looked around her helplessly. 'Come on, you'll have to tell me where everything is,' she said and was rewarded to see Mrs Greenaway dry her eyes on the corner of her apron.

Katie took a deep breath. She prayed to all the saints that Stephan would be all right, yet it was a good feeling to be able to help Mary.

There was little enough she could do except be on hand in case she was needed — and perhaps this was the right moment to be at Mary's side, for if ever she needed a friend it was now. Katie sighed; hopefully the misunderstandings of the past were over for good.

*   *   *

Later, when she returned home, Katie sat at the scrubbed

table with the oil-lamp at her side and dipped her pen into the pot of ink, trying to think of something to say to Mark without revealing her loneliness. At last, she wrote about Mary and her son and only on the last line of the letter did she tell Mark she missed him.

It was strange going to bed alone; she had become so used to having Mark beside her that she had taken his presence for granted. How soon she had slipped into the complacency of being married to Mark! Well, this was a sharp lesson to her to value what she had and to savour every moment spent with her husband.

She slept at last and dreamed that he was on a ship with sails billowing in the wind, ploughing through heavy seas, his arms held out towards her. And when she woke there were tears on her cheeks.

* * *

Paris was beautiful, the streets crooked and full of surprises, the building old and dignified. But Mark liked the river best, especially now early in the morning when he was making his way to the car factory where he felt almost certain he would find employment.

He had thought of Katie every minute of the four days he had been here in France and the picture of her bright eyes and red-gold hair was imprisoned behind his lids for him to envisage whenever he chose.

The journey from English shores had been enlivened by the presence of Margaret Francis and her son; even crossing the Channel, Mark had not been particularly perturbed for home seemed only the blinking of an eye away.

But in his small lodging-house in one of the back streets of Paris, he was very much alone. He needed to find an apartment for himself and Katie, but the first priority was a job.

The automobile factory smelled of petrol and oil and Mark, staring into the long high building, wondered if he could bear to work in such conditions.

The tinplate had been hard graft, working before the furnace for two hours at a stand with little protection for hands and face, but it was all he knew. He wondered how he could adapt to the handling of separate parts which seemed to have nothing to do with the finished product that was the car.

The foreman came out of the building, wiping his hands on a piece of rag. He spoke to Mark in rapid French, his wide face and good-natured smile giving Mark a sense of being welcome.

'Sorry, boyo, I don't know any of your lingo,' Mark said apologetically. This was a problem he had not even thought about; somehow he had assumed that everyone would be able to speak English, which was very foolish of him for weren't there pockets of folk back home who couldn't speak any other language than Welsh?

'I'm looking for a job,' he said, pointing into the building, 'working on the cars — anything going?'

The man shook his head. 'Not much jobs here, Englishman, not much jobs anywhere at all.'

Mark stared past the man, cursing his inability to communicate properly which put him at a disadvantage to start with. He made the motions of sweeping the floor. 'I'll do anything, mind, and I'm good and strong.' His voice faltered into silence, for the man was shaking his head.

'No jobs is here for French men — times very bad, go home, no good to be here now.'

Mark turned away knowing he was wasting his time and retraced his steps. His hands were thrust deep into his pockets, for he was cold. Another misconception he had harboured was that in France the weather would be warm; Margaret Francis had talked about missing the French sunshine. But Paris was not much different in temperature from Wales, at least not in the winter time.

He paused by the river staring down into the water; it was pretty, mind, but not like the bay at home which swept round the curve of the land in a five-mile stretch of golden sand. He was homesick already and his instinct was to pack up his few possessions and get back to Sweyn's Eye as soon as possible. He sighed, telling himself he must not accept defeat so easily.

The building where he had found himself a room was tall and austere, with old wooden doors full of cracks and paintwork which peeled from the walls. He had to climb up four flights of stairs and when he reached the top he was feeling far from well. He realised that he had eaten nothing that morning — nor the previous night, come to that. He could not make his landlady understand what he meant and when he asked about food, she just held out her hand waiting for money.

He sat on the creaking bed and stared through the window at the long street below. There were more people on bicycles than he had ever seen in the whole of his life. His mouth was dry and he longed for a hot sweet cup of tea, but it was coffee folk drank in France — and strong black coffee at that. He wondered if he should go back down the stairs and find somewhere he could have a meal . . . yet he was tired, so very tired. He lay back on the lumpy bed and closed his eyes and in a moment, he was asleep.

When he awoke, he thought for a moment that he was back home but then as he looked around him at the bare room with very little furniture and not even a rag mat on the floor, his spirits sank. He felt hot and his eyes didn't seem to focus very well; when he tried to sit up, it was as if the world was spinning away around him and it seemed easier simply to close his eyes and sink back once more.

It was a loud knocking on the door which brought him out of the mists of sleep. 'Come in!' He thought he called the words, but they came out like a croak.

'You sick?' The girl was young, about nineteen perhaps, and even through the mists that fogged his mind Mark registered the fact that she was beautiful. He tried to lift his head, but the effort was too much and he lay back again wearily.

'I go bring the doctor,' she said but Mark held out his hand to stop her; he couldn't afford a doctor — he had little enough money as it was. All he wanted was to get to the coast and catch the next boat home.

'Then I look after you.' The girl seemed to float around the room and Mark felt his face being bathed with cold water. She disappeared and then returned with some food in a bowl; he sipped the thin stew just to please her for he had no appetite.

She gave him a drink which smelled of herbs and then plumped up his hard pillow and tucked the bedclothes around him. 'You sleep now, I come back later.'

He lost count of the number of days that he lay sick in his bare, impersonal room, looking forward only to the ministrations of the girl who was a stranger to him but who undoubtedly kept him alive . . .

* * *

At last the fog which had clouded his brain seemed to clear. He felt weak and unutterably weary, but he was in possession of his mind once more. He smiled at the young French girl as she came into the room with a tray on her arm and her answering smile was one of relief.

'You come well again, the fever he is gone.' She touched his forehead with the back of her hand, nodding in satisfaction. 'All we need now is to get you strong.'

'What is your name?' he asked and she rubbed her hands along her apron as though to smooth out non-existent creases.

'I call Thérèse.' She glanced over her shoulder nervously. 'My mamma own this building; she very cross you sick, but I say I take care of you and she agree.'

'Well, Thérèse, I don't know how I'm going to repay you, *merchi*, but I owe you my life, I reckon.'

She laughed, but rich colour suffused her face and she looked down at her hands shyly.

'No, you owe nothing,' she said as she glanced up at him mischievously, 'except a week's rent to Mamma!'

The hours he spent convalescing were the longest of

Mark's life, but once he was stronger he asked Thérèse to bring him writing paper. She watched him and her eyes were suddenly shadowed.

'Who do you send letter to — is it your mamma?' she asked and her feelings were transparently clear. Mark held out his hand and as her fingers curled in his he smiled.

'I'm writing to my wife,' he said simply. 'Her name is Katie; she's beautiful and good and I love her.'

She leaned forward and the scent of her was like roses on a summer's morning. 'Give a kiss for me properly — just this once, please, Mark.'

He put his hands on her shoulders meaning to push her gently away, but then their mouths met and she was lovely and sweet and innocent and she had nursed him back to health.

'Oh, Mark,' there were tears in her eyes, 'your wife is so very lucky, her I envy much!'

'Go now, Thérèse,' he urged softly. 'I don't want to hurt you.' He smiled down at the paper wondering what to say to Katie, his beloved wife; she would be frantic with worry, not knowing what had happened to him. He picked up the pen and began to write.

*　　*　　*

Katie had made up her mind very quickly and had packed a small bag without even stopping to consider what clothes she would need. Mark had been sick, he had been nursed by a French girl and it seemed that Thérèse had saved his life. Katie had died a thousand deaths until the letter had come, worrying her heart out over her husband and not knowing where he was. Well, she would not rest until she could bring him home, for there was the danger that she might lose him to this foreign girl who had cared for him so well. The fare would take the rest of their meagre savings, but that meant nothing compared with the fact that Mark had been sick and Katie as his wife should be at his side.

As she locked her door and made her way down the path, she stared around her at the softly folding hills. She could smell the stink of the copper works and see the billowing green smoke from the multitude of stacks that jutted upwards invading the skies. She felt as though she was saying goodbye to her home for ever, travelling to far distant lands. But France was only just across the English Channel — hadn't Mark assured her that the journey would not take very long?

She began to walk towards the station with quick determined steps. Mark was her man, her husband and they would never be parted again — she would see to that.

CHAPTER TWENTY-THREE

The moon was a large silver orb in a soft sky and the land of Ram's Tor lay in soft shadow and highlighted curves, falling away to a peaceful sea. In the bed Morgan stirred and opened his eyes and Catherine, at his side, drew a ragged breath. He held out his hand and tentatively she clasped her fingers around his.

Catherine did not speak. She was filled with thankfulness as tears, hot and foolish, brimmed in her eyes. He smiled and touched her cheek and slowly, she leaned towards him.

His mouth was strong, his hands caressing her spine seemed on fire. How long she remained locked in his embrace she did not know, for time had no meaning any more. And now she knew without doubt that she loved Morgan Lloyd.

She found herself beside him on the bed, clinging to him with passion. Her being was alight as her hands touched his cheeks, his shoulders and the silk of his thighs. She heard herself moan softly and wondered at the sensations which were unleashed as Morgan continued to caress her. She was naked — though she scarcely remembered removing her clothes — and alive with feelings, her nerve-ends tinglingly aware of the man who held her close.

She wanted him to possess her now, for the first time, she knew what desire was. It was the sweetness of wine, the gold of the sun and it had all the beauty of a rose in full bloom.

'Morgan!' She spoke his name as though she was in torment and so she was. Hungry for him, she pressed closer, straining to become one with him, knowing only the heady sensations of love unblemished and pure.

It was beautiful: the rhythm of the sea as it rolled upon the shore, the piercing of the clouds by the sun, the fact of being one flesh with the man she loved. Colours flashed against her closed lids and she cried out but softly, her mouth against his shoulder.

When she looked at him at last, he lay silvered by moonlight, beautiful as a marble sculpture — but his eyes were alive and drinking her in and she knew he found her beautiful too.

He drew her beneath the sheets and covered her carefully, brushing back strands of hair from her face. Still they did not speak; there was no need of words as they clung together, her head nestling against his shoulder.

Catherine had not known that loving could be so sweet. She lay in her bed staring up at the dark beams with Morgan beside her and closed her eyes with the pain of her joy.

She had brought him home, saved from the dark face of Mumbles Head, and he had slept for more than a day and a night while she sat watching over him, for she would never forget that she had almost lost him to the sea.

Then he had woken and looked at her and taken her into his arms and now she was a whole woman. For the first time in her life she knew the joys of passion and love and, drowsily content, she drifted into sleep.

The rosy light of dawn was warming the room when she awoke. For the first time, Catherine was frightened; she had given herself outside the marriage bed and now there was no turning back.

Turning to Morgan, she saw that he was silently watching her. She caressed his cheek, sprinkled now with hard, strong bristles needing the attention of a razor.

'My lovely!' She smiled up at him, drinking in his closeness, tingling with happiness. 'My lovely boy!'

He took her hand and kissed it and his mouth was warm. 'Don't look at me like that, Catherine — or I swear I'll never let you out of this room.' He turned to her holding her close as her head fell naturally into the hollow of his shoulder.

'Do you love me, Morgan? Tell me the truth now.' She was afraid to look into his face, but he leaned up on one elbow and caught her chin gently between his fingers.

'Don't ask silly questions. Would I be lying here with you if I didn't want you?'

She was silent for wanting was a different thing from love, but she was afraid to pursue the matter. She kissed his mouth, closing her eyes and praying he would learn to love her as she loved him.

'There's soft I am, staying by here with you all this while.' She smiled at him as she moved away. 'Work there is on the farm — I don't know how they've managed without me these past days but Gladys, young William and Doffie have worked like slaves.'

'You're not going to leave me.' Morgan smiled at her, his eyes alight with mischief. 'I'm not strong enough yet to be alone.'

'Nonsense — like a bull you are, Morgan Lloyd!' She felt shy standing before him without her clothing and turned her back as she washed, her hair hanging over her shoulders.

'So lovely, so very lovely,' Morgan said softly. 'Please come back to me.'

Catherine pulled her skirt up to her waist and buttoned it quickly. 'We'll be together tonight and every night, remember? Now be good and rest, for tomorrow I'll expect you to pull your weight on the farm, mind.'

'What a little monster you are, Catherine Preece,' Morgan said half-seriously, 'one minute all soft and pretty and sweet and then coming the tyrant farm-owner the next. There's no fathoming you.'

Gladys had laid the table for breakfast and was stirring a pot of porridge over the fire. She looked up, her eyes shadowed but without censure. Doffie moved her chair a little to allow Catherine room to sit and William leaned forward — his young face honest and open, his eyes eager.

'Is Morgan coming downstairs soon, Catherine?' He didn't wait for a reply. '*Duw*, fancy him being stuck in a cave under the Mumbles Head all those hours 'til the tide went out.'

Catherine shuddered and took the bowl Gladys handed her, seating herself at the table with arms resting on the snowy cloth.

'Be quiet, *bachgen*,' Gladys said softly. 'Let Catherine have her food in peace, she's eaten little enough these past days.'

'But Mam, I want to ask why it was that Morgan didn't drown. When the tide came in, didn't the cave fill up with sea water?'

'It's all right,' Catherine smiled at the boy. 'You see, William, the cave sloped upwards. Towards the back, the land was high. Soaked he was, mind, but there was air enough for Morgan to breathe.'

Doffie pushed her bowl away. '*Duw*! It's like the story of Lazarus rising from the dead, isn't it?'

Gladys got to her feet and clattered the empty bowls together into a pile. 'There's soft you are, Doffie, talking like that. Morgan Lloyd was saved because the cave was big enough to hold him, so don't go making something magic out of it now.' She moved to the sink. 'You'll be down at Maggie Dick's or the Mexico Fountain getting drunk on the story, if I know anything.'

'Don't be spiteful now, Gladys Richards!' Doffie spoke up angrily. 'And me not leaving the farm all this time, but working like a slave by here to help you all.'

Gladys sighed heavily. 'I know and I'm an old bitch, it's just that my boy David . . . oh, I don't know!' She began to cry and Catherine went to her side.

'Don't, please Gladys, none of us are going to forget David and what a brave man he was right to the end of his life. Respect I have for him, mind, whatever you might think of me now.'

'Oh, lovey, I'm sorry — not blaming you for nothing, don't think that.' Gladys wiped her eyes with her apron. 'I'm an old fool to be so miserable. Come on, no long faces round here, now.'

It took Catherine only a few hours to find that the storm had ripped up the land, tossing the newly planted crop to the four winds. They would have to replant, using Bearded

April which would germinate as late as the middle of April. It would be an added cost and one she would find difficult to meet. She sighed heavily knowing that Morgan's safety was what mattered most to her now.

It was Morgan who discovered the next day that the sow lying in her pile of clean straw was biting at the wire encircling a limb which had withered and died.

'We'll have to get Gethin to slaughter the animal.' Catherine's voice was edged with impatience, for if she had not been neglecting her duties the sow would have been saved.

Gethin was used to the job of slaughtering animals and he arrived with an armful or buckets and a long evil-looking knife. Catherine went with him to the sty, keeping the boar at a distance with a pitchfork while Gethin drew the reluctant sow out into the yard.

Catherine wanted to run and hide. She had no stomach for the killing and she felt an affection for the animal who had provided two good litters a year and never eaten her offspring as some sows did.

Forced on to her back, the sow began to squeal in fear and then when Gethin's knife plunged and swiftly cut her throat the animal's cries were almost human for what seemed to Catherine the interminable moment it took for her to die. Quickly then he sliced the plump belly and the blood bubbled and steamed. Gethin worked fast, for he was as good a butcher as any man and could cleave the meat from a shoulder faster than most.

'Salt her down and hang her and there'll be meat aplenty for months to come,' he said in his taciturn way. 'Only the leg gone to waste and it's a crying shame that; I usually has the legs.'

'Take it all,' Catherine said quickly. 'It will be time for lambing soon and I'd prefer lamb to pork any day.' She cleaned the yard and spread fresh straw, but the stench of blood seemed to linger in her nostrils like a reproach.

*   *   *

The blossoms came to the trees and Catherine began to wonder if Morgan would ever speak of marriage. They had been alone on the farm for some weeks, for Gladys and William had gone home to Oystermouth and Doffie had left in search of a more stimulating way of life. But it was time now for lambing and that was more important than any personal consideration. And she would need help . . .

When Catherine walked down into Oystermouth and saw the ketches lying against the sand, bathed in the clear sunlight, she felt as though she had come awake.

Gladys's welcome was warm. 'Come and sit down, *merchi*, I must say you're looking well — putting on weight, are you?'

Catherine smiled. 'It's you I want to talk about,' she said, leaning forward in her chair. 'I want you and William to come and help with the lambing; I can't manage without you.'

Gladys flushed with pleasure. '*Duw*, and there was me thinking you didn't want us!' She pulled the already strained straps of her wrapover apron more tightly around her plump waist.

'Don't want you! Gladys, for shame! You and William are my family — more than even my own dad or my sisters, come to that.'

Gladys took a dark brown bottle from the bottom shelf of the pantry. 'Have some ginger ale — made it myself, I did, so I know it's good!'

'Glady's you don't usually bring out the ale in the daytime and you seem agitated — is there something you're keeping from me?'

Gladys flapped her hands. 'Oh, it's nothing much except that no-good flossie is telling folks around the village about you and Morgan being alone together day and night. You only got to give folks a crumb and they'll make a loaf of bread out of it.'

Catherine sighed. 'Well, does it matter? Doffie's not exactly a pillar of the chapel or anything, is she?' But for all her calm words, she could not help feeling a dart of apprehension and not a little disappointment, because she had believed Doffie was her friend.

Gladys poured the fizzing drink into a glass and handed it to Catherine. 'You're right, she's not important. Of course Will and me will come up and help with the lambing — stay for a day or two, shall we? That will hush the gossip — for a while anyway.'

'Is it as bad as that, then?' Catherine asked miserably and Gladys shook her head so hard that her fat jowls quivered.

'No, don't be so soft. I'll have something to say to anyone who talks about you in my hearing!'

Catherine put down her glass, suddenly feeling a little faint. 'I'd better get back then. Morgan's on his own up there and there's such a lot to do.' She rose to her feet, drawing her knitted cardigan around her shoulders. 'See you later then, Gladys — come up tonight, will you?'

'Aye, we'll be there. Don't you go worrying now, about what I've said — let folks talk, for when they talk about you they're talking to your backside.'

Catherine did not return to Ram's Tor at once. She walked to the sea edge and sat on the warm sand, looking at the waves so small and gentle now that it was difficult to imagine they could ever be swollen and angry. Though not surprised, it hurt her to think that she was the subject of gossip being spread by Doffie.

'Yoo, hoo! Hello, Catherine, it's me!' The voice was filled with laughter and wine and Catherine wrinkled up her nose as Doffie sank on to the sand beside her. Behind her trailed a man with a bottle in his hand, his hat falling over one eye and his shirt collar open.

'What on earth are you doing here, Doffie? I thought you'd be back in town by now.' Catherine rose to her feet, feeling embarrassed and uncomfortable. The man eyed her curiously, taking out a packet of Woodbines and holding it towards her; she shook her head.

'No, thank you,' she said as she stepped away. 'I'd better be going now.' She felt her feet sinking into the soft sand and Doffie turned to look at her with arched eyebrows.

'Oh, come on, have a little drink with Doffie then — don't be so stuck up, Catherine Preece!'

'You've had too much already if you ask me,' Catherine said, beginning to feel angry. 'Fancy you talking behind my back, for shame on you!'

Doffie tried to get up and sank back into the sand, her smile vanished. 'Oh dear — offended you, have I? Only telling the truth, mind. There you are, warming Morgan Lloyd's bed — and I don't blame you, but perhaps you should have held out for a ring, lovey!'

Catherine turned away, the hot colour coming into her cheeks. She knew there was nothing she could say — how did you explain love to a girl like Doffie?

'I'm sorry. I didn't mean it.' Doffie scrambled to her knees. 'You're a nice girl and you deserve a little bit of happiness after all you've been through. Come up to the farm and see you some time, shall I?'

Catherine backed away, aware that the man was sneering at her and looking her over as though undressing her She turned and ran back to the road, her breathing rapid.

Thoughtfully, she walked up the steep hill. Was Morgan taking advantage of her love for him? But then, what man would turn down what was readily offered? And adding to her confusion was the knowledge that the people in her own village, indeed the congregation at the chapel might all be whispering about Catherine Preece.

She was relieved to see the squat whitewashed farmhouse come into view. It was a haven where she could be alone and sort out her thoughts before Gladys and William came up later in the evening.

Unable to sit still, she began to prepare the food for the hens. Strangely the mixture of three parts of middlings to one of bran seemed sickly, the smell offensive though she had never noticed this before. When it was ready, she put it on the pantry floor to stand until morning. At nights she gave the hens green food and oyster shells — as much as they wanted — and the system seemed to work very well.

She took out her record of the winter laying from November until February, noting that the total cost in food had been eighteen shillings and ten pennies and the total number of eggs produced was in the region of three hundred which was very good. She snapped shut the book; at least she was doing something right!

Morgan looked tired when he entered the farmhouse; he sank into a chair and rested his hands on his knees.

'Put on the kettle for some hot water, Catherine,' he said, leaning back and closing his eyes, 'I think every bone in my body is aching.'

She obeyed without answering, but he did not even notice. He shrugged off his shirt and bent over the enamel bowl — his broad back muscular, his skin like brown silk. It occurred to her quite suddenly that she had become used to him: the strength of his legs, the strong line of his backbone, the slimness of his belly. His body was as familiar to her as her own. She longed to kiss his shoulder, to feel his strength . . . and yet the thought that he might simply be using her stuck in her craw.

They ate their meal in silence and after a time, Morgan looked up at her with his elbows on the table, his fork dangling from his finger.

'Come on, out with it! What have I done wrong?' His eyes were warm and smiling, sending her signals and she looked away, flushing.

'You don't seem to take anything seriously,' she said quickly. 'We've lost the sow, the land has to be replanted, yet you seem to have only one thing on your mind and that's getting me into bed.'

'For God's sake, we're not going to have a row, are we?' he said. 'I'm too tired to argue with you right now.'

'I'm sorry,' and she was. She saw the weariness in his face and the slump of his shoulders and knew now was not the time to talk to him. So she changed the subject deliberately.

'I think we'll plant Bearded April in the top field.' She smiled at Morgan cheerfully. 'We'll need a lot of seed, for spring wheat must be sown thicker than autumn wheat.'

Morgan was interested at once. 'How do you know what

quality seed to buy?' he asked, leaning forward in his chair.

'That's not too difficult. There was a testing of seeds order that came out in 1918, saying that farmers selling seed must either state that it's above a certain standard of germination or give the actual percentage of germinating seed.'

'That all sounds very complicated,' Morgan commented and Catherine heard with a sense of pleasure the note of respect in his voice.

'Not really, the germinating standards are ninety per cent for wheat and barley and eighty per cent for rye.' She smiled. 'The secret is to avoid the weed like sheep's sorrel and dock.'

'Well,' he said as he leaned back, 'I knew you were a good farmer but I didn't realise you were so knowledgeable.' He stretched out a hand to her cheek and immediately she felt on edge with him again. As she rose to her feet and moved away from him, she heard him sigh.

'The lambing's gone well.' Her voice was falsely bright. 'I'll look up the far fields tomorrow for strays, but I think we can say we've had a good crop of lambs.'

'Awe, to hell with it!' Morgan drew on his coat and made for the door, brushing past as though he did not even see her. His face was dark, his brows drawn together and his eyes hidden from her.

She hurried to the door and stared after his tall figure as he moved away over the patchwork patterns of the land, her eyes hot and dry with unshed tears. What was the matter with her, that she was brushing him aside as though her being did not ache for his touch?

She longed to call after him, but knew it was pointless for he simply wouldn't listen. He was nearing the road cut from the mountain and Catherine watched until his figure faded away into the warm dusk of the evening.

Returning to the kitchen, she sat staring into the fire, shivering in spite of the balmy spring air. She had made herself look absurd to the people of the village and she was the subject of their gossip, but did that matter — did anything matter compared with her feelings for Morgan?

Catherine began to clear away the dishes, putting them into the sink and then pouring boiling water over them. She worked without thinking, so tired and confused that she didn't know how to react any more.

* * *

The evening air was soft and the salt sea smells washed inshore to where Morgan walked slowly, his head bent, lost in thought. How could he ever understand the workings of a woman's mind? He kicked moodily at a pebble which had been smoothed and rounded by many rains, staring down at it as though the answer to his thoughts could be found in its cold face. Catherine was acting strangely, as though his touch suddenly repelled her. And her giving had been so sweet. Was it marriage she wanted?

He had scarcely given marriage a thought and did not even know if that was what he wanted himself. Blast women! Why did they have to complicate matters . . .

Then he heard footsteps and looked up with a welcoming smile as he saw the coxswain of the *Charlie Medland* toiling up the slope of the hill.

'*Duw*, Morgan boy, I'm getting old I think, for this hill grows more awkward and spiteful every day!' His hand-shake was warm. 'Good to see you fit as a fiddle again — thought we'd lost you, boyo!'

'Beginner's luck,' Morgan said with a heartiness that he hoped was convincing. 'Though when I woke up once or twice in the darkness of the cave with the water lapping my feet, I thought my time had come, I must admit.'

'Well, you've had your baptism now, boyo,' Bill said, smiling. 'How's about joining us for practice tomorrow evening after work?'

'Aye, I'll be glad to.' Morgan watched the older man walk away with a sense of pride. For a newcomer to the village, a man brought up in the coal-mining valleys, he was not fitting in too badly!

He retraced his steps and on the roadway through the

rocks he saw the dumpy figure of Gladys Richards, her son William at her side. The lad was tall now and on the verge of manhood.

'*Duw*, you do meet some funny people on the road to Ram's Tor!' Morgan caught up with the pair easily and fell into step with Gladys, who was hobbling a little.

'Oh, come on, boyo — give me your arm to hold on to.' Gladys smiled a welcome. 'My knees are that bad today, it's like toothache.'

'How would you know, Mam?' William said with a spurt of amusement. 'You haven't got a single tooth in your head!'

Gladys slapped out at him playfully. 'Less of your cheek now, *bachgen*, or I'll box your ears for you!' She paused to draw breath and stared at Morgan, her eyes narrowed as though trying to see him in the uncertain twilight.

'Well, lambing's nearly finished now, boyo — good little lambs you've got there too, have fine wool from them when they're older. Catherine asked us to come up and stay a couple of nights,' she said, then paused uncertainly. 'That's all right by you, isn't it?'

'*Duw*, you don't have to ask that, Gladys. You belong at Ram's Tor more than I do! Anyway, I think Catherine will welcome you because I can't seem to do right at all.' Morgan said.

Gladys waved her hand in dismissal. 'Don't you go worrying now, boyo, for women have strange fancies at such times.' She squeezed his arm. 'Perhaps you should arrange the wedding very quick though?'

'I don't know if we're ready for that,' he said shortly. 'It seems I've suddenly become the most eligible bachelor in the district.'

'*Duw*, less of them long words, Morgan.' Gladys laughed out loud and paused again, fanning her face with her hat. 'I wish this road wasn't so long and so steep — it feels as though Ram's Tor is at the end of the world.'

And in a way it was. Morgan imagined himself up on the rocks standing staring out to sea; on one side of him was the Mumbles Head jutting out into the ocean and on the other the ruggedly sculptured rocks of the Welsh coastline.

Catherine scarcely looked at him as he came in with the others. The kitchen was lit by the soft glow of the oil-lamp, a cheerful fire burned in the grate and the kettle as always was singing on the hob. The brass fender gleamed bright without its usual coating of dust and it was clear that Catherine had been busy cleaning the house.

'There's lovely to see you!' And as she smiled at Gladys and held out a chair, Morgan had the distinct impression that there was relief as well as a welcome in Catherine's voice.

'William, go and fetch some sticks for the morning,' Gladys said and sank into the seat gratefully with her legs planted firmly apart her skirt rucking up around her plump knees.

William sighed. 'That means there's something I'm not supposed to hear!' His eyes rolled heavenward, but he walked good naturedly to the door. 'Don't take too long then; I'm gasping for a drink of tea or something — it's thirsty work walking up that hill.'

When the door had shut behind him, Gladys stared at her hands and sighed softly. 'I know I'm going to sound like an interfering old woman, but I do think you two silly fools should get together and talk this thing out.'

Catherine drew in a sharp breath. 'You're right, Gladys. This *has* nothing to do with you and I'd thank you not to say any more!'

'Morgan hasn't said anything, there's soft you are, Catherine. He's not the sort of man to go babbling about his affairs — give him credit for some sense. No. it's my own eyes are telling me what's going on and I think you two should get together; there's not only yourselves to think about now, mind.'

'Well, I'll leave you two to sort out everything to your own satisfaction,' Morgan said calmly. 'When you think you have decided my future, perhaps you will be good enough to tell me.'

He let himself out into the softness of the night, aware of the heavy sarcasm in his voice. He could hear the hens fluttering their feathers restlessly and in the sty the boar grumbled and grunted as though longing for freedom. Morgan's eyes felt hot and dry with weariness; he had worked hard on Ram's Tor and with very little to show for it. He put his head back and stared up at the stars. 'To hell with women!' he said out loud and began to walk towards town.

* * *

It would have taken him an hour at least to walk into Sweyn's Eye, but when he was striding through the curving road of Oystermouth village an open-topped charabanc pulled up beside him. A figure leaned out, hat askew, and a hand grasped his arm.

'Hey, Morgan, it's me, Doffie! Want to come for a ride with us?' She smiled down at him, smelling of whisky and Woodbines.

'Aye, all right.' He swung himself up on to the seat and Doffie giggled, nestling up against him.

'I'd like to keep you for myself but I'm with Len, see. Judy over there now, she's by herself — her chap got sick and we had to drop him off. Here, have a drink, Morgan, and take that black cloud of gloom off your face, there's a good boy.'

The whisky was raw and cheap and clung to the back of his throat; it felt like fire as it assaulted his gullet. He handed the bottle back just as the girl Judy took Doffie's place at his side and slipped her arm into his. She was older than he, a woman of perhaps twenty-eight or more. Her hair was upswept, her eyes bright and full of merriment. Morgan could not place her; she hardly appeared to be the type to be bought for a few shillings.

Yet she was not backward in leaning against him so that the softness of her breast touched his arm. Feeling desire flare within him as raw as the whisky, he put his arm around her shoulders and smiled into her eyes.

'Hello, Judy.' Her teeth were white gleaming in the light shed from the street-lamps. 'Where are we going?' he asked and she shrugged her shoulders.

'Don't ask me, I'm just along for the ride!' She glanced provocatively at him from beneath her lashes and Morgan felt himself grow warm. It was good to be admired, not to be cast out like a leper. The thought urged him to draw her closer and kiss the softness of her mouth. Judy giggled and, taking his hand, pressed it to her bodice.

'*Duw*, you're a real man.' She edged even closer, the warmth of her thigh touching his. 'A different cut of man to the usual.'

'Usual?' he said lightly and Judy put her hand on his leg running her fingers over his trouser buttons.

'God, what if we get off by here?' she suggested, glancing around her. 'Plenty of shop doorways now that we're in the town — can't wait I'm that eager to have you!'

He caught her face between his fingers. 'And what is it going to cost me, Judy?'

She pouted at him. 'For you, I'll do it for nothing, boyo, can't you feel how desperately I want you?' When she opened her bodice, her nipples stood proud beneath his fingers. Suddenly he thought of Catherine, of her cotton nightgown that buttoned up to her throat. Of the sweet bashfulness she had shown when first they had made love. And how even now, she would turn her back to dress.

'I think I'll pass this time, Judy,' Morgan said and couldn't help smiling at the look on her face. 'I'm right off cheap whisky and women.'

He tapped the driver on the shoulder. 'I'm getting off here,' he said and then as the man hesitated, he leaned forward menacingly. 'Right here!'

The charabanc jerked to a halt and as he jumped off Judy leaned out, staring at him with her bodice still awry. 'You're a gelding, do you know what that is?' She paused, her eyes narrowed with venom. 'It's a man with no balls, see?'

Morgan laughed. 'I'll take your word for it, Judy. I expect you've seen enough of those to last you a lifetime.' He leaned over the edge of the vehicle and pinched her cheek. 'Get on with you then and see what else you can find — there should be plenty of trade down in Sweyn's Eye.'

'Don't mind him,' Doffie called as the charabanc began to move. 'All right he is, living tally with that Catherine Preece! Gets enough of it, see, Judy, don't want no spare.' She laughed uproariously. 'But give him time, they all does a bit of straying when the newness wears off. Show me an old married man and I'll show you a ram!'

Morgan stood in the silent empty street and stared round him. He was a damned fool ever to have come into town and now he would have a long walk back home again. He moved past the Bay View Hotel and along the Mumbles Road, his hands thrust into his pockets. He reckoned he'd saved himself some bother with that Judy; she would have taken all he had in his pockets, given half a chance.

He smiled to himself in the darkness. Catherine had certainly been acting oddly, but now he thought he had a glimmering of the reason why. If Doffie was talking about him 'living tally', as she called it, then what must the villagers be saying?

The sea washed gently inwards and the ketches lay like fallen beasts, shadowed against the sand. He lifted his head and stared across to the soft hills of Devon. One thing was for sure: he would not be pushed into marriage by anyone. And yet the memory of Catherine's sweet softness brought desire pounding through his being and cursing, he kicked out at a pebble and sent showers of glimmering sand flying through the night.

CHAPTER TWENTY-FOUR

The noisy clatter of the train wheels against the track was giving Rhian a headache. Never had the journey from Sweyn's Eye to Yorkshire seemed so tedious, so wearying and she was impatient to see her husband again. It had been her duty to remain in her home town until Carrie's death — so terrible in itself — had cut her ties with Sweyn's Eye, but their separation had been much longer than she had anticipated. His letters, at first frequent, had become random and almost casual and Rhian had grown afraid.

She had visited her husband of course, but each time she had arrived at the new house — appropriately named Mansel Heights — she had felt more and more of a stranger. And Mansel Jack had seemed to draw further away from her.

It troubled Rhian too that Mansel Heights was uncomfortably close to the home of Charlotte Bradley. Once betrothed to Mansel Jack, as far as Rhian could see Charlotte still loved him — and who could blame her for that?

At last the train drew gasping to a halt at the station and eagerly, Rhian looked round for the tall familiar figure of her husband. She climbed down on to the platform and put down her heavy bag, pushing back a curl of hair which fell across her forehead.

"Scuse me, are you Mrs Mansel Jack?' The man who spoke had a cap between his fingers which he twisted nervously and Rhian smiled at once, putting him at ease.

'Yes, I am, have you come to fetch me?' She concealed her disappointment well as the young man ducked his head in a gesture of assent and led the way out of the station on to the road where a horse and trap waited.

'Let me help you up, missus.' The young man was courteous, his thin face revealing his eagerness to please. 'There's your bag, I'll put it at your feet there.'

The clip-clop of the horse's hooves against the roadway was pleasant and had a calming effect on Rhian, who sighed and sat back against the cold wooden seat, closing her eyes. Soon now she would be home and in her husband's arms.

But even there she was doomed to disappointment, for when she climbed down from the trap at the large front door there was no sign of Mansel Jack. The hallway was warm and welcoming, smelling of lavender polish, and as there was no one about Rhian made her way into the drawing-room.

She glanced at the clock on the high mantelpiece. It was ornate but in impeccable taste and Rhian thought she saw the hand of Charlotte Bradley at work there, as well as in the silk wall hangings and the fine curtains at the windows.

Startled by the opening of the door, she rose to her feet, brushing the creases from her skirt. As Doreen entered the room, leaning heavily on a stick, Rhian was bound to concede that Mansel Jack had been needed at home for his sister was clearly ailing.

'Is that you, Charlotte?' Doreen's watery eyes were half-closed in an effort to focus and pity mingled with Rhian's anger that Charlotte was obviously a frequent visitor at Mansel Heights.

'It's me, Rhian.' She moved forward quickly to help Doreen to a chair and the older woman's expression altered as she brushed Rhian's hand aside.

'Don't fuss, girl, I'm perfectly able to manage on my own.' Nevertheless, it took her a good five minutes to locate her chair and settle herself in its depths.

'Where's my brother?' Doreen asked imperiously, without any word of welcome.

Rhian bit her lip to check her anger. 'I expect he's gone out on business.' She spoke with forced politeness and exaggerated slowness, for Doreen complained often that she could not understand Rhian's 'heathen tongue'.

'Nonsense! It's the Sabbath and my brother always

visits dear Charlotte on Sunday mornings.'

'Well, in that case why ask me where's he's gone?' Rhian's patience was wearing thin. She glanced out of the windows to the sun-splashed garden where the early daffodils swayed, elegant and golden and reminding her of home.

'Tut, tut — petulance is an unattractive trait, girl, learn to curb it.' Doreen pointed her stick and waved it to emphasize her words and Rhian sighed; it was useless to argue.

'Ring for some mint tea for me, I'm parched!' Doreen's abrupt change of subject was confusing and for a moment Rhian stood still, staring down at her sister-in-law's pale face. 'Well, go on, I suppose you could do with some refreshment too,' she added grudgingly.

Rhian rang the bell and moved towards the door. 'I'm going for a walk,' she said. 'Tell my husband I shan't be long.'

Doreen's sniff of indifference somehow managed to convey the impression that Mansel Jack would not care a jot either way. Rhian pulled her coat round her and did up the buttons with shaking fingers.

The cold but clear air was like a balm as Rhian set out over the fields. The pale sun warmed her and the scents of early spring were all around. She should be happy here in her husband's country with him at her side . . . but he *wasn't* at her side. Rhian wondered uneasily if the enforced separation had made him indifferent or, worse, made him realise that Charlotte Bradley was more the sort of wife he should have got for himself. At any rate he seemed to spend a great deal of his time with her.

She saw the blue of the distant hills and felt homesick for Sweyn's Eye. She badly missed the twin hills of Kilvey and Town Hill and the dipping valley edged by gentle seas. Perhaps she should return home and let Mansel Jack come to her, but then wouldn't that be giving up — allowing Charlotte Bradley to have him without a struggle?

He did not return home for lunch and Rhian hardly tasted the roast meat and the succulent vegetables diced in butter, for Doreen seemed to be watching her with amused interest.

'I wonder what's keeping Mansel Jack,' Doreen said at

305

last. 'He usually returns for lunch, I'm beginning to be a little worried about him.'

Rhian stared at her sister-in-law unflinchingly 'It's as you said, he's probably still with Charlotte.'

'I should say so, she's very good company you know, such a lady.' Doreen lifted a lace handkerchief to dab at her forehead and with sudden concern, Rhian realised that the older woman was sweating profusely.

'Are you feeling ill?' she asked and Doreen waved her hand impatiently, but she was breathless and unable to speak.

Her lips were tinged with blue and she slipped down in her chair, the scrap of lace drifting to the floor.

Rhian pulled at the silk bell tassel and then turned her attention to Doreen. She loosened the high collar and as an anxious young maid entered the room, signalled for her help in lowering Doreen to the floor.

'We must loosen her corset,' Rhian said decisively 'and then you must run and fetch the doctor, Sarah.'

'But it's Sunday, begging your pardon, miss. Doctor James doesn't come out on Sundays.'

'Well, he does now!' Rhian said in a hard voice. 'Tell him that Mansel Jack requires him to come at once. And Sarah — don't dare return without him!'

The girl bobbed a curtsey and hurried from the room, sufficiently frightened to do what she was told. But Doreen was growing more breathless with each moment and in desperation, Rhian fanned her face with a napkin. Doreen seemed to suck in the air caused by the movement and Rhian increased her efforts, fanning more vigorously.

The cook hurried in, her face revealing her distress as she stood beside Rhian, twisting her hands together.

'Fetch some pillows, Mrs Graham. Pile them beneath Doreen's back and head, raise her up as much as possible. That's right. Now bring me a paper, anything to provide as much air as possible. And open that window wider.'

Doreen seemed to be unconscious but her breathing was a little easier. Rhian's knees hurt and her arms ached from her efforts, but she continued to work over her sister-in-law's inert form.

It seemed an age before she heard the rolling of carriage wheels on the gravelled drive outside, but then the doctor was being shown into the room, dressed casually in a knitted jacket. He knelt down at once and took Doreen's pulse, then he opened her bodice and listened to her heartbeat.

'She must be taken to the infirmary straight away.' He stared down at Rhian as he folded his stethoscope. 'I think she may well owe her life to your prompt actions, young lady.'

Rhian rose to her feet. 'Thank you, Doctor James, for coming so quickly. I don't think I could have managed for very much longer.'

He made his way through the large sunny hallway and Rhian followed him. He paused and looked around. 'Is Mansel Jack at home?' he asked in a low voice and Rhian shook her head.

'No, but anything you have to say about Doreen I think you can safely say to me.'

'Ah, yes, quite right. Well, I shall arrange for an ambulance to call as soon as possible. There's no immediate danger, but you realise that Doreen will need constant care? Even when she returns home, she will be an invalid.' He allowed himself a small smile. 'It was a very good thing you were on hand, otherwise things might have been very much worse.'

When he had gone, Rhian enlisted the help of Mrs Graham and Sarah in undressing Doreen and putting her into a nightgown and robe. She was not to be moved from the dining-room but a chair was fetched and she was lifted into it. She opened her eyes and stared up at Rhian, hostility replaced by fear.

As she watched the ambulance drive away, Rhian felt a sense of loss. It was almost as though she was reliving the days of Carrie's illness once more. She took a deep breath, coming suddenly to a decision. It was time she had things sorted out with Mansel Jack: either her husband wanted her whole-heartedly or he regretted the marriage. Whatever the outcome, anything would be better than enduring this uncertainty.

She left Mansel Heights and walked down the broad tree-lined avenue towards the big house that stood in splendid isolation in its own grounds. Charlotte was a fine woman and an honourable one but she loved Mansel Jack and she would be less than human if she did not make the most of what he offered her.

Rhian's hand trembled as she pulled on the bell. The thick oak door, carved with vine leaves and grapes, seemed like an impenetrable barrier between herself and her husband.

The maid stood back in surprise, obviously knowing Rhian by sight but not expecting to see her on the doorstep.

'I'll call the mistress,' she said and quickly hurried away, the ribbons of her white apron flying behind her.

'Rhian!' Charlotte was in complete command of herself as she came forward, slim white hands outstretched. 'What an unexpected surprise.'

Rhian held her head high. 'I would like to talk to my husband.' She spoke with unmistakable authority and Charlotte wilted beneath her gaze. Her quick look towards the drawing-room was revealing and without hesitation, Rhian strode past Charlotte and flung the doors wide.

Mansel Jack was obviously very much at home; he was reclining in a chair with a drink of brandy at his side and the newspaper on his knee. He looked up in surprise when Rhian came to stand before him.

'I was disappointed that you didn't even see fit to be home to welcome me. It's clear that matters between us are not what they should be. But I'll say this once and I'll say it plainly: you have to choose.' She met his gaze, challenging him to deny any knowledge of what she meant. He rose to his feet and stared down at her without touching her.

'I have not gone into Charlotte's bed, if that is what you are saying,' he said quietly and Rhian shook her head impatiently.

'Maybe not, but you spend more time by this fireside than by your own, and I will not have it.' She hurried on before he could reply. 'I don't want half a marriage, I want you with me wholeheartedly or not at all — can you understand that?'

He put down the paper carefully and she could see that he was unsettled by her outburst. He lifted his glass and drank some brandy before turning to face her.

'I'll spend no time trying to coax you,' Rhian said more quietly. 'If you need to think about it, then you can't love me very much.'

She moved to the door. 'I'm going to the infirmary now. Doreen was taken ill just after I arrived; she's out of immediate danger, but it was touch and go for a time and it was fortunate that I was there to look after her.'

She left the house and hurried along the curving driveway feeling as though she had just cast away the most precious thing in her life. But she had done the right thing; she was not cut out to take second place, not to anyone.

Before she reached the gate, she heard the sound of Mansel Jack's automobile crunching along behind her. At her side he stopped and smiled down at her, his eyes alight.

'Get in,' he said and she felt hope begin to grow as she climbed into the seat beside him. He put his hands over hers for a moment and she saw that the laughter had gone from his eyes.

'You're right, lass,' he said softly. 'I was trying to have my cake and eat it too.'

'And?' Rhian said, wanting him to spell out his feelings for her. His eyes crinkled and he laughed down at her.

'And, lass, you asked me to choose and I've chosen my wife — isn't that good enough for you?'

Rhian looked down at her folded hands, determined not to let him see her relief. He could just take a taste of his own medicine for a while and be uncertain about *her* feelings.

'It'll do, for now,' she said flatly and looked up at him steadily. 'Let's go over to the infirmary; I promised Doreen I would find you and bring you to her.'

'Oh, sure of yourself, weren't you?' Mansel Jack said and though there was a hint of laughter in his voice, she could tell he was taken aback.

'No,' she said mockingly, 'I was sure of you!' She sat beside him in silence then as he drove carefully through the town, within her a growing determination to be a different woman from the one who had timidly submitted to both Doreen's biting tongue and her husband's thoughtlessness. Let Mansel Jack start straying in the direction of Charlotte Bradley once more and they would all find that there was more to Rhian Gray than met the eye.

* * *

It was almost two weeks later when Doreen returned home from the infirmary. She was pale and her lips still slightly blue, but her eyes were alert and her stick was clasped firmly in her hand.

Rhian led the way along the corridor to a suite of rooms on the ground floor and flung the door wide.

'I do hope all this meets with your approval, Doreen,' she said warmly. 'I've had the rooms decorated especially for you.'

Doreen's mouth closed into a tight line and her dark eyes flashed. Rhian had been expecting opposition, but was determined not to be intimidated by it.

'Why can't I go back upstairs to my old rooms?' Doreen said at last, running her fingers over the newly installed wash-basin. Rhian put an arm around the older woman's waist and led her to a chair.

'Because the doctor tells me you must on no account climb stairs,' she said firmly. 'In any case, it's much more convenient for you to be down here — it means that I won't be rushing up and down stairs all day, waiting on you.'

Doreen glanced at her quickly, opened her mouth to speak and then at the look in Rhian's eyes, fell silent.

'Look, see what a fine view you have from your window!' Rhian said more softly. 'You can see right into the park.'

Doreen leaned forward, her attention drawn to the figure of a nanny whose white cap was fluttering as she wheeled her charge in a high-bodied pram. She was beguiled by the changing scene before her and Rhian smiled, knowing that Doreen would soon convince herself that the move downstairs was all her own idea.

'I'll go and see cook about tonight's supper.' Rhian moved to the door and Doreen's head swivelled round to look at her.

'But that's always been my job.' Her mouth folded mutinously and Rhian straightened her shoulders.

'I know, Doreen, but I'm here to stay now, you see — and I am mistress of the house, after all.'

For a moment, it looked as though Doreen would put up a fight, but just then there was a cry from a small boy in the park who had fallen on the gravel path and was clutching his injured knee with both arms. Doreen's attention was diverted and with a smile, Rhian left the room.

Mrs Graham was in her kitchen, arms covered in flour as she rolled out pastry with swift movements of her capable hands.

'I've come to discuss the supper menu with you,' Rhian said quietly and the older woman scarcely glanced at her.

'It's all in hand, I'm making Miss Doreen's favourite steak and kidney pie.' She turned the round of pastry over the rolling pin and set to work again without even looking up.

'Please stop what you're doing, Mrs Graham, I want to talk to you.' Rhian spoke slowly and loudly and the young kitchen-maid bent over the sink in the corner of the kitchen looked up with round eyes.

'Yes, miss?' The cook was red to the ears and it was clear that she resented Rhian's tone but dared not say so.

'Please understand that in future I will be consulted about the menu before any decisions are made. Tonight's supper may go on as planned, but after that any meal which does not have my direct approval will be thrown out in the bin.'

Mrs Graham bit her lip, but at last she lowered her eyes, inclining her head in an attitude of submission.

'Now,' Rhian said, 'I think for breakfast tomorrow we will have devilled kidneys with eggs poached in milk for Miss Doreen. But don't worry, I shall write everything down and you can study the list at your leisure.'

As she reached the hallway, Rhian waited with hands

clasped before her as the door swung open.

Mansel Jack smiled at her as he stood back to allow Charlotte to enter the house before him. Rhian moved forward, hands outstretched in greeting.

'Do come in, Charlotte — let me take you at once to Doreen's rooms, for I imagine it's she you have come to visit?'

'Oh yes, of course.' Charlotte glanced at Mansel Jack before following Rhian along the corridor. 'How is Doreen, much better I hope?'

'Yes, much better and will be all the more so for seeing you, I'm sure.' She knocked lightly on the door before opening it.

'A visitor for you!' Rhian called out brightly and turning to Charlotte, spoke to her in a low voice. 'I'm so glad you're here - you'll be able to keep Doreen company while my husband takes me into town.'

Ignoring the surprised lift of Charlotte's eyebrows, Rhian moved away, smiling as she heard the door close. That little encounter had put Charlotte in her rightful place as a guest in Rhian's home.

Mansel Jack was helping himself to a brandy from the glistening decanter on the sideboard and Rhian moved towards him, putting her arms around his waist.

'I want you to take me into town, please.' She spoke softly, looking up into his eyes. 'I need new nightclothes and there's a blue satin robe in Cavenor's which I've had my eye on for some time. Please say you'll take me, my love.'

'Well, yes, of course I'll take you. We can go into town when I drive Charlotte back home.'

'Oh no, that's all right,' Rhian said quickly. 'Charlotte knows we're going out and she'll make her own way home. After all, her house isn't very far away, is it?'

As she sat beside her husband in the car, her feeling was one of triumph. She sighed and looked up at the sun, drinking in the softness of the day. A new era was dawning and Rhian meant to have the reins of it firmly in her own hands.

CHAPTER TWENTY-FIVE

The softly glowing day was rich with blossoms shading from white through to pink and on to the deepest red. On the western slopes of Sweyn's Eye the grass was lush, the sea below the hillside crystalline. It was a day for rebirth and joy, yet Mary Sutton could scarcely hide her tears.

When Stephan had been taken to the infirmary it had been found that he was suffering from a fever which had nothing to do with his eyes. Careful nursing had soon restored him to health, but Mary's relief was short-lived for it became obvious that his sight was deteriorating further. Bryn Thomas had been called in for a further consultation and today Mary was due to hear the details of his report from Paul Soames.

Now Mary led Stephan gently to the Austin and when he was seated in the back, she started the engine. The trees overhead laid down patterns of light and shade which moved and shimmered as she drove. Her throat contracted when she thought that soon her son might be unable to see any of the beauty spread before them.

The town was not so lovely. Hazy clouds held down the green copper smoke, blocking out the sunshine and sending the stink of copper fumes to pervade the streets. Mary drew the car to a halt outside Paul Soames' surgery and in moments the door had opened and he stood waiting to greet her.

His windows were closed, covered with thick net curtains, and an air of mustiness pervaded the house. Mary looked at the dust and raised her eyebrows at Paul.

'Your house needs some attention, Paul. It doesn't do for a doctor to lower his standards, mind.'

313

He shrugged. 'That might well be, but the good chapel-going Mrs Billings won't work for me until the deacons say it's all right.'

'So the battle is still on, in spite of everything? I thought the deacons would have accepted that there was no ir-regularity by now, Paul.'

'Oh, I think they want me to do penance for my wrongs before they forgive me,' he smiled. 'We did share one wonderful night, Mary, and I regret none of it.'

She opened the buttons on Stephan's knitted jacket and brushed back her son's hair. 'He's worse, Paul,' she said anxiously. 'I'm so worried about him. Please tell me what Bryn has to say.' Her eyes rested appealingly on his face.

'I understand that Bryn considers there may be a little damage to the retina of the eye, Mary, but he believes that rest and good care might allow the tear to heal.'

'What do you mean by rest and care?' Mary felt a knot of fear inside her as she drew Stephan close.

'No running about for a start,' Paul said. 'I know that's going to be a tall order for an active little boy, but if you could get him to relax completely and lead a quiet life for a month or two we might see an improvement.' He paused, his eyes soft as they rested on Mary. 'It won't be so bad, I will help you all I can and it might just do the trick.'

'And if it doesn't?' Mary asked, her voice trembling.

Paul leaned over, putting his hand on her shoulder in an effort to comfort her. 'Don't look so worried! Medicine is improving all the time and new discoveries are being made, so don't look on the black side — there's a good girl.'

When Mary rose to her feet, her legs seemed to tremble beneath her. She held her son's hand tightly and Stephan peered up at her as though through a haze.

'He's so young!' She spoke heavily. She felt a sense of dread — how could she accept the possibility of Stephan being permanently blind? 'Oh, Paul,' she said, 'I feel so much alone.'

She drove home, her thoughts confused, wishing with all her heart that Brandon could be at her side to share with

314

her the fears and the anguish that only a parent could understand.

Nerys took Stephan to his room, her expression troubled, knowing from the set whiteness of Mary's face that the news was not good. She had wanted to accompany Mary into town and be with her at the doctor's surgery, but Mary — always so independent and proud — had insisted on going alone.

During the afternoon Stephan slept and Mary sat beside his bed, staring down at her son. He was so like Brandon that it hurt and she felt the tears she had suppressed for so long burn her eyes.

Impatiently she got to her feet and left the room, quietly closing the door behind her. She couldn't sit still — she must get out of the house and take some sort of action or she would go mad.

She walked down the drive, breathing in the soft spring air as she tried to calm herself. She must put her worries out of her mind and concentrate on business, for it did not do to dwell on morbid thoughts.

*　　*　　*

At Spinners' Wharf the mill was in full production, the looms clattering and spitting out woollen cloth. Mary stood in the doorway for a moment and smiled as she saw Gina coming across the large room towards her.

'Mary! There's lovely to see you — come on into the house and have a bite of tea with us.'

Mary followed her across the yard and into the warmth of the old mill-house kitchen. The table was set with a white cloth and on the gleaming hob the smoke-blackened kettle was simmering.

'Sit down, Mary,' Gina's eyes were shrewd, 'and tell me what's wrong.' She warmed the brown china pot while waiting for Mary to speak.

'It's Stephan,' Mary managed to bring out the words at last. 'I think he may be going blind!'

'Oh, Mary!' Gina put down the tea-pot suddenly so that

315

some of the water spilled on to the snowy cloth. 'Oh *cariad*, there's sorry I am!'

Mary stared down at her hands. 'I've taken him to both Paul Soames and Bryn Thomas and now Bryn prescribes complete quiet and rest for a month or so, in the hope that this may improve things.'

'Well then, you must pin your faith on that,' Gina said quickly. 'While there's something can be done, there is still hope.'

Mary nodded. 'I know, but I can't help feeling it's all my fault.' She paused, her eyes filling with tears as she looked into Gina's concerned face. 'It was an accident in the car, I crashed into a tree stump when I was not paying attention. He didn't seem to suffer at all then, it was me who was hurt.'

'Now don't go blaming yourself, Mary, accidents do happen for all that we try to be careful.'

'I know that,' Mary replied, 'but I can't get it out of my head that if it had not been for my carelessness, Stephan would be all right. Deprived him of his father I have, too, by my own foolishness. I'm just a bad mother to that boy — no doubt about it.'

'There's nonsense you talk, Mary.' Gina took her hand. 'You've got money and a good business to leave to him, which is more than any of us started with, remember?'

Into the silence that followed Gina's words came the sound of an engine as the van drew round the back of the house and shuddered to a stop.

'There's Billy!' As Gina moved to the door her face was alight with happiness and Mary sighed; it seemed that other people found love in their lives, whereas in that respect she herself was a failure.

'Well, Billy — and how are the sales going?' She forced herself to speak cheerfully. 'I'm sure you're doing very well.'

It was Gina who spoke first. 'Got all the valley women after him, he has, a real Romeo. Talk about sales, he could sell sand to the Arabs!'

Mary concealed a smile as Billy sank into a chair, his face flushed as he swept off his cap.

'Take no notice of Gina, she always did exaggerate.'

'Oh, I don't know; you're a handsome man, Billy Gray, and I'm not surprised the women like you. Do they buy from you? That's the point!'

'Oh yes, I'm out of stock — was coming up to see you later, Mary, to ask you for some lightweight underclothes for the summer as well as a few bolts of calico and another couple of sets of pans.'

'Very good.' Looking at Billy, Mary could scarcely credit the fact that he had once been her sweetheart. They had both been very young then and perhaps she had lived a romantic dream, knowing underneath that they were not meant for each other.

'Have you heard from Rhian?' Uncomfortable with her own thoughts, she changed the subject and Billy nodded.

'Aye, living the life of Riley in Yorkshire, though she was a bit worried because her sister-in-law had to spend some time in the infirmary. But her and Mansel Jack seem to be getting along fine. Good luck to her, say I. She's found herself a fine husband and I wish her every happiness — she deserves it.'

'Yes,' Mary said softly. 'I suppose she does.' She rose to her feet. 'Well, I'll expect to see you later. We can go over the books together, Billy, and then sort out some stock at the warehouse.' She smiled at Gina. 'Where are the children, it seems very quiet here?'

Gina smiled. 'Oh, Doris takes them out most days when it's fine. I give her a couple of shillings and we're all happy.'

Mary did not go directly home, instead she drove down to the curve of the bay and stared at the soft sea lapping meekly on the golden sand. Her life seemed destined to lurch from one drama to the next and she wondered where she had gone wrong.

Once she had appeared to have everything: a husband, a thriving business and her own pride. How different a person she was now! She had been granted her wish to have a child, yet with the coming of her son everything had

317

changed. She had lost Brandon's love and respect, become in his eyes a fallen woman.

And now her sense of values had altered and the business no longer seemed important. Stephan was what counted now and he must *not* go blind — she would not allow it, she thought on a surge of determination.

She drove the car up the slopes of the hill towards her home. The beauty which lay all around her — in the blossoms, in the calm of the sea far below and in the clear evening sky — producing a feeling of inexplicable sadness. She climbed from the seat of her car and let herself into the cool sweet-smelling house which seemed to fold welcoming arms around her.

Nerys appeared at the top of the stairs, holding a finger to her lips. 'He's asleep!' she said in a stage whisper that could be heard all over the house.

Mary smiled up at her and moved into the drawing-room. The lights had not been lit and there was a bluish glow from the windows reflecting the skies outside.

She sat in her chair and stared around at the emptiness which was her home. Lonely for love and for her husband's arms around her, she no longer felt strong and able to cope with everything.

* * *

It was a relief when Billy interrupted the evening meal for which she had no appetite and she left the dining-table quickly, leading the way into the study.

'I think you'll find the figures in order, Mary.' Billy placed the accounts book on the desk and stood back in respectful silence while she studied the pages before her.

'That's fine, Billy,' she said at last. 'We seem to be making an excellent profit.' Billy nodded in satisfaction, but twisted his cap between his hands and seemed a little ill at ease.

'What is it, Billy?' Mary asked, bewildered by his attitude. He stared at her, his face sober, pausing a moment as if searching for the right words.

'I've heard rumours, Mary,' he said at last, 'and businesses are beginning to fail all over the place. I just wanted to let you know, so that you can invest your money sensibly, somewhere out of the country perhaps.'

Mary nodded. 'It's all right, Billy, I've had the feeling for some time that fortunes would take a swing downwards.' She smiled at him, wanting to talk to someone about her plan; there was no feeling of achievement if triumphs were not shared.

'I've put all I have into property, Billy.' She glanced up at him, waiting for his approval. 'There's not much harm can come to bricks and mortar, is there?'

'Perhaps not, Mary, but folk won't be able to pay rents if there's no money coming in.'

She pondered on this for a moment. 'Well, what would you do then?' she asked doubtfully.

He leaned forward eagerly. 'Buy one or two small pits, Mary. We'll always need coal to run factories and such. In any case, there's no harm in spreading money about a bit. The run I'm on now — that will be enough to keep us all in bread and butter, but it won't pay for your fine house, Mary.'

'Yes, I see there's sense in what you say.' She smiled. 'Then I think I'll leave it up to you, Billy. I'll empower you to handle some of my capital, buy what you think fit and supervise it all for me. Get someone else to do the valleys run if you like — and while we're at it, you'd better have a rise in wages too!'

He rubbed his hand through his hair. 'I never expected all this, Mary. I was thinking of you.'

She put her hand over his. 'I know you were, Billy, and I'm grateful to you, but you must see to your own life as well.' She smiled warmly. 'It's about time you married your little Gina, isn't it?'

He grinned sheepishly. 'Aye, you could be right. She loves me, I know that — more than I deserve, what with the mess I've made of my life.' The smile vanished. 'I was a fool to ever let you go, Mary and I still . . .' his words trailed into silence as Mary held up her hand.

319

'Don't say any more, Billy, what's past is over and done with; that's the best way of looking at it. We've all made mistakes and now you've got a chance of happiness, don't let it slip away.'

He sighed and rose to his feet. 'Right then — I'll be off and I'll get to work at once, looking for some good pits going cheap. Thank you, Mary, for your confidence in me. I hope I can justify it.'

It was silent in the small book-lined study when he had gone and Mary rubbed her eyes wearily. She would go in to see Stephan and then have an early night, for she was very tired.

The lamps were lit in the small bedroom and Stephan was sitting up against the pillows, his eyes open.

'Mammy, where are you?' His voice was low and as she watched, he scrambled from beneath the sheets. His small bare feet made no sound on the thick carpet and, smiling, Mary held out her arms to him.

He stumbled, bumping into the wooden bedpost, his head turned as though seeking her. And then the truth came to her; Stephan could not see her. She gathered him into her arms and cradled him close, hot bitter tears running down her cheeks and falling salt into her mouth.

*   *   *

It was growing dark as Billy made his way back down the hill. He had left the van at Spinners' Wharf, tired of driving the huge vehicle and determined to enjoy the softness of the spring air. He moved lithely with quickness of step, for though he was nearing his fortieth year he had kept his slim build and agility. No doubt serving for four years in the Army, eating meagre rations and hoofing it through the hilly countryside of France, had contributed to his fitness.

And yet he was aware of the passing years, particularly now when he had spent time with Mary. She was lovely still, but a mature woman and not the young eager girl he had once known. He had always shown her the respect she had somehow commanded, even in the early days when she lived in what was little better than a hovel, but now she had earned his admiration too for she was an astute businesswoman. He smiled, remembering her dignity, the way she held her head high and her back iron-straight. And she had had young men aplenty panting for her favours.

She was right to tell him he should marry Gina and settle down. Gina was like a mother to his daughter, for Cerianne had known little of her mother and had grown up with the gentleness of Gina Sinman as a pattern for her behaviour.

Yet now at this moment, even contemplating settling down, Billy felt a certain restlessness rise within him. He had been given more power, more authority by Mary and the knowledge made him feel like celebrating.

The doors of the Flint Mill stood open and from inside came the sounds of feminine laughter. These were not the good women of the parish, but the flossies who would give a man a good time for a few shillings. And that's just what he needed, he told himself firmly: a good time!

The bar was crowded with men and smelled of sweat and Woodbines. Over the snug, through the open door he saw a familiar figure with glittering hair and rouged cheeks. He did not know Rosa personally, only by sight, and she had never appealed to him. She was tawdry and cheap, plying her trade with little grace and eager only for the money which came at the end of the night. But with her was another girl who looked young and clean and fresh. There was no doubt that she too was for sale, but perhaps she was not yet utterly incapable of enjoying life.

He pushed his way through the crowd and stood near the table. Rosa lifted her painted eyebrows at him and he grinned. 'A drink, ladies; what'll it be — a couple of gins?'

Rosa nodded, her interest fading as she saw his eyes roam over her companion. 'This is Doffie,' she said flatly, 'and the charge is the same as for me — for all that she's not very good at it yet.'

He leaned towards the girl, breathing in the scent of roses as she smiled up at him. Her teeth were clean and even and her breath, unlike Rosa's did not smell of tobacco.

'How about spending the whole night with me?' he asked and Doffie's eyes lit up in anticipation. Glowing with the quickness of her smile, he failed to hear Rosa's sniff of derision.

'Couldn't afford more than an hour, you!' she said coldly but Billy dipped his hand into his pocket and brought out some money.

'You're place,' he said and Doffie got to her feet, coming only as high as his shoulder.

'Is that all right by you, Rosa?' She bit at her nail as she waited for a reply and finally the older woman nodded.

'Aye, go on then, take the back bedroom but mind and don't go cooking no food — he's there for one reason and one reason only.'

In the darkness of the streets, Billy put his arm around Doffie's slender waist. 'You're too pretty for all this,' he said gently and she glanced up at him with a rueful expression.

'Aye, so they tell me, but what else is there for a girl who don't know nothing different? I don't want to go waiting on folks in service, washing and cleaning after them — and I don't want to scrub floors neither.'

Billy thought of Mary, who had risen from the squalor of her background to be a rich successful woman. But then Mary Sutton was a remarkable person.

The room in the fading house in Canal Street was surprisingly clean and neat and Billy stared round him curiously. It seemed an unlikely setting for a girl of Doffie's type.

'Come and sit down by here.' He patted the bed and Doffie obeyed him, her eyes wide as though she was a little afraid. He took her hand and smoothed her fingers gently.

'You're not used to this, are you Doffie?' he asked gently and she looked away from him quickly.

'No, but I'll try not to disappoint you.' Her voice was small and a feeling of pity engulfed him. He did not see beyond the girl's wide eyes and pretty mouth, nor realise that her attitude was calculated to deceive him.

'Have you had many customers?' he asked, putting his

arm around her and drawing her close. She shook her head.

'No, not many. There was that Morgan Lloyd from Ram's Tor — nice young man he was too, kind to me, like you. Kept me up on the farm with him for a while — right keen on me he was.' Her voice trailed away and she bit her lip as tears welled in her eyes. 'What I'm feared of is having fat old men take me; I don't think I could bear that.'

She looked into Billy's face and then as she wound her arms around his neck, burying her face in his shoulder, she concealed a smile — men were so easy to fool!

'Come on to bed, my pretty girl.' Billy said softly, feeling mingled passion and tenderness surge through him. 'Let me show you what a real man is like.'

He opened her bodice and stared at the cool marble flesh. The small innocent rise of her breasts was sweet, the nipples pink and delicate like rosebuds in the spring.

'Oh, Doffie,' he said raggedly, 'you're lying by here like a young virgin.' He kissed her mouth and she was not too eager, but warmed to him as he smoothed and caressed her.

'Billy, my lovely,' she breathed in his ear. 'I didn't know it could be like this — honest to God I didn't.'

'By morning, Doffie, I'll make a woman of you, that's a promise,' Billy whispered as he gently moved down to her. She gave a little cry, resisting at first and then slowly yielding as if trusting him and he felt fire burn in his loins.

By the time he left Doffie in Canal Street by the early light of morning, Billy recognised that he was entranced by the young girl. Thank God, he thought wryly, that he was a single man and could take his pleasures where he wished.

CHAPTER TWENTY-SIX

The softness of summer laid colourful fingers over the lands of Ram's Tor. The Bearded April had flourished and now swayed green and strong in the gentle breezes with the appearance of sea waves. A riot of flowers — wild roses pink, white and red — intertwined with the hedgerows and above all soared the clear blue arc of the sky.

Catherine had the door ajar and the windows flung wide, for she felt strangely sick and weary of the heat in the kitchen as she heaped more coals upon the fire which was needed for cooking and heating the water to wash.

For a long time she had been ignorant of what was happening to her, knowing only that the rhythms of her body were awry and there was a heaviness about her waistline which she had been slow to understand. It was Gladys with her blunt earthiness who had crystallised the fluttering uncertainty within Catherine.

'You're going to have a babba and it's about time you told that man of yours, Catherine Preece!' Gladys had smiled her sympathy while Catherine stared at her uneasily.

'How do you know I'm going to have a baby?' Catherine could scarcely bring herself to say the words; she was trembling and suddenly she needed to sit down.

'There's a soft question, *merchi*. For a start I can see it by here,' she patted her own ample waistline. 'And for another thing there's your eyes — you can always tell by the eyes.' She had paused. 'You did know, didn't you?'

Catherine's heart seemed to spin with the fear inside her. 'Not for sure I didn't, I was afraid to think.'

Gladys was staunch in her support. Quickly she put

324

her arms round Catherine and offered her help.

'Anything I can do, you only have to ask. Like the daughter I never had you are, Catherine — and only me and God knows how good you were to my poor boy when he came home from the war.'

Now as Catherine moved towards the door, she felt heavy and breathless and deep within her there was a great sense of fear, for it was as though she had deliberately laid a trap for Morgan to fall into.

As she looked out into the dazzling sunshine her vision blurred, panic gripped her and she longed to run away from Ram's Tor and hide herself from the world; she was not ready for motherhood.

But this was nonsense and there was work to be done; the bedclothes put to soak in the tin bath; eggs to be collected from the hens and bread to be baked; standing about feeling sorry for herself would not solve anything.

It was hot in the hen-coop and heavy with the smell of meal and potato peelings and a wave of nausea swept over her. Catherine was impatient with her own weakness and collected the eggs doggedly, knowing that the task should have been done hours before.

And then a shadow fell over her and she looked up quickly. 'Oh, Morgan, you startled me!'

He took the basket from her hand and without a word led her back into the farmhouse.

'Sit down.' He put the eggs into the cool darkness of the pantry and came to stand before her.

'Is it true that you're having a baby?' Morgan sounded stern and rather frightening and Catherine blinked rapidly at the abruptness of the question. After a moment she nodded her head; what was the point of denying what would soon be patently obvious?

'Then why didn't you tell me, Catherine — why leave it to Gladys to let me in on the secret?' he asked impatiently. He crouched down before her and took her hands — cold in spite of the heat of the day — in his own warm fingers.

'We must arrange to be married as soon as possible.' He

325

sounded businesslike; it was not the sort of proposal a woman dreamed of receiving, but then she had put herself in an invidious position.

'Don't go marrying me out of pity or duty or a misguided feeling of charity, for I can manage, mind.'

'I'm not offering charity, Catherine. I'm offering you my protection and my name — how can I put it any more clearly than that?'

Why didn't he take her in his arms, hold her close and tell her all the things she longed to hear? She bit her lip, trying to control her emotions.

'Just let me think,' she said softly and he stood up, staring away over her head. His face was set and there was an angry line running from his nose to his mouth.

'If you need to think all that much about it, then perhaps we'd be better off forgetting the whole thing.' He strode to the door and turned to look back at her. 'I don't know how to reach you, Catherine — you treat me like a stranger.' When she did not reply, he shrugged and strode out of the kitchen.

Alone in the silence of the room with only the ticking clock for company, Catherine berated herself for being so foolish. He had offered her respectability if not his love and she should have accepted if only for the sake of the unborn child.

But if marriage was what he genuinely wanted, he had had ample time to make his plans before this. He was young and handsome; he could have his pick of the girls and if he married her, would he always feel trapped?

Longing to run into the sunshine after him, to cling to him, beg him to love her and cherish her, she almost rose to her feet. But no, she would not force his hand.

'Catherine, it's me!' Gladys peered round the door and smiled broadly. 'Have you made your plans then?'

Catherine brushed her hair away from her hot face. 'No, we haven't made any plans. Oh, Gladys, I'm so confused.'

Gladys took Catherine in her arms and sighed heavily. 'I'm sorry, *merchi*, there's soft I am barging in on you like this, but I saw Morgan with you and I thought . . .'

Catherine turned to stare at the older woman, her

eyes large so that the pupils were dark pools.

'Oh, Gladys, why try to make him go into a marriage that he doesn't want?' she cried, slumping back in her chair. Morgan was a decent, honest man and wanted to treat her right, but she wanted more — she needed his love.

'Don't look so hurt, *merchi*, I just had to tell the boy the truth that he'd fathered a babba on you. He had the right to know, mind, Catherine and he was eager to marry you too.'

'I don't think he's in love with me, Gladys,' Catherine said in a low voice. 'Oh, he's prepared to do the right thing and make an honest woman of me.' A ghost of a smile turned up the corners of her mouth for an instant. 'But I can't go into another loveless marriage.' She squared her shoulders and sat upright. 'But, I'll be all right, don't you worry. I'm used to taking care of myself after all. Now then, let's forget my problems and get some work done, shall we?'

*   *   *

Morgan stared up at the redness that was trailing across the sky, turning the clearness of the day into a rich sunset. He had worked like a slave all day, venting his feelings of frustration on the land. And now he was tired, weary even of Catherine in that moment.

She was stubborn as a mule and filled with silly pride, he thought. Perhaps he wasn't good enough for her: an ex-soldier, a man who had had his fill of war and woman. Well, he wouldn't lower himself again. He would work the land, bring in the harvest and take his profit and go. Catherine could have Ram's Tor to herself if that was what she wanted.

But then there was his child, the baby she carried within her; at this thought his face softened. Catherine had no right to keep him at a distance; their lives were bound up together and in spite of his angry reaction to her coolness, he knew it would be difficult for him to walk away from her.

He began to make his way down to the pier; he could see the men below moving about like tiny ants and assumed they were working on the lifeboat. The *Charlie Medland* was on the slipway as though about to be launched and it suddenly seemed important to be in the company of men. Women were so complicated — they made a mountain out of any molehill they could find.

His pace quickened as he left the farmlands behind him and hurried down the roadway that led steep and sharp to the pier. The masculine voices called to each other, carrying on the evening air; Morgan paused, hearing his own name.

'That'll be enough about gossiping,' the coxswain said. 'Come on, we're here to work, not to chew the fat like a lot of old women.'

'But she's carrying his babba and him running about making free with flossies! It isn't right . . . and him coming among us God-fearing men.'

Morgan moved nearer and recognised the tones of Joe Beaver, nicknamed 'the lamb' because of his name. He recognised too that he and Catherine were the subject of the conversation and anger curdled in his gut.

The man stood tall against the night sky, but Morgan had no shred of fear in him. He could take care of himself, the war had taught him that much.

'Got religion all of a sudden, is it?' Morgan's hands hung at his sides but he was tense, ready to spring. Joe spun around and had the grace to look sheepishly into Morgan's face.

'Just saying, that's all. Not right it is to let a woman carry your babba, and her a respectable widow before you came along.'

'Don't cause no arguments by here now,' the coxswain warned. 'I'm not having you two act like a couple of nippers in a tantrum.'

'It's all right, Bill,' Morgan said slowly. 'Not in a temper at all, just telling this whey-faced fool that his mouth better stay buttoned or I'll button it for him.'

Joe moved forward aggressively. 'You and whose army, foreigner?' He was big, Morgan noted, at least two stone heavier than himself and tall with it. But nothing to be afraid of.

'Army, why should I need an army?' Morgan's tone was

328

bland, his face calm and almost smiling. Joe hesitated in his tracks, not sure how to deal with the other's change of tactics.

'Don't go telling me to keep my mouth shut then, not if you want to stay healthy,' Joe grumbled. Morgan stepped nearer holding out his hand.

'Let's shake on it, is it?' he said and Joe, nonplussed, took his hand. Morgan held him fast, drawing him forward, his fist shooting into the man's belly. 'We both agree that you're a fat pig and need to be cut into slices of bacon, don't we?' And Morgan smiled again as Joe fell into an undignified heap at his feet.

Joe gave a bellow of rage and lumbered up from his knees, rushing forward with his arms outstretched. Morgan side-stepped him easily and kicked him in the backside, adding his strength to the man's own momentum.

Joe lay on his stomach for a moment, winded by the fall, his eyes bulging from his head. Bill moved towards Morgan, holding out a restraining hand.

'No more of this now, boyo,' he said, not without sympathy. 'I think you've more than proved your point.'

But Joe took advantage of the distraction to leap forward, his great weight bearing Morgan to the ground. His fist lashed out and Morgan saw lights blaze across the line of his vision.

He heaved mightily and slipped from beneath the crushing weight of the man, his slimness and agility helping to keep him out of harm's way until his sight cleared. Then he saw Joe lurch towards him, hands outstretched like a great animal.

'Do you never learn, Joe?' Morgan asked as he moved to one side and stuck out his foot, sending the heavier man sprawling once more. Joe leaned on his elbow, his eyes almost red in the evening light.

'You'd better keep me down next time, you bastard, or I'll tear your head from your shoulders!' He made to rise and while he was bent forward Morgan aimed with his boot and caught Joe neatly on the temple. He fell back spreadeagled, his body limp.

'*Daro!*' Bill bent over him and slapped Joe's face without

any reaction from him. Morgan went across and stood next to him.

'He'll be out for about fifteen minutes,' he remarked conversationally, 'and when he wakes up, tell him next time I catch him discussing my affairs I'll put his light out for good.'

Morgan left the pier and moved back up the hill. He was sorry it had been necessary to whip Joe Beaver the way he had done, for he would have liked to be friends with the lifeboat crew. But he could not have them putting their tongues to Catherine's good name.

It was only when he entered the cottage and saw Catherine's horrified face that he realised his eye was bruised and bleeding. She gave a small cry and ran towards him, then her arms were around his waist and she was crying against his stained shirt.

'You've been fighting over me, haven't you? Now don't bother to deny it!' After a moment, she moved away from him and began to fill the tin bowl with water. 'Let's bathe that eye then, is it, otherwise you'll have a job getting anything done on the farm come morning.'

He gave a short laugh. 'My God, don't you ever think of anything but getting the maximum amount of work out of me, woman?'

'Oh, I do sometimes.' Catherine leaned against him, dabbing at his eye gently with a cloth soaked in cold water. She smiled up at him and slowly, he leaned forward and kissed her mouth.

'You know something,' Morgan said easily, 'I think it's about time we got married — that's if I can keep you off your high horse long enough to get you to the altar.'

She leaned closer to him, her arms around his neck, her mouth inviting. 'If that's a proposal, Morgan Lloyd, consider it accepted.'

*   *   *

They were married quietly, the congregation consisting only of Gladys Richards and her son William. And in the sun-washed chapel the minister of religion frowned down upon the couple, as though suspecting they were sinners but having the grace to be charitable about the weaknesses of mankind.

Catherine wore a silk cream dress, a present to her from Gladys who had been determined that the wedding should have a bit of style about it. In her golden hair, hanging loose to her shoulders, she had threaded wild pansies in place of the hat she could not afford. She glanced up at Morgan as they stood side by side before the pulpit and his smile warmed her so that she felt safe and cherished.

The ceremony was over very quickly, since the minister forebore to offer his usual advice about children binding the marriage with ties of love. It seemed somewhat unnecessary if the evidence of his eyes was anything to go by!

And in the brightness of the sunshine outside, Morgan held Catherine close and kissed her mouth gently. Catherine felt warm and safe and the world was suddenly a beautiful place.

'Come on now, you two lovebirds,' Gladys said heartily, though there was a trace of tears in her eyes. 'I've got a lovely wedding breakfast for you as a surprise like. Can't have you going back to work on a day like this, can we?'

The parlour of the house facing the sea was cool and inviting and Gladys had spread the heavy oak table with a snowy cloth upon which was set her best porcelain tea-set. Thinly-cut slices of bread spread with good Welsh butter were placed at the centre of the table and surrounded by good wholesome cheeses and fresh fruit. The curtains, newly washed, bore the scent of sunlight and the piano against the far wall was polished to a mirror-like shine.

'Everything looks beautiful!' Catherine felt touched by the care Gladys had taken. She was generous in the extreme, for not every woman would look kindly on the widow of her son remarrying.

'Sit down by here now,' Gladys said quickly, 'and don't be talking so soft — only an ordinary spread, isn't it?' She disappeared into the kitchen, calling to William to help her with the tea-tray. 'And then,' she said coaxingly, 'you can go on up to Ram's Tor and do the milking — right, boyo?'

'Well, how does it feel to be Mrs Lloyd?' Morgan took Catherine's hand and she was warmed by the way their fingers entwined.

'It feels right and proper and very, very good,' Catherine said gently, leaning towards him and resting her head upon his shoulder. His hand gently smoothed her golden hair and she felt cosseted and loved.

'There's a fine pair of nesting sparrows, if ever I did see one.' Gladys placed the tray on the table and called over her shoulder for William to hurry up to the farm, for the cows would be milking themselves if he didn't get a move on!

'Now, then, what'll you have, Catherine? A nice bit of Welsh cheese all fresh and tasty?'

Catherine felt too excited to eat, but Gladys had gone to a great deal of trouble and so she nodded her head and took the plate, setting it down before her. Morgan helped himself to a few slices of bread and ate heartily and Catherine smiled; it seemed that nothing would put her new husband off his food.

She glanced down at the shining ring on her finger. It glinted and glowed as though with a life of its own, the gold warm and rich with copper tints. Twice a wife and she was just rising twenty-one; it seemed very strange, almost unbelievable. Her life with David Preece might have been several lifetimes ago, so far removed was it from the way she felt now.

She had given her first wedding ring to Gladys, feeling it only right that David's mother should keep it. She wanted no part of David now; he was dead and gone and must only be allowed the occasional resurrection in her memories.

'Have a bit of lardy cake, Catherine, there's a good girl — need feeding up you do, small and thin except in the belly you are!' Gladys laughed uproariously as the rich colour came into Catherine's face.

'*Duw*, there's a girl for being bashful. You'll lose all your shyness by the time you birth that fine boy you've got growing in there,' Gladys said, pointing. 'The midwife will know more about your innards than you do, so just get used to the idea now, Catherine, before your time comes.'

Catherine leaned forward. 'You'll be with me, won't you,

332

Gladys?' She suddenly felt fearful for the birth of her child had been something to push into the furthest corners of her mind. But now, with Gladys's words spoken out loud, the event became a frightening reality.

' 'Course I'll be there, try to keep me away! And in any case, we've got a lovely midwife in Oystermouth; old nurse Gordon, hands like an angel she's got.'

Catherine glanced covertly down at her figure where the swell of her stomach hardly showed in spite of Gladys's teasing remarks. She was pleased, for she wanted to look beautiful for Morgan. She felt a glow envelope her as she pictured the nightgown she had bought — daring it was, with silk and lace and a low neckline. So very different from her plain serviceable cotton gowns.

'Ought to be going away together, really.' Gladys seemed to pick up some of Catherine's thoughts. 'Should have a nice holiday in Barry or even Port Eynon where your family lives, Catherine.'

'It's the farm,' Morgan said. 'Can't afford time away from it — you know that better than most, Gladys.'

'Aye, you're right, lad.' She stared curiously at Catherine. 'Why didn't you ask your father and sisters up for the wedding? I'm sure they'd have loved to come and see you married.'

Catherine shook her head. 'I know my father, he'd probably have a shotgun with him — real strict he is and in the circumstances . . .' Her words trailed away and Gladys nodded sympathetically.

'I know what you mean, *merchi*, it was daft of me to ask. Anyway, I've got some home-made blackcurrant wine, so let's drink your health, shall we?'

The sun was fading from the cloudless sky when at last Catherine and Morgan set out for home. Gladys had tried to talk them into staying the night, offering them the big front bedroom which looked out over the sea.

'Private you'll be, with me and William at the back of the house, mind, and it would be a bit of a change, wouldn't it?'

But Catherine had been determined to return to Ram's Tor and she knew that Morgan felt the same urgency to be home. They held hands as they walked along the road towards the cut, while at their side the sea murmured softly against the shore.

'Beautiful,' Morgan murmured, but when Catherine turned to look at him he was staring not at the view but at her. His arm was around her shoulder then, warm and protective and with a possessiveness that she found strangely moving.

The cottage was in darkness, but swiftly with the ease of long practice Catherine lit the oil-lamps and the soft light sent shadows leaping against the walls. She stared around her, wondering if it was worth setting a light to the fire.

Morgan made the decision for her. 'Catherine.' He placed his hands on her shoulders and drew her towards him. 'My lovely wife, let's go on up to bed, shall we? Go on, I'll give you a couple of minutes to get ready.' He touched her cheek. 'I know how shy you are!'

She closed her eyes as he kissed her and there was tenderness and passion and longing all mixed up inside her.

In the bedroom, she took off her clothes and drew on the silk nightgown which fell in voluptuous folds around her body. She brushed her hair, peering into the mirror that hung over the wash-basin, seeing only a dim reflection in the light from the lamp.

Morgan's footsteps sounded on the stairs and Catherine slipped into bed, drawing the sheets around her shoulders. She knew it was an absurd gesture, but it was an involuntary one.

When he climbed into bed beside her, he was naked. His body was warm against hers and his hands were sure but gentle.

'You smell of springtime and flowers.' He whispered the words against her mouth and she clung to him. Loving him.

He took her gently, containing his passion. Catherine felt herself possessed by him; he was reaching within her, binding them together.

The rush and splendour and rainbow colours of her shuddering delight transcended anything she had ever known. She lay back, her hair spread about the pillows, her eyes closed as she breathed his name.

334

CHAPTER TWENTY-SEVEN

The mules hummed, the looms clattered and motes of dust fell thickly in the slant of sun shafting in through the windows. But Gina was lost in thought, moving silently through the long building occupied now by young women. Twelve hours a day they worked, producing woollen goods which Billy Gray sold to the poor folk in the valleys.

She left the building and the sun fell warm on her shoulders. The singing stream beside the mill ran redly over rust-coloured stones and a sense of loneliness gripped Gina, for it seemed she had lost Billy for ever. He appeared possessed by a summer madness, infatuated — so the gossips said — with a flossie young enough to be his daughter. But Gina had no right to feel let down, for he had never promised her marriage or anything else come to that. And yet for years she had believed there was an understanding between them, a closeness of friendship and more. She had taken it for granted that when the time was right she would walk down the aisle at Billy's side.

In the kitchen, Doris was washing the dishes and at her side, young Cerianne stood on tip-toes with a drying cloth in her hands. Dewi was building up the fire, his round face running with sweat.

'There's awkward this coal is, Mam.' When he looked up at Gina there was a black smut across his broad nose and her breath caught in her throat, for in that moment he was the image of his father. Nostalgia swept over her for the warmth of the love she had shared with Heinz; she really was a lucky woman to have had such a marriage, she told herself sternly.

Cerianne had finished drying the dishes and she looked up at Gina questioningly. 'When is Daddy coming home?' she asked. 'He's been working a long time, hasn't he, Auntie Gina?'

'Aye, selling clothes out in the valleys, he is; got to earn some money to buy food and clothes for his little girl, *merchi*!'

Cerianne's small face was upturned, her eyes fringed with long lashes; she was going to be a beauty when she grew up, Gina thought with a warm feeling of affection.

'Doesn't the mill make us money, too?' Cerianne asked, rubbing her small damp fingers against her spotless white frilled apron.

'Well, Mansel Jack owns the mill and so most of the money goes to him in Yorkshire.' Gina sank into a chair, fanning her face with her hand. 'Though I do get my pay, of course.'

'And thank God for that — you'd be in queer street without it!' Doris banged the plates against the shelf, her face red. 'If you waited for you-know-who to give you money, you'd starve.'

Gina shook her head warningly, but Doris rushed on. 'Not right a man of his age taking up with a flossie. Making a damn fool of himself, he is — ought to know better than to be taken in by a simpering no-good who's only after his money.'

Gina sighed. 'What he does is his own concern; it's none of our business, is it now?'

'I should have thought it was *your* business all right, but then he was always one for the women wasn't he? Running off with that fancy piece Delmai Richardson that time, caused such a scandal he did!'

'Hush,' Gina said softly. 'Little pitchers have long ears.' She glanced at Cerianne, who was quite unaware that it was her mother under discussion.

'Well, I still say he should be ashamed of himself — whore master, that's the name I'd put to him. But the worst thing that man has done in all his life is to lead a decent woman like you up the garden path all this time. I'd not forgive him for that if I was you!'

'Please, Doris, don't say any more.' Gina rubbed her eyes with her apron; she felt weary and dispirited, a woman who had been made to look foolish. But it was her own fault for being taken in by Billy.

The sound of the hooter from the mill pierced the silence and Doris dropped a handful of cutlery with a clatter. '*Duw*, these new-fangled inventions turn me grey.' She fanned her face with a damp hand. 'Don't know they're born, these girls don't, with all this stopping for tea and finishing work while it's still light.'

'Talking of breaks, I'm dry as an old bone.' Gina rose to her feet and pushed the kettle on to the blaze that Dewi had managed to fan into life.

'Good boy, you're a real help to your mam.' Gina ruffled his hair and he pulled away, angry at her display of affection for at almost six years of age he thought himself a man.

The sound of the happy chattering of the girls from the mill as they made their way along the yard drifted in through the open door. Gina peered out, calling good evening to them and though she smiled her heart was heavy. It was clear from the pitying glances that came her way that the gossip in the mill had once more concerned Billy Gray and his young harlot.

Her colour high, Gina poured water into the pot to warm it. As she swirled the pot around, she saw in its depths herself as a lonely old woman, dried up and vinegary, living out her life alone.

But suddenly she was angry. If Billy wanted to play the fool, then she wouldn't sit around moping; she would show him that she had more spirit than he gave her credit for. For a start, she would brush out her long brown hair, put on a clean gown and go down to the chapel to join in the choir practice.

'Doris,' she began cajolingly, 'would you mind the two children for me tonight?'

Doris put out the cups, her face avid with interest. 'Aye, I will that, my boys are big enough now to look after themselves and my old man will be down at the public,

337

swilling ale. So what are you going to do?'

'Do?' said Gina softly. 'I'm going to put up a fight, that's what I'm going to do!' And when Doris began to laugh, Gina felt suddenly more lighthearted than she had done in weeks

*　　　*　　　*

'Oh, Billy, can't I have a new pair of slippers then? These are all worn and shabby.' Doffie was leaning on one elbow, un-selfconscious of her naked breasts. 'I likes to look lovely for you, Billy boy; now don't be mean with me, there's a sweetie.'

Billy laughed and pulled her to him. 'I'll trade with you: a new pair of slippers for a bit of loving then, is it?' He put his mouth over the soft pink nipple nearest him and with a cry Doffie pushed him away.

'You're a proper ram, Billy Gray, don't you ever think of anything else?' In spite of her smile, there was an edge to her voice that Billy did not fail to notice.

'What's wrong?' he asked sharply. 'Aren't you in the mood again?' He knew he was using sarcasm against a girl who was not really very bright, but for a moment his irritation outweighed his love for her.

She melted into his arms at once. 'Oh, love, I didn't mean it, you're being an old softie. Come on, let Doffie show you what a good girl she can be!'

She swung herself on to him and lay spread over his body, her breasts almost touching his belly. Her mouth was a fire, rousing him, torturing him so that his blood pounded in his ears like thunder. At such times he felt young and new like a boy with his first woman, a heady sensation which swept away all his doubts and uncertainties about Doffie.

He turned her over and she gave a small cry as he thrust into her. There was no tenderness, no sense of loving, just the wine of desire driving him and manipulating him so that he groaned with the sweetness of his pleasure.

Beneath him, Doffie screwed up her eyes, pretending a feeling that did not exist — had never existed, for she had

338

been with so many men that one became very much like another. All that mattered was what they could give her materially and this one, this Billy Gray, might just be coaxed into marriage if she handled him right. And so she moaned and twisted the way Rosa had told her to, and when Billy fell at her side, spent, instead of revealing her scorn at his concupiscence she smiled and cooed over him, praising his vigour and strength.

When he rose, it was almost morning and she curled over and put her head beneath the pillow, trying not to hear the sound of his ablutions. She wanted nothing more than to sleep the morning away and then rise from bed, paint her eyes and go to the public bars with Rosa.

Billy, though generous, did not seem to think that she needed to be out and about meeting people, drinking gin and having a bit of fun. It was all right for him, he went into the valley's selling goods to the womenfolk and no doubt enjoying their company. Well, she had no intentions of being tied down — at least not until she had a ring on her finger.

'Give us a kiss goodbye, Doffie.' Billy nuzzled into the bedclothes, his lips warm against her cheek. She grumbled a little and turned her head and was relieved when he went out and closed the door.

Billy climbed into the seat of the lorry, feeling uncomfortable in the shirt which he had worn for two days now. He was used to fresh linen, washed lovingly by Gina. Later he must return to the mill house, for he had not been home for several days. And suddenly as he set the van into motion, the thought of coming face to face with Gina Sinman made him feel uncomfortable. But he had made her no promises, he told himself.

He did well with his sales that day. His eyes were bright and his manner flirtatious and more than one of the valley women with their dimpled cheeks and dark hair gave him a come-hither smile from beneath lowered lashes. He felt the blood surge in his veins; he had been acting the old man for too long, he needed to enjoy himself while he could.

He knew that Mary Sutton would be pleased with his efforts. She had given him a great deal more responsibility and soon he would be finding a replacement driver while he took up his new duties. He would be a man of standing as well as modest means and he felt that this had not come too early — he had had more than his share of bad luck.

Later, in the softness of the evening, he turned toward home and had the satisfaction of knowing that he had done well. He had even shifted the woollen turnovers which had stuck a bit since the onset of the warm weather. All day his tongue had been silver, his wit sharp and he felt alive and full of energy . . . and it was all thanks to Doffie.

Sweyn's Eye was beautiful by the silver light of the moon. The sea rippled along the five-mile stretch of glittering sand and the lights from the Mumbles pier spilled over into the water. Billy took a great breath of air into his lungs and felt alive and vital; love was a great thing for the system!

The door of the mill house was open and light splashed out into the yard as Billy drew the van to a stop and climbed down a little stiffly from the driving seat. He needed a bath and already he anticipated the heat of the cleansing water lapping around him. Gina always made sure there were fresh towels ready for him and clean linen hung neatly over the chair in the kitchen.

But today Gina scarcely glanced at him. Her hair hung long and glossy down her back and she was wearing a summer dress of soft cotton sprigged with delicately coloured flowers. Her eyes were bright as she twisted her hair into a bun and pinned it at the nape of her neck, while he stood for a moment uncertainly in the doorway.

'Good evening, Gina.' He sounded stiff and formal and pompous, yet he was taken aback by the picture she made — all soft and feminine and looking much younger than he had expected. 'Going to have a bath later on, if that's all right by you.'

'Oh, no, the fire's gone out Billy. Why don't you bath at your lodgings or down at your girl-friend's house?'

340

Billy swallowed hard. He had not anticipated that Gina would speak out about Doffie but then gossips had doubt-less been busy — they spared no one, hadn't he learned that long ago?

'Is there a clean shirt for me then?' he asked and Gina turned to him, passing him swiftly on her way to pick up a light shawl. Her perfume, not heavy like Doffie's but fragrant with the scent of flowers, drifted towards him and he felt a sense of anger that she was preparing to go out instead of sitting at home by the fire, mending or some such thing.

'No clean shirts, sorry.' She picked up a brown-paper parcel and placed it in his arms. 'Your dirty linen,' she smiled brightly. 'Perhaps you could get someone else to wash your shirts, Billy? I'm so busy these days.'

He blinked rapidly, not believing this could be hap-pening. Gina was usually so sensitive to his needs, so ready and willing to do anything he asked. He watched her go to the door and pause, waiting for him to step outside.

'Where are the children?' he asked curtly and Gina raised her eyebrows at his tone.

'Doris is minding them; not babies no longer, are they?' She ushered him outside and drew the door close, her hand resting on the latch, her face suddenly serious.

'Look, I'll mind Cerianne as I've always done, Billy, but I do think it's time you paid a little something towards her keep.' She moved away up the yard, still talking. 'Eating hearty she is now — a fine strong girl, thanks to me.' She paused and Billy could not see her face in the darkness. 'Though you might prefer Doffie to be minding Cerianne — I mean you and she are so close now, aren't you?'

Billy was suddenly angry. 'You're jealous, Gina, being spiteful and awkward because I'm going out with another woman.'

Gina's laugh tinkled out into the quiet evening air. 'That's wishful thinking, my boy. I'm walking out with a nice young man from the church choir, so why should I be jealous? In any case, Doffie isn't so much of a catch, is she? Anyone can buy her services — indeed they do, for I saw her coming out of the Flint Mill clinging to the arm of a sailor boy fresh in from the docks.' She seemed to take pity on him then for she held his arm a moment, her hand soft and gentle.

'Wake up, Billy, before it's too late. Don't make yourself the laughing-stock of the town, boyo.' She took a deep breath, 'Well, I'm going now, can't stand by here talking all night can I? Got better things to do.' She laughed again and Billy followed her, a mixture of emotions running through him.

'What's this nonsense you are talking about walking out with some prissy fool from the choir? When did all this happen? It's only two days since I saw you.'

'Been going round with your eyes shut lately though, haven't you, Billy? And I wouldn't call Thomas prissy — plays rugby he does and him built like the Mumbles train!'

She began to walk rapidly away and Billy stared after her, a mixture of emotions raging through him. He wanted to rush after her, take her in his arms and tell her that she was his woman and belonged to no one else . . . but then what about Doffie?

Anger burned in his gut then as he remembered Gina's words, that she had seen Doffie with a sailor. What was the girl playing at? Torn, unwilling to believe in Doffie's betrayal, he moved away from the mill house and began to walk through the darkened streets.

Doffie was not at home in the house she shared with Rosa, for the windows stared darkly back at him as he approached the doorway. Billy knocked hard, hoping against hope that he was mistaken and that Doffie was inside — perhaps asleep, for she was not expecting him until later that night.

At last he gave up, anger mounting within him as he remembered Gina's words once more; was it possible that Doffie was playing her old game behind his back?

He began to make a systematic search of the public bars Doffie usually frequented, starting with the Flint Mill. There was no sign of her or of Rosa either and Billy's rage increased as he moved up towards Green Hill.

The Dublin was full of the Irish and a tenor was singing heartrendingly about taking his Kathleen home again. Billy stood at the bar and took a mug of ale, for the evening was warm and he had not had any food or drink for hours. As he swallowed thirstily and slowly, he became aware that he was the subject of ribald merriment and turned on the men standing behind him, his jaw thrust forward.

'And what's so funny then, boyos? My shirt-tail hanging out or something?' The ale had gone to his head and he saw the grinning faces waver before his eyes as though they were some distorted creatures from a nightmare.

'No, nothing wrong with your back, man — it's where you put that thing in the front that's so funny!'

'Perhaps you'd like to explain that remark, you Irish tinker!' Billy's voice was dangerously low and the man who had spoken moved forward.

'I'm no tinker, I'm proper Irish and proud of it!' He thrust his face closer. 'And as for explaining, are you so dull then that you don't know that the doxie you're spending your money on is rutting with every man she can lie on her back for?'

Billy's pent-up anger and frustration burst inside his head, so that he saw flashing lights before his eyes. His fist connected with the man's chin, sending him flying back into the crowd; then all hell broke loose, a boot caught his knee-cap and Billy doubled up in agony. A chair was lifted and he saw it crash down on him, splintering into pieces. He tasted the sawdust from the floor in his mouth, mingling with his blood; he tried to rise to his feet but a heavy boot lashed out at him, catching him in the back.

With a bellow of rage and pain, Billy was up on his feet, lurching forward and grappling with the man, clinging to his throat, shaking him in spite of his stature like a cat with a mouse. It took three burly Irishmen to haul Billy away and by that time, the constable had arrived and for the second time in his life, Billy found himself in prison.

*   *   *

Gina sat in the polished wooden pew with her hymn-book clutched in her hand, but she was not seeing the words before her, only the pain and bewilderment in Billy's eyes as she had spoken to him. She didn't know what had hurt him most: her revelation that she was walking out with Thomas or the tit-bit of gossip she had so spitefully reported to him about Doffie being with a sailor in the Flint Mill.

There was a rustling of pages as the books were put away and Gina realised that choir practice was over. She forced herself to smile as Thomas left his place with the baritones and came over to her.

'The choir was in fine voice tonight, *merchi*, though you didn't seem to be singing very much — anything wrong?'

She shook her head. 'No, nothing that you can do anything about, Thomas, but thank you for asking.' She picked up her shawl. 'I'd better get off home because of the children, see.'

'There's no need to make excuses. I know well enough that I'm knocking my head against a brick wall by trying to get you interested in me, but I'll walk you home anyway.'

Gina wrapped the light shawl around her shoulders. 'I'm glad to have your company, Thomas, and it's not fair the way I'm taking advantage of you.'

'I wish you would.' Thomas leaned forward with his eyes alight and it was several moments before the full import of his words registered on Gina's mind.

'There's no need to blush!' Thomas said softly. 'Come on, let's get out of here or everyone will think I'm making improper advances to you.'

'Well and so you are, Thomas — you ought to be ashamed of yourself.' She walked out of the arched doorway of the chapel, shyly aware of the curious glances that a few of the choir members were giving her.

It was a fine silvery night with the moon riding the clouds as though they were stallions with flying lacy manes. She breathed deeply, wishing it was Billy and not Thomas at her side, wondering how it was that all the years of growing close to Billy had been shattered by the appearance in his

344

life of a flossie. Men could be such silly little boys at times.

'You're far away there, Gina.' Thomas's deep voice brought her back to the fact that she was walking home with a man she did not love.

'I'm sorry,' she said quickly. 'I'm not very good company, am I?' She smiled up at him apologetically. 'Don't bother to come any further; I can go the rest of the way alone.'

'Not bloody likely, pardon my language. No it's not good for a lovely woman like you to be out alone in the darkness.'

When the mill house came in sight, Thomas took Gina's arm. 'Wait a minute, don't go rushing off now. There's a shy girl you are mind.'

'Not rushing off at all, just got two little ones to look after — not a free woman, am I?'

Thomas drew her towards the light washing down from one of the street lamps. 'Well, I don't know about that, do I? That's just why I want to talk to you, girl.'

He put a warm hand on her shoulder, his fingers caressing. 'Just like a little filly that's frightened, you are. I'm not going to hurt you, *cariad*, you must know that.' He paused and ran a finger round the high collar of his shirt.

'The fact is, Gina, I think I'm falling in love with you. No, don't say a word, not yet, just hear me out.' He cleared his throat nervously. 'A widower I am, as you well know, and no children to my name. You lost your man in the war, so what would be more natural than us settling round the same hearth together?' He smiled down at her, his eyes bright. 'I'd like children and you are a young strong woman — we could make a go of it if we tried and love can grow, mind.'

Gina was too confused to reply at once. She had never thought it would come to this; all she had done was to strike up a friendship with Thomas, she liked the man. 'And used him' a small voice within her added.

'Thomas, I can't promise anything, but will you give me time to think it over?' What was she saying? She should be turning him down flat — of course she couldn't marry him — and yet 'Why not?' the small voice continued.

He drew her closer and chastely kissed her cheek. 'I'd be a good man to you and the little ones, Gina. I'd honour you and care for you and you'd never be alone again.'

She touched his cheek softly. 'Thank you for that, Thomas, you are a fine handsome man and a good one too.' She put her hand to her head. 'But I must think, just give me time.'

He nodded. 'I'll be round tomorrow for tea; now how will that do you, my lovely?'

'Yes, that'll be all right. I'll bake some Welsh cakes especially for you and I'll try to get Doris to take the children off my hands again, then we'll have some peace to talk.'

'Right, that's settled then.' He beamed down at her from his great height, such a strong man and so gentle, but he was not Billy Gray . . .

'I must go on in.' She stood on tip-toe to kiss his cheek and then before he could reach towards her, she was hurrying down the slope towards the house.

Doris was sitting in the chair near the fire, her knitting idle in her lap. She got up at once and pushed the kettle, which was already singing, on to the flames.

'Sit down by here, girl, and have a nice strong sweet cup of tea, 'cos I've got bad news for you.'

Gina felt fear drag at her and she stared around anxiously. 'The children — they're all right, aren't they?'

'Oh, aye, they're tucked up in bed as snug as two fleas. No, put your mind at rest there, girl.' She paused and bit her lip and Gina wanted to scream at her to get on with what she had to say and put her out of her misery.

'It's Billy.' Doris poured the water into the pot and set it on the brass holder on the hob. 'He's been arrested — almost killed a man, at least that was what they were all saying.'

Gina felt cold as she sank into the chair and clasped her hands in her lap. 'Who's saying this, Doris?' Surely there must be some mistake — Billy was sweet and gentle, he couldn't hurt anyone. 'It can't be true, Billy wouldn't be involved in a fight,' she said, her voice hoarse.

'Well, he was in prison for murder one time before,

mind, and folks are not going to forget that, are they?'

'But he was pardoned!' Gina felt as though she was in a nightmare from which she must surely wake at any moment. 'What happened before was an accident, everyone knows that.'

Doris put a cup of steaming tea by her. 'Drink that — it's good and strong and sweet, it'll bring colour back into your cheeks.'

'Doris, are you sure that Billy has been taken to the prison?' Gina asked, praying that there was some mistake and the other woman was just exaggerating.

'Definite! I saw Mr O'Connor and he was in the Dublin when it happened. He said Billy just went mad and was strangling this Irish bloke for something he'd said about that Doffie.'

'I see.' Gina felt sick, it was as though the bottom had dropped out of her world. Billy must really be in love with the girl to fight over her.

'Come on, have your tea and then get off to bed. Sleep on it all, you'll sort it out in the morning.'

Doris was tucking her shawl around her shoulders and pushing her knitting into her bag. 'I think I'll be off home, but I'll come in and see you tomorrow and you can tell me if you want anything doing.' She put her hand on Gina's shoulder. 'Perhaps you're better off without 'im, love — been a holy terror in his time, what with prison and running off with married women an' now this trouble over a common old flossie. You stick with that lovely Thomas; he may be a bit quiet like, but he's a good 'un and you can depend on him.'

When Doris had gone, Gina closed her eyes wearily, leaning back in the chair. Doris had spoken a great deal of sense, for Thomas was a good man and Billy had proved himself unreliable, a fool for a pretty face. And yet even as she told herself not to be as foolish as him, she knew that she loved Billy Gray and nothing would ever change that love.

CHAPTER TWENTY-EIGHT

The skies of Paris were filled with clear bright sunshine that threw a deep blackness between the buildings, making patterns in the narrow streets and alleyways. Katie sat in the room at the top of the old house, wearing only her shift for she was wearied of the heat in the dusty room in the roof of the building.

She was low in spirits, for she had hoped by now to be back home in Sweyn's Eye. But by the time she had made the journey across the sea to be with Mark, he had not only recovered from his sickness but had found himself a job in a clothing factory.

He was working all day through to late evening and though he was cheerful in spirit, Katie knew that the job was dull and unrewarding. All he did each day was to carry bales of garments from the factory to the vans waiting in the street outside and sometimes his back was bruised with so much lifting.

She sighed softly, knowing that her mind was made up and that when he returned this evening she would ask him to go home. They had only one room — sharing a privy and the use of the kitchen. Whatever efforts she had made to improve the look of the place proved fruitless, for not even bright cushions and curtains could hide the peeling paint on the walls and the great cracks in the ceiling. And always there was the lovely Thérèse watching Mark with eyes bright with love.

Katie felt near to tears now as she stretched out restlessly on the sagging bed, enduring the heat with bad grace. She wanted her home, the greenness of the grass, the soft rain that fell over folding hills. She longed for good nourishing *cawl*, soup made from Welsh mutton with whole baby carrots and shredded cabbage that remained crisp between the teeth. And more, she wanted her mammy and daddy and the noise of her brothers around her.

As the shadows lengthened and the air grew cooler, Katie rose from the bed and drew on a soft cotton frock. She sighed heavily, knowing she must go out into the streets which seemed to retain the heat of the sun, for she needed bread for the evening meal.

After the silence of her room, the babble of voices in the small shop almost hidden in a back street was like a physical blow. Katie found that she was becoming tongue-tied; knowing nothing of the French language, she could communicate with no one and her sense of loneliness was intensified. She pointed to one of the long, thin loaves that jutted from a huge basket and carefully counted out the foreign money. She invariably made a mistake and the scrupulously honest woman behind the counter with her hair clipped up at the back of her head always took great pains to give her the correct change.

When she was outside once more, she breathed deeply of the cooler air. She was later than usual, for the sun was dying and longer shadows crept between huddled buildings. She had imagined it was always hot in France, but to her surprise she had learned that sometimes the weather turned chilly just as it did at home.

Rounding the corner, she saw a couple hand in hand and in that moment her feelings were crystallized; she and Mark were apart for too much of the time and when he did come home, he was so tired that all he wanted to do was to fall into bed and sleep. Their marriage was being eroded and the days that should be filled with love and laughter were spent working out figures on sheets of paper. What good was money if the making of it drove a wedge between them?

On an impulse, she entered a large dark cave of a shop and bought a bottle of wine. She had no idea it if was a

349

good wine, but she and Mark would drink it together and they would talk, really talk, for the first time since she arrived.

She waited for him impatiently and when he came in she went into his arms, resting her head against the warmth of his body.

'Hey, what's all this in honour of?' He looked round at the candle-lit room and the glasses on the table and a smile tilted the corners of his mouth. 'It isn't our anniversary, is it?'

'Sure, it's crazy you are and us practically still on our honeymoon.' She pushed him away. 'Go and wash now, you smell of cotton and lime.'

The wine soothed them both and leaning forward, Mark caught her hand in his. 'You're very beautiful, Mrs Evans — have I ever told you that?'

She slipped to the floor and rested her head on his knee. Absently his hand stroked her hair and for a moment she felt despairing, sensing that he was far away from her. And then she raised her face to his and looked up into his eyes.

'You say you love me, Mark me darlin', but sure there's no better time than the present to prove it!'

He took her in his arms and she clung to him eagerly, feeling love surge through her. He was her man, her husband and nothing mattered so long as they were together.

It was but a few paces to the bed and there Mark set her down gently, his face shadowed and strangely unfamiliar in the candlelight.

'I love you, Mark,' she whispered against his mouth and his hold tightened.

'And I love you — never forget it, my lovely Katie.' He smoothed back her hair and kissed her eyelids and she sighed softly with happiness.

'We're hardly ever close like this, do you realise that?' Her words were not intended as an accusation, but he seemed to retreat from her. She reached out for his hand and held it tightly.

'I know you're working hard to get us a nest-egg for the future, but isn't the here and now more important? We're not getting any younger, are we?' She turned in his arms so that she was lying on her stomach and staring into his eyes.

'Look, Katie, I know you want children and a family takes money — you know that better than I do.'

She was suddenly huffy. 'If you're talking about Mammy having a lot of us kids, then be careful, for we're Catholics and follow the rulings of our church. In any case, my father kept us fed and clothed even if we didn't have a posh house.'

'All right, I didn't mean anything. I was just trying to make you see things my way.'

'Well then, you just try to see things *my* way for a change.' Katie sat up and drew her blouse around her shoulders. 'I sit in here all day by myself and then at night you're too tired to even talk to me.' She climbed from the bed and stood staring at him. 'And I've forgotten what it's like to make love with you . . . I've become a nun over the last weeks and I don't like it, Mark.'

He groaned. 'Is it too much to ask that I have some peace when I get home from slogging my guts out all day? And why don't you try to make friends, get talking to people — you might find they're very kind and generous.'

'Oh, I see, I just start spouting French like a native, do I? For that's what it would take for me to be able to make friends. She turned away from him and doused the candles with angry jabs of her fingers. 'Well, I'll tell you this, Mark Evans, I'm not staying here and that's final! I'm going to pack my bags and leave for home first thing in the morning — so put that in your pipe and smoke it!'

She couldn't even run away to hide her tears for there was nowhere to go except the street, so she climbed into bed and turned her back on him, her nerve-endings alive to Mark's every movement.

After a few moments, he turned and took her in his arms and she clung to him, burying her face in the warmth of his neck. She closed her eyes, tasting his mouth as love ran pure through her veins. When he touched her breasts,

351

caressing her urgently, almost with a sense of desperation, she pressed herself against him more from the need to be close to him than from any feelings of sensuality.

She ran her hands over the smoothness of his shoulders and down his spine to the curve of his buttocks. But something was wrong; he was moving away from her, turning away with his face towards the wall.

'I'm sorry, Katie, I don't know what it is. I'm too tired or perhaps the wine . . .' His voice trailed away and she felt she should reassure him.

'It's all right,' she said in a whisper, 'I understand.' But she didn't; it seemed to her as if she had been rejected, had suddenly become undesirable to him. She fell back against her pillows, her eyes hot and dry, despair overwhelming her. And when she heard the soft sound of his breathing and knew he had fallen asleep so easily, unaware of her pain, then the tears came and with them the resolve that tomorrow she *would* leave France behind her for good.

In the morning, Mark rose up from bed and prepared for work as usual. Katie sat up against the pillows watching him as she did every morning, drinking him in so that she could bear the loneliness of the day. But no more . . .

'I meant what I said.' Her voice was calm and Mark stared at her questioningly. 'I'm going home today, I can't bear it here any longer.'

He looked harassed as he drew on his coat. 'Please, Katie, don't start a row now — I haven't even got time to eat any breakfast. We'll discuss it tonight.'

'Like we did last night: I say I want to go home and you say we can't. Sorry, Mark, the time for discussion is past.'

He crossed the room and pressed his lips to her cheeks and suddenly she grasped his face in both hands. 'Can't you even kiss me properly now? Has that place made a eunuch out of you?' Appalled by her own words, she fell back against the pillow and silently, Mark left the room.

She half-climbed out of bed to call him back, but then she sighed softly — what was the use? She washed and dressed and sat staring at the shadowy room, for the sunlight never entered it.

'Mark, my darlin', I love you but I have to go,' she whispered into the lonely silence. Later, she packed her small bag with her few possessions and wondered if she should leave him a note? But why? He would know where she had gone.

Katie opened the tin box where Mark kept the money and took out only enough for her fare home. Let him keep his savings, for they were all he would have.

She left the apartment building without a backward glance; it was not and never could be home and she would certainly not miss anything about it. On the street, she saw Thérèse staring at her oddly.

'You going away, madam?' Thérèse said breathlessly. Her eyes were wide and eager and Katie felt a flash of anger followed by a sense of hopelessness.

'Yes, I'm going home, it seems that Paris . . . and you . . . have beaten me,' Katie said quietly.

'I don't understand,' Thérèse said quickly, her cheeks suddenly pink.

Katie bit her lip and turned away. 'Oh, I think you do.' As she walked towards the railway station, her one crumb of comfort was the knowledge that by this time tomorrow she would be back in Sweyn's Eye.

*   *   *

Mark felt bone weary by the time his shift came to an end. He was resented by some of the men because he was a foreigner taking a job that a Frenchman could be doing. He could understand this but as a result of the prejudice the foreman felt compelled to give Mark the dirtiest and heaviest jobs in the factory.

As he brushed the dust from his hands, Mark thought back unhappily to the events of the morning. He could see that Katie was upset and he didn't blame her — what good was a husband too tired even to make love to his wife? He understood a little of what she must be feeling; she was so alone and so lost in the strangeness of a new place. But why go home to face a life with no job and no money coming in — were they to starve then? Women could be so impractical.

His step was slow and dispirited as he walked back home, if one room could be called a home. He often thought longingly of the town where he had been born. Even though Sweyn's Eye stank of the copper works, there was the lovely side of the place in the folding hills and the beautiful curving bay. There the rain was soft, the breezes coming in off the sea tangy with salt. A man could take time off to fish in the river or simply walk over the hills, but this France was more like slavery than living.

He mounted the stairs slowly, his feet aching and the bones of his spine feeling bruised and crushed. Katie could just be right, he thought: perhaps even work down the pits couldn't be this bad and at least he would be amongst his own kind.

The room was dark and empty and for a moment, Mark pictured it as it had been the night before. The candlelight had shone on the wine-glasses and Katie's eager eyes had begged for his approval. Suddenly, his gut melted with love for her.

He went to the cupboard beside the bed and opened it. Her clothes were gone, so were her shoes and the soft bag she had used to carry her belonging. He hardly needed to look in the tin — he knew that she would have taken only what she needed to get her back home. Sinking down on the bed, he put his hands over this face and then he was crying like a little child . . .

It did not take him long to make his decision. Quickly he packed his own few clothes and went to see the landlady. Her heavy jowls quivered with indignation when he told her he was leaving and somehow she made him understand that she would need a month's payment in place of the notice he should have given. He counted out some money and ignored her angry words as she saw there was just two weeks rent. When he kissed Thérèse her eyes were full

354

of tears and for a moment he held her close. Then he left the ugly building behind him and strode into the street.

* * *

Katie had been waiting on the quayside for hours, for the ship was due to sail on the evening tide. She watched the sailors busy with ropes, calling instructions to each other in the strange-sounding French tongue and she knew that she had done the right thing — she was going home.

She shivered a little in the breeze coming in off the sea, the waves rising dark and ugly against the harbour wall. Wastage thrown from the ship lifted high on the water, an invitation to the calling seagulls which screeched overhead. She was lonely and afraid, missing Mark so badly that she ached.

Then there was a sudden sound of footsteps coming towards her and she looked up, her heart pounding.

'Mark!' For a long moment she studied him, noting the luggage he carried and realising that he was coming with her. She held out her hand and slowly he entwined his fingers in hers and they were together just as they should be.

The *Terra Neuva* was a graceful, three-masted barque. She dipped and bowed in the swelling seas, the rising wind singing in her rigging. Katie held on tightly to Mark's hand as he helped her along the gangplank and on to the swaying deck. He smiled at her reassuringly, but she saw him glance up at the darkening sky with anxious eyes.

'Will the weather stay fine, do you think?' Katie asked nervously and Mark shook his head.

'I don't know but don't worry — they're used to all sorts of weather, these chaps.' He led her below and they sat on the narrow seat within the cabin, staring at each other as though neither of them could believe they were really going home, together.

CHAPTER TWENTY-NINE

The summer heat brought days of splendour, with the fields of Ram's Tor rich with corn that was splashed here and there with the red of poppies. The cattle thrived and even the foolish sheep showed some sense, remaining within the confines of the farm instead of running heedlessly over the cliff-top to the sea below. And Catherine felt her child grow and flourish within her.

'Morgan, come and put your hand here and feel how he kicks.' Catherine could scarcely contain her happiness; she felt it radiated from every pore of her being as Morgan, smiling, laid his hands on her. As if in response to the warmth of his fingers, the child moved again and Morgan smiled and kissed Catherine's mouth.

'There's a real hellion in there, my girl; need a firm hand he will, if I'm any judge.' He held her close and Catherine wound her arms around his waist, closing her eyes, cherishing the moment, for once she left the breakfast-time untidiness of the little kitchen, she would be engulfed in work and so would Morgan come to that.

A shadow fell over her happiness. It was the one thorn in her flesh that the villagers of the Mumbles had turned awkward, ignoring her in the shops, falling silent whenever she appeared, giving the impression that she and her swollen belly had been the subject of the hushed conversation.

'What's wrong, love?' Morgan lifted her face up to his, sensitive to her mood as always. 'Not still worrying because the foolish villagers won't talk, are you?'

'They may be foolish,' she answered, 'but if they carry

356

on ignoring us we shall get no help with the harvest. And then how shall we manage?'

'We shall get your father to come up from Port Eynon,' Morgan said firmly. 'He seems the sort of man who would believe it a sin to let good corn go bad!'

Catherine sighed. 'I suppose you're right, but for now we'd better do some work. I'll see to the milking before old Betty and her two helpers arrive.'

'Right then and I'll shift some of those potatoes from the lower field. They look fine and healthy enough, don't they?'

Catherine nodded, 'Aye, they do.' She wound an apron around her waist, grimacing at her size. 'I'll need a sheet from the bed if I get any bigger!' Then she laughed, suddenly happy again. It was strange how her moods fluctuated between the heights and depths of emotion.

'Our William is coming up to help out this morning. You'll need him in the fields — backbreaking work, picking potatoes mind. Get on out with you now and make a start, or half the day will have gone.'

Morgan moved towards the door. '*Duw*, did ever any man have such a bossy woman as I've got for a wife?'

When he had gone, Catherine went into the sheds and saw that the newly calved cows were heavy with milk. For the first time it occurred to her that she had never stopped to wonder what a cow felt like when deprived of its calf. But she was being fanciful and silly; cows were there to yield milk and their calves were sold in the market as stores to other farmers for finishing.

She worked solidly through the morning: feeding the hens, baking bread, cleaning the small house until at last she sat exhausted in her chair. Tomorrow she would have to bring in the standing bowls of cream to churn into butter for selling in the market. The income from butter and eggs was small enough, but it did come in regularly and she frugally saved the money in a tin box under the shelf in the pantry. It was her 'rainy day' fund, not much good if the crop failed but at least it would buy them a new sow for the boar was getting restless alone.

She sighed and looked around her. The grate gleamed with blacklead and the brass shone because of her diligent rubbing with a mixture of ash and water. She closed her eyes, knowing that soon she would have to prepare a meal — Morgan would be sure to come in starving, as he always did these days. Filling out, he was now. Thin when he came to Ram's Tor first; worn down by the ravages of the war, his face had borne small lines of tension.

She had seen the same look on David's face as it shadowed her happiness to think of him now when she had not done so in months. Rising, she entered the coolness of the pantry, yet thoughts of her dead husband persisted even as she tried to push them from her mind. What would he have thought of her and Morgan, of their love made legal by the minister with the long face of disapproval down in Oystermouth?

Surely he would have understood? David was part of her past, never close to her soul but she had given him her respect. And now because it seemed she had spat on his grave by conceiving a child with another man, the villagers chose to ignore her. 'But I meant no disrespect, David,' she said into the dark marble slab of the pantry shelf as she lifted the flat round cheese.

It was then that pain cast a circle of steel round her belly and she dropped the cheese abruptly, gasping a little in fear. She backed out from the pantry and knelt upon the rag mat on the floor before the fire, clutching her swollen body. The pain receded and Catherine took a deep breath, wondering what strange things were happening to her. Experimentally she rose to her feet and found that now she moved more easily.

Placing the cheese on the table, she removed the muslin cloth and cut several slices. Set out with fresh bread and pickle, it would make an easy but nourishing meal for Morgan.

But when the pain came again, Catherine realised that her baby was going to be born several weeks too early. She looked around her as though seeking help, but the silence was hostile and frightening. Where were Gladys and

William? They should be here soon, so there was no need to be afraid, was there? And yet the hands of the clock moved mercilessly onward, the pains growing more forceful.

Catherine, telling herself to be calm, found that in between the contractions she was all right. She pushed the kettle onto the flames — hot water was always needed at the time of a birth. She thought of the calves and lambs she had seen come into the world and told herself that if animals could accomplish the job with such efficiency, then so could she, but her hands were trembling and her mouth was dry.

She went to the door and stared out into the sunshine, but the horizon wavering before her bore no sign of human life. It was as though she was the only person in the entire world.

When the pain gripped again, with it came the rush of her waters, which told her the birth was imminent. She crouched in the doorway, her eyes frantically searching the fields for some sign of Morgan, but there was nothing but the calling of the seagulls wheeling over the sea.

She moved cautiously back into the kitchen and poured water into an enamel bowl; it seemed the only one to help her baby come into the world would be herself. Yet fear dragged at her as she bent forward, holding her swollen belly and groaning through her teeth as the circle of steel closed even tighter. She wanted to scream out in panic, but what was the use when there was no one to hear her cries?

Catherine took the bowl up into the bedroom and put a fresh clean white sheet — smelling of soap and sunlight — over the patchwork quilt, just as another contraction caught her. She moaned softly, bending over the bed, clinging to the brass rail and fighting her fear. Birth was a perfectly natural event, she told herself fiercely, so she must not struggle against the pains.

She lay on the sheet and turned on to her side, wondering if she was doing the right thing, but the position was unnatural and she knelt up instead, holding on to the bedrail for support. It seemed that her bones were being dragged apart; she hurt everywhere, but most of all low in her stomach.

Time lost its meaning and her head felt light, her senses blunted to anything but the need to bear down. She growled low in her throat, feeling she would be torn asunder as sweat ran into her eyes. Surely it shouldn't be taking so long? She began to cry, silly useless tears which ran along her cheeks and mingled with sweat that beaded her face. Unable to bear it any more, she put back her head and wailed like a demented creature, but there was no help, no release from her agony.

And then she felt as though she was on fire and her body took over from her mind, wresting the child from her. Her screams died to a low moaning which sounded as if it came from a distance. Dark clouds veiled her mind, yet a great strength flowed into her as with a last effort, she thrust her baby into the world.

'I have a son,' she said softly in wonder and as though in response to her voice, the child began to wail.

For a few moments Catherine simply lay still, her son resting sweetly heavy against her breast. The pain had gone and a great calm seemed to flow through her. She breathed deeply, grateful that she had prepared for the birth.

Struggling into a sitting position, she tore strips from the clean linen she had placed on the bed. The cloth was old, well-washed and ripped easily. Carefully, her hands trembling, she tied the umbilical cord. Two separate strips of linen about an inch apart she fastened as tightly as she could around the cord, to prevent bleeding from herself or her child. Then she took up the scissors and here her nerve almost failed her.

She stared down into the small face, screwed up tightly with eyes puffy and closed. What if she made a mistake when she cut the cord that joined him to her? But it must be done and taking a deep breath, Catherine severed the cord with a decisive movement of her hands.

Holding her breath, she watched for a moment and her son still wriggled and cried in her lap, none the worse for her ministrations. She wrapped him in a sheet and put him on the bed at her side, for now she needed to see to herself.

360

It was some time later when the door downstairs opened and after a moment, heavy footsteps sounded on the stairs. Gladys entered the room, her mouth wide in surprise.

'Good God in Heaven!' She came towards the bed, scarcely able to believe her eyes. 'Can I hold the little darling?'

'It's a boy,' Catherine said proudly as she put him into Glady's waiting arms.

Gladys sniffed a little, blinking rapidly against her tears. After a moment, she went to the door and called down the stairs.

'William, come here! I want you to find Morgan for me, there's a good boy.'

He came rushing into the bedroom, his face creasing into a smile as he saw the crying infant.

'It's a boy,' Gladys said proudly. She paused to take a deep breath. 'But let Catherine tell Morgan all there is to know and you mind your tongue.'

William nodded, but paused to reach out a finger which the baby grasped immediately. 'Look, Mam, he likes me!' he cried in delight.

'Get on with you and find the father and don't be long about it. Now tell me everything,' Gladys said as she returned the baby to Catherine's arms. 'You did well mind,' she said in awe. 'The midwife couldn't have tied the cord any neater.'

'Will the baby be all right though, Gladys?' Catherine asked worriedly. 'He's a bit before his time and he's very small.'

'Nah! Perfectly all right, he is. Got your dates wrong — missed your courses earlier than you thought, I expect, 'cos that boy's an eight-pounder any day!'

There was a sudden banging downstairs and Gladys got to her feet, winking at Catherine.

'I'll leave you alone to tell your Morgan the good news.' She bundled up the sheets. 'I'll wash these and then everything will be neat and shipshape.'

Morgan had eyes for no one but his wife when he entered the room. He was unaware of Gladys going out and closing the door as he came to the bedside and put his hands

361

on Catherine's cheeks, kissing her mouth tenderly.

He sat down beside the bed, aware of Catherine' weariness. 'There's beautiful you are,' he said softly.

She reached out and drew back the bedclothes, her eye warm with tears. 'Aren't you curious about your son, then?

In wonder Morgan stared at the infant swaddled in a multitude of sheets, the tiny face rosy and serene. He ben forward almost reverently and kissed the petal-soft ski and when he looked up at Catherine, his eyes were warm

'What are we going to call him, Morgan?' Catherine asked gently. 'It's up to you to give our first-born a name

Morgan did not hesitate. 'John, after my father?'

'That suits him,' Catherine said at once. She held out he hand to Morgan and he took it, kissing each finger in turn

'I go cold thinking of you giving birth to our son alone. should have come back to the house and kept an eye on you

'Oh, so that devil William talked, did he?' Catherine said, smiling. 'Remind me to give him a box round the ears will you?'

'He didn't tell me we had a son, only that when he and Gladys arrived everything was over and you were tucked up in bed neat as a flea in a rag mat. You are a wonderfu woman, Catherine, have I ever told you that?'

There was a knock on the door and Gladys came in with a tea-tray balanced on her plump arm. 'A hot drink for the new mam,' she said, 'and for the dad too, if he's good.'

She took the baby away from Catherine and tucked him into the wooden crib which had held both her own sons

'No spoiling now, let the boy sleep a bit and you Catherine — drink your fill, for you'll need good milk to feed such a hearty child.'

Catherine had not even begun to imagine what mother-hood would mean to her. She stared longingly towards the crib with a rush of emotion, wanting her son in her arm: for they were suddenly empty without him.

'You look very tired, love,' Morgan said gently. He glanced at Gladys, who was bending over the crib. 'She'l need to rest for a while, won't she? After all, I've got to

362

have her fit again as soon as possible, for what would I do without my little farmer?'

'Aye and she needs some sleep now; birthing a babba — especially on your own takes the stuffing out of you, so go back to the fields and get that William to go with you out of the way.'

Morgan rose to his feet with a sigh of mock resignation. 'I'd better do what the old dragon tells me,' he said loudly. 'Worse than a nagging mother-in-law, is that Gladys.' He kissed Catherine and smoothed back her hair. 'See you tonight — and do as you're told now.'

When he had gone, Catherine lay back on her pillows feeling weary but filled with joy. After a moment Gladys sat next to her and took her hand.

'A few words of advice, girl,' she said as she smiled at Catherine. 'Don't go making the mistake of putting all your attention on that Babba there in the crib, give some thought to your man as well. It would be sad if the first-born child should come between a man and his wife, which sometimes happens, mind.'

Catherine smiled, though her throat was constricted with tears. 'Gladys,' she said softly, 'has anybody ever told you what a wise and wonderful woman you are?'

'Another thing,' Gladys brushed the praise aside, 'on the third day, when the milk flows so do the tears.'

Catherine was bewildered. 'What on earth do you mean? There's ominous that sounds.'

'Ah well, it's only a warning. A mother gets to be sad on the third day after the birth — no one knows the reason why, but if you are told about it then it's not half so bad, see?'

'All right,' Catherine said, smiling, 'but I feel really happy and so wonderful that I can't imagine ever feeling sad again.'

'That's as may be,' Gladys straightened the sheets, 'but don't say I didn't warn you, my girl!'

And Gladys was proved right, for Catherine suffered great pain with the engorgement of her breasts, her milk being too plentiful. Gladys promptly brought in a basket of beans from the garden and crushed them to a floury substance.

'There, we shall put this all over your poor old lilies and the flour will take away the soreness.'

Catherine, though in pain, laughed up at Gladys who was holding the bowl over her. ' "Lilies", that's a funny word for them and they never did feel less like flowers!'

'Laugh you, but this is an old remedy for soreness caused by the milk. Let me put it on you carefully now and after a bit, you'll begin to feel better, I'm telling you.'

Strangely enough Catherine did feel the pain easing as she lay back on the pillow with only her nightgown covering her, for she could not bear the weight of the blankets to touch her breasts. And after a time, she closed her eyes and slept.

* * *

Morgan was filled with delight at the perfection of his son. John was strong of feature, masculine already — and yet with the look of his mother about him, for the boy's hair was golden like ripe corn, the colour of Catherine's hair.

Catherine, watching them together, knew that John would grow up to love and respect Morgan without the fear which had soured her relationship with her own father. Parents should be close to their offspring, not make enemies of them. And yet now, Catherine had a glimmering of an understanding of the difficult task with which her father had been faced in bringing up daughters on his own.

'When shall we have the christening?' Morgan laughed at Catherine's look of surprise. 'We must have him properly christened in the chapel where we were married.'

'Aye,' Catherine said dryly, 'where we were very recently married.' She looked up into Morgan's face. 'We'd only be giving the villagers more room to talk.'

'To hell with that!' Morgan said shortly. 'No gossiping villager is going to stop me having my boy named in the proper manner by a minister of the chapel.' His face relaxed into a smile. 'However po-faced he might be!'

'Will we invite my father and my sisters to come up from Port Eynon?' Catherine asked uncertainly and Morgan nodded.

'Oh, aye, we must have all the relations and friends too — we still have friends in Sweyn's Eye, mind.'

'Well, you do.' Catherine replied, 'and most welcome. I'll be only too glad to have smiling faces around again, me.'

'That's settled, then. I'll walk down and see the minister in the morning and you write a little note to your dad.' Morgan leaned forward and kissed her gently and Catherine clung to him, her head buried in his neck.

'I love you, Morgan,' she said, 'and I need you more than I ever did.' She closed her eyes against her tears, telling herself not to be so soft.

He stroked her hair. 'I'm a hell of a lucky man.' He moved away from her, his back towards her and she knew that he too was moved by the moment; only one more thing she asked: that Morgan love her as much as she loved him.

During the afternoon, she spent an hour or so writing out a list of people whom she would invite to the christening. There would be her own family, of course, though Catherine felt sure that her father at least might flatly refuse to come. But she could rely on Gladys and William, she thought warmly.

She was not sure whom Morgan wanted to come from Sweyn's Eye. He would doubtless ask the O'Connor family, for they had been good to him and his father, but she didn't really know if there would be anyone else. Her hand trembled as she wrote down the O'Connor name, for this was Honey's family, the girl Morgan had once loved. But that was a long time ago, and she was being foolish.

As Catherine settled herself down to write, from outside the window came the hum of bees drunk with nectar and the feel of the soft scented breeze whispering through the net curtains . . . and she was content.

Once Catherine was out of childbed, the christening was quickly arranged. It was agreed that Gladys would cook a huge ham and garnish the dish with chopped vegetables and herbs. There would be lavish amounts of *Teisen lap* as well as fresh fruits and there would be dandelion pop for the children. The adults would be served home-made ale and wine, with the more abstemious among them falling back on a good strong cup of tea.

The morning was exquisite, crystal clear, with the sea below Ram's Tor azure hazing to palest violet against the coast of Devonshire. Catherine had dressed the baby in the clothing provided by Gladys. There was the long cream flannel coat which tied around the baby's body and folded up at the foot, making a loose bag which covered John entirely. On top of this was a gown of softest linen pin-tucked and embroidered, with a matching bonnet. And Catherine laughed into her son's face, which seemed screwed up in disgust at the fuss she was making over him.

Catherine took just as much care over her own appearance. She found her new slimness intriguing and wanted to please Morgan, so she wore her best blouse and a soft summer skirt. Finally, she brushed her hair until it shone, tying it back loosely with ribbons.

The light in his eyes when he saw her with John in her arms brought a blush of pleasure to her cheeks. She smiled at him and he folded her in his arms, just for a moment. But then he was smiling and leading her out to the horse and cart, helping her up into the seat.

'My wife must be the loveliest girl in the whole of South Wales,' he said brightly.

The chapel was virtually empty. Gladys sat in the front pew with William at her side and across the aisle was Catherine's father seated alone. She felt a knot of pain that her son's christening was to be witnessed by only a handful of people; she had realised that the O'Connor family would not be present at the chapel, for they were good Catholics, but she had hoped her sisters might come up from Port Eynon.

The ceremony was quickly over and when Catherine emerged into the bright sunshine once more she saw that some of the villagers were standing watching her and they were bristling with hostility. She thought she heard the word 'whore' but then Morgan was pushing his way through them and making a path for her. A woman in a striped apron hissed at her and Catherine, undaunted, stared back at her.

'Got a snake's tongue as well as his voice, have you?' she said sharply. Then she climbed up into the well of the cart and seated herself with the baby cradled close to her breasts.

'Ought to be sent to the workhouse, you,' the woman said, her eyes flashing. 'Respectable folk we are and don't hold with the widow of a hero falling with child and her husband not cold in his grave.'

Gladys moved forward, her plump face red. 'Shut your mouth, *Miss* Dower, for I know a thing or two about a woman not very far from here — living with a man and pretending they wed up in England, which is a lot of rubbish!' The woman's eyes bulged but, red of face, she retreated into the crowd.

Morgan whipped the horse into movement, his face grim. 'If they had been men, I would have battered the lot of them,' he said through his teeth. 'For spite, you can't better a woman who has sinned herself!'

'Take no notice,' Catherine said, though her cheeks were hot. 'Come on, Morgan, let's enjoy the day; we musn't let anyone spoil it for us.'

As Morgan took the road between the rocks up towards Ram's Tor, Catherine hugged the baby close, promising him silently that nothing and no one would ever hurt him.

The O'Connor family were waiting on the grass outside the farmhouse and Catherine looked at them with mixed feelings. The girls, growing now into young ladies, might have been her own sisters; they each had the same shower of bright hair which crowned her own head. From this family had come Honey, Morgan's first love . . . and once again she felt a dart of jealousy which was absurd and wicked of her.

But almost immediately she was swept up in the warmth

of Stella O'Connor's welcome. The Irishwoman took John from her arms and stared down at him in wonder. Then she looked from her husband and back to the infant in her arms and even Catherine felt awed at the resemblance between Brendan O'Connor and her own son. But as they were not related by blood, it must be simply one of life's coincidences.

And yet Stella appeared to hug John to her almost as though he was a part of her family. Smiling, Catherine held out her arms and reluctantly, Stella put the baby back into them.

'Sure and he's a fine boy,' she said in hushed tones, 'Ti lucky you are — I never did make a son.'

Gladys appeared as if from nowhere, her cheeks flushed '*Duw*, I swear that hill gets steeper every time I walk up it!' She leaned closer to Catherine. 'Didn't let them bitches down at the chapel upset you, did you? They're not all like that, just the spiteful few who got room to look at their own backyards if you ask me.'

'It's all right, Gladys,' Catherine smiled. 'There's no point in my worrying about them — got enough with my own . . . and talking of which, here comes my father.'

'Oh, well, I'll get the kettle on to boil.' Gladys permitted herself a smile. 'Though I think I might try to tempt your dad with my home-made brew — blow your head off, it will, though it tastes innocent enough!'

Catherine braced herself to face her father and Phillip Carver looked down at her, his mouth a thin line in his beard. His glance rested on the boy in her arms and Catherine understood the reason for his being at the christening: he was curious to see his grandson.

'Where are Connie and the rest of my sisters?' she asked in a small voice, but her father did not look at her as he replied.

'I thought it best if I came alone — there's a lot of work to be done and the girls can't spare the time, Catherine.'

'I see,' She held John close to her, aware of her father's scrutiny of her son.

'He's very fair, like you.' There was a note of disapproval

368

in his voice. 'The rest of the children are dark like me and I had prayed that the boy would follow my side of the family.'

Catherine forced a smile. 'You can't order those things Father, just thank God that he's a strong healthy boy.'

'Yes, indeed.' Phillip Carver seemed to hesitate. 'I shall hold him for a moment and give him my blessing.'

'Of course.' Catherine gave her son into her father's arms and watched in surprise as Phillip Carver's face seemed to soften from stern set lines into what was almost a smile.

'He's a fine boy, all right, and a good weight on him too — grow up sturdy, he will, if I'm not mistaken.'

Catherine felt her throat burn with tears. It seemed her father was human behind his hard exterior and impulsively she touched his arm.

'Please come up to see us as often as you can, for I'd like John to grow up knowing his grandfather better perhaps than I ever knew him.'

Gladys, who was busy handing out plates of food, had entrusted William with the ale and wine set out on a long trestle table just outside the farmhouse door. He poured with a liberal hand, enjoying himself hugely, Brendan O'Connor being his most frequent visitor.

Catherine saw Stella chide her husband, her face pinched as she fought a losing battle, for Brendan was a man fond of his drink. Phillip Carver's face had resumed its stern, set look and he stared at Catherine for a long moment before placing his cap on his head.

'I think it's time I left.' His tone rang with disapproval as he stared disdainfully across at Brendan O'Connor, who was once again refilling his mug. 'Some people have no self-control.'

He made no attempt to lower his voice and the words fell into that sudden silence which occurs from time to time when people are together in a crowd.

'Are you talking about me by any chance?' Brendan asked belligerently. He weaved his way across the grass and Catherine instinctively held the baby closer.

As Brendan lurched towards Catherine, Phillip Carver

369

held out a restraining hand.

'Be careful of my grandson, you lout!' His tone was strong and fierce, his eyes alight with anger; Brendan looked at him for a long time and then began to laugh.

'Well, Mr High-and-Mighty Carver, that's where you're wrong! I have news for you: the boy *isn't* your grandson!'

Stella hurriedly crossed the grass to be at her husband's side. 'Come away with you, Brendan, let things be as they are.' She tugged at his arm, but the Irishman stood firm.

'You are talking absolute gibberish!' Phillip Carver said disdainfully. 'I would advise you to get a good strong cup of tea and sober up a bit, for this is a christening and not an Irish wake.'

'Aw, looking down on us Irish now, is it?' Brendan said angrily. His face was flushed and his eyes seemed to bulge from his head. 'Well, just let me tell you something then.'

'*No!*' The cry came from Stella, but Brendan pushed her aside, determined to say his piece.

'That little blonde-haired girl there, Catherine — and sure isn't that a good old Irish name — well, she is my child, fruit of my loins not yours.' He swayed a little, pushing aside Stella's attempts to restrain him and smiling as he looked at the baby.

'Can't you see the likeness, man. or are you deliberately being blind? You must have guessed something was wrong a long time ago when your little wife stayed out all one long summer's night. I took her to me that night . . . ' He paused, his eyes vague, then went on. 'At one of the fairs I met her — and she all pretty and dainty and coming up fresh from the country. Only once it was and she very ashamed, sure enough, but then this girl was born nine months later and looking like the O'Connors as anyone with eyes can see.'

Catherine felt as though the world had turned a somersault before her very eyes. The grass tilted towards the sky and she would have fallen if Morgan had not appeared at her side, his arm warm and protective around her.

Phillip Carver stared at Catherine and then at the baby

370

in her arms and lastly, his gaze focused in hate on Brendan O'Connor.

'May the devil take you for the harm you've done!' His voice shook as he turned and strode away.

'Go after him, Morgan! Please try to stop him, we must talk. Tell him he's my father — the only one I'll ever know.'

'Gladys,' Morgan called, 'take Catherine into the house and look after her, I shan't be long.' He turned to look at Stella, shaking his head. 'Get him home, there's a good girl.'

Catherine sat in the kitchen and in spite of the warmth of the day and the fire glowing in the grate, she was shivering.

'Is it true, Gladys?' she asked in a small voice and the older woman took the baby from her arms and put him in the crib, tucking a shawl around the small sleeping boy.

'I don't know what to say to you, *merchi*. The Irishman is right enough, that boy is the spit out of his mouth. You too, come to that — all those little O'Connor girls look like they're your sisters. But I don't know the truth of it, probably none of us ever will and do it matter much now?'

Catherine shook her head. 'I don't know what to think, Gladys, I just feel so tired and bewildered.'

'Look,' Gladys took her hand, 'kinship is a funny thing. Take us now, not blood of each other's blood, but I love you like a daughter all the same. Forget all this upset and go on up to bed. Try to sleep a bit and it will sort itself out in good time.'

Catherine nodded her head wearily, knowing in her heart that Phillip Carver would not return to the farmhouse, perhaps not ever again. She would do as Gladys suggested; she would climb into bed, pull the sheet over her head and hide away from the world.

371

CHAPTER THIRTY

The long hot days of summer brought forth a profusion
of flowers: roses abounded in the hedgerows and, in the
well-kept gardens of the big houses on the western slopes
of Sweyn's Eye, flag irises waved delicate purple petals at
the sun. And in the fields of Ram's Tor Farm the corn was
turning gold. The summer had given a bounty of plenty
to the land, but it had also given scarlet fever.

The epidemic spread rapidly through the ill-ventilated
courts and narrow cobbled streets of the poorer quarters
of the town. Doors and windows were closed in fearful
superstition of miasmas entering the house. And in Green
Hill the poor Irish suffered.

Stella O'Connor had believed she had had enough of
grief, for had she not given her eldest daughter to the
ravages of war? She had endured the pain of seeing her
sweet girl laid to rest, knowing that there was her pride
in Honey's bravery to sustain her.

She had experienced the hurt of her husband's peccadilloes
in the past and had come to terms with Brendan's intem-
perate nature. And her final humiliation had been to
witness the scene between her husband and Phillip Carver
at the christening of Morgan Lloyd's baby.

But fate held yet another blow, for now there was the
sickness that provoked a red angry rash accompanied by
excess heat in the body, a feverishness that was frightening
to witness.

It was her youngest girl, Maureen, who fell ill first;
she was vomiting and her ears were giving her pain. And
then the dreaded widespread rash covered her body.

Maureen was quickly followed to her sick-bed by her sisters, but their symptoms were less severe. Stella had been visited almost at once by Father O'Flynn who had helped greatly by offering advice on the way the sickness should be dealt with.

'Keep the child cool, put her away from the heat of the fire and feed her plenty of water sweetened by a small amount of honey.'

Stella was grateful for his kindliness and practical advice, since to pay for the doctor to call would be a strain on the small resources of the family. In any case, Dr Soames was working from morning till night in an attempt to contain the epidemic.

But Maureen grew worse, her fevered eyes saw monsters and snakes and other nameless horrors which caused her to cry out in the night in fear while Stella hung over her bed, grieving.

The following day the girl's tongue had turned a brilliant red and her throat was so sore she could scarcely swallow. And at last Stella could bear it no longer. She fetched her one good pair of shoes and wrapped them in paper; then, with instructions to Brendan O'Connor to care for his girls, she left the house.

She took the back roads, unwilling to let her neighbours see that she was making for the shop of Manny Cohen. The O'Connor family had never been surrounded by luxury but because Stella had taken in lodgers, there had been enough to keep a respectable house with clean linen on the beds and the smell of polish in the parlour. But now there were no lodgers; the young man who had been roomed with her had fled the streets of Green Hill at the first sign of the scarlet fever — and who could blame him?

As Stella rounded the corner into *Stryd Fach*, her heart sank for there was a queue to the doorway of the pawn-shop such as she had never seen before. Like herself, the men and woman in the crowd were carrying anonymous parcels. And all avoided each other's eyes.

'Look!' a man nearer the front called anxiously. 'Manny's

closing the door — don't want no more stuff today, go a shopful he has.'

Stella bit her lip, fear dragging at her heart and as she felt the hardness of the shoes against her side she knew that they would have little appeal for a man who was being offered good china, lace tablecloths and other precious objects which had been passed from generation to generation.

'Stella, what's wrong, my lovely?' Morgan Lloyd was standing near and in her despair she had not seen him stop beside her.

'My girls are sick, especially Maureen the youngest — 'tis the scarlet fever, like a plague it's running through the streets of Green Hill.'

When Morgan looked at the bedraggled queue of people and at the sign of the pawnbroker hanging over the shop door, all was clear to him. Stella saw him put his hand into his pocket and bring out a leather pouch.

'Let me give you this gift, Stella, there's a good woman.' Morgan drew her away from the shop, leading her into the wider street away from curious stares.

'You were good to me when my dad died, I had no one else but you then, Stella. And we shared the grief of losing Honey, so surely you won't be too proud to let me help you now?'

Stella felt the tears run down her cheeks and fall salt into her mouth; she could not help but cry, for Morgan was offering her hope. Tentatively she held out her hand and he gave her the pouch hesitatingly.

'I don't know what to say to you, Morgan — 'tis so kind of you . . . ' her voice trailed away into a whisper as he squeezed her arm encouragingly.

'Go on, you, get the doctor to see those lovely girls and they'll soon be as cheeky and bright as they ever were!'

Stella nodded and hurried away from him, fearing even now that she would be moved to return his money; she knew it had been earned by the sweat of Morgan's brow and that he was not a rich man. One long downpour of rain now would spoil his harvest. She faltered and then as she thought of her Maureen, with eyes staring in a face that was hot and dry, she forced herself on towards Canal Street to the surgery of Doctor Soames, a ray of hope beginning to flicker in her heart.

*   *   *

Paul Soames sank into the chair beside the unlit fire and allowed his head to fall back against the cushion. He was weary unto the bone and yet there was a glow of accomplishment that warmed him. He was coping well with the epidemic of scarlet fever which had its roots in the overcrowded streets of Green Hill. The sickness might spread to the boundaries of the town and beyond, it was difficult to say, but at least Paul knew that his own patients were in the main making a recovery.

He smiled as he thought of the way the deacons had come to him, led by Alfred Phillpot whose own family were sick. They had begged him to help them. Gone was the wish to punish him for conduct unbecoming to a doctor; it seemed that when death stalked the houses of the godly, they were just as afraid as any other man.

But it would do Alfred Phillpot a power of good to worry about the fever, though somehow his sort were usually the ones to escape. It was a sickness which most affected the very young and the very old and it was inevitable that there would be a few fatalities.

Paul thought of Mary Sutton and hoped she would have the sense to stay out of the heart of the town, for she had enough problems with her son Stephan as it was. The period of rest and quiet had done nothing to improve matters and it was strange that nothing could be found to indicate why the young boy was losing his sight. It could be delayed shock to the retina from the fall Stephan had suffered, but the automobile accident had occurred quite a long time ago. Of course Mary used it to berate herself, but that was out of a maternal sense of guilt.

He was used to mothers taking the blame for what their

children did, from cut knees to turning to crime. And the lengths to which a mother would go to protect her children never ceased to amaze him. But he was a doctor, he knew bodies rather than minds — and he was a hungry doctor, he knew himself ruefully. He pushed himself out of his chair and made for the kitchen, deciding he would have a bite of cheese and some bread, for he was far too tired to begin to cook anything.

His housekeeper was sick with the fever herself and he had spent a good half an hour of his precious time at her bedside, telling her how tough she was and that she was certain to make a full recovery within a few weeks. He knew nothing of the kind, but a little reassurance went a long way he had found.

Paul ate heartily, finishing up his simple meal of bread and cheese with a little wine. He needed to bath himself, but he could not face the effort of lighting the fire to heat the water and so he settled for a scrub-down in cold water, shivering a little in spite of the warmth of the evening.

He was dressed casually in a pair of trousers and a shirt open at the collar when he heard a knock on the door. Sighing with fatigue, he was at first tempted to ignore the sound, but it was repeated forcefully and he made his way to open it.

A tall dark figure stepped into his hallway, his leonine head and jutting thatch of dark hair unmistakable.

'Brandon Sutton! It took you long enough to get here, I was beginning to think you'd not received my letter.' Paul stepped back. 'Come and have a glass of wine with me — I was just relaxing after a very difficult day. You know about the epidemic, of course?'

Brandon's eyes were hostile. 'I came straight here from the station. The cabbie did say something about a fever, but I didn't think anything of it. Is it serious then?'

'Could be; it may continue to spread and then we'll be in trouble, for there are not enough doctors to go round everyone even if we call in outside help.'

'I see,' Brandon paused. 'Had I known that, I would have

kept away from the town. As it is, I can hardly go up to see Mary — not until there is no longer any risk of infection. I suppose I should thank you for informing me about my son's eye condition.'

Paul felt a mingling of embarrassment threaded through with a little apprehension. Brandon would never know how much it had cost him to write that letter, knowing that the result might be a reconciliation between Brandon and Mary.

'Please sit down, we must talk,' Paul said, handing the American a glass of wine and refilling his own. 'You've come back to her?' he asked bluntly.

Brandon nodded. 'Sure, you could say that.' He twisted the cut glass between his fingers, staring down into the redness of the wine, his black brows furrowed. 'It seems to me that a father's place is with his boy at such a time.'

'And with the boy's mother,' Paul said quietly and saw Brandon's fingers tighten on the stem of the glass.

'Ah, yes, Mary, how is she bearing up?' Brandon asked levelly. 'Have you been seeing much of her?'

'I'll be honest with you,' Paul said slowly. 'I fell in love with Mary and I would marry her tomorrow if it were possible. But — and it's a big but — she loves *you*.' He leaned forward in his chair, knowing he must make Brandon believe him, that it was the only way he could ensure Mary's happiness.

'She was devasted by that telegram which came from the War Office informing her that you were dead. She came to see me and knowing nothing of her grief, I took her in my arms.' He paused as he saw the other man's face darken and then went on quickly. 'It was the one time *and one time only*, whatever anyone else might say — and afterwards Mary bore such a great burden of guilt that she could hardly live with it. Haven't you ever done anything you've regretted afterwards?'

'Spare me the homespun philosophy,' Brandon said, but he was smiling. 'And tell me, can you put a traveller up for the night?'

Paul relaxed and smiled. 'I think I can manage that,

but you'll have to make your own bed.' He rose and picked up the bottle of wine. 'Come on, let's celebrate, for once I've got this epidemic licked you'll be free to go back to your wife.'

Brandon held out his glass. 'And not before time, too. I've been a fool . . . but if you ever repeat that to anyone, I'll break your goddam neck!'

Paul was up early next morning and was not surprised to find that his head was throbbing. He made a rueful face at his reflection in the mirror and glanced at his tongue, looking away in disgust. He had no time to eat; he would leave a note arranging to meet Brandon Sutton in the Mackworth Hotel in the *Stryd Fawr* and they could enjoy a luncheon together.

His first call was at Green Hill at the home of the O'Connor family. He had liked Stella O'Connor on sight, for when she had come to his door there had been something in her manner which had impressed him.

The streets were unusually empty, there were no children playing in the dust and no sound of music from Dai-End-House in Market Street. He was an old man living alone and Paul decided he would call there later to see how he was.

Stella O'Connor opened the door and smiled with a warmth that pleased him. She had not the servility which marked some of the poorer people, 'the lower orders' as some of his colleagues would put it. He stepped inside the small but neat house and followed Mrs O'Connor up the stairs.

'Maureen's been so much better since your first call, doctor — and as for the other girls, sure they're as right as rain again now!'

'Well, I'll just look at them later to see if there are any infections remaining, but the youngest one is my main concern.'

The girl was looking much cooler, he could see that at a glance and the feverish look had gone from her eyes. 'You're right,' he said with a smile. 'She is much better, well on the road to recovery.'

Stella O'Connor was flushed with delight. 'I'm so glad

to hear you say that, doctor, though 'tis only what I was thinking myself.'

'Let me see down your throat, Maureen, there's a good girl.' The rest of the O'Connor girls were patently well and over their attack of the illness. Indeed, it seemed doubtful now if the girls had had anything more than a mild cold and a little attack of the panic which was becoming as widespread as the actual fever.

He left the house and made his way down the hill — there were a few more patients to see and then he would break for lunch; he would need a rest and a glass of iced tea for the weather was hot, the clouds kept low by the copper smoke. He glanced towards Market Street and paused . . . no, perhaps it would be better to see Dai-End-House last of all, for the old man was none too clean these days. Paul sighed and moved determinedly on.

Later, when he arrived at the Mackworth Hotel, Paul was a little more cheerful about the situation, for the epidemic seemed to be on the wane — at least in the area that his practice covered. It pleased him to think that he had done some little good with ideas which the old doctor Bryn Thomas used to call newfangled.

He found that Brandon had accepted his invitation and was waiting for him in the foyer of the hotel. Sutton was a tall, handsome man and it was no wonder that Mary was so unshakeably in love with her husband.

Paul found himself following Brandon Sutton into the dining-room. The man had a way of taking charge, whatever situation he found himself in. He should be irritated, but he saw in Brandon a great deal to respect.

'What are your plans?' Paul asked as he set down his knife and fork after eating a particularly good piece of halibut; it was a long time since he had had a square meal, he realised quite suddenly.

'I will go to see Mary of course, once this damned epidemic is past.' Brandon was not eating much, Paul noticed, he was probably too impatient to see his wife to think of his stomach.

379

'Oh, I don't think there'll be much danger if you go up there now,' he said lightly and Brandon's eyes were suddenly fixed unnervingly upon him.

'Are you serious?' he asked. 'Surely it's possible that I could carry the disease with me.'

'Perhaps, but then so could the butcher, the baker and the candlestick-maker come to that. Your family can't live in isolation — it's just not possible — and we all take risks of some sort every time we step out of the house.'

Brandon drank a little of the coffee put before him and, grimacing, set down the cup in the saucer again.

'When will you people learn to make proper coffee?' he said absently. Then he leaned forward with elbows on the table and looked directly at Paul.

'Why didn't you tell me this last night?' he asked and Paul shook his head.

'I thought it would be a good idea to get something straight first of all. You see, I want Mary's happiness and I know that's going to sound weak and pathetic to a man like you, but I am sincere about it. Why else should I have written to you?'

'You and half of Sweyn's Eye!' Brandon smiled suddenly and he was a man full of charm.

'You mean I wasn't the only one?' Paul was incredulous. 'You can see just how popular Mary is then, can't you?'

'Yes, I can.' Brandon paused. 'You're not weak at all, it's just that you're a nice sort of guy — at heart. And I wouldn't make the mistake of underestimating you; any man who can go where there's sickness earns my respect, sure enough.'

Paul found suddenly that he was growing to like the big American. He had changed and become more sympathetic, as though the hard edges had been knocked off him. It could have been the result of the war, he supposed, or even the long separation from Mary. But whatever it was, Brandon was certainly more human.

'Well, I'd like to sit here all day and talk, but I've more work to do,' Paul said reluctantly. 'But I wish you all the

380

luck in the world, you and Mary.' He rose to his feet and grinned. 'I'll let you pick up the bill in exchange for last night's board and lodging. In any case you're better heeled than I am — I'm just a poor town doctor and you're a rich businessman.'

Brandon waved his assent and sat back in his chair. 'Go on your errands of mercy, then. Me, I'm going to have another brandy!'

It was cooler in the streets than it had been all morning, Paul decided as he stepped past the jardinières decorating the doorway of the hotel. He took out his pocket watch and wondered if he should take a cab up to Market Street; he did want to look in on Dai-End-House before he returned home. But there was no sign of a cab and it looked as if he had just missed a tram, so he decided to walk.

The canal ran turgidly between weed-fronded banks and even as he watched, Paul saw a small boy kneel down and drink the evil-smelling water.

'Hey, you!' he called, wanting to warn the child of the dangers of consuming foetid, almost stagnant waters but the boy was startled and scuttled away.

Paul sighed. How long would it take to educate the people of the town to discriminate between clear-running streams and the much-fouled water of the canal? Even some doctors saw no harm in the practice, working no doubt on the old principle that everyone must eat a peck of dirt before they died.

The hill seemed to rise sharply to his left and he slowed his step, realising that the sun had reappeared and was shining down on him as fiercely as ever. He crossed the road into Copperman's Row and then moved to the adjoining Market Street.

'Morning, Doctor Soames.' One of the Murphy boys, red hair aflame in the sunlight, was swinging to and fro on the back gate. Paul patted his head and then held his breath against the smell of fish that emanated from the child's clothing.

'What are you doing there, boy?' Mrs Murphy, her face

screwed up against the sunlight, called to her son. Then she caught sight of Paul and bobbed him a curtsey. 'Oh, it's yourself doctor — no one sick here, thank the holy Virgin!'

'Well, that's good to hear,' Paul smiled. 'And how is your daughter — Katie, isn't it?'

'Jesu, Mary and Joseph — she's gone off to foreign parts to be with her husband! I'm hoping she makes him come back for she misses us all, so she does. But it's taking her a mighty long time to convince him.'

Paul not knowing what he was supposed to say, resorted to platitudes: 'There's no accounting for the ways of the young, she'll come home when she's good and ready.'

'Go on with you, doctor — just a young babby yourself are you not?' She absentmindedly cuffed her son across the head. 'Get indoors with you and wash yourself — you stink of fish, child!'

'Glad to hear you're well,' Paul said hastily, 'I'd better get on with my rounds — lots of people to see before I can go home.'

Mrs Murphy's face lit up with undisguised interest. 'And who's the latest to get the fever then? Is it anyone in Market Street?'

'No, nothing to worry about there, Mrs Murphy. Everything is under control.' He hurried away before she could ask any further questions and once he was out of sight, went to the home of Dai-End-House.

He knocked several times and when there was no reply, he pushed the door open. The air inside the room was foetid and the curtains drawn. There was a rustling in the corner and when Paul pushed the window open wide, the sunlight spilled on the sunken face of the old man crumpled in the makeshift bed on the floor.

Paul knelt down at once and put a hand against the man's heart; it was beating faintly like that of a frightened bird.

'I must get you into the infirmary, my old friend,' he said softly, but Dai-End-House shook his head weakly.

'No, too late.' He was gasping for breath. 'And anyway up, boyo, I'm going to die in my own house.'

He could very well be right, Paul decided, for he was very weak. The sickness had drained his energy and the lack of water compounded the damage done to his feeble old body.

'Only one thing, doctor . . .' Dai's voice was dry like the wind sighing in the trees. 'I want to have my old accordion by me — perhaps I'll be playing it in heaven, isn't it?'

Paul looked around him and saw the instrument, keys gleaming like teeth in the gloom of the corner. When he picked it up a harsh sound issued from it, as though commiserating with the plight of the old man.

'There we are, then.' Paul stood beside Dai and watched his gnarled hand reach out to touch the keys lovingly.

'No strength to play you now, old pal,' he gasped, for his accordion had been his constant and sometimes his only companion. 'No puff left to play any more music, so it's time I was going, indeed.' His voice trailed away and slowly, the thin hand slipped from the instrument.

'You've given many folks pleasure with your music, old man,' Paul said gently, covering Dai's face. And his words rang hollowly in the silent room.

Paul rose to his feet and excluded the sunlight by closing the threadbare curtains. He moved heavily towards the door, knowing that great though his joy had been with the controlling of the fever, he must always be ready to look in the face of defeat, for there would be those who were past his help.

*   *   *

Mary was sitting in the cool of the garden, with Stephan asleep at her side. He had played all morning — rolling about the grass, using up his boundless energy as though there was nothing in the world wrong with him.

Only Mary realised how restricted his vision had become, for she watched him endlessly and tirelessly, noting every single occasion when her son collided with a piece of furniture or stumbled over his pet dog lying unseen on the floor.

The sun was over the other side of the house and now, as Mary sat in the shade facing the glittering sea with the rugged coastline of Devon sharp against the horizon she thought there must be rain coming. During the heatwave the sea had been hazy, blurring into the sky.

She heard voices behind her and smiled, shaking her head a little at Greenie's excitement and wondering which friend had come to visit. Mali Richardson perhaps, for they had seen a great deal of each other lately. She worried very little about the epidemic of scarlet fever for it was far removed from her, being centred on the other side of the town where she had been born but which was no longer part of her life. And Mary had heard but little of the ravages of the sickness, for these days she remained mostly at home.

And so it was with a smile of welcome that she rose to her feet and turning, put her finger on her lips in a gentle warning that Stephan was asleep. Her hand fell to her side and her breath seemed suddenly torn from her body as she saw the man standing before her.

Brandon had changed, imperceptibly perhaps, but there was a different look about him. — a new gentleness, a trait which had ever been missing from his character.

'Mary, how are you?' His eyes searched her face as if trying to read her feelings, then he looked to where his son lay sleeping on the grass and Mary saw him swallow hard.

'I . . . was informed of Stephan's eye-sickness by your friend, the doctor,' he said slowly, 'and I want to take the boy to America where our doctors have made great strides in the treatment of eye ailments. And Mary, I want you to come too.' He took a step towards her and held out his arms. And slowly, as if waking from a long nightmare, Mary went into them.

CHAPTER THIRTY-ONE

The prison was high-walled, the old stone darkened by abrasive dust from the industrial side of the town, and even in the brilliant sunshine the building seemed menacing.

Gina moved inside with the other visitors, shepherded into the prison block like sheep by stern-faced warders. Her first sight of Billy brought a constriction to her throat, for his eye was swollen and the bruises on his face were fading to violet and yellow, giving him a strangely vulnerable look.

'Gina, there's good of you to come and see me.' He did not look up at her, but kept his eyes fixed on the floor. Was there disappointment in the slope of his shoulders? Had it been Doffie he was expecting? But his next words dispelled her fears.

'I knew you'd come *merchi* — always there when a man's in trouble, salt of the earth you are, girl!' It was not a very romantic statement, but the words of praise warmed Gina, encouraging her so that she leaned forward and took his hand.

'Billy, love, don't look so hangdog. Fighting is not a serious crime and they will be letting you out in a few days' time — I asked them.'

'I'm ashamed, Gina.' Billy still did not look up. 'Me, a grown man, going daft over a flossie. I ought to have my head read!'

Gina sighed with relief. 'Then you've come to your senses, Billy, is that what you're saying?' She held her breath as he sought for words to explain his feelings.

'Aye, I suppose so. What I felt for Doffie, it was nothing like love, Gina, just the need to possess.' He shook his head.

'A bout of madness over a young girl that comes to many man in spite of him loving a good woman.' For the first tim he looked directly into her eyes. 'And I do love you, Gina He sighed. 'I've sat by here in the jail with plenty of tim to think, see, and I've wondered what I'd do if you wer off to marry that Thomas fellow. I'd be lost, Gina, los

'Well, that's not going to happen, Billy. There's only on man I love and he's sitting by here with bruises all ove his face because he's been a silly old fool.'

Billy's eyes were moist. 'I don't deserve you, Gina.' H eyes met hers. 'You know what? I think part of the troubl is that you and me . . . well, we never were lovers, lik Now don't blush — I'm trying to explain things that ar inside me. We were together a lot and me knowing yo for a good woman didn't try anything on — and damn i I should have done! We let things get stale between us, fo if they don't grow then they can die.'

'You're right, Billy, there's been many times I've lai awake wanting you. I'm human too, mind.'

'Right then, when I get out of here we'll be marrie as soon as possible — and very quiet we'll keep it too, n fuss, agreed?'

'Agreed!' Gina smiled through the ache of tears in he throat. 'And I'll be a tyrant, mind — no more going to th Dublin to fight with Irishmen or I'll take to the rolling-pin

Billy pressed her hand. 'One thing troubles me, thoug Will Mary still let me have my job, will she trust m after this?'

'Of course she will, silly,' Gina said at once. 'Didn't sh stand by you before and you were in worse trouble then

'Aye, you're right, love, as always.' He winked wickedl 'Anyway, getting back to more pleasant things, you and m will make lovely babies!'

He was a different man from the dejected, hangdo creature he had been when Gina first came in and she fe some small measure of comfort that it had been she wh had wrought the change in him. Perhaps there woul always remain a seed of doubt in her heart, for the memor of his passion for Doffie could not be so easily erased.

The warder was ushering people away, for the visiting time was over. Gina rose to her feet and stood looking across the table at Billy, wanting to be in his arms, to have his passion spent on her and not some foolish little flossie.

'I will come to you as soon as they set me free,' Billy said gently. 'And Gina, I'll try to be a good husband to you.'

'I know you will, love.' She moved away then without looking back, for she did not want him to see her tears of pain and doubt. How many times would he have to tell her he loved her before she could really believe him?

Instead of returning to the mill, Gina began to walk towards Green Hill, her step sure and firm. She had never entered a public bar in her life, but today she meant to visit quite a few of them. The sun was hot overhead, the air heavy with the sulphurous smoke from the copper works, but Gina did not even notice.

The Dublin was full of smoke and smelling strongly of beer, plenty of which was spilled into the sawdust on the floor. A quick glance around showed her that there was no other woman present and, with a swiftly beating heart, Gina moved towards the bar.

'What you want, missus?' The landlord looked her up and down curiously. 'Don't look the sort to be in a place like this; lost your way, have you?'

'I'm looking for the woman they call Doffie. Got a nasty sickness she has — catching it is, mind, worse than the scarlet fever.' Gina looked round at the men, who had fallen silent and were now giving her their full attention. 'I'd advise you men to give her a wide berth — pass it on to you she could, see, and you'd take it home to your good wives!'

Some of the men shifted uneasily, eyes downcast, and Gina felt exultant. By the time she had finished, Doffie wouldn't have a customer left!

It was easier the next time and systematically Gina went from one public house to the next, growing in confidence. It was in the back room of the Flint Mill that she came face to face with Doffie herself. Gina stared at her with outward composure, though she was trembling inside.

'Out of your class by here in a public bar,' Doffie said, eyeing Gina's neat skirt and blouse in amusement. 'Not setting up in competition with me, are you?'

'Oh, no, I wouldn't do that,' Gina said smoothly, her anger growing. Doffie appeared not one whit contrite because Billy was in prison. 'You see, I know you've caught this dreadful sickness from going with men and I wouldn't want to end up like you.'

'What sickness? What the devil are you talking about, you stupid cow, I 'aven't got no sickness!'

'It's no good denying it,' Gina said loudly, 'because no one will believe you. Not going to take any chances, I shouldn't think, you not being that much of a beauty. Quite plain in fact, with that terrible dyed hair!'

'Why, you . . .' Doffie was speechless, staring at Gina as if she had grown two heads.

'Well, I'm going home now and you be careful — look after yourself, now, and go to see the doctor — not that there's much can be done for what you've got, I shouldn't think.'

Doffie suddenly found her voice. 'She's lying, don't any of you believe her! Just jealous she is because her bloke fell in love with me, wanted to marry me an' all. That's why he's in jail, because he was fighting over me.'

Gina smiled pityingly. 'Don't fool yourself, *merchi*. I've just come from the prison and Billy has asked me to marry him just as soon as he comes out.' She paused, her head on one side. 'I suppose he might have fancied you a bit, though I can't think why. But it was only a passing phase with him, just as with all your other men — can't keep any of them for long, can you?'

Suddenly Doffie began to cry; tears rolled down her cheeks and her mouth trembled. In that moment, Gina felt almost sorry for what she had done, but there was no taking it back now.

'Come on, stop crying like a babba,' she said sharply. 'Find yourself a proper job and be respectable while you're still young enough to change.'

388

Doffie stamped her foot. 'I don't *want* to change, I like my life the way it is; can't you understand that?'

Shrugging, Gina turned away and walked out into the sunshine. There was no hope for Doffie, she would go to hell her own way. Then she heard the sound of running footsteps and turned to see Doffie careering down the street after her.

'Why did you do that, tell those lies about me being sick and all?' she said breathlessly, her jaw jutting belligerently as she placed her hands on her hips.

'I thought it would be a good idea to put your customers off a bit, that's all,' Gina smiled. 'And I've been into lots of other public bars doing the same thing. Pay you back a bit for Billy being put into prison over a little flossie like you!'

'Oh, I could hit you!' Doffie said through her teeth and Gina raised her eyebrows.

'Well, you could try but I'm bigger than you, mind — and I do hit back if I'm hurt. In any case, if we did have a fight it would only convince people that what I said was true. No, I should leave it be, if I were you.'

To Gina's surprise, Doffie began to smile, then she flung back her head and laughed out loud. She was just like a little child with her sudden changes of mood.

'I got to hand it to you, mind,' Doffie said at last. 'You're a cool one, going into the pubs like that and putting out that story. I couldn't have thought up a better revenge myself.' She dabbed at her eyes with a scrap of lace. 'Well now, if you wants me to go straight and get all pure-like, why don't you give me a job down at your mill?'

'I'm not daft!' Gina said quickly. 'And have you around Billy all the time offering him temptations? Not likely! Anyway, it's not my mill, it belongs to Mansel Jack and he's up in Yorkshire, so forget it.'

Doffie shrugged, 'Well, I was only halfway serious, so don't get knotted knickers over it,' she sighed. 'Now I suppose I've got to try to convince my customers that you've been pulling their leg, like; and that isn't going to be the easiest thing in the world.'

'Good, then perhaps some wives will have their husbands back for a little while, isn't it?'

Doffie shook her head. 'Sometimes you good women can be very catty and spiteful, mind.' She rolled her eyes heavenward. 'Preserve me from good women, God, and don't let me ever become one!' She moved back up the street still giggling and Gina smiled at her retreating back. She had glimpsed a little of what Billy had seen in the girl and it made her slightly uneasy. Would she ever lose the feelings of jealousy that the affair between Billy and Doffie had aroused?

* * *

Billy was released from prison two weeks later and Gina was outside the gate waiting for him. He embraced her warmly and she put her hands on his cheeks.

'I love you, Billy Gray,' she said simply. He took her hand and led her towards the beach. The sand was golden, the sea reflecting the blue of the cloudless skies above.

The jutting arms of the pier cast stark black shadows and it was there against the wooden struts that Billy proposed to Gina. He spoke solemnly and formally.

'Gina Sinman, will you do me the honour of becoming my wife?' He took her hand and caressed the palm with his thumb, his eyes looking into her. Gina responded warmly.

'I'll accept your proposal, boyo!' She leaned towards him and kissed his mouth gently; then Billy held her close, smoothing back her hair, pressing his lips to her eyelids, her cheeks and her throat.

'Only a little while to wait now, Billy,' Gina said softly. 'I want it all to be right and proper with us.'

'I know.' He released her and stared out towards a ship on the distant horizon. Gina looked at him anxiously, wondering what he was thinking about, but after a moment he smiled.

'Let's get off home, I'm just pining to see the children — have they missed me?'

Gina nodded eagerly. 'They're all excited because Doris is making us all a special tea.'

Hand in hand they walked away from the beach and left the murmuring sea behind them. The heat seemed to bounce up from the cobbled roadway and Gina felt lightheaded with happiness; she was with her man and he had asked her to be his wife — what more could she possibly want?

It was only later, when she sat in the kitchen alone, that the misgivings returned. The children had gone to bed exhausted with excitement and Doris at last had said she must be getting off home. And when Billy had taken his silk scarf and slipped it round his neck, she had thought nothing of it.

'I'll just see Doris to the end of the road,' he had said cheerfully, but that was over an hour ago and still he had not returned.

Restlessly, Gina opened the door and stared out into the night. The sky was lit up by the sparks from the chimneys of the copper works so that even the stars were distant and looked insignificant in comparison with the ruddy glow. She stared up the road, listening for the sound of footsteps, making a silent wish for Billy to come to her. Was he with that flossie again? Jealousy seared her and she bit her lip, longing to run out into the night and find him.

'There's daft you are,' she said out loud. 'Behaving like a babba, you, Gina Sinman.'

She went upstairs at last and looked in at the children, hearing their gentle breathing and taking comfort from their presence. In her own small room, she lay on the bed fully dressed and quite suddenly, she began to cry.

*　　*　　*

The morning brought sunshine and a change of mood for Gina. She had been silly and unfair to think that Billy could be doing anything wrong. There would be a perfectly reasonable explanation for his failure to return last night, she was sure of it.

It was Doris who brought the bad news. She came t the door panting with exertion, for she had become plum over the years, and sank immediately into a chair, fannin herself with her hand.

'There was a terrible rumpus in Canal Street last nigh someone set fire to Billy's van and all that stock went u in flames — the stink of burning wool was terrible. Onl a few old saucepans were saved.'

'What about Billy, is he all right?' Gina was trying to spea in a low tone so as not to alarm the children, but she hear the note of fear in her voice as she asked the question

'Oh, aye, he's fine, but only because the constable cam along, for Billy was out to kill the man who set fire to th van.' She picked at a jagged nail with worried concentratio and Gina wanted to shake her.

'What man was that? For goodness sake, Doris, pay atter tion to what you're telling me and leave that silly nail alone

Doris looked up in surprise. 'All right, no need to g all het-up like, is there? It was the Irishman that Billy gav a hammering to over that slut Doffie, who'd yer think.

So it was still there: the pain and the hurt and th humiliation of Billy's fling with a flossie. Wasn't it ever t go away?

When she saw Billy that evening, she had just finishe putting the children to bed and her head was achin abominably. She let him into the kitchen and stood befor him, her hands clasped together to stop them from tremblin

'You've heard of the fire, then, *merchi*?' He sounded little sheepish and Gina sighed softly.

'Yes, I've heard, Billy and I'm sorry; quite a bit of damag done, wasn't there?'

He nodded. 'Aye, woollens burnt and the van useles now, burned to a hulk. A bad blow for Mary Sutton though she took it very well like the woman of characte she is. It's a big setback, but I expect we'll survive especiall now that Mary and her husband are together again.'

'Would you like a cup of tea?' Gina asked, wonderin why she did not just come out with it and tell him she kne who had fired the van and why.

'Yes, love, that would be very nice.' Billy was acting as though he was walking on eggs, Gina thought as she pushed the kettle on to the flames and stood the tea-pot on the hob to warm. When she turned he was right beside her and he took her swiftly in his arms, burying his face in her neck.

'I need you, Gina, don't turn against me.' His voice was muffled. 'I can see it in your eyes — you're angry with me, aren't you?'

She closed her eyes in pain; she loved him so much, yet how could she live with her doubt of him?

'Please let me go, Billy, we have to talk.' She gently disentangled herself from his arms. 'I'm not angry — not now, though I was last night. I imagined you were with Doffie and I couldn't bear it.'

'That's over and finished with,' Billy said softly, but his tone was unconvincing.

Gina shook her head. 'No, it's not over, is it, Billy? You and that Irishman, you were going to fight; it was over her, that Doffie and it was a good thing that the constable was there to stop you.'

Billy looked down at his hands. 'I need you, Gina,' he said again, but he did not meet her eyes.

'Well, we will talk about it more later.' She rubbed her head. 'I'm that tired now, Billy, I can't think straight. Just leave me be for a while, will you?'

He rose without another word, his tea forgotten, pausing at the door to look back at her. After a moment, he left the house and she heard his quick footsteps hurrying away across the yard.

She sighed and put her head down on the smooth wood of the table. Jealousy was a hateful thing, yet it was an emotion she could not fight. Perhaps it would be better if she ended the relationship between herself and Billy. For it might just be too late for them to find happiness together.

CHAPTER THIRTY-TWO

The unexpected torrent of rain beat down on the ship a
she heaved and rolled in the turgid water of the docks, bu
Katie felt a sense of calm and happiness for she and Marl
were together.

He came up behind her and put his arms around he
waist, leaning his chin on her hair. 'My lovely girl, I'll b
glad to get home again to Sweyn's Eye. I even miss the stinl
of the copper!' He sighed. 'Who knows — perhaps I ma}
find a decent job there now.'

Katie turned into his arms and hugged him. 'I'm sure you
will, boy *bach*, you're a very clever and determined man

The ship, an old square-rigged sailing barque, wa:
swaying on the heavy swell of the sea and inside the cabin
the rolling motion seemed intensified.

Mark smiled ruefully. 'Think you can stand it for a
few hours, *merchi*?' He held out his arms and she clung
to him happily.

'I can put up with anything so long as I'm with you an(
all *I* can think of is that we're going home,' she said firmly
'In any case, the captain seems a sensible sort of man; he
wouldn't put to sea if there was any danger, would he?

Mark shrugged. 'Well, I'll say this for him, he certainl}
knows how to charge! Now sit down and make yoursel
comfortable before you fall over — got no sea-legs, you, girl.

No, it wouldn't do for her to fall, Katie thought with a
feeling of warmth, but aloud she said, 'Where are you going?

He smiled and kissed the tip of her nose. 'Just to watch
the shores of France receding — don't mind, do you, or
have you become one of these bossy wives who won't allow

heir husbands out of their sight?'

Katie slapped his hand playfully. 'Less of your lip, boyo, r you'll feel the weight of my hand good and proper!'

When she was alone, she closed her eyes and sighed ontentedly; she felt secure in Mark's love, he was truly er very own husband again. Probably she would never now the truth of his feelings about Thérèsa; would he have esponded to her, Katie wondered? But those thoughts were o be put aside, for they only led to doubts and fears.

As she felt the tilt of the boat beneath her and the oporific slap of the waves against the hull, she hugged to erself the knowledge that she was going to have Mark's aby. But there would be time enough to tell him that piece f news when he had found a job and was settled. She made erself comfortable in the softness of the plush seat and fter a time, she slept.

*   *   *

The heat of the late summer brought a ripeness to the land; orn stood tall and golden, blackberries began to flourish n thorny patches and the festival of the harvest should have been triumphant. But the scarlet fever which had begun n Sweyn's Eye had pressed a deadly hand over the village of Mumbles and its people were afraid.

In concern for her baby, Catherine would not venture ar from home and at least for the moment, the farm was self-sufficient, providing butter, eggs and cheese and a plentiful supply of vegetables. She wanted a new sow and ndeed had given Morgan the money to buy an animal at the market, but he had not yet seen one that was to his liking.

Sitting in the kitchen, listening to the sound of the clock in the stillness, Catherine felt a surge of protective mother love as she took John from his crib and, opening her blouse, began to nurse Jim. He suckled contentedly, his small face screwed up as though in concentration.

'Well, there's a lovely sight for a man!' Morgan stood in the doorway, his eyes alight in the tanned face. As he

came and knelt beside Catherine and kissed her cheek sh
noticed that his hair had become sun-streaked with golde
lights which made him look even more handsome.

'And there's a lucky woman I am, Morgan Lloyd.' Sh
touched his face with her hand.

'I know I don't say many pretty things to you,' Morga
spoke softly, 'but you're a wonderful mother to our boy
Catherine.' He kissed her cheek gently and the baby's sma
fists struck outward, catching him a small blow to the chir

'*Duw*, the boy's jealous of me already!' He laughed i
delight and put his finger into the tiny hand which grippe
and held tightly. 'Just see how tenacious he is, Catherine

She felt silly tears burn her eyes, tears that came all to
readily since the birth of her son. How it had changed her
motherhood had made her so vulnerable and all she wante
to hear was that Morgan loved her and then she would fee
secure.

'I'm going down to see Gladys.' Morgan got to his feet.
know you're frightened of me mixing with the villagers, bu
I've got to see her — William too. You understand, don't you

Catherine nodded. 'Yes, you're right, Morgan, we'll nee
them both and in any case, I can't hide away in my ow
little world any longer. I suppose I've been selfishly conten
to sit by here and forget the outside world.'

Morgan smiled ruefully. 'Aye and we're going to nee
some of that outside world if we're to bring in the harvest
We can't do it alone, Catherine.'

Fear laid cold hands upon her as she thought of th
hostility of her neighbours. 'We can if we have to,' she sai
stoutly. 'You, me and Gladys and William, we can do it
She stared at him for a moment in silence and wished sh
could draw him to her, have him take her in his arms an
tell her he loved her . . . for she had never heard the word
pass his lips, not once.

'When are you going to get me that new sow?' she aske
lightly, changing the subject. 'Perhaps you'd best go to th
next cattle show in the town — there'll be one once th
sickness is past.'

Morgan stared at her for a moment, his eyes meeting hers. 'I should have told you — I haven't got the money for the sow.'

'What do you mean?' Catherine said, bewildered. 'I gave it to you myself out of the milk and egg money; it was all I'd saved up for the year.'

'I should have told you at once,' Morgan admitted as he thrust his hand into his pockets. 'I didn't bank the money. The truth is . . . I saw Stella O'Connor trying to pawn some things because her youngest child was sick, so I gave her the money.'

'You fool!' Catherine was coldly angry. 'That wasn't just money, that was part of our livelihood, earned by toil and sweat. Now my profit on the herd and the poultry is gone and worse than that, I'm out of pocket because of the feeding of the creatures. Where's your sense, Morgan?'

'I'm going now, and I'm sorry to find that my wife sets more store by a sow than by the saving of a child's life!' He strode out of the kitchen and the door swung shut behind him.

Alone in the farmhouse, Catherine listened to the silence as she put John back into his crib and stood looking down at him. He was so strong and handsome that it took her breath away. Moving to the doorway, she stared out and sighed deeply as she saw the fertile rolling fields of Ram's Tor, knowing she would sacrifice anything for the farm and knowing that one day it would all belong to her son.

* * *

Morgan walked briskly down the roadway between the rocks staring up at the grumbling clouds that were racing in from the sea, reflecting his mood. It looked as though the lovely spell of hot sunshine was about to break, but then a little soft rain would be good for the land, he reflected.

He moved down into the street that wound through the village and stood for a moment looking at the oyster ketches bobbing on the incoming tide. A wind was whipping the waves which were usually so docile into a flurry of white capped foam. Morgan frowned as he looked beyond Mumbles Head and saw the sea racing crossways over the Mixon Sands which rose hump-backed, swelling just below the waves.

Gladys welcomed him with a smile. 'Come on in Morgan, boyo.' She opened her door wide. 'There's a po of tea just made and a big pile of Welsh cakes, for that boy of mine eats me out of house and home. How's my little babba there up on the farm?'

'John is flourishing but missing you.' Morgan sat in a chair near the open door, for the kitchen was warm and fragrant with the smell of hot fruit cakes.

'Afraid to come up, I was,' Gladys said sombrely. 'There's a lot gone down with the scarlet fever here and me and Will quite healthy, thank the good Lord!'

Morgan sighed. 'I suppose the sickness will run its course before it dies out.'

Gladys poured the tea, spilling a little on to the spotless white cloth. '*Duw*, there's clumsy I am — it's my legs giving me gyp, they are.' She grinned. 'But it's a lot better than falling sick with the fever, I suppose.'

Morgan took a cake from the plate and it was still warm from the griddle. 'Has it been bad, the fever I mean?' The cake was delicious melting in his mouth, the fruit hot and spicy.

'Oh, aye, lots of the villagers gone down with it, even the men. Very bad it's been, but the doctor says it's under control, whatever that means. Only one little babba died of it, so things could have been much worse I suppose.'

Morgan nodded. 'Catherine's frightened that John might get it, that's why she won't come down into the village herself.'

Gladys lowered herself painfully into a chair. 'Tell her not to worry, babbas that are breast-fed don't get no sicknesses.' She sat for a moment in silence and Morgan noticed the beading of sweat on her forehead.

'You really are in pain there, aren't you?' he said gently

'Is there anything I can get for you?'

Gladys made a rueful face. 'Aye, get the bottle of brandy from the parlour and pour some in my tea — dulls the ache a bit, it does.'

Morgan was just about to rise from his chair when William rushed into the kitchen.

'Mam, there's a boat stuck on the Mixon, a Frenchie boat by the looks of it!'

Suddenly, shattering the stillness, came the sound of the maroons exploding, calling the crew to man the lifeboat.

'*Duw*, how many men will be well enough to go out to sea?' Gladys said softly. 'Most of them are sick in bed.'

Morgan moved towards the door. 'Well, at least I can be of help. I don't think any of the villagers will worry about being offish to me in an emergency.'

William followed Morgan outside and Gladys called to him anxiously. 'Come back, boy — you can't go, you're too young.'

'No, I'm not.' William paused: 'I've got to do my bit, can't you see that?'

Morgan hurried across the road and ran along the sea-front towards the lifeboat station with William at his heels. The rain was beginnning to fall, heavy drops like tears were running down Morgan's face and his vision was blurred. When he slipped on the wetness of the roadway, William was behind him putting a steadying arm on his shoulder. The boy was growing up, Morgan thought in surprise.

The coxswain was handing out life-jackets to a handful of men and his face lit up when he saw Morgan.

'Come on, boyo, could do with your help and no two ways about it!' he called through the noise of the rising wind. He hesitated when he saw William, then counted his men and looked down the roadway which was empty.

'Right then, William, if you're half the man your dad was then you'll do. You just make up the thirteen that I need.'

Morgan glanced up at the sky and then out to sea and almost tasted the fear of the unknown. He had fought a war, killed men when he had to, but his facing the sea, taking on the rising waves after what happened to him before, was a far more fearsome prospect. But what of the people aboard the stranded *Terra Nueva* — what fears must they be facing?

*   *   *

Katie had been awakened by a strange bumping sound and she sat up, wondering for a moment where she was. The ship seemed to be lifting and dipping more heavily and the wind was swooping and diving amid the sails.

She suddenly felt queasy, for she was no sailor and the constant and varied movements of the ship were distressing to her. She pushed herself upright with difficulty, staggering on the heaving floor. Suddenly tossed sideways, she fell to her knees, knocking her head against the wooden side of the bunk.

Where was Mark? Katie struggled to her feet once more and made her way slowly towards the door of the cabin. It was difficult to open, but at last she managed it and then the full tilt of the wind took her breath away. Waves washed upwards and the sky seeemed to reel around her head.

'Get back inside!' Mark was holding her arms, drawing her back into the cabin. His hair was soaked, flattened to his forehead and Katie felt fear grip her.

'What's happening?' She had to shout to be heard and when Mark touched her cheek, his hand was icy cold.

'It's just a storm,' he said, struggling to be heard. 'Nothing the captain hasn't dealt with before. Get in you and stay there safe and warm and I'll be easier in my mind, then.'

Suddenly, Katie clung to him, oblivious of the wetness of his coat as his arms closed round her. She was frightened, not for herself but for Mark and she didn't want him out of her sight for a moment.

'Please Mark, stay with me,' she called but even as she clung, he was drawing away from her.

'I must see if I can help.' He pushed her gently back into the cabin. 'Now stay here where you're safe; the wind is bound to drop soon and then I'll come back.' When he kissed her mouth, his own was cold and salt — then the door was closed and he was gone.

Katie returned to the bunk, clinging to the wooden sides, closing her eyes, hoping to ease the feeling of sickness and dread that held her in an icy grip. Her mind was out there on the sea-washed decks, as though her force of will could keep him safe.

How foolish seemed her doubts about him now. What if Mark had succumbed to the flattering of the young French girl — it surely meant very little to him? If only she could be with him safe on land, then she would be forever happy, Katie told herself.

She clasped her hand to her mouth, feeling faint with nausea. Then a roll of the ship sent her spinning to the floor and she lay there for a moment, listening to the slap of the water against the boards as though searching for entry. She shivered as she imagined the coldness of the sea, the hugeness of the waves which could snap a mast as though it were a twig.

Katie had seen wrecks from the safety of the hills above Sweyn's Eye, seen how ships were tossed against the rocks of Mumbles Head. She had thought little then about the men aboard those vessels, but now she tasted the same fear, smelled the evil scent of it.

The wind, far from abating, seemed to be rising and the ship creaked and groaned as though in pain. A table detached itself from its fastenings and careered across the cabin, but Katie stifled her scream for the men up on deck had more to be worried about than her silly fears.

*   *   *

The sea was much rougher than Morgan had expected, running at about thirty feet beyond the shelter of the bay. The coxswain of the *Charlie Medland* was guiding the boat through the inner sound and the rush of water seemed to mock the puny efforts of the crew to reach the stranded ship.

401

By now the French barque had struck the rocks of Mumbles Head full on and there was a cracking of timbers as the sea broke the back of the ship. Morgan remembered from his brief training that the practice was to bring the lifeboat windward and for the bowman to use the anchor rope, hauling in and playing out to counter the effects of the waves and the backwash.

The vessel seemed to move up on to the rocks as though of her own volition and the coxswain of the lifeboat shouted a command to his men.

'Prepare a lifebuoy and a line!' Even as he shouted, the foremast of the barque came crashing down into the sea.

The ebb was growing stronger and the crew of the lifeboat — most of them as inexperienced as Morgan and young William — were having difficulty keeping the head of the boat towards the seas. Morgan felt as though his arms were being dragged from their sockets and he glanced behind to smile encouragingly at William who was pulling with all his strength.

'*Duw*, this is some adventure, Morgan!' The boy called to him cheerfully, though his face was white and his sea-soaked hair was plastered down across his forehead.

The line was thrown and snaked uncertainly through the air, but it found its mark and Morgan sighed in relief for the lifeboat was bobbing like a cork in the swell of the seas.

He gasped as he realised that there was a woman being pulled from the dying ship. Her skirts billowed like sails and her grip seemed precarious as the wind sang through her tangled hair. At last she fell into the well of the lifeboat where she lay gasping, unable to speak. When she struggled to sit up, Morgan recognised her.

'Good God, it's Katie Murphy!' he said as her anguished eyes looked past him to where a man was struggling across from the ship, battling against the gusting wind.

A great wave reared up, dark and dangerous, lashing at the man as though in sudden fury. The line grew taut and suddenly snapped and the man disappeared.

'*Mark*!' Katie screamed the name and if Morgan had not

caught her arm she would have been overboard and into the raging seas.

Another line was cast, but at that moment the *Charlie Medland* went out of control as the mountainous waves towered threateningly before crashing down on the boat. Morgan felt the sea drum into his ears and it was as though he would never stop falling . . . lower and lower he sank into the water. He grasped a piece of cloth and when at last he surfaced, found he was clinging to Katie's skirt.

Miraculously the lifeboat had righted itself, but only three of the crew were left aboard. Katie was dragged back into the lifeboat half unconscious, her eyes closed in an ashen face.

Morgan tried to grasp the oar held out to him by one of the men, but he was swept away by the heavy swell. He saw the cruel black of the jagged rocks ominously close to him, then he was washed upward and seemed to be lifted by a giant hand and carried beyond the outer rocks. The breath was knocked from him, but as the sea ebbed he found himself safe on land. Gasping, he forced himself to his feet, for the next water would grasp him and pull him into the boiling seas once more.

When he was on higher ground he stared seaward, trying to locate the *Charlie Medland*, but in the whipping wind and the rushing seas there was no sign of the lifeboat. Morgan moved up towards the roadway, shaking the blur of water from his eyes. As he went he became aware that his head was bleeding and that his entire body seemed to burn with the grazing of the rocks against his flesh, but otherwise he was unharmed.

In the calmer waters of Bracelet Bay a crowd had gathered on the shore — old men mostly and women in grand-mothers shawls who were trying to snatch survivors washed in by the sea. Even as Morgan watched a man was brought ashore, miraculously unhurt. Morgan made his way towards the water once more, searching for any sign of William and was about to plunge into the waves when hands grasped him.

'Bide by here, boy *bach*,' one of the old women said firmly. 'You've done your bit and any fool can see there's no strength left in you.'

Morgan stared into the darkness. The wind which had sprung up so suddenly seemed to be dropping, the storm dying away as quickly as it had come. He saw Gladys hobbling along the sand, her eyes wide as her gaze rested on him.

'Where's my boy?' she asked in a low voice and Morgan took her hand in his.

'I don't know. We were swept overboard, all of us; the sea just swamped the boat, but don't worry — he's tough, is William!'

Gladys put a hand on her mouth. 'The water's taken him like it took his father before him, hasn't it?'

'I'll find him!' Morgan's body was on fire. His legs moved stiffly as the sand clung to his feet but he needed at least to try to find the boy.

The sea was becoming calm now, the moon slipping from behind clouds silvering the sand as Morgan walked waist-high into the water, joining the chain of rescuers who were bringing out the survivors from the French barque.

Suddenly he became aware of a woman beside him and turning he saw Katie, Mark's wife, blood smearing her face but with her hands held out to help the men from the stranded ship. And he knew that she was driven by the futile hope that she might find her husband alive.

CHAPTER THIRTY-THREE

As morning came, the sun washed the fields of Ram's Tor. The corn was straightening, heads lifting in the warmth and the only sign of the storm of the previous night was the stark hulk of the French barque on the rocks below.

But the village of Mumbles was counting its dead. Most of the thirteen-men crew of the lifeboat *Charlie Medland* had been drowned and one passenger from the French ship had met his death in the rough seas which had pounded him mercilessly against the rocks.

In the kitchen of the farmhouse, Catherine put her son in his crib, her eyes drinking in the sight of her husband standing in the doorway. She had not known until this moment if Morgan was alive or dead. And what did it matter if he did not love her? She had enough love for both of them.

'Thank God!' She drew Morgan close, uncaring of his rain-soaked clothes and hair matted with salt water. 'I waited for you, keeping the fire going all night,' she said at last, recognising that the words were pitifully inadequate but how could she speak of the love that overwhelmed her?

She moved away from him then. 'There's water been heating and I've fetched in the bath — I knew you'd need a good scrubbing.' She tried to speak lightly, but her eyes were asking him questions.

'William's gone.' Morgan's hands clenched into fists. 'When the boat capsized he disappeared along with most of the crew. I hoped he had been saved, but just before dawn his body was washed up on the beach at Sweyn's Eye.'

Catherine's eyes burned and a terrible pain gripped her,

for she had not spared thought for William. Morgan stood looking down at her, his shoulders slumped in fatigue.

'One of the neighbours took Gladys in, gave her some brandy and put her to bed. I'll go to her later, bring her up here to be with us.'

Catherine saw his sense of guilt mingled with defeat and roused herself. 'Come on, we've got to get you out of these wet things.' She gave a small cry of distress as she saw that much of his body was raw and the grazes were bleeding afresh as she pulled the wet clothes from him. 'Morgan, I didn't know you'd been hurt!'

'It's nothing that won't heal,' Morgan said, his voice hoarse. Catherine touched his shoulder gently, unable to speak, then she fetched the water and it drummed steaming against the ridges of the zinc bath.

Later, as Morgan lay on the bed having fallen into an exhausted sleep, Catherine wrapped the baby in his shawl Welsh fashion, which secured the boy to her body while leaving her hands free. The cows still needed to be milked, the hens to be fed and the life of the farm must go on.

When she went to the fields she saw that the corn had not been badly damaged by the storm. Now, with the sun hot again, the heads were high on the stems as though reaching for the warmth; it would be a good harvest, if they could bring it in.

At harvest times the farmers would help each other; it was an age-old custom which had its roots in sound common sense. But things were different now, for she had been ignored and insulted by her neighbours . . . moreover they had their own griefs to contend with, for most families in the village had lost a loved one to the sea during the night.

Catherine lifted her head high, resolving she would not be daunted — even if she had to cut down every head of corn herself, she would bring in the crop for she owed it to her son.

And then, as she thought of young William's eager face and clear eyes and the fervour with which he had promised o help with the gathering of the corn, her tears came. She had been planning to teach him how to make the specially shaped stooks, with small 'hats' in the form of thatching to protect the corn whilst it dried. But William would never see the fields, never breathe in the summer scents of Ram's Tor . . . not ever again.

When Catherine returned to the farmhouse, Morgan was awake and he smiled and came to take the baby from her. The boy stirred and grizzled a little in protest at being removed from his comfortable nest as Morgan laid him gently in his crib.

Morgan sighed. 'I must go to fetch Gladys home. You know, Catherine, I just can't get the look of her from my mind.'

Catherine busied herself making tea and as she lifted the pot she looked at her husband, achingly aware that he too might have perished in the storm.

'Drink some of this first, Morgan, it's good and hot. *Duw*, my throat is parched, the work can wait a minute.' She looked at him anxiously; he was pale and abstracted, his eyes not seeing the room in which he was sitting.

Morgan sat beside her at the table. 'You know Katie Murphy from Green Hill — I was at her wedding, remember?'

Catherine could not fail to remember, for she had burst in on the celebrations, worried because David and William were missing.

'On the French ship she was, poor girl. Lost her husband to the sea, yet she was so brave standing there in the water with the rest of us pulling the survivors. Never gave up hope of finding Mark until the last.' He paused. 'And then she just quietly made her way back to the road and began to walk into town with the sun beginning to rise in the sky.'

'Oh, Morgan.' Catherine said softly, 'I'm so sorry for her. I don't think I could have been strong.' Filled with a renewed awareness of how near to disaster her own life had come, she wanted to hold him close — but he was far away from her, untouchable and unreachable and she was afraid.

* * *

407

Market Street was bustling with life and Murphy's Fresh Fish Shop was doing a brisk trade, for the people of Sweyn's Eye had heard of the shipwreck at the Mumbles. The news of interest in itself, became a source of avid discussion when it was known that Katie Murphy had been seen on board the French barque and had lost her husband in the storm

Upstairs in the room which had been hers since child hood, Katie sat listlessly on the bed, staring out of the small window but seeing nothing of the street below. In her head was imprinted the picture of Mark leaving the ship and the thin line which had held him snapping as he was sucked into the waves.

When the lifeboat had overturned she had felt a moment of elation, for she wanted to join Mark beneath the waters. Then strong hands had caught and held her, lifting her back to a safety she did not want.

She had stood with the rescuers, pulling men from the water looking into strange faces and praying that the next one would be that of her beloved husband. It was only when the seas had calmed and the sun had begun to rise that she had realised there would be no more survivors

Then she had walked home, driven by instinct to the house where she was born. Her mother, never a demon strative woman, had led her indoors, changed her clothes as though she was a baby and put her to bed.

But she had not slept; she sat up against the pillows, dry eyed, waiting for news of Mark. Until he was found, dead or alive, she could not rest for she was not willing that the sea should keep him.

When the loud knock came on the door and the huge voice of the constable penetrated the floorboards, she was ready.

'There's sorry I am to ask you this, Katie.' Freddie-Cop Shop was red-faced, his uniform appearing too tight round the collar; there was a sympathy in his eyes that pained her

'I knew you'd have to come for me some time.' She felt calm but with a sense of purpose, for she would not believe that he was dead. When she glanced towards her father Tom was frowning, his greying ginger eyebrows drawn together.

'Shall I come with you, girl?' he asked but she shook her head firmly, her eyes begging him to understand.

'No, Daddy, I have to go alone.' She walked out into the glare of the sunshine and the pitying, curious glances of her neighbours, her head held high.

'There's a good girl,' Freddie said, his voice booming as usual. 'Katie Murphy, you've got plenty of guts!'

'Where do we have to go?' Katie asked, hoping her strength would last. It was a fragile thread of self-control which might snap at any moment.

'Just down to the infirmary, girl — won't take a minute, this, just got to be sure which of the men we've found.'

The bodies were laid out in a long room, some still incongruously dressed in oilskins and boots. Katie saw the young smooth face of William Richards and bit her lip in pity. And then Freddie was drawing her to a halt.

Half fearfully she looked down at the figure on the bed — he seemed incredibly tall — and drew in a ragged breath. Her husband's face was bruised and cut and a jagged wound ran across his head, cutting through the thick hair as though with a scythe. Dumbly she nodded, not looking at the constable.

Suddenly she was trembling. The feeling began in her head and travelled through her shoulders to her arms and hands, and lastly her legs became to weak to support her.

'Take me out of here,' she dimly heard herself say and then she was being half-carried into the sunshine where she sank on to the warm stone of the wall outside and stared down at her feet until the feeling of faintness passed. She was gripped by a sense of unreality: none of this was really happening, it was a dreadful dream from which she must awake.

'Come on, Katie, let me take you home.' The constable was helping her to her feet as though she was a very old lady. 'Home' — the word rang in her head. She had no home, her home was lying in the infirmary battered by the sea.

'Now, come on back to Market Street where your mam

409

and dad can look after you.' Freddie spoke kindly, his stron
arm around her.

Obediently, she moved forward, aware that she wa
walking away from all that she held dear.

*   *   *

Catherine sat in the cart with the baby in her arms an
stared at Morgan intently as he climbed up into the sea
She was worried about him for he still walked stiffly, h
body weakened by the battering he had received from th
seas.

It was almost a week now since the night of the storr
and so far, Catherine had been unsuccessful in her hop
of persuading Gladys to come up to the farm. But perhap
now that the dreadful day of the funeral was past, she migl
change her mind.

Morgan guided the horse carefully down the stee
roadway that twisted into Oystermouth and the soporif:
sound of hooves against the roadway in the silence of th
sunlit day made Catherine feel drowsy. She had been u
since early morning catching up with her chores on th
farm, for when the harvest was brought in other thing
would have to be left.

Gladys was slow to answer the door, but she forced
tired smile when she saw them, though her legs appeare
swollen and were giving her great pain.

Catherine put a hand on the older woman's shoulde
'I need you,' she said softly and saw the tears spring readil
to Glady's eyes as she sank back in her chair, her plum
face seemed shrunken.

'I miss him, my lovely boy and that's all I can thin
about.' She waved her hand around her in a wild gestur
'Emptiness, that's all I see, is emptiness.'

'Come on home to the farm then, Gladys, please
Catherine held her hands and rubbed them gently. 'I nee
you very badly, mind, for I don't think anyone will com
and help us with the harvesting. But if you will have th

410

baby for me, I'll be able to put in a good day's work beside Morgan, see?'

Gladys stared at her as though coming awake. 'Of course you need me, girl, what have I been thinking of?'

Catherine sighed in relief, it seemed that she had penetrated Gladys's grief. 'Aye, and ruined we'll be if this harvest don't come in good,' she said quickly.

'Go and pack some things in my bag for me, Catherine,' Gladys asked, the light returning to her eyes. 'And you, Morgan — you just get me up into that cart, right?'

The sun shone gloriously on a calm glittering sea, so innocent now without the rain and wind to throw it into a rage. Catherine sat beside Gladys, clinging gratefully to her arm; perhaps now Gladys would begin to overcome the first bitterness of the loss of her son — at least some progress had been made.

Tomorrow they would bring in the corn. They would start early next morning, she and Morgan, for it would take days for them to work the fields alone. And what if it rained before they were finished? But there was little point in meeting trouble half-way.

Gladys had decided to make a few stops on their way through the village and she climbed from the cart with difficulty, to be swallowed up into the houses of her neighbours. Catherine knew what she was up to — asking for help with the harvest, she was, but not likely to get it. And yet she ached with gratitude, for her mother-in-law was putting aside her own pain and giving her utmost in order to help Catherine.

The baby began to cry and no wonder, Catherine thought, for it was past his feeding time and she could scarcely sit on the cart in the middle of the village and put him to the breast.

As she rocked John in her arms, crooning to him softly, she became aware that Morgan was watching her with a strange expression on his face.

Later, as she settled Gladys in the room that used to be David's, Catherine kissed her warmly.

411

'Thank you for everything, Mam.' It was the first time she had addressed Gladys that way and she was rewarded by a tearful smile.

'We'd better have an early night,' Catherine continued, a catch in her voice. 'There's a dawn start for us all in the morning.'

'Well, I'm going to have a nice noggin before I go to sleep,' Gladys said. 'A slight chill in the tummy, you know!'

'I think I'll join you.' Morgan winked at Catherine as he poured a liberal measure of brandy into a glass. 'Here we are then — get that down you, it will warm the cockles of your heart.'

Gladys smiled up at him with sadness lingering in her eyes. But at least she knew that she was needed and that she had a home with them for as long as she wanted to stay.

When at last Catherine lay in her bed, with John settled in his crib and Morgan breathing evenly at her side, she found it difficult to sleep. Moonlight slanted through the open curtains and fell in a silver streak across the room. Hearing Gladys coughing downstairs, she wondered if she should go down to see how she was.

But she continued to lie staring up at the ceiling, wondering how they would manage the harvesting; the work was back-breaking and the fields unusally rich with corn, but she aimed to cut at least one acre before breakfast. She had managed during the war years, hadn't she? But *then*, a small voice said, she had had the help and goodwill of her neighbours.

At last, sighing, she settled down beside Morgan and closed her eyes. She felt herself relaxing for whatever happened tomorrow, she could go to sleep tonight surrounded by her loved ones.

*   *   *

The weather held, but a cool breeze was blowing across the fields of Ram's Tor when Catherine woke next morning. She took John in her arms and snuggled him close so that his round mouth clamped on to her nipple. At her side, Morgan stirred and leaned up on his elbow, watching her in silence. Their eyes met and she looked away at once, suddenly shy, for what did she really know about this man who was her husband?

Morgan slid from beneath the sheets and stretched his arms above his head; the sight of the huge bruises and abrasions on his bronzed skin was a physical pain to Catherine.

'Sounds as if Gladys was up before us,' Morgan said as he drew on his shirt. 'At any rate, I can smell bacon cooking — makes my mouth water, it does.'

Catherine moved the suckling baby higher in her arms. 'If I let him have his fill, I can spend more time in the fields,' she said.

Morgan frowned. 'It's not right, Catherine; you should be resting by here with the baby, not gathering corn.'

She thought of the flour-bin growing emptier and the meagre supply of coal which was all they had to see them through the coming winter, and she forced a smile.

'You forget, I'm a farming girl born and bred in the country. I'm used to the work, so it doesn't come so hard for me as it does to you — and see how the sun shines, the time is right for harvesting and we must take advantage of it. Anyway,' her voice sank, 'we have no option but to do the work ourselves, boy *bach*!'

Gladys was just finishing the cooking and as Catherine entered the kitchen, she put a platter of bacon and eggs on the table.

'Hold the baby 'til Morgan fetches his crib down from the bedroom,' Catherine asked and watched the glow come into Gladys's eyes as she stared down at the infant cradled in her arms.

'I've given him a good feed,' Catherine said wryly, 'and now I know how the poor old cows feel when I take the milk from them.' She sat down and helped herself to bacon and eggs; she would need a good meal inside her as she was to work in the fields all day.

413

Morgan came in from the yard, his hair glistening with water, his face fresh-washed — the very scents of him those of cleanliness and sunshine. He sat beside Catherine and ate his breakfast in silence.

Later, Gladys waved them goodbye from the doorway, the baby cradled against her ample bosom. Her eyes seemed clearer now, as though looking to the future.

Together Catherine and Morgan walked to the top fields, those which lay nearest the sun and where the corn was ripest. 'You start on that side of the field and I'll follow you and put the corn into stooks,' Catherine said. 'And remember, bend into the scythe and don't fight against it.'

Morgan smiled and the sun streaked his hair to gold. 'There you go with your bossiness again!' He brushed past her and to Catherine he smelled of sun and the grain.

She worked steadily behind Morgan as the sun rose higher, burning down on Ram's Tor. Only a small part of the fields had been cut and put into stooks, but already her breasts ached as though they were on fire. Milk soaked her bodice and trickled into her waistband.

She glanced across to where Morgan was doing his best to cut the corn, knowing he must be in pain from the newly opened grazes on his skin.

'Rest time!' she called loudly and made her way wearily to the edge of the field where she had left a bottle of home-made dandelion beer.

'Not getting on very well, are we?' Morgan said softly and Catherine bit her lip, covering her soaked bodice with her arms.

'Not doing badly at all, so don't go worrying, there's a good boy.'

There was bitterness in his eyes as he stared down at her. 'It's my fault we've come to this,' he said. 'Me that gave our money away and me that put all the neighbours against us.'

Catherine turned to face him. 'I thank God every minute for giving you to me! Now no more talk, let's get back to work — we'll harvest this corn if it kills us.'

Morgan picked up the scythe and began to swing it

nexpertly against the stalks of the corn as, with a sigh, Catherine bent to tie the cut corn into the stooks. They worked silently then, each unwilling to admit defeat. After a time, Catherine looked up and saw that the sky was lowering and a fresh breeze had begun to come in from the sea.

'Morgan, we're working against time too now, boy *bach* — let's try to hurry a bit, is it?'

But despair and weariness sapped her spirit . . . they were done for, lost, it was not possible for them to work fast enough to bring in the harvest before the rain came.

Then she heard a sound from across the field and, shading her eyes with her hands, she saw Gethin from the next farm walking towards them with a scythe swinging at his side. He smiled at them sheepishly and pointed up at the sky.

'Seems we might have another storm like the one you risked your life in, Morgan Lloyd!' And without another word, Gethin began to cut the corn, expertly and swiftly. Catherine looked at Morgan in sudden hope and he smiled even as he eased from his back the shirt that was patch-worked with blood.

And then, after a few moments, Joe Beaver strode across the land and shame-facedly held out his hand to Morgan. 'I'm no farmer, but I'm strong and can carry loads right enough,' he offered in his big voice. He jerked his thumb over his shoulder. 'There's more company on the way!'

Minutes later Denny-the-Stack came striding through the corn singing at the top of his voice, and with him his four sons and two daughters. The girls, with a shy smile at Catherine, began to gather the corn into bundles at her side.

Slowly the villagers came to Ram's Tor — men with their womenfolk and children ready to harvest the corn for Morgan Lloyd, a newcomer with strange ways but one who had braved the seas alongside them.

As Catherine paused for a moment to ease her aching back, she looked into the distance and there unmistakably was the lean figure of her father striding towards her, his face as dour as always. He stood before her and for a long moment, their eyes met and held.

'I've come then, girl,' he said. 'Can't let my family down in time of need, it's not Christian!'

'Thank you, Dad,' she said softly and for a moment, she leaned her head against his shoulder. He moved away then and joined the other men who were swiftly bringing down the standing corn that was full with ripeness.

Catherine held up her head, listening as the sweet voice of one of the girls rang out into the silence of the day, singing the song of harvest home . . . and slowly other joined in, deep masculine voices all in harmony.

Morgan came towards Catherine and took her in his arm as weary but jubilant, they clung together. 'We've won,' Morgan said. 'Damn it, we've won!'

He looked down at her, his face suddenly sobe 'Catherine, have I ever told you how much I love you?' H eyes were alight as they looked into hers and joy swept ove her. She put her hands on his cheeks and as his mout touched hers, she knew he spoke the truth — he did love her

Above them, the clouds cleared from the face of the su and a great slant of light shafted downwards, washing th fields as though in benediction. And on the golden fertil lands of Ram's Tor, the harvest was gathered in.

THE END